BITTER SWEET VENGEANCE

MADDISON KINGS UNIVERSITY

LUCA & PEYTON DUET

USA TODAY & WALL STREET JOURNAL BESTSELLING AUTHOR

TRACY LORRAINE

THE VENGEANCE YOU CRAVE

MADDISON KINGS UNIVERSITY #4

1

LUCA

Since coming back to Maddison after the holidays, I've been out here in the dark every night.

The fury I felt when I discovered that she'd managed to slip out the back and avoid me still burns through my veins.

I'm still desperate to stand in front of her, to demand that she finally tells me the truth, finally confesses to lying but I've settled for watching her.

I might have only had glimpses of the woman—the girl—I gave my heart to all those years ago, but it's easy to see the differences. Starting with the hair. Peyton always had the lightest, softest, prettiest honey blonde hair.

The pink is cute, sure. She's clearly trying to make some kind of statement with it.

But it's not my Peyton.

And while I might hate her, I also crave that girl with the easy, infectious smile who could make me laugh without even trying and light up my entire day with only that smile.

Reaching up, I run my hand through my hair as I think back to those years, how easy they were.

Sure, I had pressure from Dad pressing down on me even back

then. At the time I thought it was awful. I remember demanding that Mom make him take a step back, but what I didn't appreciate was that he was going easy back then. Because the years that followed, right now, are unbearable.

A part of me wishes that I wasn't any good on the field. That the first time Dad threw me a ball, I fumbled, tripped over my own feet and shattered all his dreams. Although, I can't help but wonder that if that was the case then he'd have gone out of his way to 'fix' me.

Dad's game days might have been over, but by the time Lee and I were old enough to catch a ball, he knew his dream was going to continue, just through us.

It's exhausting.

The second he discovered that I was quarterback material, he turned all his focus onto me. He wanted me to be his protégé. Leon was still very much on his radar, but I was the one he really turned his attention to. Lee has no idea how lucky he was, how lucky he is, not being constantly told that you're not good enough, that you called the wrong play, that you made the wrong decision.

I blow out a long shaky breath, my fingers wrapping around the wheel in front of me until they hurt. I need to feel something other than the anger, the disappointment, the crushing loss of everything that's gone fucking wrong recently.

That's why I need her.

I need something that I can control. I need to feel like I can be the one making the decisions, pulling the strings, causing the pain. Because everyone has taken everything else away from me. The pressure, the failure, the lies, the cheating, the bullshit. All of it needs to end.

A roar of frustration rips up my throat, filling the silence of my car as I try to expel the growing feelings within me. I don't even know what they are. Desperation probably.

I'm drowning. Falling deeper into the darkness, and I have no idea how to claw myself back.

I remain in my car, in the darkest corner of the parking lot like I have for the past week and wait. I thought I wanted to stand before her and demand answers, but watching her and knowing she has no idea settles something inside me.

Maybe if I watch for long enough, I'll discover the truth.

I'll catch her out in a lie.

But I know that's unlikely, we haven't seen each other in almost five years. I have no idea who the girl I once knew is now. I have no idea why she's even back here.

I've run through all the possibilities in my head. I've searched for her on social media. But I haven't found an account in her name, let alone any answers.

For those, I need her.

My fingers twitch with the thought of reaching out and touching her. My mouth waters for all the ways I want to show her just how much her lies hurt. How badly she broke me back then before Letty turned up like a guardian fucking angel and helped me put the pieces back together.

I thought when Letty arrived at MKU it was for me. I truly fucking did.

But now I know differently.

Because all this time, I've been waiting for *her*, and I had no idea.

The second someone pushes the back door open casting a bright glow across the parking lot, my eyes snap toward it, praying that it's time for her to leave.

When it's not her, but a guy taking some trash out, my teeth grind in frustration.

I need her. I need my fucking fix.

I've never been addicted to anything—okay, maybe the game—but this is different. This incessant need for her, the excitement about seeing her wide, fearful eyes when I finally catch up with her. Fuck. It makes me feel more alive than I have in weeks and I fucking love it.

I've lost everything else, but this, this right now, is mine and only mine.

I have the control when I reveal myself. I have the control with what I do and what I say for when that happens. No one can take this away from me.

2

———

PEYTON

I chew on my nail as I sit in the parking lot watching the other students around me head toward the buildings ready for their first classes of the day. But I'm frozen. My stomach is in a tight knot with fear racing through my veins.

I'm a mess. Everything is a fucking mess and nothing makes sense other than wanting to hide. But that's not who I am. I'm stronger than that. Mom raised me to face my demons and to tackle them head-on, not to run like others... like her.

I lower my hand when I have no nail left to bite. It's a habit I thought I cracked in high school, but with everything that's happened in the past couple of months, they're as red and sore as they've ever been.

However, this could be the worst decision I've ever made in my life.

I know that Aunt Fee is right, that I can't just turn my back on everything I've achieved so far, but starting here, at MKU where I know he is. It already feels like a disaster waiting to happen.

As I stare at the smiling students as they catch up with their friends after the holiday break, the dread only gets heavier in my stomach.

I think back to Christmas Eve at The Locker Room and the look in Luca's eyes when he realized it was me. I expected the shock the first time he laid eyes on me again, but what I had hoped was that he'd have moved past what happened between us before I left Rosewood all those years ago. But the second his shock morphed into anger I knew it was only wishful thinking.

I blow out a long breath, my fingers wrapping around the steering wheel in front of me.

Maddison Kings University is huge. The chances of me bumping into him are slim. That knowledge is one of the reasons why I allowed Aunt Fee to convince me to fill out the transfer papers.

"You can do this," I tell myself. "Mom would want you to do this."

With my head held high, I climb from my car, dragging my purse with me and throw it over my shoulder.

I studied the campus map before leaving the house this morning so I think I know where both of my classes today are.

The huge, imposing Westerfield Building looms before me as students funnel through the huge double doors at the front. All my classes this semester are here. Seeing as I was starting over, I decided to make my life as easy as possible and choose classes in my comfort zone. English.

Reading and writing have been the only things that have allowed me to get out of my head these past few weeks, and without them, I have no idea how I could have come through it all.

As the majority of the students inside head for the elevator, I go for the stairs. I don't have time to work out so I've got to get exercise in, wherever I can. My job requires me to be in top form because my boss is a pig and I can't risk losing it.

He's already taken a risk by allowing me to start working before I turn twenty-one. The last thing I need to do is piss him off by adding an inch to my waist.

I make quick work of the two flights of stairs and I'm soon approaching room 305 for my morning class. I follow the other students inside and find myself a seat about halfway back.

I scan every face as I climb the stairs. I don't know why I bother, I already know he's not here. I'd feel it if he were. Just like I did that night.

I felt his presence as I worked the room, clearing empty glasses and taking orders, but I refused to turn around and discover who was causing that kind of reaction within me. Nothing good could come from someone paying me as much attention as I knew the man behind me in the shadows was.

When Bry, the bartender, passed me over his order, I almost refused to take it over. But knowing I didn't have a choice if I didn't want to draw attention to myself, I swallowed down my apprehension and turned his way.

I knew that at some point it was likely to happen. I wasn't going to move to his territory and get away without him finding out. But this was the last place I was expecting to discover the ghost from my past.

I applied for the job on a whim, thinking it was probably one of the only places surrounding the university where students might not hang out. How wrong was I because not even a week into my position and there he was. My old best friend, the boy who used to know me better than I knew myself. He was sitting there mentally imagining all the ways he could make me leave as fast as I had the last time.

Only, he's going to be disappointed because this time, I'm not going anywhere. I need to be here. I've got people depending on me not to screw this whole thing up.

My life has changed in ways I never could have imagined since Mom packed up mine and my sister's shit and drove us out of Rosewood without looking back.

I understand why she did it. She thought that getting Libby away would help to put her on the right path. She had no idea that the months and years that would follow would only get worse.

I pull my notebook from my purse and rummage around the mess for a pen as I keep an eye on all the students who continue to stream into the room.

There was a time when I wouldn't have needed to even think about what class he might have taken. I knew everything there was to know about Luca Dunn. I knew his dreams, his fears, I knew exactly what made him tick. That was true until I confessed what I had discovered and I realized that maybe I didn't know everything about him after all. Or more so, that he didn't know me because I thought he knew that I'd never lie to him. That no matter how hard something was to tell him, that I'd always do it if I thought it was the right thing to do. Turns out, that wasn't how it was because instead of accepting what I'd said as the truth, he fed into every one of my insecurities and turned against me.

I wished so hard that what I told him wasn't true. But I knew in my soul that it was and that no matter what his reaction was to it, that it was going to change all of our lives. And I couldn't have been more right because only days later, I returned home from school to find Mom packing up our belongings and the three of us drove out of town, never to return.

To this day, I have no idea if it was the right thing to do, but I understand why she did it.

She wanted to protect us. Our safety was more important to her than anything else.

But a part of me wished she'd handled it differently.

I wished we could have stayed and fought for what was right, to stop it from happening again. Maybe if we'd have stayed, I wouldn't have been in this position now.

Eventually, the stream of students comes to an end and our professor joins us before setting up his presentation and starting the class.

The second he starts talking, even if it's to lay out what we can expect from the course this semester, I forget about everything that's falling apart around me and focus on him.

This is my safe place, my escape from reality. I soak up every single word he says, and already I can feel the tingle of excitement when he talks about the assignments we're going to be expected to complete. Anything that involves me tapping at my keyboard immediately makes me feel lighter.

———

Folding up the campus map and sliding it back into my pocket, I walk around the corner of the building. The scent in the air makes my mouth water.

The sight of the beans on the sign hanging above the door makes me smile and without a second thought, I head inside.

Thanks to classes just ending, the line is almost out the door. I join the line prepared to wait until my next class if it means getting my hands on the biggest cup of coffee this place has to offer.

Much to my relief, the line moves quickly and before I know it, I've got a cappuccino in one hand and an oatmeal raisin cookie in the other.

I walk through the seating area in the hope someone is about to leave so I can sit. It's not all that cold outside but I'd rather be in here, ideally at the back of the room so I can watch the people coming and going, but there's nothing.

Balancing my cookie on my takeout cup, I pull my purse up higher on my shoulder and take a step to leave. I guess it'll have to be a bench outside after all.

"You can sit here," a soft female voice says from behind me, making me look over my shoulder to see if she's actually talking to me.

Spinning around, I find a petite blonde smiling at me and pointing to an empty chair at her table.

"A-are you sure? I don't want to interrupt."

"Of course not," her friend says, clearing away some of their trash from the other side of the table to give me space.

"Thank you," I say sincerely, looking between the two of them.

"I'm Ella and this is Letty," the blonde says, tilting her head to her dark-haired friend beside her.

"H-hey, I'm Peyton, and this is my first day," I add, in case it's not already abundantly clear that I have no clue what I'm doing.

"We guessed," Letty says as I lower my ass to the chair.

"I transferred from Trinity Royal," I explain.

"Ah, South Carolina, right?"

"Yeah." I pull a chunk of my cookie off and throw it into my mouth. Neither of them asks why I've moved here and I don't offer up any information either.

"I only started at the beginning of the year. I was at Columbia before that."

"Oh wow, Columbia."

"Yeah, it was pretty incredible, but things... things didn't work out."

"Life doesn't always turn out as we expect, huh?" I ask, more to myself than anyone else.

"You got that right," Letty mutters, lifting her coffee to take a sip.

"So," Ella asks. "What classes are you taking this semester?"

The three of us fall into easy conversation and before I know it, we're having to clear our table and head to class. Ella and I walk back toward the Westerfield Building while Letty heads elsewhere.

"Where are you living? In dorms or..." Ella asks after a few minutes of comfortable silence as we get ourselves set up for class side by side.

Making friends here wasn't all that high up on my to-do list. Surviving has been my most pressing issue the past few months. But I can't deny that having someone beside me, who I think could potentially become a friend, doesn't feel incredible.

It seems like forever ago that I could let my hair down and have a night with the girls without the stress of real life weighing me down. And although I may have found a couple of possible friends, I still can't see a carefree night out happening any time soon. I've got too many responsibilities now, too many people relying on me.

"I'm actually living with my aunt off campus. Well, she's not actually my aunt but..." I trail off realizing that Ella probably doesn't care about the finer details of my life. Well, not bullshit like that anyway. I'm sure she'd more than happily listen to the dramatics because even after living through it all, I still find it unbelievable as if I'm living out a freaking movie.

"That's good though, it'll save you a ton of money."

"Y-yeah, it will," I agree because she's right, and if it weren't for Aunt Fee, then there's no way I'd be able to be here right now. She really is a guardian angel. I dread to even think what my life might be like right now if she didn't reach out and offer to help me.

"The Kappas are having a toga party Friday night to kick off the new semester. You're in, right?"

"Uh," I hesitate. "Actually, I have to work."

"What?" she says, but I can tell from her face that she understands. "That sucks."

I shrug. "Yeah, but I need the money."

"Fair enough. Where do you work?"

Thankfully, our professor follows a couple of latecomers into the auditorium and immediately demands all of our attention and puts a stop to me having to answer.

I won't lie about my job. I'm a waitress in a bar. I might just skirt around the name of said bar because even from only being here a few weeks, I know that the girls who work at The Locker Room have a certain kind of reputation. To be honest, from the things I've both heard and seen, most of them warrant it. But I'm not like them. Yes, I'm there because the pay is better than any other bar in Maddison County, but I have zero interest in the extracurricular activities that can come with the job. I might want the money, but not that bad.

Much like my morning class, I lose myself in the lecture and everything the professor has to say about the course. I eagerly write down our first assignment, already excited to get some words down onto paper to argue my case about whether fraternities promote misogyny. It's an interesting topic seeing as I was just invited to a party where we all have to wear nothing but sheets, of which I'm sure would cover up as little skin as possible.

"What classes do you have tomorrow?" Ella asks as we make our way out of the building surrounded by others who are equally excited to get out.

"Um... I've got a morning lecture, then I'll probably spend the rest of the day in the library."

"I'm in all day, but do you want to meet us for lunch? I'm pretty sure Letty is free in the afternoon, maybe she could study with you."

"I don't need babysitting." My voice comes out harsher than I intend and Ella's brows pull together, her shoulders dropping in disappointment.

"No, no. I know. That wasn't— fuck. I'm sorry. It's just... you seem like our kind of girl, you know. I didn't want you to be lonely."

"I know, I'm sorry. I'm just not used to..." I gesture between us. "This."

"I know I can be a little full-on at times. But when you know, you know. You know?" She wiggles her brows in amusement as a small laugh passes her lips.

"Yeah, I know." Although really, the only one I thought I knew that with, turned on me, so maybe I'm clueless. "Lunch tomorrow sounds great."

"Yes," she hisses. "And see if you can get Friday night off. It's gonna be a banging party, and I know a few guys who'll love you."

"Oh, no, no. I'm not—"

"I'm not setting you up, don't worry."

"It's fine. Just... just tell me they're not football players," I beg.

She studies me for a beat, one of her eyebrows lifting in curiosity.

"Some are, yeah. They're good guys though."

I can practically hear her silent question, but I speak before she gets a chance to ask.

"I'll take your word for it. Listen, thank you for today. I really appreciate you taking a chance on me, but I really need to head out."

"Work?"

"Yeah."

We quickly agree on a time to meet tomorrow and after Ella taps her number into my cell and calls herself to get mine, she leads me toward the parking lot.

Feeling much more positive about this fresh start than I did when I pulled up this morning, I head home to grab some food and check-in before heading to work.

———

I stare at myself in the mirror in the staff bathroom at the bar. I hated the dress code—if it can even be called that—from the moment I first stepped inside the building and saw the girls. I knew what to expect from the internet but still, seeing it in real life was entirely different.

But equally, I knew that if the manager would give me a chance that there was no way I was going to turn it down. People do much worse than show a bit of skin for extra tips. Hell, I could be doing a hell of a lot worse for it. But I draw the line here. The paycheck means I get to do fewer hours and hopefully continue with college.

Win-win—I hope.

But since seeing *him* here that night, I seem to spend all my time looking over my shoulder. He warned me that I wasn't getting away, yet, but by some miracle, I was able to slip out of the back door unnoticed at the end of my shift. Luckily I spent my time at the other side of the bar so I didn't have to serve him again.

I lied to Bry, told him that Luca was an ex that I didn't want to be anywhere near, and thankfully, he allowed me to switch with another waitress for the rest of my shift.

Touching up my lip gloss, I tuck the loose strands of hair from my updo behind my ears and square my shoulders.

He hasn't been here since, much to my amazement. He seemed pretty adamant that night that he'd wanted something from me, but it was also clear from his glazed expression that he was drunk.

I convinced myself more each day when he didn't show his face that it was just the drink talking. That just like the day I confessed what I knew, that he didn't want anything to do with me anymore.

I'd hoped that when the time came, that if he turned his back on me once more that it wouldn't hurt as much as it did the first time. And while our time apart and the distance between us has softened the pain somewhat, knowing that what we once had has well and truly been severed, still sends a searing pain through my chest.

I thought Luca was the one. I truly thought we were going to live out everything we'd planned over the years. We were going to go to college, he was going to go into the NFL, we'd get married, have two kids, two dogs, and live happily ever after. We'd even chosen the style of house we wanted. The only thing we never pinned down was the location. Luca had a few top teams he was desperate to be signed by, but he was sensible enough back then to keep his options open. His dad, however, had other ideas and wanted him to follow in his footsteps and join the Atlanta Falcons. Luca was open to it, but he hadn't put all his eggs in one basket, or he hadn't back then. Everything could have changed now.

But two weeks from that night, and I'm still waiting—hoping—that he might show back up and follow through on his threats. I've lost count of how many times I've planned what I might say to him when we come face-to-face once more, but now that time is closer than ever, I'm questioning everything.

I want to believe that time's a healer and that we can move past what happened. I'm not stupid, I know we'll never have the kind of relationship we did when we were kids. What he did when he walked away from everything we had is something I'm not sure I'll ever truly forgive him for.

Shoving my purse into my locker, I tuck the key into my bra and head out.

He's not been back—at least not when I've been on shift—since that night, so I have no reason to think that he'll be here tonight.

3

LUCA

I'm sitting at the island in the kitchen when the guys spill through the front door a few hours after our last class of the day.

They all went to a diner for burgers seeing as the season is out and we actually get a bit of free time. Me though? I headed straight for the training facility to put in my second gym session of the day.

"Ah, here he is. Our dedicated QB," Colt barks, eyeballing the remains of my chicken salad that's still on the plate in front of me.

Lifting my hand, I flip him off as he yanks the refrigerator door open and begins tossing bottles of beer at the others who are loitering by the door.

A few look at me with their brows drawn in concern and others with confusion, but none more so than my twin brother.

"You coming to hang or continue being a boring fucker?" Colt continues, ignoring the death stare I'm shooting his way.

"I'm busy, asshole," I mutter, casting a glance down at the textbook in front of me.

"Alright, fuck, Luc." He holds his hands up in defense as he and the others disappear in favor of the den.

"Taking this semester seriously, huh?" Leon asks, closing the door and cutting off the noise from the others.

"Something like that," I mutter.

Things are still strained between us since I discovered that he's been lying to me for years about sleeping with Letty.

I know I should probably just let it go, but I can't. I didn't think Lee and I had secrets. Hell, I didn't think Letty and I did, not back then anyway. I know we kinda went our separate ways a little after high school when she left for Columbia, but still. To know that they'd been together and I had no clue.

Fuck.

I scrub my hand down my face, my anger with both of them threatening to explode once more.

If I discovered this at any other time, I'm sure I'd have just dealt with it. Right now, it's just another thing on top of a whole pile of shit I don't know how to work through.

I hoped that getting back here and taking it out in the gym would have helped. Although it took some of the need to fight out of my body, my head is an entirely different beast and that wants to hurt anyone who comes close.

"Did you need something or are you just loitering to piss me off?"

"Mom's worried."

"Right?" I ask. This isn't news. She either calls or messages me daily after I skipped out early on the holidays, preferring to be back here and stalking The Locker Room for sights of Peyton.

She probably has every right to be worried, but like fuck am I confessing to that.

"Luc, I wish you'd just—"

"Just what? Forgive you for fucking my best friend and lying to me about it for years?"

"We never lied to you," he says with a sigh.

I get it, I'm fed up with having this same argument too but no matter what, I can't get past it.

"No? So how come I didn't have a fucking clue about it until that cunt told me?" That's the bit that really stings, that I had to find out from someone I can't stand. Someone who now claims to love Letty more than life itself. Fuck, he even fucking proposed.

My teeth grind and my fist curls around the pen in my hand as I think about that image of her with her black diamond engagement ring on her finger.

A fucking black diamond. What fucked-up kind of asshole buys a girl a black fucking diamond.

"We were in the wrong, okay. We should have told you. We know this. We've both told you this. But it's in the past. She's not even yours."

The memory of what happened in my bedroom with the three of us last year slams into me. I can still smell the scent of her perfume and remember just how soft her skin was. I can also vividly remember exactly how my brother looked with his head between her thighs.

Letty was mine. At least, that's what I thought.

Turns out that I never really stood a chance.

They always say the bad boys always win, and I guess Letty and Kane are just proof of that.

She loves him for some fucking reason I've yet to see after the way he's treated her. I just really fucking hope that he doesn't screw it up and hurt her even more. Despite being pissed at her, she doesn't deserve to have her heart ripped to pieces.

"You need to talk to her," Lee says, being able to read exactly who I'm thinking about.

"And you need to leave me the fuck alone."

His eyes hold mine as he lifts his hand to push his hair out of his eyes. The anger and frustration, along with a hint of disappointment, reminds me so much of our father that it actually makes my chest hurt.

Even miles away, that controlling fuck manages to get into my head.

"Luc—"

Standing so fast, the stool I was sitting on crashes to the floor, I stand nose to nose with him.

We're the same height, the same build and I know we're matched in the strength department, so when we go at it, we can both hold our own.

My chest heaves in anger that he has the audacity to stand there and tell me to just put everything behind me.

My fists clench and unclench as my heaving breaths wash over his face.

"Go on, asshole. Hit me if it'll make you feel better."

My jaw pops with my restraint.

I know that for a few seconds after the pain shoots up my arm that it will be really fucking worth it, but having to look at his fucking bruised, smug face afterward, no fucking thank you.

"You need to get out of my face," I warn, my voice low and rough.

"I wasn't the one who put myself here, Bro," he quips with a smirk that I really want to wipe clean off.

Lifting my hands, I slam them down on his chest, forcing him to back up.

"You need to focus on your own bullshit life, Lee, and keep your fucking nose out of mine."

He throws his head back and laughs.

"Yeah, because it's that fucking easy when I'm watching you self-destruct, Bro. We didn't make playoffs, so what? You're still one of the best QBs in the country. You didn't get the girl. Yeah, well, I think we both know that you were always better off as friends anyway. Letty was never it for you. I 'lied' to you. I'm fucking sorry, okay. But you can hardly stand there and tell me that you've never lied to me."

My lips twist in frustration as I take another step toward him.

"Like... where have you been sneaking off to every night since I got back here, huh? Who are you fucking?"

All the air rushes out of my lungs knowing that I've been caught.

"I'm not fucking anyone," I scoff.

"Yeah, I know because you're acting like a whiny little bitch who needs to get laid."

"Fuck me, Lee. Tell me how you really feel," I mutter.

"Will it make a difference?" he asks, his eyes wide. When I don't respond, he takes it as my answer. "You need to sort your shit out. No fucking team will want you next year if you're acting like a fucking pussy."

Snatching up my shit from the counter, I abandon my half-eaten dinner and blow out of the room, more than fed up with Leon's opinions about my life.

The guys are all shooting the shit in the den when I pass them on my way to the stairs. They hear me coming and their voices drop for a beat but when they realize that I'm not joining them, they soon start up again.

Taking three stairs at a time, I finally hit the top floor and lock myself in my room.

It should be a new year, a new semester, and a fresh start, but I can't seem to drag my ass out of last year.

Pulling my cell from my pocket so I can put some music on in the hope of drowning out my misery, I find a stream of messages from Dad.

"Fuuuck," I roar, throwing the thing across the room until it collides with the wall with a satisfying bang.

Stumbling back, I crash into the door and slide down until my ass hits the floor.

Tipping my head back, I suck in some deep breaths.

Leon's right. I know he is. But that knowledge pisses me off as much as all the other shit.

As kids, I was always the one who appeared to have my shit together while he was the loose cannon with his emotions. But as the years have passed, we seem to have switched roles and I fucking hate it.

He manages to keep a lid on everything and moves through each day smoothly. Whereas I feel like I'm wading through quicksand, sinking faster than anything else.

———

"Oh look, it's booty call time again," a voice says from the darkness behind me.

"You a fucking stalker?" I shoot over my shoulder.

"No, but you could well be. That or you're about to rob a bank," he says, appearing from the kitchen. He walks around me, taking in what I'm wearing.

"What I'm doing has fuck all to do with you, Bro."

"I'll remind you of that when I'm bailing you out of whatever shit you're getting yourself into."

Shaking my head at him, I march toward the front door without so much as a glance at him.

Where I'm going is the only place that makes sense right now. Seeing her is the only thing that makes everything fade into nothingness. The anger of my life dies out and gets replaced with something even more toxic.

My need for her.

As I have been every night, I'm in the space at the very back of the almost empty lot. Hidden under the low-hanging tree that scrapes across the roof of my Audi when I park.

I turn all the lights off and slide down in my seat as I begin my wait for her to slip out the back.

Thanks to Leon's interruption, I'm later than I have been the past few nights, and she doesn't make me wait long.

My heart jumps, my pulse thundering so hard I can feel it in every part of my body as the light from inside the building fills the other end of the lot. She emerges, with her head down, heading for her own car.

My fingers curl around the wheel with my need to get out and see her, but once I do that, all of this is over.

She's wearing an oversized hoodie. A man's, probably. A boyfriend's? That thought makes bile rush up my throat.

The thought of someone else having her makes me feel murderous.

She was always so pure, so innocent. There's not a second of our time together that I've forgotten before she ruined everything with her lies.

But all that's gone now, hasn't it? She's working in Dad's seedy, exclusive sports bar, shaking her ass for any asshole who wants to look at it.

What happened to her?

The Peyton I knew would never have done that. She was desperate to hide in the shadows and it took all of my persuasive skills to get her to dance with me at school dances. She preferred to just let me get molested by the cheerleaders than to be up there and being judged by them.

I never cared though. I loved that she wasn't one of them, that she cared more about a person than their appearances or the hobbies or sports they played. Same with Letty.

I know for a fact that if Peyton never said what she did, if her mom didn't drag her away then I never would have touched a cheer slut, or a jersey chaser.

She was it for me. Even at fourteen, I knew that. Hell, I'd known a lot earlier than that, I just didn't understand it then.

Reaching down, I palm my dick as I think about everything we shared together. The firsts we gave each other.

Fuck. What I wouldn't give to get a little bit of that right now.

But who else has had a piece of my sweet girl since then?

The second she starts her car and pulls out of the lot, I turn my lights on and follow her out.

To this point, I've only followed her to the end of the street and allowed her to turn left while I've gone right and back to the house.

But tonight is different.

Tonight, I need more.

So when she turns left like usual, so do I.

I hang back, but not too much. Quite honestly, if she wants to pull over and confront me, I'm all for it. Not that I think she'd have the balls. I'd fucking love it if she did though.

The thought of looking into her scared silver eyes again gets my dick hard every single time.

I follow her through town until she turns up a street lined with houses that I really wasn't expecting.

She pulls to a stop alongside the sidewalk of an old bungalow. The building itself looks dated but really well-loved, with lights illuminating the porch and flowers that cover the deck out front.

I park on the other side of the street a few cars down and kill my lights.

There are two other cars parked in the driveway and all the lights are on. Whoever lives here are either night owls, or they're waiting for her.

My heart thunders in my chest as I think about the possibility of the owner of that hoodie waiting to welcome her home from work with open arms.

My hands wring the steering wheel as she throws her door open and heads for the house.

She's not even halfway up the driveway when the front door opens and a man emerges. It's too dark to make out much about him, but Peyton's excitement is obvious as she takes off running and jumps into his arms.

My stomach churns, bile rushes up my throat to the point I think I'm going to have to open the door to puke.

They hold each other for a few seconds and thankfully, my stomach settles and I'm not forced to look away from them.

He takes her purse from her and leads her up to the front door, closing it behind them and cutting off my view of them.

"Motherfucker." I slam my palm down on the wheel time and time again in my need to expel my pent-up aggression. But right now, nothing short of marching up to that door and letting it out on whoever he is will suffice.

4

PEYTON

I can barely keep my eyes open as I drive home after my shift. Once again, there was no sight of Luca, so I can only assume that he's got better things to do than to come after me for shit that happened between us years ago.

Part of me is glad. My life is hard enough right now. The last thing I want to do is rehash the past and try to plead my innocence and convince him that I only told him what I found out because I thought he deserved to know. But the other part, the part that deep down still misses the boy who stole my heart and touched my soul, craves that connection we once had.

In all our years apart, I've never found anything close to what we had.

He was my best friend. My everything. And I'm pretty sure it would have continued that way. We certainly never did anything wrong, anything to deserve to be ripped apart as we were.

Every muscle in my body aches as I throw the door open and climb out.

All I want to do is curl up in bed, but I know I've got a few hours to go yet. I've got assignments that I need to make a start on. This isn't going to work if I fall behind on day one. And I have to make this work.

The future isn't just about me anymore. I have people relying on me to provide a future.

It's not unusual that Aunt Fee is still up and the lights are on, so I don't think anything of it as I walk toward the house. That is until the front door opens and someone steps out.

"Oh my God," I squeal when I register who it is.

My exhaustion is suddenly forgotten as I run into his arms.

"I didn't know you were coming," I say as he returns my embrace, holding me tight.

"I didn't tell anyone. Surprise," he says, releasing me and holding his arms out to the sides.

"Aunt Fee must have lost her shit."

He chuckles at me. "She was pretty excited."

"Man, I wish I was here to see her face."

"Come on," he says, wrapping an arm around my shoulders. "She's made you something to eat."

Guilt floods me, I hate that she feels like she needs to stay up and make sure I'm okay. The deal with moving in here wasn't for her to look after me.

"My boy's home," she announces with a wide smile on her face as we enter the kitchen.

Elijah's a Marine and has been on tour for months after being based on the other side of the country. I know that Aunt Fee is mega proud of him, but she also misses her youngest something awful.

He's the same age as my sister, and although they were always closer growing up, the two of us connected after she left. He was at Trinity Royal, and Mom insisted on cooking him a decent meal once a week and doing his laundry as a favor to Aunt Fee. He obliged because, well, what male college student could turn down the offer of free food and laundry services. But it gave us a chance to chat. He was the only real friend I had after leaving Rosewood, which is kind of embarrassing because he's basically family. But my heart and trust were in tatters post-Luca so it's not all that surprising really that I didn't let anyone in.

Aunt Fee places a bowl of mac and cheese in front of both of us and excuses herself for a few minutes.

"Mom says you're working at a bar," he says, suspicion evident in his tone along with his raised eyebrow. "How'd you swing that?"

"My charm, I guess."

"What bar, Peyton?" he growls, putting on his protective big brother act.

I shake my head at him, really not wanting to get into it. Elijah grew up in Maddison so I have no doubt he knows all about the things that go on behind closed doors inside The Locker Room. "It—"

Thankfully, Aunt Fee walks back in cutting off whatever I was going to say in the hope of changing the topic of conversation.

"It's so nice having you all here," she says, going to the cake tin on the side and pulling the lid off.

"Is everything okay?" I ask, knowing that she went to the back room.

"Perfect. Nothing to worry about." She smiles at me softly, but although she says the words I want to hear, she knows full well that I'll still worry. "How was work?" she asks, completely ignoring the obvious tension radiating from her son because there's no way she'd miss it, she's too perceptive.

"You know, the usual. Busy."

"Have you cut your hours yet? You know it's going to get too much, now classes have started." She pins me with a look while Elijah's eyes burn into the side of my face.

"N-no, not yet. I want to do as much as I can."

"Pey," she warns.

"I know what I'm doing," I argue. *I have no clue what I'm doing.*

"I trust you, but I'm worried. I know you're strong, but you can't take on the world single-handedly."

I pick at my mac and cheese, still full of the food she packed for me and sent me to work with. When she pulls out her homemade cake, Elijah's eyes light up but I make my excuses and leave them to get caught up.

I quietly poke my head into the back room to make sure everything really is okay before I make my way upstairs to my room.

It's tiny, barely more than a closet, but it's got everything I need and it's a hell of a lot more than I'd be able to afford if I were out on my own right now.

Ripping the hoodie from my body—one of Elijah's I stole years ago when he stayed with us for a week or two—I grab a clean pair of pajamas and head for the shower to wash the scent of the bar off me.

———

I walk onto campus the next morning already feeling like I belong. Meeting Ella and Letty yesterday was exactly what I needed. Just like the day before, I lose myself in class the second our professor starts talking and the morning flies by.

Before I know it, our class is drawing to an end. I'm taking notes on our first assignment before following all the others from the auditorium and heading out of the building.

The winter sun blinds me as I step out into the coolness and suck in deep lungfuls of fresh air.

Checking my surroundings, I head in the direction that Ella and I walked from the coffee shop I met them both in yesterday. I can't see either of them when I pull the heavy door open and step inside. I once again join the line and order myself some lunch. My stomach growling loudly as I wait, seeing as I woke up too late to grab any food this morning.

I stayed up long after I should have, trying to get on top of yesterday's assignment. When the alarm went off this morning, I turned it off and rolled over. Needless to say, it was the wrong move and I ended up running around like a headless chicken to get here on time.

With my veggie wrap and cappuccino in hand, I make my way over to an empty table for four at the back of the coffee shop and get comfortable.

I push down concerns that Ella and Letty might bail on me. They have every right to do so, we don't actually know each other, but I really want to trust them and tell myself that their class just has run over.

Sitting back in the chair, I look around at all the students eating their lunch and chatting with friends. I don't recognize anyone. It's no surprise. Aside from Ella, Letty, Luca, or Leon, I would probably struggle to recognize anyone I went to school with in Rosewood if they're here, just like I wouldn't expect anyone to give me a second glance. It's not just my hair that's different these days. I'm older, wiser, hardened to the realities of life and the pain that comes along with it. I barely recognize myself in the mirror some days, anyone else doesn't stand a chance.

Moving my eyes to the windows, I gasp in shock when they land on a very familiar figure.

Luca.

My heart jumps into my throat and my stomach knots, threatening to bring up the few mouthfuls of lunch I've already had.

He's standing with three other guys. I don't think I know any of them, but I find it hard to really focus on them because I'm still too drawn to Luca even after all these years.

His hair is shorter than it was back in high school and instead of flopping down on his brow, it's styled away from his face. His jaw is squarer, sharper, and covered in dark scruff from days of not shaving. His lips are just as full as I remember and I can't help running my tongue along my bottom one as I wonder if he still tastes the same. His nose is still straight and just the perfect size. Seriously, if football didn't work out, he could totally be a model. But what I really want to see but can't from this distance, are his eyes. They were always the most mesmerizing green. I could get lost in them for hours and I'm sure that's something that's not changed.

I'm so lost in watching him with his friends that I don't notice when Ella and Letty join me. The movement of them pulling the chairs out around me causes a small shriek to fall from my lips.

"They're pretty distracting, right?" Ella asks, her eyes locked on the same guys that mine were on only seconds ago.

"U-uh..." I stutter, really not wanting to get into anything about the reason behind my fascination. "Y-yeah. Don't tell me, they're part of the football team?"

"What gave them away?" she asks with a laugh. "The arrogance they ooze or their over-the-top confidence?"

"B-both," I confess.

Letty looks over at them, but she shows much less interest than Ella whose eyes seem to linger on one of them a little too long.

"One of them yours?" I ask Ella, the thought of her being Luca's girlfriend—or anyone being with him really—makes my stomach knot painfully.

"Pfft," she says, ripping her eyes away from them and focusing on her lunch. "All they do is fuck and chuck. Fucking pigs."

"Ignore her, she's been burned by number twenty-two," Letty chips in.

"I have not been burned, thank you very much."

"Riiight, so you don't spend most of the day looking around for him," she deadpans.

Ella's back straightens but her anger is hard to take seriously with the smirk playing on her lips.

"Oh, did you want to revisit your issues with certain members of the team, Miss Hunter?"

Ella's eyes hold Letty's for a beat before they drop to the table. Intrigued as to what's holding her attention, I follow her stare.

"Holy crap, are you engaged to a football player?" I blurt without thought.

Letty chuckles as I admire her stunning black diamond engagement ring. I can't help but wonder the reason behind the color of the stone. It's stunning, unique and I just know there's a story there for him not to have gone for the standard.

"Yeah. Not one of those guys though."

Relief floods me. I have no say in what Luca does or who he's attached to anymore. That ship has long sailed but I can't help wanting to hear that he's not a player, that he's single, that he's held out for me.

I almost laugh out loud at my thought—okay, fantasy.

I already know it's not true, I've spent enough time scrolling through his social media over the years to know that he's always got a girl on his arm.

"Kane's... different," Ella explains, making Letty snort a laugh.

"You can say that again."

With a soft smile playing on her lips, Letty gives me the CliffsNotes of her relationship with her fiancé. The story makes my chest ache hearing about how they grew up together but spent most of their teen and young adult years at each other's throats. That was all before figuring their shit out after finding themselves at MKU together unexpectedly. I'm sure there's a hell of a lot more to the story than she lets on in her five-minute run down, but even still, it gives me hope. Probably naïvely, but my teenage heart still craves my all-American boy from the fancy house a few streets over who stole my heart with one cheeky smile.

"Sounds like you two have quite the story," I force past the giant lump in my throat.

"It wasn't love at first sight, that's for sure. So what about you? Got a boy on the scene?"

I chuckle, thinking of the boy who's taken over my life recently. "Nope. Boys are off my radar right now."

"We'll fix that Friday night, right, Let? You got the night off, right?"

"Umm..." I hesitate. "My boss wouldn't let me switch," I lie, guilt eating me as I do. I really want to make the most of this budding friendship, but equally, I don't want to be at a party where he's likely to be. The longer I can remain hidden in the shadows the better.

"Damn, girl. You're just going to have to come after. We're going to sort our costumes tomorrow after class. Wanna join?"

My lips part to refuse, but tomorrow is my night off and I'll feel like a jerk if I pass up this opportunity.

"S-sure, I'd love to," I say, not having to force the smile that appears on my face at the thought of spending time with them off campus.

"Perfect. We'll have you looking like such a goddess that all the boys will be tripping over themselves to get to you," she says, rubbing her hands together as if I've just turned into a little pet project for her.

"Uh... that's okay. I don't—"

"You can argue as much as you like," Letty interrupts. "But I should warn you that she'll still get her way."

"Hey, you make me sound like a control freak," Ella argues.

"I'm not trying to make you sound like one, you are one."

Ella huffs in frustration but movement outside the window stops me from focusing on her response to Letty.

My heart picks up speed as the guys head this way.

My pulse thunders through my body and my chest begins to heave as panic assaults me.

He can't come in here. He just can't.

I wring my trembling hands under the table, my eyes tracking the group's movement as they get closer.

My eyes flash to the only door, the one they're about to walk to.

I can't even escape.

My head spins as the thought of coming face-to-face with him once more in public becomes more and more a reality. But he claps his hand on one of his friend's shoulders, says something briefly and then takes off in the opposite direction without looking back.

Holy fuck. That was close.

"Peyton, are you okay? You look like you've just seen a ghost."

"Oh, um... yeah, sorry. I just remembered something that I..." I trail off, not able to finish the sentence. Not only because it's all a lie but because I literally can't form words as I watch his back retreat around the corner.

The realization that I need to man up and talk to him slams into me.

I'm two days into this new start and I'm already a mess.

I hoped that I'd be able to avoid him.

This campus is huge. We should be able to live entirely separate lives without ever bumping into each other. But of course that's not how this is going to work because fate is a bitch and for some reason the universe thinks that we need to be close once more.

They both look at me with concerned expressions while I fight to get myself under control.

"Everything's fine, I promise."

They both smile, but neither of them look like they believe me. Thankfully, though, they let it go. For now. I have no doubt that if this budding friendship continues then they're going to want to know more about me and if—when—Luca and I collide again, they're going to have even more questions about me seeing as he's the King of MKU. Hell, they've both probably already slept with him.

Once we've finished eating and thankfully started gossiping about things that don't involve me, my past or a certain quarterback, Ella excuses herself to her afternoon class, and Letty and I head for the library.

Thankfully, she seems to be as dedicated to her studies as I am and not much is said between us as we sit at a table together and tap away on our laptops. We work in comfortable silence and I can't help feeling more at home than I have in quite a long while, just in her presence.

I slump down in my chair, my shoulders aching from the position I'm sitting in and let out a sigh. The time is ticking by and it's impossible to forget that I've got another shift tonight.

And it's Tuesday. I silently groan. For some reason, Tuesday nights are the busiest of the week. But, while it might be crazy, it also comes with extra tips. Money is the reason I'm there, so I swallow down my dread.

"It'll get better," Letty says softly.

"Huh?" I ask, still lost in my own head about what tonight is going to hold to have a clue of what she's talking about.

"Starting over. It'll get better."

"Oh, yeah. I know. I've just got a lot of family shit going on right now. It's kinda dragging me down," I say, risking opening up to her.

"Ugh, that's the worst. Do you want to talk about it?"

The thought of telling my truths, exposing my pain is about as terrifying as looking directly into Luca's angry eyes again.

"N-no, not really."

"Okay. Well, if you do. We're here. I know how hard it is so if there's anything I can do."

"Th-thank you," I whisper, my voice cracking with emotion.

I haven't told anyone my reality. Everyone in my circle knows what happened because they've been a part of it. The thought of just saying the words shatters my heart. I can only imagine how painful it'll be when I finally run out of excuses and have to confess everything.

"I need to head out."

"Work again?"

"Always. Gotta pay for all this somehow."

"It'll be worth it in the end," she says, closing down her laptop to walk out with me. "I've got a shift tonight too while Kane's at practice."

Her entire expression changes when she says his name and I can't help but smile knowing she's found that.

There have been times over the years where I thought true love and happily ever afters were a myth. I thought I had it, but it was ripped from under me before I knew what happened. We might have been young but I knew. And what if that was my only chance? Am I now destined to a life as a spinster?

I shake my head, pushing away my insecurities about my life and my future.

We chat about her job in a coffee shop and the apartment she shares with her fiancé as we make our way to the parking lot.

"See you tomorrow for toga construction?" she says as I open my car door.

"Yeah, sounds like fun."

"If Ella is involved then you can guarantee it."

5

———

PEYTON

I'm filled with the same trepidation that I am every time I step out of the staff area and out into the main bar, but on a Tuesday night, it's always worse.

I've only been here a few weeks, but I already know some of the regulars, and I'm fully aware of exactly what they expect from me.

My stomach turns at the thought of what I'm going to have to do tonight to get the tips I need.

I feel their burning stares as I step out into the lights and make my way over toward Bry who's working the bar.

"Evening, gorgeous," he says, dropping his eyes down my body. "You on a mission tonight?"

"I'm always on a mission, Bry. To get out of here as soon as possible."

He chuckles at my response as he passes me a bottle of water.

"Your favorite table awaits." I take a sip of the water before stashing it on the shelf at the end of the bar for when I need a breather in about... two minutes.

"Great." I grab my notepad, not that I'll need it, they never order anything different as they sit there and strip me naked with their eyes.

Disgust rolls through me as I make my way over.

"Here's our girl," the most cringeworthy one of them says directly to my tits. He's got the bushiest eyebrows I think I've ever seen and I'm desperate to get a trimmer on them.

"Evening, gentlemen. What can I get for you tonight?" I pop my hip and lean against the booth they're sitting in, close enough to the least scary one of the group. The scent of his cologne fills my nose and my mouth goes dry.

I fucking hate this.

"You already know what we want, princess," the one with the greasy slicked back hair says.

They're all office workers and turn up on a weekly basis in their suits with their designer watches, but I can tell you that that is where their class ends. I'd put money on that all of them have wives and kids at home, yet they choose to spend their evening here getting their rocks off looking at my tits and ass and making me as uncomfortable as humanly possible with their lewd comments.

"Macallan all around then, boys?" I purr.

"Don't forget our hot wings," Eyebrows adds.

"Would I forget?"

Placing my notepad on the table, I stick my ass out as I write down their order as if I'm some dumb airhead that can't remember two things on the short walk over to the bar.

My skin prickles as they eat me up and as soon as I've finished my little show, I flash them a seductive smile and saunter off. But I don't make it back to the bar before Slick calls for me.

"We're celebrating tonight, princess, and we're feeling generous. Show us a good night and we'll make it worth your while."

My stomach churns at his words but I force a smile onto my face and retreat to the safety of the bar.

"You are aware of how much they'd probably pay you if you took them to the back room, right?" Bry asks.

"I'm not that fucking desperate," I mutter, not even needing to tell him their order. He knows as well as I do.

"Just saying, it would get you out of here quicker."

I want to be annoyed at him, but I can't. He's one of the only people who really seems to understand my need to be here despite the fact we've never shared our stories, there's just something about him that makes me think he gets it.

Helena, one of the other waitresses, approaches us. Her filled lips are painted bright red and her fake tits damn near pushed up around her neck. Resting her elbows on the bar she flashes her cleavage at Bry who pays her very little attention.

"Order's up, sweetie," she purrs, sliding her order over to him. "What's up, girl?" she asks, blatantly running her eyes over me disapprovingly.

I know I don't look like most of the other girls here. I don't have a fake thing on my body. Okay, aside from my eyelashes. I roll my eyes at myself. And while I might try my best to flirt with the customers, it's glaringly obvious that I have no idea what I'm doing and that I'm totally uncomfortable doing it. Bry tells me that that's my whole appeal, that I've got the innocent virgin vibe going on. And while I hate the thought of the men who leer at me thinking about ruining my innocence, I know it's what gets the tips and ultimately what landed me the job here in the first place.

I wish I could have just got a job at a coffee shop like Letty and serve normal people their caffeine and sugar fixes daily.

"Going for the big tips tonight, love?" Helena asks, her eyes zeroing in on my breasts, much like the men.

"Well, I might not have as much as you, but I figure I should work with what I've got."

Bry snorts a laugh, quickly covering it up with a cough, but it's too late, Helena heard it loud and clear.

"Well, enjoy the tips you can get. When you're ready to play with the women, you just let me know."

She spins around with her notebook poised, ready to take more orders from her adoring customers when Bry calls her back.

"Helena."

"Yes," she hisses, clearly done with both of us.

"You've got a little..." He taps the corner of his mouth. "Cum, maybe."

"Oh my God," I cry as her face twists in frustration. She storms off to the sound of our laughter.

"She's going to kill you with the heel of her stiletto," I tell him once she's out of earshot.

"Meh, it would be worth it. She's a bitch. I'd have you over her any day of the week."

"Bry, you're gay."

"Yeah, I'm not fucking blind though." He drops his eyes down my mostly exposed body and I can't help it heating up with his attention.

"Stop it," I snap.

"I fucking knew it. You want a bit of this, don't you?" he says, lifting his shirt to show off his abs.

"Ew, as if. I have no idea where you've been."

"In some really, really fucked-up guys," he deadpans.

"Ah, got a thing for the bad boys, do you?" I ask as he continues to put me off, grabbing the glasses I need for my table of assholes.

"Who doesn't?"

My lips part to argue but the words die on my tongue.

Luca was vicious that first night, but fuck if he didn't call to me even more so than he did back in the day. The wicked glint in his eyes, the snarl on his lips. Hell, if I'd have turned him down.

"Yeah, alright. You gonna finish this for me before they expect extras for me being late."

"Yes." He turns his back on me and grabs the glasses before sliding the tray over. "Pey," he says when I take off, holding the tray with one hand over my shoulder.

"Yeah."

"Be careful with those guys, I don't like the way they look at you."

"I've got this, Bry. You don't need to worry about me." I put as much confidence into my voice as possible, covering the fact on the inside I'm a terrified wreck who would rather hide in a dark closet than serve those sleazy jerks. But that's not going to pay the medical bills that are racking up faster than I can cope with.

Throwing my shoulders back and holding my head up high, I make my way over.

———

As expected, under the disgusting stares of the regulars, my night drags. Even the banter with Bry doesn't turn my night around. By the time my shift comes to an end, I can't run out of the building fast enough.

Thankfully, my fan club left about fifteen minutes ago, allowing me to step out of the back door of the club without too much concern about them still being back here. From the amount they all put away, there's no way they should be anywhere near a car anyway.

But as I take my first steps toward my car, I can't ignore the shiver that races down my spine.

The majority of the parking lot is illuminated by the security lights lining the building, but there are still plenty of dark spots that someone could hide in if they wanted to.

My eyes fly around in the hope of seeing whatever it is that's making all my hairs stand on end, but I don't see anyone. The parking lot is mostly empty, just a couple of the regular's cars who are still inside along with the remaining staff.

Swallowing down my fear, I continue forward. I tell myself that it's just the memory of the way those men looked at me tonight that has me on edge, but still, I don't believe it.

Someone is watching me.

Someone is—

The scream that erupts from my throat when a hot body presses against my back not a second later is cut off when a hand wraps around my mouth.

I'm shoved forward as my heart pounds so hard in my chest that I feel it in my toes.

My entire body trembles with fear.

Stupid, stupid girl, I think to myself. I knew I was playing with fire tonight in the hope of getting more tips, but all I've done is make them think they could take whatever they wanted.

I whimper beneath the hand as a strong arm wraps around my waist and I'm lifted from the ground.

I manage to get a look at the arm around me and even in the dull light, it's clear to see that it's not a suit jacket or even a shirt.

The man who has me is wearing a hoodie.

Oh God.

Together we slip into the darkness and somehow my pulse picks up even more speed knowing that even if someone did come back here, they'd never see us.

The front of my body presses up against a car and his long, hard body pins me in place.

"You didn't think I'd forgotten, did you?" a familiar voice growls in my ear.

The shudder of fear immediately turns into something else entirely as his breath caresses my ear and down my neck. Despite his obvious anger, there's still something there that calls to me, that feels right. Although everything about this is so very, very wrong.

I whimper again, wishing I was able to say something, anything, to get me out of this right now.

"I've been watching you, you know. Watching you leave every night. Wondering exactly who you've spent the night shaking your ass at for some cash."

Emotion clogs my throat, shame washing through me for the depths I've lowered myself to. Only a few months ago, I never would have considered a job like this. But needs must and all that.

"I guess it's true what they say, the apple never falls far from the tree."

No, I want to scream.

I know what people thought of my mom. I spent years having to endure the guys ribbing me over her job. But that's all it was. A job. A job to ensure that her girls had a roof over their heads and food in their bellies.

I don't want to hear anything bad about the woman who gave her life to look after us.

Suddenly, I'm moving. My front leaves the car and I'm spun around until it's my back against the cool metal.

Luca's hand leaves my mouth, his fingers curling around the top of his car and pinning me in.

"Don't even think about calling for help, Little Girl."

A weird mix of comfort and hatred races through me at his use of the name he used to call me all those years ago. It was always a joke because I was a couple of weeks younger than him. But right now, it feels anything like a joke and everything like a threat.

I am little compared to him. I always was. But in our time apart he's grown, both in height and bulk, and I already know that I don't stand a chance against him.

My lips part, but no noise passes them, just a large exhale as I stare into his dark eyes. I know they're the most incredible green, but right now, hidden in the darkness, it's hard to see.

He stares at me as if he can't believe I'm actually standing before him.

His chest heaves, his full lips parted as he fights to keep his cool.

"You shouldn't have come back here," he warns, his voice low and cold in a way I remember all too well from the last time we spoke.

"I-I—"

"No," he barks. "I don't want your pity story, Peyton."

I swallow down the argument that was on the tip of my tongue, although I already know that it was weak at best because there is no way I'm telling him the truth. I'm not giving him any more ammunition to hurt me than he already thinks he has.

"Did you think you would turn up here and I wouldn't find you?"

I stare at him, willing him to see the truth in my eyes.

I didn't have any other option.

"Or is that exactly what you wanted? That I would find you and that I'd have forgotten? Did you think that I'd put all your lies behind me and that we could just pick back up where we left off?" He spits the words as if even saying them disgusts him. "Did you really miss me that much?"

Internally, I scream yes. Yes, I really missed him that much. When we first moved away, I'd have done anything to have my best friend back. Literally anything. But I knew there was no way it was going to happen. Just like I don't think it's going to happen now either.

"Let's see what you've had on offer tonight then. See if we can make all of this worthwhile for me."

"W-wha—"

I'm frozen in shock as he lifts his hand to the zipper on the front of my hoodie and pulls it down.

Unlike last night, this one actually belongs to me. The moment I put it on, I missed the comfort of Elijah's. It's crazy but it's like some weird security blanket.

The cool winter air washes over my exposed skin, making me shiver. That is until his eyes drop from mine and scorch a trail over my skin.

Then I'm burning up. My blood boiling from the inside from the way that he's making me feel.

But it's not for him. It's not lust or my desire for him to touch me.

It's shame.

Red-hot shame for the person I've become, the woman he's standing before after all these years and what I've lowered myself to.

It's no surprise he doesn't like me. Every time I come to this place and put in a shift, I hate myself a little bit more.

It's just a means to an end, I tell myself. My family needs me, and this is the best way I can help.

But that knowledge doesn't make it any better.

A growl of disapproval rumbles at the back of his throat before he clicks his tongue.

"You were showing those boys a good time tonight, huh?" he mutters.

Unable to even look at him as he judges me, I turn my head to the side and stare into the darkness, wishing like hell that it would swallow me up.

Why did it have to be like this?

The lump in my throat is so large, it's hard to even breathe as he continues studying me.

"Tell me..." he starts, making my stomach sink for what's going to come next. "Did you make a lot of tips tonight?"

I don't answer him. I don't even look at him. Too mortified by the knowledge of just how much I made from merely showing off a little too much skin.

Not happy with my lack of response, Luca shoves his hand into the pocket of my hoodie, correctly guessing where I stashed the cash.

"Fucking hell," he gasps when he pulls the wad of bills out. "What did you do tonight, you filthy slut?" he growls, leaning in and whispering in my ear.

"N-nothing."

"Bullshit," he spits, moving closer still. We're not touching but the heat of his skin burns. It makes me tingle with my need for him to actually touch me. To know if it's still as electric as it was back then.

When he does finally connect with me, it's not at all in the way I'd hoped, or longed for, after all these years.

I swallow down the whimper that wants to erupt when his hot fingers wrap around my throat.

They squeeze lightly in warning, making my eyes burn with red hot tears.

I'm sorry. I'm so sorry, I scream internally. I know full well that what happened between us was what created—or at least contributed to—the angry, vicious, dark boy who's standing before me. He was always there, hiding under the surface. Whenever someone pissed him off—mainly his dad—he would emerge. But only ever behind closed doors, and only ever alone or with me or Leon. His safe places.

What the rest of the world saw when shit hit the fan was an entirely different person to the one I knew. He was ashamed of the place he went when he was really angry, and I knew why, even without him ever telling me.

It made him like his father.

His temper, his ability to lash out. It was just like Brett Dunn, and Luca hated it.

I got it. His dad was a douchebag of epic proportions. I just always wished he found a way to deal with it instead of hiding and taking it out on those he loved. Me, Lee, his mom.

It makes me wonder if anyone else has been there for him over the past five years with me gone.

My heart aches considering that there might be a woman out there right now who understands this side of him. Who helps him through it much like I used to.

"Don't act like a stupid little girl, Peyton. We both know you're not. And, we both know exactly what happens in there to earn this kind of money. So... What. Did. You. Do?"

"N-nothing," I repeat.

"Who touched you?"

"N-no one." It's not entirely true. Slick did get a little handsy after the fourth bottle of whisky was delivered to their table, but he didn't touch me like I'm sure Luca is thinking right now.

He shakes his head at me, disappointment rolling off him in waves.

"So, all this money just to look, huh? They must really think you're something special."

"I-I'm nothing, Luc. I just... I just give them what they want."

"Trust me. If you didn't let them touch you, if you didn't touch them, I can assure you that you got nowhere fucking close to giving them what they wanted."

I swallow down my response because we both know any argument I might have would be a lie.

"You're a tease, Peyton. Walking around like this, giving guys ideas." His eyes drop to my breasts, and even in the dark, I know exactly what he can see and it makes me want the ground to swallow me whole.

My hands curl into tight fists and I squeeze my eyes closed, wishing that I were anywhere but here right now. That we could have collided again in any other place than this. Any other time than tonight.

"Tell me, P. Were these as hard for them as they are for me right now?"

I gasp when his soft touch brushes over one of my nipples.

His fingers tighten around my throat when I don't immediately respond.

"I-it's the cold."

"Fucking bullshit, P. We both know that if I were to push my hand inside your panties right now that you'd be dripping fucking wet for me."

My eyes fly up to his in shock. His words rocking me to my very core and reminding me that I'm not dealing with a fifteen-year-old Luca anymore. I'm dealing with a man with more anger and hurt than I know how to navigate.

"Wait..." he says before I have any time to fight my corner. "You are wearing panties, right? You're not that desperate for those cunts' money that you've been bending over in this short skirt all night and showing them what's mine."

"Y-yours?" I stutter, ignoring the rest of his statement. My shock at his ownership of my body is too much to brush aside.

A low, menacing chuckle rumbles up his throat. A terrifying smirk curls at his lips.

"Yeah, Peyton. *Mine.*"

I swallow, trying to force down the ever-growing lump, but it's pointless. Even long after he releases me, I know it's going to remain.

I hold his eyes, dragging up as much confidence as I can muster while refusing to dignify his question with an actual answer.

That all goes to shit though when he lowers his hand, skimming his knuckles along the edge of my skirt.

"Yes. Yes," I cry. "I'm wearing panties."

Pulling his hand away, he lifts the cash he's still got in his fingers.

His lips curl once more before he pushes it all into the pocket of his sweats.

"Luca, please. I need—"

"What you need is to stop looking like a cheap whore, P."

"It's my job. I need the money."

"Tell me why and maybe I'll go easier on you. Assuming I believe a word that comes out of your lying mouth."

6

LUCA

My heart is a runaway train in my chest as I stare into her silver eyes, watching her internal battle. She wants to tell me her reasons for being here because she wants to get away. I don't need to be able to feel the tremor wracking her body to know that she's scared of me right now. I can practically taste her fear and it feeds some part of me that I wasn't aware needed sating quite so badly.

I knew standing before her, looking into her eyes was going to calm the war raging inside me. But I had no idea her fear was going to be this... addictive.

"Tell me," I demand again as footsteps in the gravel of the parking lot sound out. I have no idea if it's some of tonight's late-night customers or staff, I don't rip my eyes from Peyton's to find out.

I don't need to say anything to warn her against calling out or asking for help. She seems to know that it would be a really bad fucking thing to do.

She swallows once more, her delicate skin rippling against my hand, making me want to tighten my hold to terrify her even more. But I resist, for now.

I still want to address the fact that even in the fucking dark I can clearly see the imprint of her nipples through her shirt. Why she thought for even a second that it was a good idea to step outside of the house looking like that, let alone spend the night around the disgusting cunts who spend their Tuesday nights at The Locker Room.

"Fuck you, Luc. I owe you nothing. What I do has nothing to do with you. You made your place in my life very clear five years ago. You don't get to storm back in now and shame me for doing what I need to do."

Her fire makes my cock swell. It always took a lot to rattle her. I think that's one of the reasons we just worked so well. Whenever I'd lose my shit, she'd always been the one to cool me off, to make me see things from a different perspective. I can probably count on one hand the number of times I saw her angry. The worst of those times was the last time I saw her.

Memories of that afternoon still haunt me. But I did the right thing. I couldn't let her poison me with her lies. Even if she had no idea they were lies.

A huge part of me knows that she doesn't really believe it, that she's just putting too much loyalty on those she loves.

What infuriated me back then, and still does now, is that she had the audacity to stand there and make those bullshit claims as if she actually believed it.

What she told me... it was... it was serious.

There's no way... no fucking way...

"What the hell are you doing?" she hisses when I lift my hand once more and gently rub at her nipple through the thin fabric of her shirt with the pad of my thumb.

"Did you even look in a mirror before you stepped out in this?" I ask, my eyes locked on my movements as her peak hardens even more with the sensation.

I'm not the only one who's changed since the last time we saw each other. She was a young woman back then. Now she's all woman. The curves she's developed threaten to fucking ruin me. Sadly for her, the only one here who's getting ruined is her.

I've waited years to finally have this out between us and now she's right here.

My prey.

She keeps her lips pressed into a thin line, refusing to speak after her little outburst.

"So I'll assume you did then and you wanted every man in that place to imagine how they look bare. If your nipples are as pink and rosy as they're imagining. I bet they were wondering just how you would sound if they were to—"

Her gasp of shock rips through the air as I pinch down hard on her sensitive peak.

Her eyes narrow in warning but it's impossible to miss how much they darken at my move.

"You like that, P? Is what you were hoping for? For someone to take away that innocence you seem to be trying to convince everyone of with this little act."

Leaning forward, I brush my lips against her ear.

"Is that it? Have you told them all that you're a virgin?"

A growl vibrates up her throat. I'd miss it if I weren't holding her so tight.

"Just another lie to add to all the others you spill because we both know you're anything but a virgin, don't we, P?"

Her chest heaves as she stares at me. Memories of us together, figuring each other's bodies out all those years ago, are almost visible in her gray depths.

"How much do you think they'd pay you for this?" I ask, switching to the other side which is already at a hard point for me.

She shakes her head, still trying to claim her innocence.

"What about a taste, P? How much does that cost?"

"I don't sell my body, Luc." The plea in her voice only makes me want to push her more. And I realize for the first time just how much I want to break her.

Just like she broke me.

Everything changed for me the day her mom dragged her out of Rosewood. My trust was in tatters, my life imploding on me, and everything I thought I knew was in question.

I've trusted no one with the darkest part of me since that day.

I found a vault deep inside and locked it all down because I couldn't risk anyone betraying me like that again.

Letty thinks she knows everything about me. But she doesn't. There are parts that I've never exposed to her. Parts that even Leon hasn't seen for a very long time.

They both just think I'm a little hot-headed, and I am, I can't deny that. But it's what happens when I lock myself into my room after that outburst that they have no idea about.

Peyton knows it all though. She's seen every dark and twisted side of me and despite knowing that, she fucking broke me.

"You're fucking right there. You've already taken enough from me. It's time for me to repay the favor."

Releasing her throat, I wrap my fingers around the cropped hem of her shirt and push it up, exposing her bare tits.

They're fucking perfect and everything I've spent years dreaming about but like fuck am I about to tell her that.

Before she has a chance to protest, I lower down and suck one into my mouth.

Her sweetness explodes in my mouth and my cock weeps for her.

I remember the image of her lips wrapped around my length all too well. I remember her hesitation, her nerves. It makes me wonder how much more confidence she might have now. How much practice she might have had.

The thought of her on her knees for some other motherfucker makes my fists clench but I soon realize I've something better right before me to release my frustration on.

"Luc," she cries as I bite down on the nipple deep in my mouth as I pinch the other.

Her fingers thrust into my hair, pulling hard and making my scalp sting as she tries to fight me off.

"And to think, you tried to deny being a whore," I mutter against the fullness of her breast.

"I'm not. Get the hell off me."

"Stop lying to yourself, P. You want this. You're wet for this."

"No. I hate you, Luc. I fucking hate you."

Her words send a tsunami of anger racing through me.

"You hate me?" I roar, forgetting all about where we are and that anyone could hear and come rushing to her rescue. My hand finds her throat once more but my grip is much more brutal this time and her eyes widen in fear. Once upon a time, she'd have every confidence in me never taking things too far, never hurting her. But times have fucking changed and she deserves all the pain I can deliver. "I did nothing, P. Fucking nothing," I bellow, the hurt fifteen-year-old boy inside me rearing his little head. "You ruined everything with your bullshit lies. I loved you, P. I loved you so fucking much and you fucking broke me."

Need, hunger, anger, depravity, it all swirls around me like a dark cloud making me forget who I really am, where we are and what I should be doing.

"Luca, no," Peyton cries as I rip her panties aside. Kicking her legs wider with my feet, I sink two fingers deep inside her. Her velvet heat surrounds me and immediately something settles because I was right.

I was fucking right.

"Fuck, P. You're fucking dripping right now."

"Luca," she whimpers. Her body is clearly on a different page than her head because as I bend my fingers inside her, she clamps down on me, a rush of liquid running down my digits and to my hand.

"You enjoy walking around looking like a filthy slut, don't you? Does it make you feel powerful knowing that all the men want you?"

"No," she cries.

"Let's make a deal."

She thrashes her head from side to side trying to ignore what my fingers are doing buried deep inside her.

"We'll let them look... for now. But no one else touches what's mine."

"Luc." Her voice is raspy, her body teetering right on the edge of her release.

The need to push her over. To watch her fall once again because of me is almost too much to deny.

Almost.

"Oh shit. Luc. No," she cries, sagging against the side of my car as I rip my fingers from inside her.

Her chest heaves, her nipples still glistening from my attention. Her eyes are blown and I know if I could see better her cheeks and chest would be bright red with her almost-release.

Lifting my hand, I make the most of her parted lips and push them inside.

"Suck them clean."

Her eyes widen once more in surprise but whatever she sees in mine ensures she does as she's told.

I damn near come in my pants like a fucking schoolboy when her tongue laves at me.

Grinding my teeth, I rip my fingers away again.

"Good girl." I take a step back and she sags lower, her knees barely holding her up. "I meant what I said, P. No one else touches you." Bending to her height, I look into her eyes so she can see how serious I am. "Even your cunt of a boyfriend." The word is bitter on my tongue but I can't leave it unsaid after seeing them yesterday.

"My b-boy—" She slams her lips shut, probably realizing that I really have been watching her. She swallows nervously.

"Now, get off my car. You're making it look cheap."

Her jaw drops in shock as I wrap my hand around the fabric of her hoodie and pull her away.

She stumbles back away from me, wrapping it around herself to cover up.

It's a damn shame but I'll let it go. For now.

"Luc, wait. Please."

I take two steps toward the driver's door before I realize what she's begging for.

Digging my hand into my pocket, I pull out her cash, along with my wallet.

"This all you care about?" I say, throwing the bills at her.

She wants to look down, to gather them up, but she doesn't. Her eyes remain on mine, begging me to stop.

She can try that all she wants. What she really needs to realize is that this is just the beginning.

Opening my wallet, I stare her straight in the eyes when I ask my next question. "So how much for the fingerbang?"

A garbled cry falls from her lips and I pull a few bills from my wallet. I have no idea how much is in there but I really don't give a fuck.

I throw the money at her before ripping my car door open and dropping into the seat.

I look in the mirror as I pull out of the lot and find her in a pile on the ground with her head in her hands.

My stomach knots. The little boy within me wanting to go and scoop up the girl who was his entire life. To help her put the pieces back together and tell her that everything is going to be okay.

But he's long gone. The man in his place is nowhere near as caring to the person who killed that sweet boy.

7

PEYTON

Tears continue to cascade down my cheeks as I make the drive back to Aunt Fee's house. My body trembles as those few moments with Luca play on repeat in my head. Every vicious word taunts me, every barbed insult and insinuation about being a whore hurt more and more every time I hear them. Yet, despite all of that, my skin still burns from where he touched me. My core muscles tighten with the memory of his fingers inside me.

I was so close. So close to just forgetting about my reality for just a few seconds and he took it from me.

A sob erupts as I pull to a stop outside the house.

I can't walk in there like this, Aunt Fee will take one look at me and demand to know what's wrong.

I could lie, sure. I've got enough to cry about in my life right now, but she'd see straight through it. She'd know that this was different. It is. It's different because it's about him. The only person I've ever given my heart to.

Instead of turning the engine off, I throw the car back into drive and pull off again.

I can't sit out here in case one of them notices, and I can't walk inside until I've got myself under control.

I drive around town, wishing that I was back in Rosewood and that I could go and sit on the beach. Listening to the crashing waves is perfect when you need to get out of your own head.

Luc and I used to spend hours down on the beach after dark just laying on the cool sand putting the world to rights.

My chest tightens. What I wouldn't give to go back to easier times with him.

I find a coffee shop with a drive-thru in the center of town and order myself the biggest hot chocolate with all the trimmings that they have before pulling into the parking lot, sliding my chair back and just allowing myself a moment to breathe.

My time with Luca was intense. Part of me is surprised by his brutality, his need to hurt me. But another part isn't. I've seen that side of him before. But in the past, it was only ever directed at his dad or occasionally an opposing player who touched a sore spot. It was never —other than just before I left—been directed at me quite like that.

A shiver races up my spine as I think about his electric touch. Although vicious and tinged with hate, it was exactly as I hoped it would be. The second he brushed his thumb over my nipple, the same electric sparks I remember all too well zipped through my body, assaulting my nerve endings.

My nipples harden once more, the throb in my clit returning from my lost orgasm. Resting my head back, I close my eyes and blow out a long, slow breath. I can almost feel the ghost of his fingers still deep inside me.

My head flies up as I realize what I'm doing.

What the fuck is wrong with me?

I didn't want that. I didn't ask for that. Why am I sitting here fantasizing about it?

Shaking my head, my cheeks burn red hot in the knowledge that I'd have let that continue tonight, and possibly so much more given the chance.

It didn't matter the malicious words he'd spat at me. I was with Luca again. Something about his presence just spoke to my soul.

He knew it too.

It's why he played me like he did.

My hot chocolate is long gone by the time I start the engine once more, feeling like I'm going to be able to walk through Aunt Fee's front door and not give myself away instantly.

I don't realize just how late it is until I pull back up outside the house and notice that it's in darkness.

It's not often that Aunt Fee heads to bed before I'm home, but clearly, she got bored with waiting tonight.

With a heavy heart and a knot that seems to be a permanent fixture in the pit of my stomach, I head inside.

The house is as quiet as I expected, and I tiptoe down the hallway toward the kitchen to grab a glass of water to take upstairs with me.

I'm standing at the sink, staring at my reflection in the window before me, still questioning myself over how I felt tonight with Luca when a voice makes me drop the glass in my hand.

"Holy sh— moly," I curse when I spin around and see a small face looking at me with his brows drawn in concern. "You scared me, baby boy."

His lips twist in the way they always do when I call him that.

"You're late," he states.

"Err... yeah, I got held up. You should be asleep," I warn.

"I know." He stares at me with sad eyes. "I was waiting for you."

"I'm sorry. You're okay though, right?"

He nods, but the sadness never leaves his face. I understand why. I feel the same pain on a daily basis too.

"Come on, let's get you to bed."

I help him back to his room and tuck him in.

"I don't like you working late, Pey."

"I know, baby. But sometimes we have to do things we don't like. It will get better, I promise."

"I miss her," he says, his soft voice cracking with emotion and shattering my heart all over again.

"I know, baby. I know."

I hold his small hand in mine, allowing his warmth to ground me. He holds my eyes for a minute but they soon become too heavy once more and he drifts off to sleep.

I watch him for a long time as he snores lightly, his raggedy lamb tucked under his head.

As I sit there, I make him the promise I have done a million times over in the last couple of weeks.

I promise to make everything okay. I promise to give you everything they couldn't.

With tears in my eyes, I drop a kiss to his forehead and slip silently out of the room.

While I might have been through hell in the past few months, that little boy has had it even worse.

All of this is for him. All of it.

I'll take everything Luca throws my way. All his vicious accusations and wicked touches because Kayden is my endgame here. He's lost too much for me to give up on him too.

I arrive at Ella's dorm later than I agreed because, after the night before, I knew I needed to have dinner at home.

It would be too easy to get swept up into college life while working as many hours as physically possible. But that's not my life now. I have responsibilities, and that little boy needs me.

I knew it was the right decision the second I stepped foot into the house after class and saw his little face light up.

He was working on his phonics with Aunt Fee, but she called time on their little lesson so the two of us could hang out.

He talked my ear off the entire time and then insisted on sitting beside me while we ate. It was like he was scared that if he even looked away for a second then I might vanish.

I got it. Hell, I more than got it. There were times in the past few weeks where I felt exactly the same.

Not wanting to disappoint him, I stayed and put him to bed. And I'm so glad I did. It was the reminder I needed for why I'm doing this. For why I'm putting myself through bullshit like last night.

I shudder, still able to feel the eyes of those guys on my skin.

I scrubbed every inch of my body twice as I stood under the scorching heat of Aunt Fee's shower once I left Kayden last night.

I told myself that I was washing Luca off me, but it was all lies. While a huge part of me might hate him for how he treated me, there was something about his scent clinging to my skin that just felt so right.

He might have been vicious, but I also know that while he's watching me, the other men can't touch me. Or at least, that's what I hope anyway.

I knock on the door to Ella's dorm before pushing it open and poking my head inside.

"Well, well, well," a guy says, immediately turning his stare on me. "What do we have here?"

My skin burns as the other two guys in the room hear his comment and also turn to look at me.

"Uh..."

"Don't even try it," a familiar voice barks from the end of the room.

After a beat, Ella emerges haphazardly wrapped in a bedsheet and gives each of them a look they probably should be scared of.

"Damn, girl. You are looking—"

"Finish that sentence and lose a testicle." She pops a hip, putting a hand on her waist.

"Jeez, who pissed in your margarita?" one of them growls.

"Peyton," she says, a smile turning up the corners of her mouth when she looks over at me. "This is West, Brax, and Micah. They're something akin to our dorm pets."

I snort a laugh at the incredulous looks on two of their faces.

"Hey," I squeak, trying to keep my amusement locked down.

"She's off-limits to you pigs, so only engage the brains in your heads, please."

"Not sure these two have anything up there," the one who's been the least interested in my arrival deadpans.

"Fuck you, man."

"Jesus. Come on." Ella holds her arm out and gestures for me to follow her.

I hear the hysterical laughter before I get to her room, and when we walk through, I discover Letty sitting on the bed with tears rolling down her cheeks while another girl that I've yet to meet is rolling around on the floor wrapped in a bedsheet.

"What the hell happened?" Ella demands.

"I think your margarita is too strong," Letty says innocently.

"When isn't it?" the other asks, finally getting to her feet, leaving the bedsheet behind and confidently standing in just her white strapless bra and panties.

"Hey, I'm Violet," she says with a smile.

"Uh... hey. I'm Pe—"

"Peyton. I've heard all about you, Pink. I think you're going to fit right in with this bunch of reprobates."

"You're aware that includes you, right, Vi?" Ella asks with a laugh, filling an empty glass from the pitcher sitting on the side and offering it over to me.

"I'm driving," I say, not taking it.

"It's okay, it's virgin for you and Letty."

"Oh, well. Thank you."

"Come sit down. Ella promised us mad skills with this but all I've seen so far is a girl wrapped in a bedsheet." She glances over at Ella, who admittedly does look exactly as she described.

"Don't worry, I've got it. Right, Vi? You remember last year? I'm just finding my flow."

She flips open a pink box and pulls out a huge pair of scissors.

"I really hope she knows what she's doing with them."

"Me too," Letty whispers back. "But at least Vi is first."

"Yes, but just how many margaritas is she going to have had by the time she gets to us?"

Letty's lips part to say something but she quickly realizes that I'm right. "Shit."

———

It's well past midnight when I leave their dorm with a sheet and firm instructions on how to wear it come Friday night. My face hurts from laughing so much.

I can't remember the last time that happened.

I cast my mind back but come up blank for anything over the past five years.

Memories from before I left Rosewood hit me. Laughing with Luca. Acting like complete idiots until we laughed so hard we couldn't breathe.

A smile curls at my lips thinking of those two young kids who were still naïve about real life and just loving every day.

I'd give anything to go back to then. To running around the backyard with water pistols, to making dens and camping out overnight. To thinking that what the two of us shared would never break.

How wrong were we?

Everyone is once again asleep when I get home. Knowing that I was just hanging out with friends instead of working, Aunt Fee told me that she'd be able to relax properly, knowing I was safe. As much as I love her concern, I wish I wasn't putting any more stress on her shoulders. She's already had her life changed enough by us turning up here, I don't want to do anything to make it worse.

Unlike the night before, I fall asleep with a little bit of hope filling my veins. Things with Luca might be fucked up beyond belief, but I've actually made some friends. Some friends who might just be able to make my life here more bearable.

8

LUCA

Not going to sit in the parking lot of The Locker Room last night was weird. It's become something of a sanctuary for me over the past couple of weeks. Just seeing her walk out of the building and to her car settled something inside me. But that was nothing compared to the feeling of standing in front of her Tuesday night.

My fists curl as I walk toward my morning class with my need for a repeat.

Her scent. Her taste. The little whimpers that involuntarily fell from her lips as I brought her right to the edge, they're all I can think about.

My cock swells as the image of her pressed up against my car, her tits exposed and my hand disappearing up her skirt fills my mind.

Fuck. I really needed that last night. But, watching her the past couple of weeks, I knew that it was her night off.

The hallway is empty as I make my way down to the elevator. I'm hardly surprised. I got sucked into the gym this morning and it wasn't until one of the coaching staff poked his head in to say something that I realized the time.

I needed the release. I needed something other than my own right hand that was doing very fucking little to take the edge off.

I need her.

Reaching down, I palm my growing cock, rearranging myself so I'm not about to walk into class, not only late but with a raging boner over the girl I should have forgotten long ago.

Hitting the call button for the elevator, I step inside and slam my hand down on the button for the correct floor.

Leaning against the back wall, I close my eyes as the doors shut, shutting me off from the rest of campus for just a little bit.

Right before the doors close, I hear a curse before the doors audibly stop moving.

Blowing out a breath that someone is about to ruin my peace, I rip my head from the wall and look to see who's joined me.

She glances up at the same time I do and we both suck in a sharp breath.

"Letty," I breathe.

"Shit." Her eyes widen in surprise and she quickly takes a step back but she's too late. The doors have already closed, caging us in together. "Um... h-how are you?"

I stare at her, my heart aching in my chest.

I hate how things turned out between us. I hate that she's now with that jerk. But what can I really do about it? She was never meant to be mine. I think deep down I always knew that, but I really wanted to believe that she was here for me.

Turns out fate had other ideas because she just put her and Kane in the same place, allowing them to sort their shit out. Although not before making me want to end the motherfucker for the way he treated her. And I know for a fact that I only know the basics of the situation.

Reaching up, I wrap my hand around the back of my neck as she steps into the enclosed space a little more.

The elevator jolts as we begin our ascent, and her scent fills my nose.

"I-I'm good. You?" I hate the awkwardness, and I know that most of it—hell, all of it—is because of me.

"Y-yeah. Things are really good." Unable to stop it, a soft smile spreads across her face, I assume, as she thinks about Kane.

Asshole.

"I'm glad."

We fall into an uncomfortable silence and I hate it. I hate everything that's happened between us. After Peyton left Rosewood all those years ago, Letty turned up like a fucking angel. I was in a bad place when our teacher decided that I'd be the perfect partner for the new girl. Fuck knows what he was thinking. Maybe he hoped she'd be a good influence on me because hell knows I was fucking up all over the place back then. Even my place on the team was at risk at one point when I was caught skipping, preferring to go to the beach to get fucked up instead of dealing with the fact I'd been betrayed and abandoned by my best friend.

My lips part to say something, but I can't find the words I want to say to her. An apology doesn't seem enough after all the shit I've put her through.

She's tried to reach out to me time and time again, and I've only pushed her farther away. It's probably best for her in the long run if I do.

I think it's pretty obvious that Kane and I are never going to see eye to eye, and I'm not sure where that leaves a friendship between us.

"Luc?" she whispers after what feels like the longest silence of my life.

Dragging my eyes from my feet, I look at her. My breath catches at how happy she looks, despite the concern that's currently causing a frown to mar her brow.

"I-I'm sorry," I whisper, utterly defeated where Letty is concerned.

Her eyes hold mine. The sparkle that was within them when she first stepped into the elevator has vanished, replaced with worry, pity even, and I hate it.

"Luc, it's—"

I suck in a breath waiting to hear the words I don't deserve from her when the doors open and reveal a large group of students waiting to get inside.

Silently, we move past the group and make our way down to our lit class.

Seeing as we're both late, the professor has already started and we both slip inside and find the first two empty seats we can, side by side.

It's the closest I've been to her in weeks, and I can't deny that it feels good to have her there.

Everything in my life is fucked beyond belief right now. I know most of that is my fault, and that the situation we've found ourselves in is entirely on me. But I'm starting to wonder if it's time to put it all behind me. Letty is the least of my concerns now that Peyton is in town.

She's happy. I can see that without even having to ask her. A few weeks ago, I was drowning in jealousy that she'd found in Kane what I wanted to give her.

I have no idea what our professor is saying, and seeing as it's our first class of the semester, I really should be paying attention. With the season over, it's time for me to get some credits in the bag but I can't find it in me to focus.

My plan was always to graduate before I started playing pro football. It's just a shame that wasn't everyone's plan for me.

If Dad had his way, I'd be in this year's draft. First pick, obviously. But even if I did enter this year, I never would have been first after the season we just saw the back of.

It was embarrassing, and I know the responsibility for the clusterfuck lands on my shoulders. All the guys are pissed. I can see that just from looking at them. None of them have outwardly blamed me, but I know they do.

I fucked up. I dropped the ball—literally and figuratively. I totally lost sight of what was important as Kane stole the girl from under my feet.

But she was never my girl, was she?

I blow out a long, frustrated breath and slump down in the chair.

Movement to my side catches my eye and when I glance over, I find Letty studying me, her brows pulled together.

"Everything is going to be okay, Luc." She gives me a soft smile that

I wish would make me feel better but all it does is make my chest ache for the way I treated her.

She reaches over and takes my hand. It's not an unusual move but the heat of her fingers against my skin makes my entire body jolt.

Not missing my reaction, she hesitantly pulls her hand back, muttering an apology as she does.

Every muscle in my body locks up tight as I stare at the door, my need to storm out and put all this bullshit behind me is strong.

I have no idea what I'm doing right now. Football, college, Letty, Leon, fucking Peyton.

I relax slightly just at the thought of her name. She's the only one who makes it all go away.

When I look at her, standing before her, everything else that's falling apart in my life goes quiet.

Dad's voice disappears, and all my failings as a friend, a captain, a teammate, a brother, all vanish.

It's just me and her. It's like I'm a kid again without the pressure of real life, only that my best friend is no longer that. She's a girl who lied to me. Betrayed me. And the fun we used to have together has morphed into my need to hurt her, to show her what her words, her accusations, did to me back then.

Aside from Leon who was existing in the same hell as me, she was the only one who got me. The only one who knew what my life was really like. The only one who knew how hard I battled with family issues and how badly I wanted things to be different.

And then she shattered all of it.

The pencil that was in my hand snaps under the pressure of my grip, the splintered wood digging into my skin.

My heart races as I stare down at it, feeling exactly like I did the day she dropped the bomb on me.

The auditorium around me blurs as I fight to get a grip on reality.

"Luc?" A warm hand lands on mine and fingers begin to pry mine open.

Her scent fills my nose and I blink a few times as Letty's image clears before me.

I glance around, finding that the seats are almost empty around me and the professor is nowhere to be seen.

Fuck.

"Come on, I'm buying you a coffee and a cupcake. And don't even think about arguing with me."

Even if I wanted to, I couldn't right now.

The darkness from my past is clawing at me, threatening to consume me.

I once again look around the room, willing her to appear to put it all to rest, but she never does. Instead, students just leave, too many casting curious glances my way.

When I still don't move, Letty wraps her hand around my bicep and does her best attempt at pulling me from the chair.

My lip curls up in a smile as I watch her efforts.

Blowing a lock of hair from her face, she looks up at me, exasperated.

"You're gonna need to help."

Running my eyes down her body, I'm relieved to see that she's finally putting some decent weight on. When I first ran into her at the beginning of the fall semester, she was skin and bones. But even with all the drama of the past few months, she seems to have managed to find the time to look after herself, or more likely—and I hate to even admit this—Kane has.

I might not like him. I might not trust him or think he's good enough for Letty. But since they've become official, he only seems to have treated her exactly as she deserves. And for that, I'm beyond grateful because of anyone I know, Letty deserves the happily ever after.

Having pity on her, I grab my still unopened notebook, shoving it into my bag, and then scoop up the shards of my now ruined pencil from the desk and slide out behind her. I drop the remains in the trash on the way out, looking at the pieces for a beat, seeing the resemblance to my life.

There's a massive crowd waiting for the elevator, so when Letty looks toward the stairs, I follow her lead, not wanting to be stuck in an enclosed space with a group of people right now.

I trail down behind her and then out into the winter sun. I squint against the brightness, feeling a little better getting some fresh air.

Nothing is said between us as we stand in line to order our coffees. Everyone else's stares and interest burn into me. The girls—the jersey chasers—blatantly strip me naked while the guys either stare at me with angry eyes for having that effect on their girls or for the fact I've lost them their season. Either is a valid reason, to be fair.

"Dunn," the server calls, her cheeks turning a deep crimson when I look at her and take my coffee.

"Thanks," I mutter, giving her zero special attention, but still she damn near pisses her pants.

Don't get me wrong, there are many, many times where I've lapped up this kind of attention. The adoring fans, screaming crowds, girls who would sell their left tit to have a night with me. I'm a college guy, of course I've made the most of that over the years, who fucking wouldn't. But right now, I want them all to go away. I need the pity in their eyes to vanish and their attention to dwindle. I'd hoped it would after I lost us the championship, but now instead of everyone looking at me like they either want to be me or bang me, they're looking at me and wondering where it all went wrong. How their golden boy went from the epic high of last season to the pitiful low of this one.

I blow out a frustrated breath as I fall down into a chair that ensures I have my back to the rest of the coffee shop. I know they'll still be staring, but at least I don't have to watch them do it.

"It's still weird seeing you as such a celebrity," Letty says lightly, unable to miss the fact that the volume of the place dropped and all eyes turned on me from the second we entered.

I scoff, reaching out for one of the cupcakes she loves so much and pulling the wrapper off.

Taking a huge bite, I let the sweetness explode in my mouth in the hope it'll help sweeten my mood.

"What?" I mutter with a mouthful of cake when I pull it away.

"You really need to shave." Letty laughs, reaching over and wiping a generous blob of icing and sprinkles from the overly long scruff above my top lip.

I watch as she puts her finger in her mouth innocently to wipe it off. Not so long ago that move would have done things to me, but right now I feel nothing. But I don't think that's because I've accepted our reality and more just because I'm dead inside right now. The only thing that gets my blood pumping is the thought of torturing Peyton some more.

I shift in the chair as I think about Tuesday night once again before remembering that Letty said something.

"Y-yeah," I say, lifting my hand to my chin. "I know, I just..."

"Don't make excuses, Luc. I know you, remember." She pins me with a look that makes me feel about two inches tall.

"Let, I'm—"

"Don't," she snaps. "Don't apologize and assume everything is just going to go back to how it once was."

"It won't though, will it? You're with him."

"Luc," she breathes, looking up to the ceiling as if she needs some strength for this conversation.

"That wasn't what I meant. I get it, Let. Okay? I fucking get it." Pushing the rest of my cupcake away, I rest my elbows on the edge of the table and shove my fingers into my hair. "It was never meant to be us."

"You know, if it were four years ago then maybe it could have been." Slowly, I lift my head and find her dark eyes.

"Oh come off it. As if you didn't know I had the biggest crush on you." She rolls her eyes at herself, embarrassment heating her cheeks and down her neck.

"You slept with Leon," I blurt, pain slicing through my heart as I remember that revelation.

"And you slept with half the female population of Rosewood High. It's all in the past, Luc. We did some stupid shit. I'm sure we'll continue to do stupid shit. But I want to do it knowing that you've got my back." Her expression softens and my frozen heart begins to melt a little.

"Does he really make you happy?"

"Yes, he does. He really does."

I nod at her, reaching for my coffee and pulling it closer.

"I know the two of you will probably never see eye to eye. But if you could at least try to tolerate each other, it would mean the world to me."

"I tolerate him just fine," I mutter, thinking of him being a much bigger part of my life than I ever wanted or expected him to be.

I thought exchanges with Kane Legend were done once I graduated. I thought he'd disappear into the pits of hell that was Harrow Creek, destined for a life of gangs, drugs, and crime. But no, apparently the universe had other ideas. As if I didn't already have enough to deal with.

Letty scoffs. "That's what you call tolerating? You're gonna have to get used to it. You're not going to be getting rid of him next season."

"I know," I mutter. The truth of it is, while I might be worried about Letty being with him, I'm not stupid enough to deny that he needs to be standing beside Leon and me on the Panther's offense. Unfortunately, he's the best man for the job. While I might place the majority of last season's failing on my own shoulders, I can't lie and say that his name also doesn't feature seeing as he ended up on the bench injured more than he played. And as much as I might hate it, the three of us are a good team on the field. If we have any chance of making a comeback next season then we need to solidify them, and sadly, that means that we're going to have to spend some time together. Assuming I want to be back on the field next season.

Letty's cell bleeping cuts off whatever she was going to say. She pulls it from her back pocket, opening the message and almost instantly laughing to herself at whatever is on the screen.

"His cock that small, huh?" I ask, although I've probably seen that motherfucker naked as many times as she has, so I know it's not true. Asshole.

"Nah. Ella insisted on a toga fitting last night. There was a lot of tequila involved. Look." She turns her cell around and my eyes land on Ella and Violet, two of Letty's old roommates, dancing around in their dorm room wrapped in what looks like cut-up bedsheets.

They're laughing and joking, clearly totally wasted but it's not the sight of them that makes my heart jump into my throat, because that's the flash of pink hair in the bottom left of the screen.

All the air rushes from my lungs but I quickly tell myself to get a grip. Loads of girls have pink hair on campus.

She's not even here. She spends too much time shaking her tits for assholes to attend classes.

But it was her night off, a little voice says in my head.

Shutting it all down, I look back to Letty as she takes her cell back.

"Looks like it was quite a night."

A genuine smile curls at her lips and I can't help but copy her. There were so many times she looked utterly miserable after she first started here last year, I love seeing her looking more like her fun-loving old self.

"Oh yeah, it was something. Those two were trashed."

The question about the pink haired girl is right on the tip of my tongue, but I swallow it down, not wanting to alert Letty to something —something that I'm sure is nothing more than me jumping to conclusions.

The two of them never met. Letty arrived only a few weeks after Peyton left, and although she's aware that my old friend left on bad terms, Peyton never came to visit. Even talking about her turned me into a dark, angry beast that I needed to keep hidden behind closed doors. I found that the best way to deal with that was to do my best to forget any of it even happened, that Peyton never even existed.

Letty's probably heard her name many times over the years, and now understanding just how close her and Leon were, it makes me wonder if she knows more than she ever let on. Not that Leon ever knew the whole truth. It was bad enough that I had to deal with Peyton's lies. I wasn't poisoning my brother's mind with them too.

"You're coming Friday night, right?" she asks after putting her cell away.

"Uh..." Honestly, I'd mostly planned to sit outside The Locker Room like a sad motherfucker and wait for my daily hit of Peyton.

I wrap my hand around the back of my neck, realizing just how fucking pathetic I'm becoming needing a look at a girl in the dead of night to settle the darkness within me.

"Oh come on. Everyone is over the season. You need to stop sulking and enjoy your free time before it starts all over again."

"I'm not sulking," I mutter, earning myself a raised eyebrow in return. "Okay. Fine. I'll be there."

We finish our coffees and chat about bullshit like classes and assignments, both of us skirting around the more serious topics that we've only touched on.

The two of us are going to need more than this little coffee icebreaker until we're back on some kind of level footing again.

When it's time for us to head to our next classes, I pull her in for a hug and hold her tight. I breath in her familiar and comforting scent as my heart aches once more and confusion clouds my brain.

"I'll see you soon, yeah?" she asks hesitantly as if she's about to walk away and it'll shatter the progress we've just made.

"Yeah. Maybe you and that guy of yours should even come and hang at the house sometime," I offer, although I'm not entirely sure if I mean it or not.

I walk away with a heavy heart, but the knowledge that I'm closer to seeing Peyton again puts a bit of a spring into my step as I walk toward my afternoon class.

9

———

PEYTON

I feel him the second I step out of the building, just like I did last night when my shift ended. But just like last night, he remains in the shadows, lurking, watching me, probably scheming up all the ways he can torture me.

I try to force myself to be scared, but I'm not. I might not be able to predict Luca's actions, the things he's thinking like I once could, but one thing has not changed. When I'm with him, I feel safe. Which is ironic because he should be the person I'm most terrified of right now.

Keeping my eyes focused on the dark corner of the lot, I move toward my car waiting for him to emerge. But he never does.

As I drop down into my driver's seat, I can't deny the disappointment that races down my spine. I shiver, my skin prickling with coldness that he's keeping his distance.

It's what I should want. But I don't.

At least if he's in front of me then I have half a chance of making him see the truth, of being able to convince him that I never once lied to him. That what I told him, although hard to hear and accept, was the truth.

I sigh, thinking of that sweet little boy hopefully tucked up in his bed at Aunt Fee's. He never asked for this. He doesn't deserve this. It's why I do this. I look up to the building, my fingers curling into fists. Tonight wasn't bad. It wasn't like Tuesday night, but still. It's not good. It's still not where I actually want to be.

With a long sigh, I start my car and pull out of the lot. I'm hardly surprised when headlights come on behind me and follow me out.

My heart jumps into my throat that he could be going to the same place as me. I didn't want to go to this party, but if he's going to be there, then... shit. Then it's exactly where I want to be.

"Shit," I hiss to myself as I turn down the street for the frat houses.

I glance in my mirror, expecting him to still be tailing me, but he's gone.

My heart sinks. Does he not care now I'm away from The Locker Room? What exactly is he waiting for, the opportunity for someone else to accost me like he did the other night?

The thought that he could be protecting me flickers through my mind. That's what the old Luca would have done but I squash the thought immediately because there's no way it's that.

He just wants to torture me, punish me. Prove that I'm nothing better than a filthy liar.

The knot in my stomach grows as I pull up somewhere close to where tonight's party is being held. The street is lined with cars and people all dressed similarly to how I should be.

All I've got to do is send one message and my little makeover team will appear to ensure I look the part.

Or I could make some excuse and head home to curl up in my bed.

"Argh," I scream when someone bangs on my car window, making me jump off the seat in fright. But when I look up, it's just a group of drunk guys enjoying their night.

They soon move on, leaving me in the solitude of my car but I know I can't sit out here all night, so I need to make a decision.

Pulling my cell from my purse, I send the message I need to and wait.

Not six minutes later do Ella and Letty come racing down the street. Letty looks relatively sober but Ella looks about as wrecked as she was on Wednesday night. This is not going to be good.

They both look like goddesses as they get closer. The pristine white sheet looks insane against Letty's bronzed skin and Ella's toga shows off every one of her wicked curves.

I feel completely inadequate as they descend on me.

Ella rips open my door and smiles down at me.

"Get in the back, girl," she slurs. "I need to work my magic."

Somewhat reluctantly, I climb from the seat.

"Here, you might need this," Letty says, handing me a small bottle of vodka.

"Thank you," I say, taking it from her.

She takes my seat, although sits backward so she can watch me get attacked by Ella in the back.

"Makeup," she demands and Letty throws my purse through the seats to her.

It's dark out so I have no clue how I'm going to look after this, but I go with it. Ella might be trashed but I trust Letty enough not to let me walk into the party looking like Frankenstein.

"Off," she demands, shoving the last of my makeup back into its bag.

I pull my tank off and shimmy out of my skirt.

"Off," she says again, looking down at my boobs.

"Umm..." Glancing over her shoulder, I take in the people that are still loitering out on the street.

"We've seen a pair of tits before, girl."

Reaching behind me, I unsnap the fabric. "It wasn't you two I was worried about."

"No one will see anything. I'll be like lightning."

I stare at her in the shadows now Letty has turned the interior light off so my naked breasts aren't like a homing beacon for horny college guys. She doesn't respond to the incredulous look on my face. She is way too far gone to do anything at the speed of light, other than falling face-first to the floor, I'm sure.

But much to my surprise, no sooner has my bra left my skin does the softness of the sheet wrap around me and I breathe a sigh of relief.

"I don't know what you're worried about, your tits are insane. If I swung the other way, I totally would." Ella winks.

"Oh my God," Letty groans with a laugh.

"What? She's got a great rack. Any guy would be lucky to have a pop on those babies."

"You need to be cut off," Letty tells her, reaching for the bottle Ella stashed amongst my discarded clothes.

"Nah, what I need is to get laid and that is certainly not going to happen while we're hiding in here. So come on, I'll pin the rest outside."

I look down at myself showing off way more skin than I was when we had our little fitting session the other night.

"Are you sure this is—"

"You look hot, now get out."

Unable to do anything but what I'm told, I slip my shoes on and slide out of the back of the car.

There are a few shouts and whistles as I emerge. I have no idea if it's a coincidence and I don't dare look up to find out.

Ella attacks the back of my toga, making me feel a little more secure in the thing now before running her fingers through my hair and making me twirl around to show them both the final look.

"Banging. Now let's go get drunk and dance the night away."

"Get drunk?" I mutter, much to Letty's amusement.

Ella throws my purse at me, allowing me to lock my car, and with them on either side of me, we head toward the house. To my first college party at MKU.

I'm sure it's a cookie-cutter duplicate of the ones back at Trinity, drunk college kids making memories that will embarrass them for the rest of their lives. There's only one difference here. I have no idea if Luca is inside this building or not. And if he's not here right now, he could turn up at any moment.

My heart tumbles in my chest and my steps falter as we get to the front door.

"Are you okay?" Letty asks.

"Y-yeah. That vodka hit me. I need food," I admit.

I went home between classes and work. Aunt Fee had made dinner but I could only pick at it, too anxious about what tonight was going to hold to really stomach any of it. But even though my nerves are completely shot right now, I know I need something before the alcohol hits me too hard and I make an even bigger mess of my life tonight.

At some point on the way to the kitchen, Ella disappears into the crowd but Letty makes sure I get there and deposits me by the mass of food that's been arranged on the kitchen island.

"Ah, a girl after my own heart," a familiar voice says as I reach for a handful of chips.

Looking over, I find one of the guys who lives in Ella and Violet's dorm. He's dressed in a toga—obviously—the loose fabric hanging from one shoulder and leaving very little to the imagination. If I didn't already know he was on the team then it wouldn't be hard to guess from looking at him.

It makes me wonder how well he knows Luca. If they're close. Was he one of the guys standing outside the coffee shop with him on Monday? Hell, I have no idea how well Ella or Letty know Luca.

"Hey, um..."

"Brax," he says.

"Y-yeah, of course."

"It's easy to remember. I'm the good-looking, smart one."

I chuckle at his idiocy. "I'll try to remember that."

"Our girl is looking hot, right?" Letty says, handing me a red Solo cup.

"Hell yes, shame I've already been warned off." His eyes drop down the length of me, lingering on the side boob that Ella left me with before finally meeting my eyes.

"Ah look, the ugly, dense one," I deadpan as West joins us making both Brax and Letty choke on their recently sipped drinks.

"Uh... got an issue, new girl?" he asks, although there's no malice behind his words.

"No. Brax here was just telling me that I can tell him apart from you because he's the good-looking, smart one."

"Is that right?" he asks, turning to his friend.

"Only telling the lady the truth." Brax shrugs.

"I'm banging your girl tonight."

"I don't have a girl."

"Nope because your cock is so small that no one wants to bounce on it. But whoever you end up dancing with, she's mine, motherfucker. I'll show her how a real man does it."

"Fuck you, man. You've only got all of that on display in the hopes of distracting them from the reality under your toga."

"Oookay. As fun as this little cock measuring contest is," Letty says lightly. "We've got places to be."

With her arm around my shoulders, she leads me away from the guys and out of the kitchen. The music gets louder as we weave together through the crowds and toward the back of the house.

"Oh wow," I breathe, taking in the floor-to-ceiling windows that showcase the twinkling lights and pool in the garden.

"Yeah, the Kappas have a pretty sweet thing going on," Letty says beside me. "There's El and Vi, come on." She nods to the crowd but I have no chance of seeing them with all the people grinding it up on the makeshift dance floor. I do, however, look around for someone else, but I don't see him anywhere.

Plastering a smile on my face, I follow Letty through the crowd and lose myself to the music pounding through the speakers almost the second we join the other two.

"Your man not here tonight?" I shout to Letty. I was kind of hoping to meet this enigma of a man who's stolen her heart.

"Yeah, he is," she calls back. "He's with some friends. I'm sure he'll find me before too long."

And she's not wrong because not two songs later does the crowd before us part and a hot but slightly terrifying guy marches straight up to Letty. He wraps his hand around her throat and slams his lips down on hers.

Whoa.

My temperature spikes just watching them as he crushes her slender body against his and totally consumes her.

I'm immediately taken back to having Luca squashing me between his hard body and his car. How would that have felt if it were fueled by desire, not hate and vengeance.

"You get used to them eventually. Just be glad you never experienced living in a dorm with them," Ella shouts in my ear as she rests her arms over my shoulders, encouraging me to dance with her.

"That good, huh?"

"My batteries died."

I bark out a laugh as we're joined by the other guys. Brax steps up behind Ella, his eyes flicking between the two of us rolling our hips to the music.

"Now this is something I can get on board with," he announces happily.

"Shut up, you dog," Ella snaps, but with a wink, she turns her back on me and begins dancing with him. He whispers something in her ear and she throws her head back with a laugh.

Jealousy washes through me at their easy relationship. West has Violet in his arms, the two of them enjoying themselves in the same relaxed manner.

My heart sinks as I think of years gone by when I'd have got that same comfort and enjoyment from dancing with Luc.

"Dance with me?" a voice says over my shoulder.

Spinning, I find their final dorm member. Only, he hardly resembles the guy I met briefly on Wednesday night as he ripped into the other two. His geeky glasses are gone and his hair has been styled away from his face. He looks... hot. And the fact I know that he's not a part of the team—or at least I assumed he's not seeing as he looked more nerd than jock the other night—means I'm even more drawn to him.

With a smile, I hold my hand out to him. "I'd love to."

Drinks are delivered to us courtesy of a few of the freshman team members. After being assured that they're totally trustworthy by everyone, I happily knock each one back until all my limbs begin to feel heavy and my head starts to swim.

It's the best I've felt in a long time as I move my body against Micah, a wide smile splitting my face as we all enjoy ourselves and just for a few hours, I'm able to let go.

Coming here was the right decision tonight. I have no idea what I was even so worried about.

10

LUCA

"We didn't think you were coming," Colt says when I join him and a few of the guys in the backyard.

"Here." Evan passes me a beer. "Glad to see you made an effort," he mutters, glancing down at my hoodie, Panthers jersey, and dark jeans.

I might have shown up but like fuck was I going to the effort to wrap myself in a fucking toga. In years gone by, yes, I was all over that shit. But right now? Nah. I'm here for the beer and hopefully the pussy, assuming I can get someone else out of my head for long enough to perform that is.

The memory of her looking right at me tonight despite the fact I know she couldn't actually see me hits me, and my cock swells.

What would have happened if I got out and walked toward her? Would she have run, or would she continue to play this little cat-and-mouse game we've got going on? Something tells me that it would be the latter. My cock twitches once more. I really fucking hope it would be the latter.

"Whatever," I grumble, lifting the bottle to my lips and draining half of it down in one.

"Been anywhere nice?" Leon asks, emerging from the crowd dressed like every other motherfucker here.

"You know, here and there."

"Riiight. Few more of them and maybe I'll get you to confess."

"It's none of your damn business," I snap.

It doesn't escape my attention that while I let Letty off pretty easily the other day, I'm still very much holding a grudge with Leon. What he did, the fact he's lied to me about it for so many years when I didn't think we kept shit like that from each other hurts.

You haven't told him about Peyton, a little voice screams in my head.

Lifting the bottle once more, I try to drown my conscience out. Knowing that he can easily keep stuff from me makes it easier to do.

He shakes his head at me. "Fine. You do your thing. But don't come running to me when it blows up in your face." Turning his back on me, he walks up to a couple of jersey chasers, accepting a drink from one of them and knocking it back like he doesn't care.

It's all a lie though. I can tell by the hard set of his shoulders that he does. He cares more than he'll ever admit.

There's only one person I know who's able to hide the truth about what's really going on with them better than me, and that's my twin brother.

I know almost everything about him. But there's something, something buried deep that he keeps locked up tight, I just know there is.

I used to think it was just teenage hormone bullshit, but as we get older, that darkness in his eyes never seems to vanish.

No one else sees it. They all see the slightly moody, colder version of the playboy act I put on. But I see it and I've ignored it for years in the hope that one day he'd confess to whatever it was but I'm starting to think that whatever it is, he's going to take to his grave.

He has every right to do that, even if it does piss me off beyond belief.

Lifting my hand, I drag my hair back, wondering if I should just come clean to him. Tell him everything that happened back then. I remember feeding him with some bullshit about her cheating on me and then her mom getting a better job in South Carolina, severing all our ties.

He bought it, or I think he did, because he never really questioned it.

How would he react if he knew what really went down, if he heard the lies that spewed from her lips?

A commotion from the back doors finally pulls my eyes from the dark, starlit sky above me and the house.

A group of drunk students all go down like dominoes as they try to get out of the house. On any other day it might amuse me, right now I barely give them all a second glance because something catches my eyes through the glass door.

Pink. I saw pink.

Placing the bottle on the table beside me, I snatch up a new one and take a step forward.

No. It can't be.

It's just the random girl from Letty's video.

It can't be.

I take another step forward but whoever it is has been swallowed by the crowd that's gathered on the makeshift dance floor.

But then it parts once more and this time, I'm in the perfect line of sight.

The bottle falls from my hand as I watch her dancing with Micah at her back and none other than Letty at her front, who is of course attached to Kane fucking Legend.

Glass shatters at my feet, beer soaking my jeans as people surround her once more and she vanishes almost as if she was never there in the first place.

But she was. I know she was.

"What the fuck, Dunn?" one of the Kappas barks when he sees the mess I march away from.

"Sorry, bro. I'll get one of my boys to clean it," I promise, storming past him and straight inside without a second thought.

More than a handful of people try to talk to me as I make my way through the throngs of people. But as seems to be becoming normal since our failed season, most give me a wide berth while shooting me concerned looks. I get it, I know I'm kinda volatile since everything went to shit.

I stand in the doorway of the room where she is, resting my hip against the doorframe. Waiting as I try to come up with a plan that isn't to publicly drag her out of here kicking and screaming so I can dump her back wherever it is she's crawled out from all of sudden.

But as angry as I am at seeing her here, in the middle of my life, with my fucking friends, I know I can't just storm in there. The last thing I need is the rest of them on my case.

I stand there with my heart thundering in my chest and my nails digging into my palms just waiting for the perfect time to make my move.

Does she know I'm here? And if she does, what exactly is she expecting me to do?

No one speaks to me, and I know why. Fury surrounds me like a dark storm cloud, lightning just waiting for the perfect time to strike.

"Luca, are you—" Zayn cuts off whatever he was about to ask me when my eyes meet his. "Whoa, okay. Maybe later." He backs away with his hands up in defeat before disappearing around the corner.

When I look back to Peyton, Micah has fucked off, leaving me the perfect opening to take his place.

Her back is completely bare, making my semi only get harder as I imagine what little she's wearing under that sheet. Whoever wrapped her in it did a good job of making her look like the filthy slut that she is.

My hands tremble with restraint by the time I come to a stop behind her.

Her scent floods my senses, making my mouth water as the bare skin of her back burns my front through my shirt.

She freezes before me as if without looking that she knows it's me.

"Who's your new friend?" I ask innocently, sliding my hand in the back of her hair and tugging until she has no choice but to look up at me.

"Luc, this is Peyton. Peyton meet Luca, Panther's captain, lady killer, douchebag extraordinaire."

"Hey," I complain, ripping my eyes from Peyton's narrowed ones to look at Ella who's thankfully stopped running her mouth. "What did I ever do to you?"

"Aside from not showing me heaven."

"Ignore her," Letty shouts over the music. "She's wasted. Makes her mouth a little easy."

"From what I hear, it's not just her mouth. Might want to watch that one, bro," I say to Brax, who's grinding up against her. "You have no idea where she's been."

"Fuck you, Luc," Ella hisses but sways on her feet, showing just how drunk she is.

"How did you miss the dress code for tonight?" Letty asks while Kane stares daggers at me and Peyton squirms against my hold.

I move against her with the music, my hand on her waist ensuring she rolls her hips with me, rubbing her ass against my quickly growing cock.

"Yeah, I must have missed that."

"Do you two know each other?" Kane asks, clearly not missing Peyton's reaction to me.

"Nope. But I've got a feeling we're about to. What do you say, Pink? Wanna come get a drink with me?"

My fingers both twist in her hair and dig into her waist ensuring only one answer falls from her lips.

"A drink with the famous QB1 of the Panthers. How could a girl say no?" she purrs sweetly. So much so, it's almost believable.

"Don't expect her back." I wink at Kane while Letty tenses in his hold. She probably thinks I'm doing this to teach her a lesson for being with him, but that's far from the truth. Letty isn't even on my radar right now. "Let's go," I growl in Peyton's ear, releasing her hair and steering her out of the room.

I swing by the kitchen for a bottle of vodka and thankfully, we bump into Owen, the Kappa president.

"Dunn, did you forget something?" he asks, taking in my clothes.

"Nope, I've got it right here. Listen, I need a favor." I lean into his ear, whispering my request so that Peyton can't hear.

He nods and in seconds pulls a key from somewhere in his toga. I wrap my fingers around it, trying to ignore the fact it's warm.

"Enjoy, man. And if you make a mess, clean it the fuck up."

"You got it, man. Later."

He nods at me, and with my hand still locked around Peyton's waist. I direct her outside and around the side of the impressive building, ensuring we go in the opposite direction of where I last saw Leon and head toward the pool house.

"Luca, what the hell are you doing?" she hisses, but at no point does she try to escape me. I tell myself that it's because she wants to be with me and not just because she doesn't want to make a scene in front of a massive portion of MKU.

"Shut up," I snap. "You don't need to talk."

All the air rushes from her as a disgruntled noise rips from her throat.

My grip tightens on her waist, my finger digging into her soft skin enough to leave marks.

The thought of her waking up in the morning with the evidence that I was this close to her is the final straw. By the time I push the key into the lock, my cock is trying to bust out of my jeans. Fucking good thing I'm not wearing a bedsheet right now.

"Get the fuck in," I say, pushing Peyton inside with my hand on the nape of her neck. She stumbles on her heels and falls into the couch as I once again lock the doors and pocket the key to stop her escape.

"I will ask you this once," I say, although it pains me to do so. "Do you want an audience for what's about to go down or would you prefer to keep it just between us?" I run my eyes down her barely covered body. Her chest is heaving, the fabric of her makeshift dress just about keeping her tits concealed, the skirt high enough that I can see her white lace panties beneath.

Her eyes drill into me as her nostrils flare and her lips purse in anger.

"So? I have no problem with everyone out there knowing what a filthy slut you are."

11

PEYTON

My body trembles with adrenaline, fear, and dare I say it... desire.

He stares at me with dark eyes, the muscle in his neck is pulsating and his hands balled into tight fists.

Pushing up from the couch so I'm sitting, I keep my eyes locked on his, trying not to wither under the heat of his stare.

I have no idea what's running through his head right now, but none of it is good. My stomach clenches at the thought of a repeat of Tuesday night only... alone.

My heart rate picks up even more, making my already alcohol-buzzed head spin faster.

I shouldn't want this. I shouldn't be excited about being locked in a building with this man—this stranger. Because that's what he is. The boy I once used to know and love is long gone. The man standing before me is someone else entirely. He's angry, dangerous, and lethal. Three things I didn't know I wanted but hell if I can deny that I'm not just a little bit turned on right now.

"You have three seconds to answer or the entire college is going to be witness to me ruining you right there on the couch."

"C-close th-them," I stutter, knowing that I need this to be between just us.

This isn't about anyone else. It's not about the people involved in ruining us. It's just us exorcising some demons. I just only hope that we can move past them once this is done.

He doesn't move and just as I start to think it was a trick question, that he was going to allow everyone to witness what happens next, he finally turns around.

The blinds are twisted closed and immediately it feels like the room has halved in size.

I fight to drag in the air I need but the second the air hits my nose, all I smell is him.

"Luc, what are you—"

"Why, P? Why are you here?"

I hesitate for a second but when I do try to answer he doesn't allow me. "Because I—"

"You're at MKU, aren't you?" he barks, his jaw popping with restraint.

"Yes," I confess, although my voice is so quiet I doubt he actually hears it. He doesn't need to. He already knows the answer.

"Why? Why would you come here knowing that I was here? And don't try to play the innocent, P. I know you're not stupid enough to not know where I am."

"I knew you were here. I've watched your games."

All the air rushes from his lungs at my words.

"Y-you watch— fuck. FUCK," he bellows, his fingers tugging at his hair until it has to hurt.

I stare at him wondering if I'm about to watch him shatter. Scooting forward, I'm just about to push to stand when he lifts his eyes from the floor and locks them on mine.

A shiver races down my spine at the warning I can read within them.

"Luc?" I whisper but I think he's too far gone to hear anything right now.

He's before me in a heartbeat, his long, powerful legs eating up the distance faster than I thought possible.

His burning hot fingers wrap around my throat and squeeze enough to warn me of just how strong he is but without actually hurting me.

My ass leaves the couch until I'm standing in front of him.

"You don't belong here."

His eyes are so dark as he stares into mine that they're almost black, but even still, I can't find it in me to actually be scared of him.

"I-I didn't have a choic— argh," my squeal of surprise as he surges me backward cuts off my words. An umph falls from my lips as my back hits the wall.

He crowds me against the wall, his wide chest heaving with his anger, his scent utterly consuming me and the heat from his body turning my blood to lava.

"You. Do. Not. Belong. Here," he spits.

"So what are you going to do about it?"

A gasp rips from my throat as he reaches out and tugs at the fabric wrapped around me. It falls away as if it's no more than tissue leaving me once again exposed to him. Only this time, we're standing under fluorescent lighting and he can see everything. There's no hiding in the shadows right now.

Unable to look at him as he stares down at my breasts, I focus on a spot on the floor as my cheeks burn with embarrassment. It might not be the first time he's seen me naked, but that was years ago, my body has changed since then. We were still kids when we started experimenting with each other, now we're adults.

My nipples harden to the point of pain as his attention continues to burn into them. My breathing is erratic, giving away just how I'm feeling right now.

I wish I could be indifferent to his undivided attention but I can't. It's always been the same between us. I was always super aware of him, but as we became teenagers and my hormones started to kick in. I was acutely aware if he was in the room, if he was looking at me. For a long time, I didn't understand it. But I do now. I'd just hoped it might have fizzled out with our time apart.

"Look at you," he says, his eyes finally lifting to my face once more, but I still keep my eyes on a knot in the wooden floor beneath us.

"Practically begging for it. Is that what you're like at the bar? Begging for any bit of attention those men give you."

I bite down on the inside of my lips, not wanting to have to plead my innocence once more.

"Look at me, P."

I suck in a deep breath before lifting my eyes from the floor. I gasp when I see the darkness in his eyes.

"Do they get your nipples this hard? Make your chest redden with desire?"

I shake my head, unable to find any words even if I wanted to.

"You love knowing that you're turning them on, don't you? You love that your little innocent look gets them all hard for you. So why don't you try telling me again how you don't let them touch you, because from what I see, you're fucking begging for it."

"Th-they don't— I don't—"

"Bullshit." He says the word so low that it almost sounds like a purr. The sound of it does delicious things between my thighs.

Damn him. Fucking damn him.

"At least I get to benefit from all the practice you've had," he mutters, his eyes full of wicked intent.

"Wha—" His hands land on my shoulders and I have no choice but to allow my knees to buckle.

"That's it, P. Get down there where you belong."

"Luc," I whimper but the sight of the bulge in his pants causes heat to flood my core.

"Too late to try and get out of this, P. You're already on your knees."

I watch, utterly captivated as he undoes his belt, pops the button, and lowers the zipper.

My mouth waters with anticipation and I stuff down the realization that I should not be turned on by this in the slightest.

This is Luc. Neither of us were ever very good at following the rules. That's exactly how we ended up in this position the very first time it happened when he snuck into my bedroom after Mom had gone to bed one night.

Without hesitation, he hooks his thumbs into the waistband of both his pants and boxers and pushes them over his hips.

His solid length springs free and my entire body tenses as I take it in.

Fuck, he's bigger than I remember.

When I don't move, only stare at the angry purple head that's already got a bead of precum glistening at the tip, he wraps his fingers around himself.

Ripping my eyes from the sight of him pleasuring himself, I move them up his shirt, wishing it was gone and I could get a look at what he's hiding beneath. Finally, I find his eyes as he glares down at me.

"Problem?" he asks, lifting a brow, his hand still moving up and down his shaft.

"Um..." I suck my bottom lip into my mouth, the thought of tasting him again is almost too much to deny but hell if I want to look like I want this.

His eyes lock on my lips and I bite down on the bottom one causing a growl to rumble at the back of his throat.

The second I release my lip, his restraint snaps.

Threading his fingers painfully into my hair, he moves me exactly where he wants me before pushing his steel length past my lips.

He's not gentle, not like the boy I remember who never wanted to hurt me, instead, he surges forward until the tip of his cock hits the back of my throat and I can't help but gag at the intrusion.

"Much fucking better," he says, pulling out a little to allow me to drag in a breath. "You look right at home down there, P."

Before I'm ready, he thrusts forward again.

His taste, his size, his angry thrusts are the only things I can think about as he continues to fuck my mouth.

My lungs burn with my need for air and my eyes water as I gag around him, but he doesn't let up.

"Fuck, you look beautiful, baby."

That one word sends a shudder through the length of my body. It's said so much softer than anything else he's spat at me tonight and it makes me think of the boy I used to know.

Is he still in there buried beneath the anger?

Saliva drips from my chin as his cock swells even bigger and his grip on my hair becomes unbearable, as if he's about to rip it clean from my scalp.

Just when I don't think I can take anymore, his cock jerks violently in my mouth before he shoots hot jets of cum down my throat. He holds himself deep as he finishes, his loud groan of pleasure echoing off the walls of the pool house.

The second he's done, he pulls out of my mouth and leans down, wrapping his hand around my throat once more and pulling me to my feet.

I just about manage to wipe the drool from my chin before his dark stare renders me useless.

"Not bad," he growls. "Took the edge off at least." His eyes flick down to my bare chest once more.

The tension crackles between us as his eyes flick between mine and my lips.

Surely he's not going to kiss me after that.

"Great. Can I go now?" I ask. I know I'm pushing my luck and if I'm being honest with myself. I'll be disappointed if he says yes and lets me walk out before discovering exactly what he has planned for me.

In a move I wasn't expecting, a smile twitches at his lips before it splits right across his face. It's the most beautiful sight, even with the anger still darkening his green eyes.

"Can you go now?" he repeats before laughing. It's so light and happy that anyone overhearing might think I'd just told him a joke, although I think to him, I just did. "Sure," he says, taking a giant step back. His eyes remain on mine as he tucks himself away, but he never does his fly up as he continues to back away. "You can walk out of here right now if you plan on leaving town, taking your lying, filthy mouth with you, and never show your face again."

My lips part to argue, to tell him that I can't do that but it seems I don't need to.

"But you won't, will you? You've got a loving boyfriend waiting for you at home. That is who I saw welcome you back the other night with open arms, right? Where is he now, huh? Do you think he has any idea that you've just had my cock in your mouth? Do you think he'd be happy to know that you put up zero fight about it?"

I want to tell him that Elijah isn't my boyfriend but I have a feeling that even if I tried, he wouldn't listen to me. He only wants to believe what he wants. That I'm a liar and a cheat. The reality is that I'm neither.

"I'm not leaving town, Luc. And not because of him."

"No? Because of who then... me?" he spits.

"Oh yeah, because you've been so warm and welcoming," I deadpan, wrapping my fingers around the bedsheet hanging at my waist, ready to cover myself up. I barely lift the fabric before he notices.

"Strip."

"What."

"You heard me."

"But I just..." I look down at his crotch indicating what I just did and he laughs.

"You think that was it? You think all of this is all over because you gave me one half-decent blow job?"

My chin drops but I don't have any words.

He walks back until his legs hit the edge of the couch, then he drops down, swiping the vodka he brought in with us from the coffee table and twisting the top. He spreads his legs wide and tips the bottle to his lips, swallowing down a generous amount and ensuring I focus on the muscles in his throat rippling as he does.

"Now," he says, finding my eyes once more. "Strip."

"Luc, this is insane," I try to argue.

"Okay," he says, getting comfortable for the show. "Then tell me the truth. Tell me that you're a lying cunt and apologize for what happened."

My teeth grind at his demand because he knows full well that I'm not going to do that.

"I didn't lie, Luc," I hiss, although I don't know why I bother because if he didn't believe me then, why would he now? The only way to prove it is to... no. I refuse to even consider the option. Luca hating me, torturing me, is better than allowing him into my life and revealing the truth.

It'll hurt him, sure. But he's not my biggest concern anymore.

There's someone else who's more important who doesn't need his world to be flipped over once again.

He stares at me, his face void of emotion. Reaching into his pocket, he pulls out his cell and after a second, the sexy beat of a Rhianna song fills the space.

Lifting the bottle, he tips it toward me. "Go on then. Show me how you earn your money."

"I'm not a fucking stripper, Luc."

He quirks a brow.

"Or a hooker," I add, knowing exactly what he's thinking.

"No, you just walk around with your nipples out for any asshole who cares to look. Your boyfriend must really fucking love you to allow you to do that. If you were mi—" He cuts himself off, preferring to drown the unspoken words in vodka instead of letting them hang between us.

"Yours?" I ask with a laugh. "If I were yours?"

His brows pull together as he studies me.

Every muscle in my body screams at me to cover up but I refuse to show even an ounce of weakness around him right now.

12

LUCA

"*If I were yours?*"

Her words repeat over and over in my head as she stands there trying to appear confident before me when I know that deep down, all she wants to do is cover up. Her nose twitches in a way that I used to think was utterly adorable. I'd put her in any awkward situation just to see that twitch.

YOU used to be mine. YOU fucked it up. YOU lied to me. YOU ruined us.

But still, I can't help wondering what the fuck her boyfriend is playing at allowing her to walk around looking like she does at The Locker Room.

Unless... what she's saying is true and he's not her boyfriend. She was just very willingly gagging on my cock.

Is she really a cheat as well as a liar?

I think back to her jumping into his arms only days ago. They certainly seemed close.

I lift the bottle to my lips once more, the vodka no longer burning as it goes down. But it's not doing a fucking good job of numbing everything I don't want to be feeling.

Grabbing my cell once more, I turn the volume up.

"I'm done waiting, P. I want action." I turn it louder to ensure she can't respond, or at least if she does, I can't hear it.

Pushing everything aside, our past, her possible boyfriend, the fact my heart beats that little bit faster than it should whenever I'm anywhere near her and the ache in my balls despite the fact I've only just come down her throat, I watch her.

She drops her hands to the rope around her waist, but she makes no move to undo it.

After a beat, I lean forward, resting my elbows on my knees and allowing the now half-empty bottle to hang between.

I stare at her as defiance flickers through her silver eyes.

"Peyton," I warn, knowing that she'll be able to hear it loud and clear despite the volume of the music.

She tilts her chin up and stares at me, her chest heaving and her nipples still hard, begging for attention.

Not touching them this far has damn near killed me.

I stand, killing the music in the process. Clearly, she's not going to make use of it, and I'm going to have to get involved then I want her to hear every single thing I'm going to growl in her ear.

"You're playing a dangerous game here, P," I warn.

"I can handle you, Luc."

"Nah," I say, taking another swig of vodka. "You handled me as a boy. You have no fucking clue what you're getting into with me now."

I don't need to be touching her to know a shudder just worked its way down her body.

"Open," I demand, holding the bottle up to her lips.

I pour some in, watching as it runs from the corners of her mouth and drops from her chin and onto her breasts.

Lifting my other hand, I run my fingertip through the stream of liquid.

"Luca," she breathes when I circle her nipple, making it pucker even more.

"You're so fucking desperate, P." I lean in close to whisper in her ear. "I can smell you. But I doubt you taste as sweet as you used to. Bitter and sour. I bet that's how you taste now after all your lies and bullshit."

She shakes her head.

"You can tell me the truth at any time, you know. I might even take pity on you and let you go." It's a barefaced lie, she's not walking through those doors for a very long time yet.

Her expression hardens and she once again lifts her chin slightly.

"Right choice, baby. I want to fuck the truth out of you too. I'm glad we're on the same page."

Her eyes hold mine and I can see the argument she's desperate to spit at me within them, but she never does.

Why? Why doesn't she just tell me everything?

Because she doesn't want to admit to being a liar.

"Luc," she cries as I twist her around and push her into the blinds. The wooden slats clatter against the glass as Peyton's breathing becomes erratic.

Filthy little bitch like this. My cock gets hard again just at the thought alone.

Pressing the length of my body against her back I breathe into her ear as my hands slip around her waist to the knot in the rope that's tied around her.

"Imagine how you'd look to my team right now if you didn't request I close the blinds." She swallows loudly. "They'd get to see your rosy, hard nipples pressed against the glass. They'd see the heat of your cheeks, the desire in your eyes."

"Luc," she whimpers.

"That turn you on, baby, imagining them watching you?"

Finally loosening the rope, I pull it from around her body.

"Would you want them to watch me as I fucked you too?" She trembles against me. "Or would you like them to join, is that it?"

"No," she cries.

"It could be arranged. It wouldn't be the first time we've tag-teamed. Did you have anyone in mind?"

She shakes her head violently as I run my knuckles down her arms causing goose bumps to erupt in their wake. She's like putty in my hands and fuck if it's not exactly as I've imagined for the best part of five years.

"Or maybe you want to try out the twin thing," I continue,

distracting her with my wicked words as I wind the rope around her wrists. "Letty has been between us. Did you know that?"

"No. Luc, no. I don't want them."

"No? Who is it you want then?" I ask, running my lips around the shell of her ear, a smile pulling at my lips when she trembles again. "Lie to me again, baby. I dare you," I warn.

"Y-you, Luc. I want you."

"Right answer, baby. Although I still don't think you have any clue what you're asking for."

"I know what I want, Luca," she spits.

"And what if I don't want to give you what you want?"

She shrugs but pauses with her shoulders up as she must realize for the first time what I've done.

"Luc?"

"Well, well... look at that. You're totally at my mercy now, baby. What am I going to do with you?"

Finally finding the pin that's holding the fabric around her waist, I pull it out and watch in delight as the fabric finally falls away from her body.

"Whoops," I breathe innocently in her ear.

Sliding my hands around her waist and to her stomach, I pull her away from the window and into me.

"For someone who claims not to be a slut, you're not fighting very hard to stop this."

"Who said I wanted to stop it? Maybe I want your punishment, your torture, your cock."

Her words are like fuel to the already out-of-control fire that's burning red hot inside me.

"Filthy. Slut."

Skimming one hand up, I finally cup one of her heavy, needy breasts in my hand, pinching her nipple between my fingers.

Needing to know just how badly she wants what she just said, I push the other hand lower, my fingers dipping under her white lace panties.

Her pussy is smooth as I get lower.

"I bet those dirty old men love your smooth pussy."

She tenses in my hold but any response that she was going to bite back is cut off by a soft whimper then I part her and find her clit.

I push lower and find exactly what I was expecting.

"Oh baby," I moan, pushing two fingers inside her dripping center. "Did you like sucking my cock?"

"Luc," she moans, her hips rolling, riding my hand.

Ripping my hand from her panties, I wrap it around her throat and walk backward, pulling her with me.

"Oh God," she cries when I push her bare tits against the small glass table. Pinning her in place with my hand on the nape of her neck, I rip her panties from her body with the other.

"Don't move a fucking inch," I warn as I kick her legs wide and drop to my knees, unable to resist getting just a little taste of her.

Parting her, I take in her pretty, slick pussy.

She always was fucking perfect, and I hate that she only looks better five years later.

"Oh, P. Look how swollen your clit is. You really did like my cock, huh?"

She whimpers, giving me the response I really didn't need.

Leaning forward, I run my tongue up the length of her pussy, allowing her sweetness to explode on my tongue.

My mouth waters. The taste of getting my vengeance after all these years is really fucking sweet.

"Luc, fuck," she cries when I latch on to her clit and suck it hard into my mouth.

She's so fucking wet, her juices run down my chin but I fucking lap it up, eating her until she's only a breath from her release. It's then I pull back and wipe my mouth with the back of my hand.

"No, Luc. No. No, not again. Please."

"Give me one good reason why you deserve any pleasure," I tell her, pushing to stand and once again shoving my pants down over my ass, exposing my rock-hard cock.

I stare at her pussy, imagining what she's going to look like stretched full of me. My cock jerks with its need to find out.

"Because I've never lied to you in my life," she shouts, her voice bordering on manic.

"Not good enough." Without warning, I thrust forward, filling her up in one quick move.

"Luca," she screams, her body locking up in shock.

"Don't come."

"What?" she cries as if I just said the most bizarre thing she's ever heard.

"You do not come." Reaching forward, I slide my fingers into her hair and pull her head back. "You got that?" She attempts to nod. "Good, because you won't like what happens if you defy me."

"It gets worse?" she sasses.

"Don't test me, baby. I'm no longer an innocent fifteen-year-old boy. You have no idea what I'm capable of or all of the things I told myself I'd do to you if I ever saw you again."

My body moves without instruction from my brain as I thrust into her, chasing the release I so desperately need. It might have only been minutes ago that I blew a load in her mouth, but fuck, I need more.

I fear I need more than I'm ever going to be able to get when it comes to Peyton.

"Luca," she cries, her body surging forward, her feet leaving the floor with my forceful movements.

"I said." Thrust. "Don't." Thrust. "Come."

"Oh God," she cries, her fingers curling around the edge of the table, her grip so tight her knuckles turn white.

"Yesss," I hiss as my balls start to draw up. "For a slut, you've got a tight little cunt, baby."

"Argh," she grunts, her muscles tightening around me as if she's about to fall.

Not wanting to risk her getting what she wants, I pull out of her, flip her around and jack my cock until hot jets of cum coat her tits.

"Filthy fucking slut," I mutter as I rub the sticky mess into her skin.

She watches my movement, not saying a word as I mark her with my seed.

When I finally pull back, her eyes lift to mine. Her mask has dropped momentarily and it's the first time I see how she's really feeling.

Tears fill her eyes as she looks up at me. Her makeup is smeared everywhere, her hair a matted mess, and her skin red and patchy from her almost orgasm.

"I hate you," she hisses. "I thought—"

"That I'd forget all about it? I thought you knew me better than that, baby." Reaching behind me, I pull my jersey over my head, but if she thinks I'm going to pass it over to her so she can clean up, she's going to be bitterly disappointed. Instead, I throw it toward the bedroom and swipe up my bottle of vodka.

I take a swig while her eyes track my every movement. I hate the way she studies me, as if she knows me, as if she can see past the act, the bravado and see the broken, hurt little boy who's still hiding beneath it all.

"Can I?" she asks, holding her hand out.

I stare at it for a beat, considering if I'm willing to share. But one glance at her spunk-covered tits and I pass it over.

We're so far from done right now, something tells me that she's going to need it.

"Thank you," she whispers, lifting it to her once red lips, swallowing down shot after shot.

Reaching up, I run my fingers through my hair, tracking my eyes down the smooth column of her neck, over the swell of her breasts and the indent of her waist.

Fuck, she's beautiful.

"What?" she barks, her eyes narrowing in frustration.

"Just taking in the changes."

"The biggest ones are on the inside," she confesses.

"Fucking tell me about it."

Swiping the bottle back, I drain the remaining vodka.

"So now what?"

Turning my back on her, I find where she abandoned her purse when I first locked us in here.

"Hey," she complains when I start rummaging through looking for her cell.

Holding it before me, I wake it up and find a message.

> Letty: Are you okay? Do you need me to come
> and rescue you?

Irritation once again surges through me that Letty thinks that Peyton needs rescuing from me. I mean, she quite possibly might, but I didn't think Letty would think I was capable of hurting her. But then I guess after the state I've seen her in after some of her wilder rendezvous with Kane, it just proves that maybe we didn't know each other all that well in the first place.

"Aw, how sweet. Letty wants to protect you from the big bad wolf," I say, holding up her screen so she can see it.

"You know her? Them?"

"Aw, baby. Letty was your replacement when you fucked off. She rolled into town right on cue."

"B-but she's engaged." Peyton's brow wrinkles in confusion.

"So she is. And you've got a boyfriend. Passcode?" I demand, not willing to go any farther down the Letty route because although what I just said was the truth, Letty didn't replace Peyton. No one could ever have done that back then. Hell, I'm not sure anyone could do it now either, but fuck if I'm confessing to that anytime soon.

Peyton stares at me, defiance shining bright in her eyes, but eventually she mumbles out four numbers that rattle my resolve.

They're the numbers we used to use for everything as kids. Our two birth dates.

My breathing catches but I force myself to rip my eyes away from hers and type it into the cell as if I haven't even noticed.

Opening her messages, I find the unread one from Letty at the top. The second one though, is from him. Although the name makes me pause for a beat.

Elijah. I know that name.

Elijah: Have a great night, you deserve it. x

Pushing the nagging feeling that something isn't right here aside, I allow my anger to take over.

"Aw, isn't that sweet? He wants you to have a nice night. I wonder if he has any idea just what his little slut is getting up to. That she's standing naked before me right now with my jizz running down her tits."

Her teeth grind as she wraps her arms around herself, trying to hide from me.

She's going to need to try harder than that.

"What are you doing?" she hisses.

"Me?" I ask innocently. "Nothing. You, however, are going to tell Letty that you're fine, that I took you home when you got a little too drunk. You're also going to tell loverboy that you've decided to hang out with your friends this weekend instead of returning to suck his tiny cock." My thumbs fly over the screen as I explain exactly what I'm doing.

"He won't believe me."

"Well then, let him come looking."

The second I'm done, I turn her cell off and tuck it into my pocket.

"You made a mistake letting me lead you in here, P."

"Oh." She tilts her chin, trying to appear as if she has some kind of control over what's going to happen within these walls.

I chuckle, pushing my hair back and running my eyes down her insane curves. Yeah, she's different from what's been in my mind all this time. She's fucking better.

Marching up to her, I pull her into my body, pinning her there with a tight grip on the nape of her neck.

"You're not leaving this place until every single inch of your body knows who owns it."

"You had me, Luc, and you threw me away. I'll never belong to you again." Her body trembles as she says the words, making me wonder just how forced they are. Something tells me that Peyton is very much aware of who she really belongs to. I'm more than happy to give her the evidence she needs.

"Yeah, we'll see about that, baby."

13

PEYTON

I'm thrown down on the bed, bouncing unceremoniously in the center as Luca turns his back on me and storms through a door off to the side, the bathroom, I assume.

Not two minutes later does an ice cold cloth slap down on my outstretched thigh.

"Clean yourself up, you look like a whore," he barks before leaving the room.

I wince as I press the cloth to my chest, wiping away the evidence of what he did. I try to clear the memory of him marking me in such a primal way out of my head as well, but that doesn't disappear quite as easily.

Looking around the room, I try to find something to cover up with. The closet calls to me, but a loud crash from inside the small pool house startles me and stops me from moving.

In the end, I settle for slipping under the covers. I have no idea whose bed this is but right now I really don't care. With Luca gone, my body temperature is dropping by the second.

The clock on the nightstand ticks by but he doesn't return. I know he's still here though. I can sense him.

If he's trying to drive me crazy, then I hate to admit that it's working.

I rub my thighs together as I sit with the covers pulled up to my chest. My need to finish myself off is almost unignorable, but something tells me it would be a really stupid move to do something about it.

After long agonizing minutes, footsteps begin to get louder before his shadow fills the doorway.

Thanks to the drinks I've had tonight, plus the shots of vodka, my vision swims when I look at him.

Shirtless, the ink now covering one of his arms is clear to see, his pants are still undone at the waist, his hair is a mess and his face is still set as an emotionless mask. But that's not the most shocking thing, because that is the joint he's holding to his lips.

I hate it. This isn't the Luca I fell in love with all those years ago. This Luca is cold, cruel, vicious. His need to hurt me, to punish me for something that was entirely out of our control is the only thing he can see right now.

I know that I could probably make it better, that I could explain everything that happened since Mom dragged both me and Libby away to start new lives away from the lies.

Maybe if we'd stayed and she'd fought for what was right, then everything would have been different. The truth would have been exposed. My stomach twists, bile burning up my throat as I consider how many other young lives have been tainted because Mom decided to protect her own and keep the truth from the media.

"Luc, what are you doing?" I ask, my concern for my old friend taking precedence over my anger right now. Luca doesn't do drugs. His career is too important to him. So to see him standing there with a stream of smoke billowing from his lips is shocking.

He takes another deep drag before slowly releasing the smoke from one side of his mouth.

"Football," I breathe.

"It's cute that you care. Admirable, I guess."

He pushes from the doorframe and walks around the bed, his eyes holding mine.

"You covered up," he states.

"I was cold."

"Hmm..." rumbles up his throat.

Reaching forward, he pulls the sheets with one harsh tug. His strength is no match for mine and the fabric slips out of my grip and away from my body.

Curling up into a ball, my skin pricks with goose bumps as Luca digs his hand into his pocket and pulls out his cell.

"L-Luc, what are you d-doing?" I ask, my voice cracking with a mixture of emotion, exhaustion and frustration.

He keeps the camera trained on me as he takes a step closer.

"Getting some evidence."

"Evidence for what? To prove you tortured me and got your vengeance at last?"

"Something like that," he mutters.

Reaching out, his hot fingers wrap around my ankle and he pulls until I unfold and fall onto my back.

Mortification burns through me as he runs the camera over my naked body.

Part of me wants to believe that the Luca I knew and loved wouldn't do this to me. But I fear he might be long gone and that this new, evil version of himself wouldn't bat an eyelid about making this video and then sending it out to the world.

"P-please don't. Please," I beg, hating the desperation in my voice.

"Why? Don't you want the whole world to know that you're a filthy slut just like the rest of your family?"

I shake my head, trying to keep his words out.

"You know the guys at school used to jerk off to videos of your mom dancing, right?"

"No," I cry. But it's futile because I remember all too well the gossip that used to go around about her. My only saving grace back then was Luca because if anyone was stupid enough to say anything out of line in front of him, he'd deal with it. Protecting me. Always protecting me.

"And your whore of a sister. Guys used to pay her to blow them in the locker room, did you know that?"

"Luc, please," I try again, needing not to go down these painful parts of my past right now.

"You knew this. You knew what she was up to. I'm surprised you weren't as well. We all knew what the Banks girls did to keep a roof over their heads. But then I guess, that's exactly what you're doing now, isn't it? Following in mommy's footsteps and shaking these pretty little tits for money." He scoffs, lifting another bottle from his side that I didn't notice before and swallowing an obscene amount. "You disgust me."

"Didn't stop you fucking me bare out there though, did it," I point out, knowing for a fact that he didn't stop for a second to consider protection.

His entire body tenses at my words and I can't help the satisfied smirk that curls at my lips.

My core throbs as he stares at my closed thighs.

"I'll get tested tomorrow. I wouldn't believe you even if you said you were clean."

"Fuck you, Luc," I say, scrambling to my feet and standing before him, for once in my life having a height advantage. "I'm fucking clean *and* on birth control. You're safe."

He scoffs once more, downing more vodka.

"Safe. With you. Never."

His solid arm hooks around the back of my legs and the world falls out from beneath me as I hurtle toward the mattress once more.

No sooner than my back hitting the softness of the mattress is he crawling between my thighs, pushing them wide and exposing every inch of me.

Somehow, he managed to shed his remaining clothes while I was flying through the air. My concern about my position melts away as I get my first look at him as a whole in five years.

And fuck, he's... he's... mesmerizing.

His hand wraps around my throat, pinning me to the bed.

Our eyes lock and for just a second, everything is different. Everything is just as it used to be as I stare into the hungry green eyes of my best friend.

But then he speaks, and I crash back down to reality with a violent bang.

"The only safe bet here is that your cunt is going to be obliterated by the time I allow you to hobble out of here. But—" he quickly adds. "Only one of us will have enjoyed it."

He thrusts inside me once more, clearly either believing that I'm clean or serious about just getting tested tomorrow. The thought of the latter makes my stomach turn. That he really thinks I'm that deceitful but the feeling of his length stretching me open soon consumes my every thought. It burns after his rough treatment over the table along with the fact it's not been used by anything that doesn't vibrate in... well... a really long fucking time. And because of that, I'm racing toward a release I already know I won't be allowed to ride out all too soon.

———

Pain slices through my body when I come to the next morning. I roll onto my back and just about to smother my moan as my muscles pull.

Memories of the reason for my aching body slam into me like a freaking movie. The dining table, the bed, against the wall, over the dresser, the shower.

"Fucking hell, Peyton," I chastise myself as I regretfully rip my eyes open against the harsh morning sunlight.

I blink as my eyes fill with water before looking to the other side of the bed. I already know what I'm going to find, I can feel his distance.

The sheets are a mess and there's a dent in the pillow, indicating toward the fact he was here at one point in the night. But he obviously didn't deem me a suitable sleeping partner because he's left me alone.

Sucking in a deep breath, I push myself to sit on the edge before forcing myself to stand.

Everything hurts as if I spent a night in a boxing ring, not in a bed with Luca.

Heat floods my core at just the thought of his name. It aches like the rest of me. The thought of him taking me again makes my thighs squeeze together, but hell knows I need the release. I didn't think he'd follow through. I didn't think he'd be able to because I was right on the edge time and time again. But somehow, he knew just how to play my body and every single time I was about to fall, he stopped me.

Holding onto the vanity unit, I lower myself to the toilet to pee, the tenderness of my delicate parts not surprising me as I wipe. What I'm not expecting, however, is what stares back at me when I stand in front of the mirror to wash my hands.

I look like I've been mauled by a rabid dog.

You were.

Lifting my hand, I run my fingertips over the red hickeys that run down my neck and litter across my chest and down onto my breasts.

I don't even remember him giving me most of these, but they look like I should have because they're so bright, the skin tender.

Stepping back to get a look at my lower half, I find more of the same, only when I get to my thighs, the hickeys are joined by actual bite marks, some of which have broken the skin.

"Jesus, Luc," I mutter, running a fingertip over one of the worst ones, a memory flickering in my mind of him between my thighs and giving it to me.

There is one thing I remember though.

He never kissed me. Not once.

Pain pierces my heart at the knowledge.

I wasn't good enough for him to kiss.

A sob erupts from my throat.

He really does hate me.

We used to spend hours making out as kids, it was my most favorite thing to do, well... until we started getting a little more adventurous. I didn't realize it last night, my brain was too distracted by him and the alcohol but I needed it. I needed his lips on mine.

Wiping the tears that have spilled from my eyes with the back of my hand. I reach for the toothpaste that's sitting beside the sink and squirt some on my finger to freshen up my mouth.

My temples pound steadily as I stand there. The shower calls to me, desperation to wash away some of last night down the drain is almost too much to deny, but having none of my own stuff stops me. Then another thought hits me.

I have no clothes.

I walked in here wearing a bedsheet and a pair of panties, both of which he ripped from my body.

Grabbing a towel, figuring it's my only option to hide the car crash that my body is right now.

The bedroom door is already open, so I slip through it in search of Luca. I know he's still here. I know he wouldn't have just left me here for someone else to find.

And I soon find that I'm right when I round the corner and find him passed out on the sofa wearing only a pair of black boxer briefs.

His tattooed arm is thrown over his head, making the muscles in his torso tighten in the most delicious way.

His eyes are closed, his dark lashes resting down on his cheeks. His full lips are parted as his shallow breaths pass. Lowering myself to the coffee table before him, I sit and just take him in. Noting all the differences from the boy I used to know.

His body was always a work of art. His dad ensured he was always in peak condition so Luca could follow his footsteps into the NFL. Even back then, his six-pack and V were well defined. But now, they're downright deadly.

His hair falls down onto his brow, making my fingers twitch to move it back, to feel its softness against my skin. But I can't. If I touch him. If I wake him, I'm never going to get out of here.

Ripping my eyes from his face, I track the lines of his abs before dropping lower.

I gasp when I discover that his cock is straining against the fabric of his underwear and my mouth waters.

The image of dropping to my knees, of pulling it out and sucking him while he's asleep fills my mind and my core throbs once more with its missing release.

How long would it take to wake him like that?

I'd like to think that one day I might get a chance to find out because I already know that today isn't the day. He already thinks I'm a slut. Him waking to find me doing that is only going to confirm his suspicions.

But the truth is, there isn't anyone else in the world I want to be a slut for. No one has ever turned me on or affected me in the way Luca does. Even when he's being wicked, even last night when the most sensible thing to do would have been to run, I couldn't.

I gave my heart, body, and soul over to him years ago, and he never gave it back. I fear that he never will and that I'll always be bound to him in some way.

Knowing that I need to do something before he begins to stir, I push from the coffee table and swipe up his discarded jersey then head back to the bedroom.

Dropping the towel to the end of the bed, I slip his shirt over my head. His powerful scent gives me pause for a second. My need to be wrapped in his arms instead of his number consumes me.

I'd give anything for him to tell me that he believes me and to hold me. Anything but risk the person I need to protect from all of this. Anything but that.

Finding his pants abandoned on the floor, I don't think twice about shoving my hand into his pockets to locate both the key to my freedom and my cell that he stole last night.

With both in hand, I tiptoe back through the main living area, grab my purse from the floor and head for the door.

I push the key into the lock and twist but the damn thing doesn't budge.

"What the—"

"Nice try, baby."

His deep voice, rough from sleep, vibrates through me, and damn it if my nipples don't immediately harden.

"Did you really think I'd allow you to slip away from me so easily?"

I blow out a long breath.

Yeah. Yeah, I did.

"I need to go home, Luca. I've got work and—"

"You've called in sick."

His words finally make me move and I spin toward him. I force my eyes to remain on his face as he sits on the arm of the couch, almost his entire body naked for me to feast on once more.

"I'm s-sorry, I've what?"

"You're sick. They won't be expecting you tonight."

Anger surges through me turning my blood to lava.

"You can't do that," I screech. "I need that job. I need that money."

He pushes from the couch and begins stalking toward me.

"Why, P? Why are you so desperate for the money?"

My heart kicks up a notch as he stares at me through his lashes, demanding to know all my secrets.

"I... I..." I hesitate, my gut telling me to be at least partially honest while my head screams at me to lie because he doesn't deserve the truth, especially not after last night. "I need it to pay medical bills," I blurt, my gut winning out.

His brows pull together. "Medical bills?" he asks, his eyes dropping down my body as if he's now only just going to notice I've got a limb missing or something. "But... you're perfect."

His admission floors me but I force myself to move past it because from the widening of his eyes two seconds after the words pass his lips, I'm assuming he didn't mean to say them out loud.

"Th-they're not mine," I explain but immediately regret it. I'm opening myself up to too many questions.

"Okay, so whose are they?"

"Family."

His eyes narrow. "Your mom or sister then," he surmises.

This time it's my turn to narrow my eyes in suspicion.

"Or my gran?" The reality is, she died only a year after we all moved to South Carolina to live with her, but the only way for Luca to really know that would be for him to have been keeping tabs on me and I really don't think he was.

"Oh, yeah. So..."

"I'm not discussing this with you, Luc. I just need to leave."

His smile isn't at all welcome. There's no friendly happiness in it, it's purely wicked and full of dark intentions.

"You can't keep me locked up in here like some kind of sex slave, Luc. That's insane."

"You're right. I'd much rather have you chained up in my own bedroom, but we're here now so this will have to do."

My jaw drops. He's joking, right?

But his face is deadly serious.

Jesus, have I totally underestimated this new Luca?

"So you've spent the past few weeks stalking me at work and now you're what, holding me against my will?"

He closes the last bit of space between us, the heat of his body burning through his jersey and making my skin prickle with awareness.

Reaching out, he cups my chin in his hand and tilts my head up to look at him.

He lowers his head as if he's about to kiss me and I have to force my eyes to stay open, because I know he's not going to. And I'm right, because he stops only a centimeter from my lips.

My chest heaves with his nearness, my head spinning as his scent fills my nose and reminds me of the things he did to me last night. I swear to God, each hickey and mark on my body burns hot just thinking about his lips and teeth on me.

"Against your will?" he asks, his lips ghosting over my cheek until they brush against my ear. "I think you're exactly where you want to be, baby."

A violent shudder rips through me and he chuckles, clearly noticing my reaction to him.

"Yeah, exactly as I thought."

Selfishly, if I'm being honest with myself, being with Luca again, even if he is this cold, brutal version of himself is where I want to be. But I can't be selfish, I have people relying on me. People who need me present and not locked up by some crazy boy I used to know.

"I need to go home, Luc," I plead.

"To him?" he spits, pulling back from me.

I bite down on the inside of my lips to stop me from spilling the truth.

"I need to go home."

"You're going nowhere yet. I'm not done with you."

I want to scream at him to look at the state of me, to tell him how much he's hurting me both physically and mentally but I don't. I fear he wouldn't hear a word of it even if I did.

"I'm hungry," I whisper.

"Go and shower. You smell like sex. I'll find you some food and coffee."

My argument is on the tip of my tongue but it's pointless. Nothing I say is going to convince him otherwise. I just need to bide my time until he screws up and I can make my escape.

He'll always find you now you're here, a little voice says in my head. He's clearly on a mission with an outcome in mind, he's not going to stop until he's achieved whatever it is.

14

LUCA

Walking into the bathroom, I swipe my jersey from where she's abandoned it on the floor before stepping into the shower.

Steam fills the stall, stopping me from getting a good view of her, it's probably a good thing. If I get a shot of her naked ass body right now then there's a chance I won't leave for food, or ever, to be fair.

Reaching down, I palm my hard cock through my pants.

Last night should have been enough. I fucked her seven ways from Sunday. I took out all my hate, anger, and disappointment on her but one look at her trying to escape and wearing my fucking number and all I could think about was getting inside her again.

Peyton was always smart. That's how I knew she'd go straight for the key the second I passed out. And that couldn't happen, I wasn't allowing her to get away until I'd had my fill of her, even if that meant calling in a favor at The Locker Room to get her out of her shift tonight. Like fuck is she turning up with my marks all over her body.

If I had my way, she'd never go back there again. But short of getting her fired, I'm not sure how I'm going to achieve that.

The water cuts off as I'm still standing there reminiscing on our previous night and how many times I brought her right to the edge, only to leave her hanging. Every time I felt bad. That's not the way a woman deserves to be treated in the bedroom—or anywhere to be fair. But then I would remember what she said to me that night and I'd leave her high and dry, listening to her complain as her body lost its grip on the impending release.

Sliding the door open, she steps out in a cloud of steam and the second it clears, our eyes lock and my heart jumps into my throat.

Fuck, I want to kiss her. I really want to fucking kiss her. It took every ounce of restraint I possess not to claim her lips last night, to make her mine, to remind myself of just how good it used to be spending hours just making out with her.

"Luc," she gasps, her arms lifting in an attempt to hide from me.

"A little late for that, don't you think?"

She looks down at herself, color hitting her cheeks.

"I'm going out. Be good." Spinning on my heels, I walk away from her, only to hear wet footsteps racing after me.

"You're..."

"Going out," I repeat.

"You can't just leave me here. I have no clothes, no anything."

"You don't need anything. I'll bring back food."

"Great," she mutters, and I know that if I were to turn around fast enough, I'd catch her rolling her eyes at me.

Pushing the correct key into the lock, I twist it and feel it release for me.

"Luc, you're not actually serious right now."

"Deadly. See you later."

Slamming the door behind me, I quickly lock it back up, not that I really think she'd come running out here naked to try to stop me, and suck in a deep breath.

Looking back over my shoulder, I catch her lifting her hands to her hair, and tip her head to the sky as if she's praying for strength. I stand there for a few long seconds just watching her, allowing myself to get completely fucking addicted to her once again.

"Hey, man. Good night?" Owen asks me from the deck where he's leaning against the railing smoking.

I glance back at the pool house to make sure he can't see anything before walking up to him.

"Yeah, man. Pretty fucking fantastic."

"Yeah, the hickey on your neck confirms it," he says, nodding to where the mark is.

I remember the exact moment last night when she sank her teeth into me after I pulled out of her, not allowing her to come.

"Listen, I'm not done with the pool house. Keep your boys out for now, yeah?"

"Bro, tell me you've got some girl tied to the bed or some kinky shit."

"Can't tell you my secrets, man. Just keep every motherfucker out, yeah?"

"You got it, man. Whatever you need."

"I'll be back later. Just gonna give her a few hours to really miss me."

Owen holds his fist out for me to bump and I happily return the gesture.

"Later," I say with a quick salute. I take off around the side of the house to find where I abandoned my car when I arrived last night.

I don't need to walk into our house to know it's full.

"Fucking hell," I mutter, scrubbing my hand down my face as I realize that I totally spaced on today's bowl game.

That's what she does to me. She makes me forget everything, and hell if I don't like being in that little bubble with her.

Pushing through the front door, an eruption of shouts and cries come from the den where they're watching the game.

Silently, I slip into the kitchen and kickstart the coffee maker, desperate for the caffeine hit I promised Peyton and never delivered on.

As the scent of the beans fill the room, I briefly wonder if I've done the wrong thing. Guilt about abandoning her there begins to tug at my chest. But then I think back to the way she tried to rip my family apart.

The pain I remember all too well as she lied to me, and I tell myself that leaving her there alone is nowhere near what she deserves.

It's not like I've abandoned her somewhere horrible. She's in a fully stocked fucking pool house to the biggest and wealthiest frat on campus. There really are worse places to be stuck.

"Oh, look what the cat dragged in," Leon drawls, placing his beer on the counter and leaning his ass back against it.

His arms cross over his chest as he stares at me.

"What?" I bark.

"You get lucky last night?"

"What's it to you?"

He scoffs.

"Jealous? How long's it been since you saw some action who wasn't a distressed friend needing a distraction?"

"Fuck you, man. That's got nothing to do with you."

"Yet who I was with last night has something to do with you?"

"When you're acting like a fucking asshole, yeah. It is."

"Well, in case you hadn't realized, you're not our father and you can't tell me what the fuck to do."

My blood heats at even the mention of his name and the things he tells me to do. Although, I'm not sure even he would be able to keep me from Peyton right now.

"Speaking of, you need to call him back."

"I'm good, thanks." I already know how that conversation is going to go.

"We need to talk about plan B, Son, seeing as you royally fucked plan A with the shittiest season I've ever seen. Do you even remember how to throw a football?"

I shake his words from my head. I don't care about him, I don't care about his opinions. I got what I wanted, I'm not heading for the draft. Although I never wanted a failed season to be the reason for it.

I know it's pointless but there's a part of me deep down that just wants him to tell me that it's okay, that we all have off days, off seasons, and that there's always next year. I just want him to be proud of me. To be the dad I always hoped was hiding deep down, but at every turn, he just disappoints me. I want it to stop, I need it to stop.

I just... I think of Peyton, of the things she confessed to me.

They can't be true. They just can't. I refused to believe it back then and I still refuse to now, because if it's true then... I lift my hand to my hair, tugging on the lengths until it hurts.

It can't be true.

"Luc," he sighs, rubbing the back of his neck. "I'm worried about you."

"Yeah, well you don't need to be. Everything is great," I lie. The reality is that my life right now feels like sand slipping through my fingers. I've barely got a grasp on reality. Things are getting clouded by darkness faster than I can control.

The only thing that makes sense is her.

Tormenting her, teasing her, punishing her.

She lied and she left me to drown in the knowledge. That's something I don't think I'll ever be able to forgive her for.

He stares at me, not believing a single word. I don't blame him, I wouldn't believe it either.

"Whatever. I'm going to shower."

I'm almost at the door with my mug in hand when he speaks again.

"Who was she, Luca?"

"No one. She's no one."

I storm from the room and up the stairs before he can respond. The pain of that confession tightens my chest until it feels like my lungs are about to explode.

She might be no one now, but she was someone. Someone who meant more to me than anyone else in the world. There were times I'd even have put her above Leon.

I shake my head at my thoughts. I was so fucking stupid.

"Never put a girl above your boys, Son. All they do is try to poison your mind and distract you from what's really important." Dad's words rattle through my brain. I can't count the number of times I've heard them, or similar, over the years.

Slamming my door so hard the floor beneath me shakes, I put my mug down and begin stripping out of my clothes, desperate to wash her off me. Needing just a few moments where I'm not surrounded by her and the confusion she's brought down on my already fucked up life.

15

PEYTON

The asshole never returns and when I walk out of the bathroom, once again only wrapped in a towel, I find what I already knew. He's gone.

"You're a fucking asshole, Luca Dunn," I scream into the silence.

I don't need to try it, but I do anyway. I wrap my hand around the door handle and twisting it as hard as I can in the hope it releases. It doesn't.

"Fuck," I hiss, tucking the towel around me tighter.

Hooking my fingers into the blind, I lift one of the slats and look out.

The sun is already high in the sky, telling me that it's later than I thought but there's no one to be seen.

I could shout, scream and slam my fists against the glass, but it would be pointless. No one is coming to my rescue.

My stomach growls, reminding me that Luca promised me food. The naïve little girl inside me wants to believe that he left to get some, but I know I'm only bullshitting myself. He hasn't left to do anything nice for me. He's left to torture me.

Something in a heap on the floor next to the table that he fucked me over last night catches my eye. Walking over, I pull the hoodie up and hold it to my nose.

It's Luca's.

Dropping the damp towel, I pull it over my head and wrap my arms around myself.

With each second that passes, my headache only gets worse with my lack of liquid and with no other choice, I make my way to the kitchenette to see if there's anything in here.

To my shock, the cupboards are full and in seconds I have the coffee maker working its magic and a huge bag of chips in hand. Not exactly the healthiest option but it's exactly what I need right now.

I curl myself into the corner of the couch and rip into the bag, stuffing a handful of salty chips into my mouth.

Luca was right, I did think—hope—that he would take one look at me and forget everything that happened and that we could just move past it.

Last night, I hoped that maybe he could fuck the hate out of his system. Take all of it out on me and exorcise everything, and this morning we'd be able to start over.

I don't think that's what happened, damn it.

I came to terms with our romantic relationship being over long ago, but our friendship is harder to let go of. All of my childhood memories include him. All the best parts of my life include him.

I was stupid. Deluded to even consider the fact he would want to have me back in his life, but with everything else falling apart around me, it was easy to cling on to.

Well, no more. When—if—he comes back, I'm getting the hell out of here and turning my back on him.

He doesn't deserve me to try, and he certainly doesn't deserve the truth. And as sad as that makes me, I'm also relieved I didn't spill all my secrets the second I first saw him because he's not worthy of knowing the truth.

Once the bag is empty and my coffee is gone, I push up from the couch and set about trying to figure out an escape plan. I figure there must be an unlocked window or a spare key or something somewhere.

But as the sun begins to descend for the night, I realize that I'm fucked. I have no clothes, no cell, and no fucking hope.

I've got to sit here until the jerk returns or hope someone else turns up for something.

Pulling one of the books I found from the shelf, I settle myself back onto the couch to wait it out. It's not my usual genre of choice, I'm a romance girl really, but a good thriller could be exactly what I need right now. It might give me all the answers I need for my escape, as well as a few ideas for how I can cause Luca a long painful death for doing this to me.

I quickly get lost in the pages but as engrossed as I am, it's not enough to keep my eyes open when my exhaustion from my lack of sleep the night before begins to consume me.

I awake with a start sometime later, blinking against the darkness and lifting the heavy weight of the book I fell asleep reading from my chest.

"Holy shit," I screech when I look forward and find Luca watching me. My hand covers my racing heart as I try to calm down. "Did you just touch me?" I ask, noticing that my skin is burning.

He shrugs, the indifference on his face causing anger to explode inside me.

"What the hell is wrong with you, Luca?" I scream, jumping up from the couch and storming away from him. "You're acting like a fucking psycho locking me in here like some prisoner." I throw my arms up in frustration and begin pacing, needing to do something to expel the energy that's racing through me.

"You didn't seem to mind so much last night," he mutters, his eyes following my every move.

"Last night I was drunk, Luc. I was fucking wasted and—" I slam my lips shut, not wanting to allow the next words out of my mouth free.

"And..." he prompts, lifting a brow.

"And..." I sigh. "And I thought it might help. I thought you might fuck me and—"

He throws his head back and laughs. It's not the response I was expecting. "Fucking hell, P. You really must have a high opinion of your pussy if you think a night of pounding it was going to make me forget everything." My lips part in shock. "I mean, it was good. One of the best I've had in a while." His words are like a knife through my chest, and I fight to keep my expression blank so he can't see how much he's hurting me. "But it wasn't that fucking good."

"Fuck you, Luca. Fuck you." I take off running toward the bedroom, needing some distance from him after ripping my chest wide open with his cruel words. But he's faster than me and his giant hand wraps around my upper arm, stopping my retreat.

"No, Luc. No," I scream, my arms hitting, slapping, and punching any part of him I can reach.

He allows me to hit him for a few minutes before he takes my wrists in his hands and slams me back against the wall, pinning them above my head.

"Are you about done?" he snarls.

"No. Nowhere fucking near," I hiss.

Both our chests heave as we stand only inches apart, staring at each other.

I search his eyes in the hope I'll find just a flicker of the boy I used to love hiding within the angry depths, but there's no sign of him.

"What happened to you, Luc?" I whisper, regretting the words the second they pass my lips.

His jaw tics and a muscle in his temple pulsates.

"You," he spits. "You happened to me."

"I didn't fucking do anything, Luc. I just told you the truth."

He shakes his head. "No. No, he wouldn't do that."

"Okay," I sigh, totally defeated by all of this. "If that's what you want to believe, then fine. But let me go, let me get on with my life. Spend the rest of your life living in denial and wondering if you should have believed me all along."

His eyes narrow at me. "It's not that easy, baby."

That final word rolls through me, causing goose bumps to erupt across my skin but I refuse to let it sink any deeper.

"You've done your worst, you dished out your punishment. We're done."

Taking both of my wrists in one of his hands, he grips my chin with the other and holds my stare.

"We'll never be done, Peyton. You never should have come back here."

"You think I put myself in this position by choice?" I laugh but it's bitter, full of pain and sadness. "My mom died, Luc," I confess, my knees threatening to give out as the words pass my lips. "I sat by her side and held her hand as she died."

His eyes soften slightly, but it's too late. I don't want his pity now that he knows that tiny bit about my life.

"I watched her take her last breath and leave me behind. I had no choice but to walk away from my life and start over. I'm drowning in medical debt." Most of them aren't from Mom, but he doesn't need to know that right now. "All I'm doing is trying to survive. Trying to put one foot in front of the other and ensure I have a future. What I don't need is this bullshit from you. I'm sorry you don't believe me, that's your choice. But I get to choose too, and I'm fucking done, Luc." Tears burn my eyes but I refuse to let them fall, to allow him to see just how fragile I am right now. Putting on a brave front has been my coping mechanism for weeks. I don't want to finally shatter in front of him. "What we had is dead, I see that now. All I ever did was be the best friend I could to you, but clearly, that didn't mean as much to you as it did to me."

"Pey—"

"No," I seethe, tugging my arms so harshly that he has no choice but to release me if he doesn't want to hurt me again. "It's too late. It's over."

Slipping from between him and the wall, I continue toward the bedroom.

"Peyton?" His voice is deep, rough, and full of a pain that I understand all too well but it's not enough to make me turn around. After a second's pause, I step into the room and close the door behind me.

The second the lock clicks into place, a sob erupts from my throat and the tears I was trying so desperately hard to keep from falling from my eyes finally drop.

My back slides down the door until my ass hits the floor. I fold my arms around my legs and let myself break for the first time since I sat beside my mom's freshly dug grave and said goodbye to her for the final time.

I don't hear his footsteps over my cries, but I startle when he knocks.

"Peyton?"

I sniff and try to force down the lump that's clogging my throat.

"Go away, Luc. I don't need you anymore. I learned to live without you."

Not wanting to be so close to him, not trusting myself not to turn around, open the door and fall into his arms like I once would have. I stumble toward the bed and crawl under the covers.

I have no idea how long I lay there in a ball sobbing, or at what point Luca moved from the door, if he even did. But eventually, I drift off into a fitful sleep full of nightmares that wake me up more than once covered in sweat and desperate to outrun my demons.

I wake feeling as exhausted as I did the day before. But instead of my entire body aching, it's just my eyes that sting after the inordinate amount of time I spent crying for everything I've lost.

My body begs me to turn over, pull the sheets over my head and force myself to get some more sleep, but I know I can't.

I've got a life and a certain unreasonable man to deal with.

I might have let him take over my life the past thirty-six hours, but I'm done. The girl who rolled over and let him take what he needed, let him lock me up in here like a prisoner, is long gone.

Today I'm taking back control because fuck him.

Fuck him.

I open my eyes ready to take on the world, or at least Luca Dunn, and scream when I once again find him staring down at me.

"What the fuck is it with you watching me sleep?" I bark, my fingers curling around the sheets.

He's sitting with his back resting against the headboard. His arms are casually resting at his sides as if he was patiently waiting for me to wake because he actually wanted to see me or some bullshit. But none of that is what really captures my attention. That would be the fact he's sitting there with messed up bed hair and clearly only wearing a pair of boxers.

"Tell me you did not sleep in here with me," I demand.

His eyes bounce between mine for a few seconds.

"Okay, I didn't sleep here."

"Don't try to be cute, Luc. It doesn't suit you. Not anymore."

He shrugs and it infuriates me.

Throwing the sheets off me, I rush to pull his hoodie down my body that I'm still wearing to cover up the fact I'm bare beneath.

"I'm going home, and you're going to let me walk out of that door."

His eyes eat me up, lingering on my bare legs for a few seconds too long before he shifts on the bed.

"Is that right?"

"Yeah. I meant what I said last night, Luc. We're done. You took your hate out on me, you used me, punished me. We ar—" His hand quite obviously slips under the sheets as I rant at him. "What the hell are you doing?"

"Your fire makes me hard. Always did."

My chin drops as my eyes take in the movement beneath the sheets.

"Unbelievable. Fucking unbelievable."

"If you wanna help me out, I might even make it worth your while this time."

His nice act doesn't fool me for a second.

"I'd rather fuck a corpse."

His eyes widen at my response.

"Your loss. You could really do with letting go."

"No, asshole. What I need is to go home and get back to my life instead of being locked in here with you," I spit. "I stupidly thought that there could still be something here for us, but you've shattered all that hope. You're nowhere near the same person I once knew. This new version of you, well... he's a cunt, Luc. I fucking hate him."

I swing the bathroom door closed so hard I'm surprised it doesn't fall off its hinges.

I scream in frustration, not caring that he can hear me.

I pee, brush my teeth with my finger, and rip the door open once more. I hesitantly look at the bed, dreading what I might find, but to my relief, it's empty. Instead, I find him pulling his jeans up his legs.

"I want my cell and I want you to unlock the door."

He looks up as if he wasn't aware that I was here, although I know he does.

"Fine."

Opening the closet behind him, I watch as he taps in a code to a safe and produces my cell.

"Key?" I demand, holding my other hand out.

His eyes hold mine for a beat, conflict battling within them, although I have no idea what he's confused over. He hates me as much as I do him now. Why could he possibly want to keep me here when he's made it perfectly clear how he feels.

After long, agonizing seconds where I feel like he might just be about to say something that's going to shatter all of my resolve, he places the key in my hand.

"Thank you. Me and you. Whatever this has been. It ends the second I walk out that door. You get on with your life and I'll do the same with mine." I'm aware that this means having to cut ties with Ella and Letty, seeing as they seem to be his friends, but I've only known them a few days, it shouldn't be that hard.

I spin on my heels and storm away from him, swiping my purse from the counter as I pass the kitchenette on my way to the door.

I'm halfway across the living area when a loud knock on the front door sounds before it rattles violently.

"Luca, I know you're in there. Come and open the fucking door," an angry yet familiar voice calls.

"Fuck," Luca barks behind me, clearly knowing exactly who it is.

"Too late to be ashamed, Luc. You should have listened to your conscience a good few hours ago."

Not even bothering to look back at him, I march toward the door. This time when I twist the key it actually works before Leon barges inside not a beat later.

He scans the room quickly before his eyes land on mine.

They go wide almost instantly before he does a quick lap of my body.

"Peyton?" he breathes in total disbelief.

"Hey, how's it going? You need to put that asshole on a leash."

"Shit," he breathes, lifting his hand to the back of his neck. "Fuck. How are you?" he asks, showing more concern in that one question than Luca has since the moment he found me in The Locker Room before the holidays.

"I... I'm leaving." I sidestep him and am almost free when his hand shoots out, wrapping around my wrist and stopping me.

"Has he hurt you?" Leon whispers, his brows drawing together in concern.

"It's probably best you stay out of it. It's over now, anyway. Bye, Lee."

"Peyton, wait." Luca's voice sends a violent shudder racing through me.

I hate myself for it, but for some reason, my body still reacts to him quicker than my head.

"I'm sorry about your mom."

I wait for another second as a ball of emotion climbs up my throat once more before I take off.

It might be early January but it's already late enough in the day that I don't immediately freeze, only being in Luca's hoodie.

I'm at my car and safely inside in only minutes. I hit the lock button and open my purse, needing to know what Aunt Fee's response was to me not coming back this weekend before I rock up at home looking like this.

> Aunt Fee: You deserve to let your hair down, Peyton. Enjoy yourself. Don't worry about a thing.

"Easier said than done, Aunt Fee," I mutter to myself as I quickly scan the messages I've received from Letty after not responding to her first one that Luca read out to me.

I don't reply. I can't. What the hell would I even say? I can hardly tell her the truth. *Or maybe you should*, a little voice shouts. Maybe she'll be able to fill in some of the gaps I have with how my sweet caring Luca turned into the monster who's locked me up this weekend.

16

LUCA

"You need to start fucking talking," Leon demands after watching Peyton flee from the pool house like her ass was on fire.

"Fuck you, Lee. I don't owe you an explanation for anything."

"You did just see Peyton, your old girlfriend, run from this place wearing nothing but your hoodie and looking like hell, right? Or am I fucking imagining things?"

"It's none of your business," I say, finally pulling my shirt on.

"Like hell, it's not. What the fuck is going on?"

"Nothing." Stuffing my wallet and cell into my pocket, I barge past him.

"You're not just running away from this, Luca."

"Fucking watch me."

I'm out of the pool house before he catches up to me, his palms landing on my shoulder blades and forcing me forward. I stumble but manage to catch myself before I face-plant on the ground.

"What the hell?" I boom, somehow managing to dodge his first punch. Sadly, I'm not as on the ball for the second one and his fist connects with my jaw.

"Fucking asshole." Surging forward, I plant my first hit into his stomach, causing him to double over so I can get the upper hand.

The two of us go at it like we haven't in a very long time and it's not until one of the Kappas notice and emerge from the house that we're finally dragged apart.

"You're fucking everything up, Luc," Leon hisses at me through his heaving breaths.

"It's my fucking life, I can do what I want." I go for him again but the hands wrapped around my upper arms stop me.

"You act like none of the rest of us have problems. Pull your head out of your fucking ass, Bro. You're not a kid anymore."

"Fuck you." I shrug off the hands that are holding me and storm away, lifting my hand to my split lip and wiping the blood away as I do.

My knuckles scream in pain, my face aches, but it's what's inside my chest that hurts the most.

Leon's right. I am fucking everything up.

"FUCK," I bellow, slamming my hands on the wheel of my car the second I drop into the seat. "FUCK, FUCK, FUCK." I repeat it over and over, but it never makes me feel any better.

My one reprieve from all of this shit just walked away from me. What the fuck do I do now?

I allow the vibration of my car to flow through me as I suck in a few deep breaths in the hope it might help clear my head. But it does nothing.

My knuckles split open as I wrap my fingers tightly around the wheel and pull away from the frat house right as Leon stalks around the side of the building.

I don't want to go home, but I don't know where else to go.

Letty is my first thought, but like fuck will she want me showing up at her apartment like this and there's a fucking solid chance that Kane will be there, and I really don't fucking need that.

With no other choice, I take a right and speed out of Maddison County. I need to put this place behind me for a few hours.

The drive helps clear my head somewhat but the persistent pounding of my eye socket and cheek keeps me from forgetting what happened before I left Maddison. The sight of the blood coating my knuckles does a pretty good job too.

I don't park on the driveway of the main house. I don't want to be seen by more people than I have to be in this state. Instead, I kill the engine, step out onto the sidewalk and slip around the main house to the pool house in the backyard.

The second the windows come into view, I breathe a sigh of relief when I see the little family inside all sitting on the floor playing together.

It's not until I'm at the door and pushing the handle down that I'm spotted.

"Holy crap, Luc. What happened?" Chelsea cries, jumping up from her spot on the floor, dragging me inside. "Sit," she demands, pointing to the couch before running out of the room, I'm assuming to get the first aid kit.

"What did you do?" Shane asks, moving the toys toward Nadine to keep her occupied while he grills me.

Ripping my eyes from his concerned ones, I stare down at my beautiful niece. She's seven months old now and literally the most perfect thing on the planet.

I was as shocked as the next person when we discovered that my little brother had knocked Chelsea up, but I can't deny that what they made together wasn't worth all the stress and drama.

"How's my girl doing?"

"Nice try."

Nadine stuffs a toy into her mouth and starts chomping down.

"She's teething. Had us both up all night. So..."

"Lee and I got into it."

"Again? You two haven't fought this much since we were kids," he says, knowing that only weeks ago we were at it over Letty, although our fight that night wasn't this brutal.

"What can I say, he's an asshole."

"I mean, yeah. That goes without saying but..."

"I don't want to talk about it. We both said some shit, it got messy."

"So it's over a girl again then I assume?" Chelsea asks. She rejoins us and takes the seat beside me on the couch as she opens up the first aid box and pulls out what she's going to need.

"What makes you say that?"

"Just tell me it's not Letty again," she begs. "She's with Kane now. She's happy. She doesn't need you—"

"It didn't have anything to do with, Letty, *Mom.*"

She rolls her eyes at me.

"I'm worried about you, okay? Shoot me."

"We're all worried about you. Mom especially. Can you at least return her call at some point, it might stop her nagging at me so much?"

"Everything's fine. It's—"

"Don't bullshit us, Luc. We know everything isn't fucking fine or you wouldn't be here right now looking like that. Is it Dad?"

"When isn't it about Dad?" I mutter as Chelsea presses a cool wipe to my lip, making me hiss.

"Sorry."

Shane knows better than anyone what Dad can be like. When he found out about Nadine, and Shane's plans to only attend MKU part-time this year and not to even attempt to be a part of the team, he went nuclear. But before long, as it always happens when it's to do with Leon or Shane, Dad lets it go and just turns his frustration toward me as if I'm the one who's personally fucked him over.

I get it... I think. I'm the quarterback, I'm the one to possibly follow in his footsteps, to hit heights that he never managed to in his career. But fuck... I'm not actually him and his overbearing, controlling, asshat-ness is just too much to fucking bear.

I stare at my little brother, wondering how much to divulge. He'll remember Peyton. She basically lived at our house growing up, but he never really had anything to do with her, and he certainly doesn't know anything about the circumstances under which she left.

In the end, I decide to go with honesty, or at least a little of it. I know that Leon will only rat me out later if I don't confess now.

"Peyton is back."

"Pey... oooh."

"She's at MKU. I just... I wasn't expecting to ever see her again, you know?"

Chelsea continues working to clean up my face and I have to force myself to sit still while she does it and not knock her hands away from me.

Maybe coming here was a bad idea.

But then Nadine makes this cute little gargle noise and I look down into her giant green eyes and I realize that it's exactly where I need to be.

"Let me finish cleaning you up then you can hold her," Chelsea says softly, clearly sensing that what I really need right now is cute baby cuddles with the most precious little girl in the world.

Silence falls between us as Chelsea starts to work on my knuckles and Shane pulls Nadine onto his lap. They both might be young, but fuck if they aren't the most incredible parents. That little girl has no idea how lucky she is.

"Here," he says, handing his daughter over.

"Hey, baby girl. How's it going?" I ask, looking down into her sparkling eyes. Her lips curl up in happiness and she giggles, wiggling about in my arms. "Yeah, I'm happy to see you too."

Chelsea and Shane both get up and leave me with my girl for a few minutes before bringing over cans of soda.

"So I'm assuming it wasn't a happy reunion?" Shane says, unfortunately wanting to know more.

"No. When she left, we weren't on good terms."

"I remember. But that was what... five years ago? You were just kids then. Don't you think that it's time to let go of whatever it is?"

As he says the words, I find myself fifteen years old sitting in Peyton's backyard discussing plans for our summer when she turned to me and dropped the bomb that would not only change our plans for the summer, but for the rest of our lives.

Everything we thought we were going to have together was gone the moment I looked her in the eyes and called her a liar.

Pain slices through my chest as I think of the look on her face when I adamantly told her that I didn't believe her, that she was lying to me. I had no idea why she would do that, why she'd want to hurt me, but that was the only thing that made sense because the possibility of her being right... I couldn't—I can't—deal with it.

"I don't know if I can."

"What did she do?" Chelsea asks, turning to look at me.

My lips part but I soon find that I have no words. "It... it doesn't matter."

"Exactly," Shane announces. "So just let it go. You two were so good together. I really thought this was going to end up being your life." He points to Chelsea and then Nadine.

"I don't think so, I know how to fucking wrap it," I joke, raising a brow at him. Although, it's a big fat lie because I fucked Peyton bareback without a second thought Friday night.

Out of nowhere, the image of her belly swollen with my baby pops into my head and my breathing falters. I bet she would look so fucking beautiful.

My grip on Nadine tightens as I try to get control of myself.

"Whatever. I just don't think it's worth getting yourself fucked up over. You've got enough to worry about with the new season and classes and—"

"You sound like Dad."

"Nah, man. I don't mean it like that. No girl is worth going at it over with Lee."

"Nice," Chelsea mutters.

"Baby, you know exactly what I mean. Bros over hoes." He winks and she groans.

"It doesn't matter. I don't think she's going to be making an effort to talk to me again anytime soon anyway."

"What did you do?" Chelsea asks.

"The specifics don't matter," I say, already ashamed of my actions this weekend. "We hashed out a few things and it got a bit... brutal. Lee was pissed. It was all just a bit intense."

"Right, well... Chelsea's parents are out and we were about to order dinner. You staying?"

My stomach growls right on cue. It was late by the time Peyton woke earlier, with the fight and the drive here, it's the first time I'm realizing that I haven't actually had anything yet.

"Yeah, if it's okay with you two."

"Of course. But don't get any ideas about crashing here. Firstly, unless you're going to be on Nadine nighttime duty, trust us when we say you wouldn't want to be here, and secondly, don't even think about running away from your issues. That's not how we deal with shit."

"Yes, *Mom*," I deadpan, rolling my eyes at my little, yet seemingly wiser, brother. I guess it's true what they say, becoming a father makes you grow up fast.

17

PEYTON

My heart is in my throat as I walk into work later that night. I might have been able to cover up the marks on my body enough to hide them from Aunt Fee and Elijah after managing to slip into my room before either of them caught me doing the walk of shame, but the men here—my boss—are a different story.

None of them are going to be impressed by the marks he left behind on my skin.

I'm meant to be the innocent one. That's what earns me decent money without having to accept any of the offers I get to go and make use of one of the back rooms.

I shed my hoodie and stuff it and my purse into my locker and give myself another once over in the mirror. I went all out with the outfit in the hope it would distract from the amount of concealer I've had to slather on my body.

My pleated skirt just barely covers my ass. If I bend over even slightly, then the entire bar is going to know what color my panties are. And my white shirt is unbuttoned but tied in a knot between my breasts, showing off as much skin as possible.

I hate it. I hate that men's eyes are going to be drilling into me all night. That just as Luca said, they're going to be imagining all kinds of things every time they look at me.

But that's okay, they're not going to be close enough to touch.

I tell myself this over and over as I make my way out to the bar, my skin prickling with awareness as I move.

"Whoa, girl. Someone is feeling better," Bry says, his eyes eating up my mostly exposed body.

"And on a mission," Helena mutters, also noticing me.

I just about manage to hold in my groan of frustration that she's on shift tonight.

Bry slides my water over before nodding over to my shoulder in the direction of a booth I avoided at all costs as I walked through.

"You'll be glad you put the extra effort in when you see who's waiting for you."

"What are they doing here?" I hiss. Tonight was already going to be bad, I really don't need Slick and Eyebrows here making it worse.

"Yeah, they're here but they're not the only ones."

I stare at Bry, thankful that Helena has walked off to thrust her fake tits at some guy, so she doesn't witness the panic that races through me.

Please God, tell me he's not here.

Sucking in a deep breath, I risk a glance over my shoulder at the farthest booth back. And sure as shit, there he is.

It might be dark, I might not even be able to see his face in the shadows, but I know it's him and I know he's watching me.

"Jesus fucking Christ, he needs to leave."

"Yeah, he does. If Julian finds out that you've got a boyfriend in here. A boyfriend who is Luca Dunn, I might add, then he's going to lose his shit."

"Luca isn't my boyfriend."

Bry raises a brow at me making me wonder just how much he knows. I sure as hell have never said anything to him about Luc. He figured there was once something between us from our first meeting here. The tension was palpable, Luca's blatant threat too loud for him to miss. But I shot him down every time he brought it up after and refused to talk about him ever since.

Apparently, none of that matters though, because, from the way he's looking at me, I'd say he's well aware of the situation. Well, as much as anyone on the outside can be. I'm in the middle of it and I have no freaking clue what's going on.

"Riiight," he sings with a smirk.

"If you've got something to say, just say it."

"He waits for you every night, Pey. He cares about you."

How the hell does he know that?

"Trust me, he really doesn't. He's just trying to make my life hard."

"By trying to protect you from those assholes?" Bry sends a look to my most dreaded table.

"He is the asshole."

"What happened between you?"

"Nothing," I snap. "Pass me my pad, I've got work to do."

"Want me to tell Helena to leave his table to you?"

"No," I shout a little too loudly. There's no way in hell I'm walking up to his table and taking his freaking order. "She can have him. I hope he enjoys her."

I'm gone the second I have my pad in hand and make my way over to my fan club.

"Well damn, looks like tonight was the right night, boys," Slick says, practically drooling as I come to a stop at their table.

"How are you all this evening, gentlemen?" I purr, putting on my best act that makes my stomach turn in disgust.

If Luca thinks I'm a slut who sells herself for money, then why would I want to disappoint him?

I spend way longer than I usually would at their table, stroking their egos and allowing them to get their fill of me.

They all stick to the rules of no touching the girls, but I see their fingers curling into fists with their need to reach out.

My skin itches at the thought of feeling their touch. But right now I want to hurt Luca more than anything else, so I push through it, finally excusing myself to collect their order.

"You're playing with fire, girl," Bry warns, slipping back behind the bar as I approach.

"Whatever. I'm just here to do my job and make some cash. The rest is white noise."

"You might not be saying that when Dunn takes out some of Julian's best customers because of the way they look at you."

"He wouldn't."

Bry levels me with a stare, knowing as well as I do that Luca wouldn't bat an eyelid at doing just that.

"Fucking hell."

"You need to deal with your shit. If Julian gets one whiff of this, then you'll be sacked faster than Helena gets the guy's dicks hard."

"So he'll give me ten minutes to explain."

Bry throws his head back and laughs. "Yeah, something like that."

I know he would. I might have only been here a few weeks, but already I've witnessed how cutthroat our boss is when it comes to things—boyfriends—upsetting business.

"He has no right to be here. He has nothing to do with me. You kick him out."

He holds his hands up in defeat. "I am not getting involved in this."

"Well, I'm not going over there."

He holds my stare.

"Okay, fine," I whine, throwing my hands up in frustration. "After I've delivered these."

I walk over to another couple of tables to collect up empties. I take some orders before taking the tray Bry has put together for my dreaded table and taking it over, putting extra sass into my hips just to be a bitch. I know Luca is watching my every move. His eyes burn into my back.

"Here you go, gents. Would you like anything else?"

"You know we would, sweetheart," Eyebrows says, a disgusting smile curling at his thin lips.

"I'm sorry, that's not on the menu."

"It's a damn shame," Slick adds. "I think we could all really have some fun."

All?

I have no idea how I don't lose the contents of my stomach right there and then.

Fucking pigs.

"Right, well. Enjoy your evening." I give them my most seductive smile and thankfully slip away. Although I know I'm still very much the object of their attention.

I shudder when I get to the bar but I don't get any rest because Bry slides a glass over to me.

"For your solo admirer."

I swallow down my nerves at the thought of having to look him in the eyes once more and lift the tray.

I try to convince myself that walking up to Luca right now is less terrifying than that group of sleazeball men, but it's really not. They can objectify me all they like. I don't care what they think of me. But Luca. Shit. Back in the day, his opinions used to mean everything to me. I used to care what he thought.

I shove that teenage girl deep down in the box she belongs in and hold my head up high as I step into the darkness that surrounds his booth.

There's a very good reason why this booth is situated in Helena's section. None of us can see what happens back here and we're not brave enough to come and see.

Stepping up to him, I slam the glass down on the table, making the contents splash over my hands.

"You need to lea—" My word falters when I get a look at his face.

Concern washes through me, but I bite it back.

He deserves whatever Leon threw at him for the game he played this weekend.

But as I stare at him, I don't feel vindicated in any way. I just feel... sad.

I might have been dragged away from Luca years ago. I thought I'd dealt with the loss, but deep down there was always a hope that one day we might just be able to reconnect. That he would still be the boy I remember all too well.

But he's not. That boy is dead, and the intense wave of grief that rushes through me almost takes me to the floor.

"You need to be careful with those assholes," he says as if I'm some naïve little girl who's not aware of the situation I've put myself in doing this job.

I know the risks. But right now, the benefits of the paycheck outweigh them.

Maybe if he cared a little less about himself, he'd have a better understanding of why I'm doing it.

"I know what I'm doing."

He sits forward, his elbows resting on the tables, his fingers laced together and covering what looks like incredibly sore, busted-up knuckles. His eyes hold mine. There's a softness in them that I really don't want to see. I don't want or need him to be nice to me right now. I need him to be the evil, vindictive asshole he's been since he first found me in here a few weeks ago.

"You don't have—"

"No, Luc. You don't get to show up here and do this," I explode, guessing where his question was going. "You don't get to care all of a sudden because you don't like the way they look at me, not after how you've treated me. After this weekend, I'd actually prefer to be serving their drinks and allowing them to look down my top rather than I would you," I spit. It's a barefaced lie but he doesn't know that.

"You don't mean that."

"Don't I? Do you know what else?" I ask, ready to really rub salt into his wounds. His lips twitch as if he wants to say something but I beat him to it. "I bet they'd more than willingly get me off too."

His palms slam down on the table, the glass I placed down only minutes ago rattling with the force.

"You need to leave."

"If one of them—"

"Save it, Luca. It's too late to pretend to care. You've already proved how little you feel for me now."

"They don't get to fucking touch you, P. *No one* gets to touch you."

"Oh get over yourself, you conceited jerk. Leave or I'll get security to throw your ass through the door."

"It's cute that you think they could."

My teeth grind as I barely contain my anger at his arrogance.

Reaching out, he takes his glass and tips back the amber liquid, swallowing it down in one.

The thought of him driving drunk fills me with dread but I refuse to be the kind of person who points it out now. He doesn't need me to look out for him.

"As you wish, but I'll be waiting."

"Bite me," I bark at his retreating back, but instantly regret it when I see his shoulders lift with amusement.

"Oh, baby. I fully intend to."

"I hate you," I seethe.

"No, you don't. You just hate that you're still desperate for the orgasm I kept from you."

"That's long forgotten," I spit, although from the way my pussy clenches at just his words alone, I know my statement is far from the truth. "You weren't that good, most of it was faked."

He chuckles, finally shooting me a look over his shoulder. The heat in his eyes threatens to burn me from the inside out.

With a single nod, he walks away from me and finally out the front door.

I breathe a sigh of relief until I look down at his table to collect his glass and I find a hundred-dollar bill and a note.

There's always another way.

Crumpling up the note, I throw it in the trash can behind the bar before pocketing his money. It's less than I would have earned in tips last night so it's the least he could do.

"Loverboy gone?" Bry asks, amusement filling his tone.

"He's no—" I blow out a frustrated sigh. "Whatever. I don't care what you or anyone thinks."

With every hour that passes, the place only gets busier. By the time I get off, the balls of my feet are pounding from the height of my shoes and I can barely keep my eyes open. The short nap I had at Aunt Fee's before my shift was nowhere near long enough to deal with the number of assholes I've been subjected to tonight.

Tugging my hoodie up my arms and zipping it right up to the neck, I throw my purse over my shoulder and head out.

The music still plays out from the bar and the sound of the men's chatter filters down to me. The bar stays open later on the weekends, but thankfully, I don't have to work until closing. Which is a bonus because it means I don't need to deal with the drunken idiots who don't want to go home to their wives.

I know he's there the second I step out the back door and into the parking lot. A shiver runs down my spine as my feet sink into the gravel beneath them.

Other than that one night, he stays in his car and watches me from the darkness. But everything changed this weekend.

The second I round the corner, I see him and my heart leaps into my throat.

Instead of sitting in the shadows, his headlights are on, illuminating his dark figure sitting back on the hood of his car.

His eyes follow me as I make my way to my own car to get the hell out of here.

I expect him to push off, to walk over and do something.

But he never does. He just watches me.

My hand trembles as I pull the door open and after holding his stare for a beat, I throw my purse inside and drop down into the seat.

I force myself not to look in the rearview mirror to see what he's doing and just focus on starting the engine and leaving.

I manage it until the very last minute, once I've got the car in drive and ready to go.

"Fuck," I hiss when I find he's moved and is now behind the wheel and ready to follow me out.

Putting my foot down, I speed out of the lot, desperate to be in the safety of Aunt Fee's house.

Thoughts about going elsewhere so he doesn't follow me back there flicker through my mind, but it's pointless. He already knows where I live. He saw me that night with Elijah. All I'd be doing is putting off finally getting into bed by messing with him.

With a loud sigh, I head for home, trying to ignore the fact his headlights follow me all the way there.

18

LUCA

My knuckles split once more as my grip on the pen in my hand tightens.

I should be focusing on whatever my professor is saying, but I can't get the image of her in that little skirt last night out of my head.

I might have only been in The Locker Room with her for a short period of time. But it was enough to have the image of her bending over to pass her asshole customers their drinks burned into my brain.

The thought of all the other douchebags in that place seeing the same thing made me fucking murderous.

She's mine.

Mine.

I fucking hate that she's working there. And the fact she clearly has no idea who actually owns the place because something tells me that she'd have run a mile if she knew the truth.

Our dad is nothing if not protective of his public image, so it's hardly surprising that he's not openly announced his involvement in a seedy chain of sports bars that litter the country. I always wondered why he didn't make them just sports bars but then I guess he'd lose the majority of his customers who only come for the waitresses and the extras they offer behind closed doors.

Confusion swirls around me as I once again think about what Peyton told me that night five years ago. I've been so adamant since, that she was the liar, but I can't deny the facts.

I wanted to believe that she was lying because I couldn't cope with the alternative but now she's here, openly standing before me and calling me out on it. I can't help but wonder if I did have it wrong all these years.

But if I was wrong and she was telling the truth, then it would mean that my dad... the man I've looked up to all my life is a...

I scrub my hand down my face, pushing the thought aside.

No.

No. It has to be lies.

Our father is a lot of things. But he's not that.

He wouldn't. He just wouldn't have done what Peyton claimed he did.

———

My head is still a fucking mess after hours in the gym after my classes. By the time I walk up to the front door of our house—a house paid for by our father—not only does my body ache from the beating I took from Leon, but my muscles pull from my workout.

My eyes are heavy, my body sluggish as I make my way to the kitchen for some food before I crawl into bed and crash.

I barely slept last night. All I could think about was her and *them.* I couldn't help wondering at what point she'll realize that she can make even more money to pay off the debts she has by allowing them to take what they want.

I want to believe that Peyton really isn't like that. But then I'm sure every woman thinks that until the offer of the money they so desperately need is right there for the taking.

"Bro." Leon nods when he walks into the kitchen behind me as if he was waiting for me to get home. If he wants to give me a lecture then he really can stick it up his ass because I am not interested in anything he has to say.

He doesn't know anything about the situation between me and Peyton, and as far as I'm concerned, the less he—and anyone else knows—the better. I won't have any member of my family's name dragged through the mud because of some teenager's accusations. Our father might be a cunt, but he's our father, and I'd protect him to the end, if it came to it.

Thankfully, the first words he says aren't to attempt to rip me a new one again.

"You've got a visitor."

My initial thought is that it's Peyton but then I get over myself and realize that she's never going to willingly come anywhere near me after the weekend.

"Fuck, really?" I ask, reading the truth in his eyes.

"Apparently he's had enough of your bullshit too."

"Fucking hell."

Reaching in the refrigerator, I pull out an energy drink, although I wish it was vodka for the conversation that I'm sure is about to commence.

With a weary sigh, I pass Leon and head out into the hall to find my guest.

"Take whatever he says with a grain of salt," Leon says behind me.

"Easy for you to say, he's not constantly riding your ass about being better."

"You're right because being forgotten is so much better."

My lips part to respond but I quickly find I don't have a comeback for that.

Leon tries not to let it bother him, but I know it does. I never asked to be Dad's favorite. I don't want to be the focus of all his attention but sadly, it's the way it is, and both of us just have to find a way to deal with it because it's not going to be changing anytime soon.

Walking into the den, I find him sitting on the wingback chair that's usually reserved for me and Leon, with one leg bent over the other and his arms crossed over his chest.

As approachable as ever.

I fight not to roll my eyes at him but it physically pains me.

"Son," he says, nodding but not bothering to get up or anything as I fall down onto the couch opposite him.

"What do you want?" I grunt, knowing that he's not here to catch up. He's here to grill me about the season and my failed chance to enter the draft this year.

I was expecting it to happen in person over the holidays, but it turned out that he fucked off to Hawaii with some hot piece of ass that's meant to be a replacement for our mother. She's a fucking bargain bucket Barbie doll, if you ask me. I hope he knows what he lost when he started fucking around on the woman who stuck by all his bullshit. Mom's just another reason why I want to believe he's innocent in Peyton's accusation, because she's already dealt with enough of Dad's infidelity. Finding out that it is true would kill her.

"That's not the way to greet your old man after all this time," he mutters.

I sit forward, waiting for him to get to the point. He doesn't do social visits, so he can cut the fucking act right now.

I hold his eyes, begging him just to get it over with so he can leave, and I can drown every word that he's about to say to me in whatever bottle of poison I find in the kitchen first.

"You fucked up, Son."

My body tenses at his words.

There's no, tough season, or you can't win them all, with Brett Dunn. You either win or you fail, there is no middle ground. It's one of many things I will do differently if I'm ever lucky enough to have kids of my own.

It's bullshit. Totally fucking bullshit.

All my life he's been on my ass, telling me that I'm not good enough. That I'll never be him, I'll never be as good as him or as big of a success as him. What he fails to see or understand is that he's right, I'm not fucking him and neither do I want to be because he's a cunt.

Sure, Peyton might have a similar opinion of me right now, but that's not who I am, not really. I don't usually go out of my way to make anyone's life harder than necessary. And if I end up having a football team's worth of boys in years to come then I already know that I will not give a shit if not a single one of them wants to play. They can be who, and do what, they want.

"It wasn't a great season. There were things in my—"

"Don't make excuses, Luca. You didn't work hard enough. You didn't lead your team properly."

"Things didn't go as planned," I mutter. It doesn't matter what I say right now, he won't hear any of it, even if I accept the blame.

"Seeing as you screwed up our plan to enter the draft as a first pick —" He means his plan because mine has always been to get my degree before entering, but he doesn't give a shit about what I want.

"We need to discuss the next steps."

My fists curl, my short nails digging into my palms as my heart pounds dangerously fast in my chest.

"What I think we should do is—"

"No," I blurt, ensuring his eyebrows shoot up to his hairline.

"N-no?"

"Yeah, no. I'm fed up with having my life dictated by you." I push to stand, unable to confess this and not at least attempt to expel the adrenaline coursing around my body.

"But you want the NFL, you want the life I had," he says, looking genuinely confused that there's even a chance that I don't want that.

"That's what *you* want, Dad. You're trying to relive your lost career through me and I'm exhausted. Honestly, I don't even know if I want to play again after last season." It's not a lie. It's a thought that's almost been on repeat since walking off that field for the final time last season.

Giving up everything has been a pretty consistent thought, to be honest.

It's not just football. It's Leon, Letty, Kane. Everything.

The only thing that makes it seem achievable is her. And that's so many shades of fucked up, I don't even know where to start with it.

"You what?" he roars, suddenly jumping from the couch and coming to stand in front of me, forcing me to stop pacing. "You don't get to quit this, Luca. Dunns don't quit."

"You might not, but I'm balancing on the edge of doing just that right now."

"No, I haven't worked this hard for you to just throw it all away," he booms. The muscle I'm more than used to pulsating in his temple with his anger.

"Yeah, that's just it though. It's not about you. This is about me, about my life."

"No, Luca. It's about the future, your career, your success."

"And what if I don't want to succeed, huh? What if I don't want any of this?" I throw my hands up in frustration. "What if I never wanted any of this?"

Before he gets a chance to respond with some bullshit that I already know is going to add gasoline to my already raging inferno, I storm from the room.

Leon is standing right outside, probably enjoying himself listening to the kind of bullshit Dad never spits at him.

"Did you enjoy that?" I ask, slamming my palms down on his chest, forcing him to stumble back against the wall.

All the air rushes from his lungs as he connects with the wall but he makes no move to fight back. Whatever he sees in my eyes stops him.

"Did you really mean that? You want to give it all up?" he asks, sounding genuinely concerned, unlike our father who doesn't give two shits about how I really feel.

"I don't know. I don't fucking know anything anymore."

Ripping my eyes from his, I storm down the hallway toward the front door.

"Luca," he calls before I slam the door behind me and disappear.

"What?" I bark.

"Please, don't take this out on her."

"Get your nose out of my business, Lee. You don't know what you're talking about."

The door slams behind me, cutting off whatever response he might have had to that. I know what I said, but Lee is the only person in my life—aside from Peyton—who has ever had any clue. I fear he might have more of an idea about what I'm going through right now than he lets on.

I don't leave town this time, instead, after driving aimlessly for over an hour in an attempt to calm down, I find myself pulling into the parking lot behind The Locker Room.

Leon's parting words about not taking it out on her ring out in my head, but she's the only thing right now that makes sense. She's the only one who will calm whatever the fucked up shit is in my head.

I'm out of the car and heading toward the entrance before I've even realized I've moved. It's not until I see how quiet it is that I remember it's only Monday night.

Bry notices me first as I stride toward the bar.

"Evening. Two nights in a row. You really must be desperate."

I pin him with a hard glare. We're not friends exactly, but I've spent enough time here in the past couple of years that we're at the point of it being acceptable to give each other shit.

"You have no fucking idea, man."

Without having to ask for it, a glass of whisky is pushed toward me and I knock it back without thinking.

I glance around, not even attempting to hide the fact that I'm looking for her.

"Where is she?" I finally ask not finding her pink hair anywhere.

"She's out back. She—"

"She's fucking what?" I boom, the stool I was perched on crashes to the ground behind me. The thought of her being back there with some other guy makes me fucking crazy.

"She's on break. Jesus, Luc. You need to chill your shit. I think you know as well as I do that she's not one of your dad's usual girls. They're not usually that... innocent."

Images of her in the pool house on the weekend hit me.

Innocent my ass. That woman writhing against me wasn't a woman who doesn't know what she's doing.

My chest damn near rips open, making me bleed out over the floor as I think about her with others, about her selling herself like I accused her of.

But then Bry's words register.

"She's on break."

"B-break?"

"Yeah."

My heart continues to race as I stare at Bry's concerned eyes.

"I really think you should wai—"

I don't hang around long enough to hear his warning. My need for her is too strong.

19

PEYTON

I sit at the small table in our break room and poke a carrot stick into the hummus before me. Aunt Fee always sends me to work with a healthy snack. I appreciate it, I do. But right now, I just want a bar of chocolate or some candy.

I'm exhausted, my whole body aches with my need to curl in bed and sleep for a week. But I can't. I'm halfway through what feels like the longest shift of my life.

When I walked in and saw hardly any customers, I thought I was in for an easy night, and I wasn't wrong but easy also means boring and boring equals a long ass night.

"Ugh," I groan, dropping my head to rest on my forearm and closing my eyes for a beat.

I swear it was for just a second.

The click of the door closing on the other side of the room startles me and I sit bolt upright.

"Shit, I'm sorry. I didn't mean to fall asleep," I say in a rush, quickly tidying up what's left of my food. "I'll be right there."

A tingle runs down my spine as I stand, quickly dumping everything into my lunch bag and it gives me pause.

Realizing that no one has said anything, I stop and look over my shoulder.

My breath catches at the sight of Luca standing with his back resting against the door. But it's not his presence that startles me as much as the look in his eyes.

He looks... broken.

His green eyes are dark. The fire and hate from our previous exchanges are nowhere to be seen and the hard set of his shoulders I was becoming used to has gone. He seems totally defeated.

My fists curl as I force myself to remember everything that's happened between us this past week. I repeat over and over in my head that I don't care. That Luca the man is evil and twisted and that I hate him. But it doesn't work because that look on his face right now, it's one hundred percent the boy I remember all too well.

"Luc, what—"

At the sound of my voice, he moves. He pushes from the door and storms over.

The chair in front of me clatters into the wall as he throws it out of his way to get to me.

"Luc?" My voice is weak and cracks with confusion as his warm fingers grip my chin and his lips slam down on mine.

Oh God.

My heart pounds, my head spins as he kisses my lips. His tongue sneaking out to try to part them, but despite every single part of my body screaming at me to hand myself over to him, this time, my head is louder.

I can't let him do this.

I wanted him to kiss me all weekend and he refused. Why should he get to do it now just because he's decided he needs it?

The expression on his face as he stood there only seconds ago flickers through my mind as his hot hand curls around my waist, burning into my bare skin.

"Come on, Sweet P," he whispers, and I melt.

There have only been three people who've called me that in my life and it was only a few weeks ago that I thought I'd lost them all. But he's here. He's standing right here and he needs this. Hell, I fucking need this.

The next time he tries to part my lips, my restraint slips and his tongue pushes inside as he walks me backward until I collide with the wall.

I gasp, giving him the access he needs to properly deepen the kiss.

Reaching down, his hands grip my thighs and he wraps my legs around his waist, his already hard cock pressing exactly where I need him.

The promise of finding that orgasm he denied me of all weekend forces me to forget all of my concerns. I roll my hips against him as my hands slide over his shoulders and come to rest in his hair, dragging him closer to me.

The low moan that rumbles up his throat as my tongue slides against his sends a surge of heat between my legs.

His hands slide down my thighs until he's palming my ass, pulling me even tighter against him.

I haven't got myself off since being with him. I knew that doing so would make me go back there, make me think of his tongue, his fingers, his cock, and I couldn't bear to torture myself like that. So I've suffered through it. But right now, I need that release more than I need my next breath.

"Luc, please," I whimper when he leaves my lips and begins kissing and nipping down my jawline.

He lifts me a little higher before one of his hands leaves me and the sound of his zipper mixes with our heavy breathing.

My core clenches, liquid lust filling my veins.

Fuck, I need him. I need him so bad.

I already know that I'm going to regret this the second it's over. But even with that knowledge, I don't stop. It's too late, my body is already lost to him and what he can give me.

I tell myself that it's okay to take his, because I want it too.

I'll let him do his worst, take what I so desperately need and then I can take back control.

"So wet," he growls in my ear as he hooks his finger into my soaked panties and tugs them aside. His words only make the situation worse as my hips roll, searching out some friction. "I love how impatient you are for my cock."

"Luca," I pant when the head of his dick presses against my entrance.

My legs tighten around his waist in an attempt to force him inside but before he does that, he pulls his face from my neck and stares me deep in the eyes.

For the first time since bumping into him, I feel like I'm really looking at him. The boy I knew, the man he's really grown into. Not the one full of anger and hate that he's shown me so far.

This side of him. It's vulnerable, lost, confused.

I equally hate it as much as I love it.

"Peyton, I—"

I press my fingers against his lips, cutting off what he wants to say.

Whatever it is, I already know that I'm not in any position to hear it.

Forgetting what I thought only seconds ago, I realize that if we're going to do this right now then I need to take the upper hand. I need to be the one in control or I'm not going to survive what comes next.

This needs to be on my terms.

"Give me what I need, Luc."

"Fuck," he barks, thrusting forward and filling me to the hilt in one move.

"Oh shit," I gasp, my muscles clamping around him as my nails dig into his shoulders.

My lips part to demand he fucks me but before I manage to find the words, he starts moving.

His lips find mine once more. His kisses are brutal, almost as brutal as his thrusts hit the spot deep inside me every single time.

In only minutes, I'm racing toward the release I didn't get to ride out over the weekend.

I panic right before I crash that I read this all wrong and that he's going to drop me at any minute. But that's not what happens.

Instead, he drags his lips from mine, and whispers, "Come for me, baby," in my ear.

The low growl of his voice is the final push I need, and I fall over the edge of one very tall cliff, screaming his name as I tumble into the abyss.

"Lucaaaaa. Oh God, oh shit," I chant as wave after wave of intense pleasure races through me.

My head falls against the wall. He pulls my hips out and thrusts into me a couple more times, sending aftershocks through my body before he throws his own head back and roars his own release.

For a second, I wonder if I should have forced him to back up and ruined it for him the same way he did for me time and time again over the weekend. But I quickly decide that I'm not that petty, and also, he looks insanely fucking hot when he comes and I couldn't bring myself to miss it.

Now though... now that it's over and it's time to make a stand.

When his eyes find mine, the vulnerability from before is still there but he looks a little more settled as if he needed that as much as I did.

The expression soon changes though when I open my mouth.

"Thanks, I needed that," I say coldly, unwrapping my legs from him and giving him no choice but to lower my feet to the floor.

"Peyton?" he growls as I right my clothing and smooth my hair down.

"You can leave now. I need to get back to work." I keep my back to him as I say the words, knowing that the look on his face as he hears them will gut me.

He came here because he needed me for whatever reason and I've just told him in not so many words that I'm not interested.

I tell myself over and over again that I'm not.

"W-what?" he stutters, his shadow falling over me, but still, I refuse to look over my shoulder.

"I'm sure you can see yourself out."

I rush for the door before he does something stupid like try to touch me, or kiss me again.

"Wait... I need—"

Finally spinning around, I pin him with a determined look. "I don't care what you need, Luca. You made your feelings for me very clear on the weekend. That," I say, pointing at the wall. "You owed me that. So thanks, I appreciate the gesture. But as for anything else... we're done. Over. Finito."

His lips part to respond but I'm not having any of it.

"Goodbye, Luca. I'll get security to ensure you leave if you don't go willingly." With that said, I pull the door open and all but run down the hallway as the remnants of what happened back in that room begin to flood out of me.

I fight my sob until the ladies bathroom door slams closed behind me. I lock myself in a stall and lower to the toilet as my tears spill over.

I knew it was going to hurt. I knew it was going to be a mistake but I also knew that I needed to make a point.

I'm not some toy for him to play with when he needs to hurt someone or expel some pent-up frustration.

I drop my head into my hands and cry for everything I hoped we might be able to find again but now I know is never going to happen because as far as I'm concerned, that's it for me and Luca. I meant what I said. We're done. Over. I can just only hope that I can forget as easily.

I've still got my head buried in my hands and my panties around my ankles when the door opens a while later and a familiar voice says my name.

"Give me a minute," I say, my voice shaky and weak.

Wiping at my cheeks, I clear away my tears although I already know it'll do little to make me look any more respectful. How I'm going to walk back out there and continue with my job tonight God only knows.

Pulling my panties up, I try to put myself back together as much as I can before opening the door and facing Bry.

"You know this is the ladies, right?" I quip, but my joke falls flat on its ass because the second he looks at me, his only reaction is to frown and take a step toward me as if he's going to hug me.

"No, please," I beg, throwing back my shoulders and sucking in a deep, calming breath.

"Peyton."

"No. Don't give me that look. I'm not some charity case, Bry," I snap, unable to deal with the compassion in his eyes when I know I did this to myself.

That had to happen. We needed that one final moment. But that doesn't mean allowing it to happen and taking what he owed me didn't come at a cost.

"What happened?"

"We're done. He's left."

"You don't look like you just told him to leave." Lifting my eyes from the sink, I hold his stare in the mirror over my shoulder.

"We had some unfinished business." My voice cracks with emotion and I lift my fingers to my kiss-swollen lips, remembering just how it felt with his against them.

"You should go home. Get an early night."

"I can't, Bry. I've got a shift to finish."

"It's dead out there. I'll tell Julian you got sick and I sent you home."

"No, you don't need—"

"Peyton," he growls. "It wasn't a suggestion."

His eyes hold mine, his brows lifts and I know he's not going to allow me to walk back out there.

"Take the night off, get your head together and come back tomorrow fresh."

Tomorrow... Tuesday. God, I really don't need that again.

My heart sinks with what I already know tomorrow will hold and what will be expected of me from my favorite table.

Dread sits heavy in my stomach.

Taking this job was a mistake. This isn't who I am. But I think about the tips I've got stuffed into my bra, even from our quiet night and I remember why I'm here.

"Okay," I finally conceded, knowing that I'll need to bring my A-game tomorrow night.

"Good. You need me to walk you out?"

"N-no. I'm fine. Could you just... could you just make sure he's left. I don't think I can face him again tonight."

"Of course. I'll come and let you know if there's an issue."

"Thank you, Bry. I really appreciate it."

He smiles softly at me before spinning on his heels and marching from the room.

Bry's good people. I have no idea how he ended up here. I'm sure he's got a story of his own, but it's one he keeps close to his chest and I know better than to start prying where people don't want it.

I wash my hands and throw some cold water on my face, not giving two craps about the state of me, before holding my head high and walking out of the bathroom.

"It's all clear," Bry calls from the main bar when he sees me exit.

"Thank you," I say once again before slipping down the hallway and escaping through the back door.

The second I step into the darkness, I feel him.

"You have got to be fucking kidding me?" I mutter to myself, digging into my purse for my car keys in the hope I can be faster than him.

It's a futile thought though. I'd never outrun him and we both know it.

"Wait, please," he begs, stepping up behind me, although he doesn't get close enough to touch me which is a relief.

"I meant what I said, Luc. We're done."

"I know, I just..."

It's the defeat in his tone that forces me to turn around and I instantly regret it when I get a look into those eyes once more.

"M-my dad's in town and I—"

My entire body jolts at his confession.

"And what, Luc? You thought you'd come here and take it out on me."

"No. I needed—"

"I don't care." I throw my hands up in frustration. "I don't care about what you need, and I certainly don't care about your father. He can rot in hell for all I care." Something flashes across his face but it's too quick and I don't have the energy to dissect it right now.

"Peyton, please. I'm sorry, okay. I'm fucking sorry."

"Too late, Luc. You should have thought about that before locking me in a pool house all weekend."

"Aw, come on, it wasn't all that bad, was it?" He takes a step toward me but soon stops when my entire body tenses with anger.

"Yes, Luca. It was. There's nothing you can do or say that's going to make this any better. I was stupid to think there could be anything salvageable here."

"P," he growls, closing the space once more but I'm not having any of it.

I know I can't let him touch me. It's too dangerous.

"I'm not leaving town," I tell him before he so much as suggests it. "I need to be here. I have people relying on me."

"Peyton, I didn't even—" I hold my hand up, cutting him off.

"I'll stay out of your way," I promise before pulling my car door open and dropping into the driver's seat.

"No, please. I just want to talk. My dad, he—"

"You lost any right to 'just talk' when you called me a liar and turned your back on me, Luc. Too little too late."

Slamming the door closed, I quickly hit the lock in case he decides to try and drag me out before starting the engine and flooring the accelerator.

Stones fly up behind me as I speed past him, forcing him to jump out of my way.

My hands tremble as I fly from the lot. I don't even remember if I looked to see if the intersection was clear. It must have been because I'm not sitting in a crumpled car.

My heart is still racing and my eyes still burning with the tears I refuse to shed after leaving him like that.

It's what he deserves, I tell myself.

———

"Hey, sweetie. You're home early," Aunt Fee says when I walk into the kitchen to find her doing something on her laptop.

"It was dead. Bry sent me home for an early night."

She studies me for a beat. "You look like you could use it. You're doing too much," she states.

"I'm fine," I promise, pulling a bottle of water from the refrigerator and twisting the top.

"You're not and we both know it. What's really going on here, Peyton?"

I stare at Aunt Fee for long seconds, wondering just how much I want to confess. I have no idea how much she actually knows, but seeing as Mom and her shared everything, I have to assume that she knows it all.

"It's Luca," I confess, dropping into the seat opposite her.

"Oh." She lowers the lid of her computer and folds her arms on the table.

"You know you'd run into him eventually," she says softly. "How'd he take it?"

Images of our time together flicker through my mind. "Not well."

"Silly, silly boy."

"He's loyal," I mutter, thinking of his refusal to accept the truth.

"Yeah, to the wrong person."

Her eyes hold mine, giving me all the answers I need. She knows everything.

"I just wish..." I trail off, not really having the words to finish that sentence. I wish for so many things. That Libby stayed out of trouble, that Luca believed me, that Mom exposed the truth instead of running away. But mostly, I just wish I could have my best friend back. I haven't found anything even close to the connection the two of us shared, and I miss it.

A sob rips from my throat.

"Oh, sweetie."

"I miss him, Aunt Fee. I miss him, I miss her. I just..." I blow out a calming breath. "Everything is such a mess. All I want is a decent life for Kayden but—"

"You can't ruin your life trying to make that happen, P. Kayden does have a good life. Despite everything, he's happy. He likes it here and he's making incredible progress."

"I know but he could have so much more, you know."

She nods sadly. "I do. But like I told you before, that's not just down to you. I can only tell you what I think."

"And that is?" I ask, already knowing that I'm going to regret it.

She holds my eyes, her own sparkling with unshed tears. "There's too much loss in this world. You of all people know that Peyton. Life is short. Everyone deserves all the family they can get."

I nod, the lump in my throat too big to speak around.

Lifting my bottle to my lips, I force down large gulps before looking back at her.

"And if they don't accept him?"

"But what if they do?"

I slide down in the chair, allowing my head to hang back.

"I'm scared, Aunt Fee," I confess, staring at the ceiling.

"I know. I am too. But you don't need to expose him straight away. If they refuse to accept it, then nothing has changed for him."

I know she's right, but the thought of them—of him—telling me again that he doesn't believe me, that he wants nothing to do with Kayden. It shreds me.

"I want him to be worthy of knowing Kayden."

"I know you do. I only want the best for that little boy too, you know that. But maybe knowing about Kayden will allow him to prove his worth. It might be the push Luca needs to finally pull his head out of his ass with this."

Dropping my head into my hands, I consider standing in front of Luca once again and confessing everything. But just like every time I've thought about it over the years, I'm immediately fifteen again listening to him telling me that I'm a liar and that he couldn't believe we were ever friends.

"I need to go and shower," I tell Aunt Fee, standing with my bottle and heading for the door.

"Just think about it, yeah?"

Like I think about anything else. "I will," I agree before dragging my weary body up the stairs for what I already know is going to be a fitful night's sleep once again.

20

PEYTON

Much to my surprise, when I open my eyes the next morning, I actually feel like I've slept, which is a relief.

I dress and throw my hair up into a messy bun, seeing as I fell asleep with it still wet last night and head downstairs.

Aunt Fee is in the exact same place I left her last night, the only difference is that her breakfast is in front of her, not her laptop.

"Good morning," I sing, putting as much joy into my voice as possible.

"PeyPey," Kayden sings, excitedly bouncing in his seat.

"Hey, my gorgeous boy. Did you sleep well?" I ask, dropping down beside him.

"I missed you," he confesses, making my heart ache.

"Aw, I missed you too, baby boy." Leaning over I plant a sloppy kiss on his cheek and ruffle his hair. "See, didn't miss me that much, did you?" I joke when he fights to get away.

"Breakfast?" Aunt Fee asks, pushing from the table.

"Sit down. I can sort myself out."

"Nonsense. You're going to college with a good meal in you this morning." Her eyes drop down my body. "You look like you need it."

I smile at her. I'll be the first person to admit that I haven't been eating right in a while. Well, not since Mom died and my life got flipped on its head once more.

With a stomach full of bacon, Aunt Fee and Kayden wave me off from the sidewalk as they head in the opposite direction for the store and some winter sun.

My heart is in my throat throughout the entire drive to MKU. I hated to do it yesterday, but I turned up to class at the very last minute and I left the second our professors had finished in my attempt to avoid the grilling that I know is coming from Ella and Letty.

I don't need to have read the messages that were sitting on my cell Sunday when I finally got it back to know that they are both suspicious as fuck as to what's going on.

And now I know that Letty is close to Luca, well... it makes me want to talk to her even less.

It's a shame because they seem like my kind of people. But I refuse to be the girl who puts herself in the middle of friends and tears people apart. Luca might not agree, but ruining people's lives isn't really my MO.

I pull the same stunt this morning, waiting in my car until the last second. I make my way across campus to the Westerfield Building, knowing that I share my morning class with Letty.

Unfortunately, it seems she's caught on to my little plan because when I slip into the room barely five seconds before our professor, I find her sitting in the closest row with a spare seat next to her.

"Good morning," our professor booms through the auditorium ensuring everyone's—bar Letty's—attention turns to him. Letty keeps her eyes firmly fixed on me, her brow lifting as she briefly glances down at the space beside her.

"Nicely played," I mutter when I drop down into the empty seat.

"Can't play a player," she mutters, flipping her notebook and writing down the title our professor has just displayed on the wall.

To my surprise, she doesn't say anything for the entire class. But I'm not naïve enough to think that's not because she's not got a million and one questions. I can practically hear them all spinning around her head.

It's not until our class draws to a close and she picks up her purse to put her things away when she finally speaks.

"You should have told me that you were Luca's Peyton."

"I'm not Luca's anything," I hiss as I throw my books and pen into my purse.

But it seems that my tone doesn't put her off because the second I stand and move toward the exit, she follows.

"The second he stepped up behind you on Saturday night, all the pieces fell into place."

"I'm amazed he ever mentioned my name," I mutter, following the stream of students down the hallway.

"He didn't."

"Ouch." But as much as that might hurt, it's exactly what I expected.

"But people talked about you, compared me to you. Apparently, I never quite lived up to the enigma that was Peyton Banks."

"You expect me to believe that?"

She shrugs.

"I think we need to go and get a coffee, and properly talk."

"I need to go to the library. I've got an assignment to do," I lie.

"Not happening. Ella is busy, and me and you need to sit down and hash a few things out."

I go to argue with her but the second I glance over, I watch as she lifts her cell to her ear.

"Hey," she says, a smile twitching at her lips. "Yeah. Coffee shop. Ten minutes? Great. See you there."

"Who was that?"

"Someone else who wants to talk."

"Why do I feel like this is an ambush?"

"Probably because it is."

"Great."

"Aw, come on. It's not that bad. We're just worried about Luca and we think you probably hold all the answers."

"Prior to a few weeks ago, I hadn't seen him for five years."

"That may be true, Peyton. But I'm pretty sure he's never really let you go."

She gives me a small reprieve as we walk toward the coffee shop and instead of grilling me about Luca she turns the conversation to work.

We order and find ourselves a table before the person she was speaking to on the phone appears. I know the second he walks in because the volume of chatter dips.

Glancing over my shoulder, I guess I shouldn't be surprised to find Leon stalking our way.

"Morning, ladies," he says, wrapping Letty in a bear hug when she stands to greet him. "Peyton," he nods when I don't make a move to receive the same welcome.

Leon and I were never close. Just friends because of mine and Luca's closeness. I'm sure we could be friends though, we just never really got the chance.

He twists the chair around and sits on it backward, pulling his coffee that Letty bought for him closer.

"P tell you about her weekend then?" he asks, looking between the two of us.

I shake my head.

"I was waiting for you," Letty tells him before they both turn their eyes on me.

"Jesus," I mutter.

"We just want to help," Leon says, sincerity bleeding from his tone.

I stare down at my coffee for a moment. If they expect me to spill all mine and Luca's secrets then they're going to have to think again because that's not going to happen. Leon clearly has no idea what happened between us and it's not my place to tell him when Luca obviously doesn't want him to know.

"I know, but there's no need. Luca and I, we've... put our issues to bed."

Leon scoffs. "Oh yeah because that's what was going down in a bed this weekend."

"Leon," Letty chastises.

"What? Luca locked her in the pool house at the Kappa house."

"He what?" she seethes.

"Seriously, it's over. We've said what we need to say and we're leaving it all in the past where it belongs."

"Peyton, don't lie to me," Leon growls, sounding entirely too much like his brother.

I'm sure most people can't see the similarities between them, but after being attached to Luca's hips for all those years, I see them.

"I have a feeling that things will never be over when it comes to you and Luca. You've been gone years but you were never forgotten. Letty might have done a good job of filling the void, but you're a piece of him, Pey."

I shake my head, refusing to believe it.

"That may have been true once upon a time, but it's not anymore. There is no Peyton and Luca anymore. It's over."

"What happened, Peyton? How did you go from being as close as you were to... well, nothing?"

Lifting my hand, I drag my hair back from my face.

"I just... I told him something. Something he didn't want to believe."

They both stare at me with blank expressions. "Is that really all you're going to give us?" Letty asks.

"Yep."

"He came to see you last night, didn't he?"

I nod, thinking of our brief encounter in the back room at the club.

"What happened? He never came home and no one's seen him since. He's not picking up his cell. I'm worried."

"Yeah, he did and I once again told him something he didn't want to hear."

"Fucking hell," Leon mutters, scrubbing his hand down his face. "Any idea where he might be?"

"I don't know him anymore, Lee. The Luca I used to know died a long time ago."

His lips part but he swallows the words that were on the tip of his tongue as he studies me. "Do you really believe that?"

"He hasn't shown me any differently."

"Luca's... Luca's not in a good place right now—"

"You don't say," I deadpan.

"He told our dad that he's thinking about quitting the team, everything, yesterday."

"He did what?" Letty gasps.

"Then he came to you—"

"And I sent him away."

Leon blows out a breath and drops his head.

"Okay so... where'd he go?"

"I already told you, I don't know—"

"What?" he asks, looking up as if I'm about to provide him with the answer.

"N-no. It's stupid."

"Peyton, I can't find him. None of the guys have heard from him. Mom was already losing her shit with him and now I've alerted her to the fact he's fucked off and—"

"You remember that place we all camped at once as kids?"

"Right at the end of the beach?"

"Yeah. That's the only place I can think he'd go. But that was years ago when—"

"I'll let you know." He's gone before I get to tell him that it's probably a long shot at best.

"Fucking hell," I breathe, dropping my head into my hands.

"Everything will be okay," Letty says softly after long painful minutes.

My eyes are full with unshed tears when I glance up at her and her expression softens even more at the sight of them.

"Why don't you hate me?" I ask, genuinely curious.

She chuckles, although it lacks any actual humor.

"Luca may never really have spoken about you, but others did. Leon did. I know how big a part of his life you were. It took me a while to realize why Luca shut down whenever he was going down memory lane, but as soon as Leon explained, it made total sense. Just talking about you hurt him. He—"

"I never meant to hurt him, Letty. What I told him. It was... it was the hardest thing I've ever done. But I knew I had to do it, I knew I had to confess the truth to him."

She nods, understanding shining in her dark eyes but unlike Leon, she doesn't even try to find out what I might have said.

"You're not a bad person, Peyton. I can see that. You were just kids. Crazy shit happens." I nod, knowing that she's right. "But we're not anymore. You're a junior in college about to embark on possibly the most important years of your life. Luca is..." She blows out a breath, glancing out of the window for a second. "He was drowning before you showed up, Peyton, and that's on me. I'm as much to blame here for his spiral. I did some stuff that... it's not important right now but you need to know that this... darkness, it's not solely your fault. Your arrival has only added weight to an already sinking ship."

"I never meant—"

"I know," she assures, taking me by surprise and reaching across the table to my hand. "I know, Peyton. You care about him, we can see that. I know that from living in your shadow."

She glances up again and I can't help but wonder if we're about to be joined by someone else.

"You were right to stand your ground. You deserve better than how he's treated you. But also, give him time. He's working through a lot of shit, and if he's seriously threatening to quit football, then I fear it could be worse than I thought. But you need to make a decision."

"Oh?"

"Be there for him, or don't. One way or the other." Her serious face morphs into something else entirely as she looks up once again as a shadow falls over me. "Hey."

She's swept out of her chair by a strong tattooed arm and is soon completely distracted from our conversation when he captures her lips.

She finally manages to push him away to let her up for air and the two of them sit opposite me.

"Peyton, Kane. Kane, Peyton," she says quickly, in case we needed the reminder.

I nod at him, forcing a small smile onto my lips.

"I was right," Letty says. "She is Luca's Peyton."

"I'm not—" I start to argue again but her eyes come to mine, cutting me off. "I was... I was Luca's Peyton."

"Trouble in paradise?" Kane asks with a smirk and a little too much enjoyment sparkling in his blue eyes.

"I don't know what paradise is," I mutter. I can't remember the last time I was genuinely happy. Although I know it was before Mom dragged me out of Rosewood, and I know it was because of him.

"Listen," Kane says, pulling Letty's chair closer and throwing his arm around her shoulder. "It's no secret that Dunn isn't my favorite person," Letty scoffs, making me wonder what the story is there but I don't get to pry. "But I will give you this advice. Don't go down without a fight. Make him work for it."

Letty turns to him and barks out a laugh.

"What? Got me, didn't it?"

"Because this," she says, waving her hand toward me. "Is anything like what we went through."

He shrugs, clearly seeing things differently to his girl.

"Luca hates you, right?" he asks, turning back to me.

Pain slices through my chest at his words but I nod, because he's right. Luca does hate me, and he wants to make sure I know it.

"But he can't stay away from you?"

"I... I don't know about that."

"He locked her in the Kappa pool house all weekend," Letty helpfully supplies which amuses him.

"Well then. Just like I said, don't go down without a fight. You never know what might come out at the end of it."

He drops a kiss to Letty's temple and my heart melts at the sight.

They make it look so easy, so real, so... perfect. I have no idea what they went through to get there, but I'm pretty sure it was all worth it.

"I gotta run. I've got a meeting in the study center, then I wanna hit the gym this afternoon."

"Okay. See you at home later?"

"You got it, Princess."

He leaves her with a knee-weakening kiss before nodding at me. He strides from the coffee shop, taking the adoring stares of every female around with him.

"You two are too damn cute."

She smiles goofily before muttering, "Kane is anything but cute."

"He is with you."

She shakes her head. "What are your plans for the rest of the day?"

"Other than going home to hide?"

"Peyton," she sighs.

"I was planning on the library. I've got all the work I should have done over the weekend to complete."

"Awesome. Let's go."

Just like that, I find myself walking side by side with Letty. I realize that my plan to put some distance between us all so I'm not in the middle of Luca's life and friends has already gone to shit.

I briefly wonder what Leon's going to find at the place I sent him. Probably nothing but old memories and the hopes of two young, naïve kids.

I blow out a long breath that Letty doesn't miss.

"Despite Kane's opinion, Luca is one of the best people I know. We'll get him through this. All of us."

My lips part to tell her that I can't be a part of that. That I'm already in deeper than I should be and hiding too much but I don't find any words.

Instead, I nod and follow her inside the building, hoping like hell that when the truth does get revealed, it won't tip him over the edge any more than he already is.

21

—

LUCA

Something hitting me in the stomach drags me from my fitful sleep.

"Go away," I mutter, already knowing that the second I open my eyes or allow reality to seep in that I'm going to be hit with the hangover from hell.

"Unlikely, motherfucker."

I groan at the sound of Leon's voice. He moves, his clothing rustling but still, I refuse to even crack my eyes open.

My temples begin to pound as I try to ignore the fact my mouth is like the fucking Sahara.

I knew it was a bad idea. I fucking knew, but I did it anyway. It was the only way I could see out of the hell that yesterday descended upon me.

"How did you find me?"

"How do you think?" His voice is closer, telling me that he's getting himself comfortable for the long haul.

"Fucking Peyton," I complain, hating the way my chest aches from hearing her name pass my lips.

"Talk to me, Luc." I hate the desperation in his voice. Fucking hate it.

We've never been the kind of brothers who do the heart to heart, heavy shit but it seems that might be about to change.

Unable to see a way out of this, I roll on my back and rip my eyes open.

I regret it the second the blinding sun fills them.

"What time is it?"

"Almost midday."

"Jesus."

My stomach lurches as I attempt to sit up, last night's cocktail of alcohol threatening to make a reappearance.

"Here," Leon says, passing me over a bottle of water and a bottle of painkillers. "I had the suspicion you might need them."

"Th-thanks."

Twisting the top off the bottle, I down half before throwing two of the pills into the back of my mouth and laying back down.

Silence stretches out between us for the longest time. I'm trying to come up with what to say, how to even put how I'm feeling right now into words. Thankfully he doesn't push me for it.

"I have no idea what I'm doing, Lee. All this shit is happening around me and I have no idea how to deal. Then she showed up and fuck." I lift my hands to my face, scrubbing over my skin. "I don't know. I just lost the fucking plot."

"Yeah locking her in the pool house screams fucking psychopath, Luc."

"I just..." I sit forward once more and drop my head into my hands. "Fuck."

"You never stopped loving her, did you?"

I look over at him, shocked that he's ever said the words.

"W-we were just kids, Lee. I'm not sure—"

"Don't lie to me. I was there. I saw the two of you with my own eyes. Hell, I fucking hated the two of you for a long time because of what you found."

"You did?" I ask, concern pulling at my brows.

"Yeah. I mean, I've got you, obviously. But I've never had a friend, or anything really like you did with Peyton. I was so fucking jealous."

I stare at him, floored that he's just admitted that.

"Shit."

He shrugs. "Do you really want to let that go now that she's back?"

"We're not the same people anymore."

"No one would expect you to be. Five years have passed. A lot of shit has happened. But that's not the point really, is it? Do you still want her despite whatever bullshit went down that you both still refuse to confess to?"

"I never stopped wanting her. That's not the issue. I don't know if I can trust her."

"Have you even talked about... about whatever it was?"

"No."

"Maybe you should start there instead of just punishing her for something you might not fully understand."

I look at him, stare into his green eyes that are so familiar to the ones I look into every day in the mirror.

"When did you get to be so wise?"

He shakes his head and chuckles. "I always have been, Bro. You just haven't noticed before now."

"Oh fuck off." I laugh, and despite the fact it makes my head pound with pain, I can't deny that it doesn't feel good.

"And what about the rest of it? Have you had it out with Letty yet?"

"Kind of. We spoke for a bit last week."

"A bit?"

"It was more than we have in weeks."

"It's not enough, Luc. If you wanna fix this shit, you need to sort stuff out. You need to hear Letty out, listen to what really happened with Kane. It might even help you understand how you're feeling about Peyton."

"What do you know that I don't?"

"It's not my place to discuss their relationship with you. But there are bigger things than you know about when it comes to Kane and Letty. She's happy, Luc. Really fucking happy. I know we hurt you. I know Kane hates you. But it's how it is. You need to be able to accept him in her life, and in yours."

I scoff, still not happy about that unexpected turn of events at the beginning of the season.

"Which leads me to the biggest issue here. Football."

"What about it?" I spit, although I already know where this is going and quite honestly, I don't have an answer for him.

"What you said to Dad yesterday, did you really mean it?"

"I don't know. And this isn't some overly dramatic sulk because we lost, this isn't new. I've been feeling like this for a while. I'm just tired, Lee. I'm tired of the pressure, the bullshit, the expectations."

"From who?"

"Him. I fucking hate him, Lee," I confess.

"I know and I get it." I turn to look at him, ready to rip him a new one because he doesn't know, he doesn't get even half the shit I do. "Oh no, don't even think about it," he snaps before I manage to say anything. "Don't pull the 'you don't understand it's different for you card.' I fucking know it's different because I've been forced to watch it for years, Luc. I know exactly what kind of pressure he puts on you, exactly what he expects of you. I might not be the one going through it, I'm here on the sidelines watching and feeling your pain right alongside you."

I open my mouth to argue but I have no words.

"I get it, okay. I fucking get it. And if you sit here right now and tell me that you're done with football, that you're going to walk away from all of it, then I'll support you all the way."

"Well, shit," I breathe because I was not expecting that. I thought he was going to be angry that I'd even consider walking away from it all.

"I'm not the bad guy here, Luc. I'm on your side, always."

"Did you just happen to forget that when you fucked Letty?" I mutter.

"Fuck, man. You need to let that go."

"I know. It just hurts that you both lied to me. We don't do that, Lee. We fucking don't."

"So tell me why Peyton really left town."

I stare at him, the words right on the tip of my tongue, her accusation word for word how she told it to me. But I can't do it.

"If I do, then it leaves you wide open, Bro."

All the air rushes from his lungs.

"Yeah, exactly as I thought. We all have our secrets, Lee. Until I know the truth. Until I know for sure that she did lie to me that day, I'll keep it locked down. Trust me when I say that you don't need to hear the words unless they are one hundred percent the truth because if that's the case, it's going to change things for us."

He narrows his eyes studying me as if he'll be able to read the words in my head if he searches long enough.

"That's bullshit."

"You'll thank me if it turns out to be bullshit. You don't need that poison in your head. And trust me, I ain't letting you lock her in a pool house. You've already got game with my girls."

He throws his head back and laughs. "I swear to you, Luc. I've been nowhere near Peyton and I promise I never will. Well... unless she really begs."

"She can beg all she likes," I mutter.

"Aw, Bro, you wouldn't even share with your twin?"

Images of the girls we've had between us over the years flicker through my mind before they morph into Peyton.

Could I do it? Could I share her like we did with those nameless jersey chasers, with Letty?

No. I'm pretty sure I couldn't.

"Touch her whether I'm in the room or not and I will fucking kill you."

"And there's the answer to my first question."

My breath catches. "Fuck you, Bro. Fuck you."

"So are you coming back or is your new life plan to be a hobo who lives at the end of the beach?"

I look around at the tree-covered hideaway that I could call my home.

"I dunno. It's pretty sweet here."

His eyes lift from me and I know the second he spots it because he sucks in a sharp breath.

"How about you come back, talk to her and you can make some new memories instead of having to relive the old ones like a loser."

"I'm not a loser," I argue.

"Sure. Whatever you say."

He climbs to his feet and stares down at me.

"So?"

"I'll follow you in a bit."

He nods, taking a step back. "You'd better."

I nod and watch as he pushes a branch aside and walks away. Just before he's out of sight, I call out.

"Yeah?" he calls back.

"Thank you."

"I gotta be useful for something, right?"

"Lee, I... I really appreciate it."

"I know, Bro. Just make it right, yeah. You'll never forgive yourself if you don't at least try. Sometimes, we've just got to let go of the past."

His words are laced with pain but he's gone before I get to say anything about it. I guess whatever it is he's kept covered up all these years is going to remain in the lockbox he keeps it in.

With a sigh, I fall back onto my palms and take in the view of the glistening blue ocean in the distance.

This used to be our place. A little bit of paradise for when we needed some peace from school or our parents.

Twisting around, I look at the spot on the tree behind me that Leon was looking at.

The letters P and L are carved deep into the trunk surrounded by a heart.

Climbing to my feet, my head continues to spin as I stare at my really bad knife skills.

I remember the day we did this. I truly believed it would be us together forever against the world back then. I never could have imagined that only weeks later we would be ripped apart.

With a loud exhale, I eventually pick up the bottles littered around my feet and make the walk back to my car.

I hadn't planned on sleeping out here last night. I didn't have a plan at all other than I needed to make it all stop, and the only place I could see that happening was at the bottom of a bottle.

I stop for food on the way home, shoving a burger into my mouth as I make the drive back to Maddison in the hope it soaks up whatever alcohol might be in my system. I probably shouldn't be driving right now, but I wasn't hanging around there any longer.

The house is quiet when I get back, I guess everyone is either in class or working out. That or acting like the easy-go-lucky off-season college students they are, unlike me.

It's not until I get to the third floor where mine and Leon's room are that I hear music playing from his.

I knock and push the door open before he calls out.

"Hey," I say, finding him at his desk working. "Not in class?"

"Nah, I'd have been late. I'll grab the notes off someone."

"Sorry, I—"

"Don't. It's okay, Luc. Whatever you need, yeah?"

"Yeah. I was actually going to see if you could do something for me tonight."

"Sure. What is it?"

I close his bedroom door behind me and drop down onto his bed.

"Peyton has a job at The Locker Room. That's where—"

"What?" he barks, disbelief filling his features.

"That's where I first found her on Christmas Eve."

His eyes widen at my confession. "You've known she's been in town since Christmas Eve?" He must see the guilt on my face. He places his pen down and properly turns to look at me. "Jesus, Luc."

"I went there for a drink. It seemed like a better option than pretending to be happy with you and Mom." His lips purse like he wants to rip me a new one for that but he thankfully refrains. It doesn't matter, it's too late now. "Safe to say she wasn't expecting to see me there."

"I'm assuming she has no idea who owns it?"

"No, I don't think she does. Which is why I need you to go there tonight. Dad's in town and I want him nowhere near her."

He narrows his eyes at me. "Why? What would Dad want with her? No offense, Luc, but he probably doesn't remember her. He barely remembers his own kids most days."

"I know... I just... please? She's not going to want me there, and I don't think it's a good idea I go but—"

"That's where you've been going every night, isn't it? Keeping an eye on her."

I don't answer him. I don't think he really needs the confirmation. Instead, I scrub my hand down my face, rubbing at my rough jaw.

"I just sit in my car and make sure she leaves okay."

"You're fucking whipped, man. You know that, right?"

"You haven't seen the way those scumbags look at her. It's... it's disgusting. How I haven't killed any of them yet, I don't know."

"She needs to leave. She doesn't belong in a place like that."

"She needs the money."

"There are other ways."

"I know. I'm just trying not to get involved."

He throws his head back and laughs. "That was a joke, right? You couldn't be more involved right now if you tried."

"Trust me, I could. I could throw her over my shoulder and demand she never step foot in that place again."

"Why haven't you?"

"Because she's working there to pay off her mom's medical bills."

"What's wrong with her mom?"

"She died."

"Oh... shit."

"So will you... just make sure she gets out, okay?"

He nods. "But I'm not doing it every night because you're too much of a pussy to sort your own shit out."

"I know. Just tonight."

"Okay. Now fuck off and go shower. You fucking stink."

"You're an asshole, you know that, right?"

"Oh yeah, because I do fucking nothing for you."

I flip him off over my shoulder, but when I look back, he's smiling just as much as I am.

"Thank you," I say again before slipping out of his room in favor of mine so I can do as he suggested because he's not wrong about how I smell.

22

PEYTON

As it has become normal, my stomach is in knots and my hands tremble when I walk into The Locker Room on Tuesday evening.

Thankfully, when I walk out into the bar, I find my dreaded booth empty. But I'm sure it won't stay that way for long.

"Hey, how are you doing?" Bry asks, once he's finished serving and comes to my end of the bar.

"I'm good. Thank you for last night."

"No problem. It seems you've got a new babysitter tonight," he mutters, passing my bottle of water over.

"Huh?"

He nods toward the table where Luca was sitting the very first night I found him here. Looking over my shoulder, my breath catches when I find Leon sitting there smiling at me.

It really shouldn't happen but one look at him and my heart drops. After everything, I shouldn't want Luca to be here. But I do.

"Here. He needs a refill."

Bry passes a soda over and I take it over.

"Hey," I say shyly as I walk up to his table, aware that I'm wearing way less clothing than I'd like right now. But despite all the skin I'm showing, his eyes don't once drop from mine.

"Hey. Thank you," he says politely, accepting the drink I pass over. "I assume Luca sent you."

"Yeah, what gave me away?"

I laugh, but it lacks any humor.

"You don't belong here, Peyton. This." He finally looks down at me, his eyes widening. "This isn't you."

"I'm not the girl I used to be, Lee. And sometimes, we've just got to do things to survive. This is one of them."

"I'm sorry about your mom."

"Th-thanks," I force out. My emotions are running high just from the sympathetic look in his eyes. "How much did he tell you?"

Leon shakes his head. "Not much more than that, other than he's been an asshole."

"Putting it mildly," I mutter, making him laugh.

"I know it's not an excuse. He's totally in the wrong here no matter what's happened between you, but he's in a really bad place and you just happen to turn up at the wrong time."

"He hates me, Lee. Anytime would have been the wrong time."

"Yeah, maybe. But you're wrong. He doesn't hate you, Peyton. Far from it."

I scoff, looking over my shoulder when a commotion starts at the door. The second I find them, my eyes lock with Slick and my stomach drops. Oh good, now my night can really get started.

"You don't need to be here to babysit me, Lee. I'm a big girl and I can look after myself."

"Uh... funny, because I said the exact same thing to Luca but I think I'll stay for a bit, actually." He doesn't once glance at me as he says this, instead, his eyes are locked on the men behind me. God only knows what they're doing, I dread to think but it's clearly enough to warrant Leon feeling like he needs to stay.

"Okay, do whatever. But you can't do his dirty work forever."

Spinning on my heels, I take a step away from him.

"How much do you owe, Peyton?"

All the air rushes out of my lungs at his question. It's something I try not to think about because the reality is too depressing.

"A lot."

I take off, not wanting to hear whatever he wanted to say after. I'm too scared he'll do something stupid like offer to pay it. It's no secret that the Dunns have more money than sense, but I'm not a charity case. Even if Luca and I were the best of friends again right now, I'd still refuse to take anything from him.

This is my problem to deal with, no one else's.

Leon doesn't move from his table all night and I feel his eyes on me every place I go. But it's not like having customers watching, stripping me bare and hoping I might drop something and bend over for them. Having him watching me makes me feel safe. I have a feeling that if any of the men were to step out of line that he'd get to me way before security. It's like having a brother watching me, protecting me. And annoyingly, I kinda like it.

I emerge at the end of my shift with my purse thrown over my shoulder and thankfully a hoodie covering up as much of my exposed body as possible. He pushes his half-empty drink aside and stands to walk me out.

He doesn't speak until we're at my car and when he does, it brings tears to my eyes. I tell myself that it's just my exhaustion after a stressful shift, but really, it's the sincerity I see shining in his green depths, one I wish I could see in another pair.

"You're too good for this place, Peyton. You can't stay here. The way they look at you. The way they talk to you." His lips curl in disgust and his fists clench at his sides.

"I hate it," I confess. "But other than taking up a spot on a street corner, it's the best shot I've got at getting the kind of money I need."

I know the words are coming but they still hit like a baseball bat across the chest.

"Let us help."

"No."

I cross my hands over my chest, standing my ground.

"You could—"

"No, Leon." His face drops and I realize I might have been a little harsh. "I really appreciate all this. The offer. But it's not necessary. This is my life now, and I need to deal with my own shit. Luca made his decision five years ago. Just because I was his friend—his girlfriend—once, it doesn't mean you owe me."

"Peyton, that's not how it—"

"Leon, please," I beg. "I'm exhausted. I just need to go home and sleep tonight off. Tomorrow, we can all just get on with our lives. Thank you for tonight, but you really don't need to do his dirty work."

Without waiting for a response, I pull my car door open and drop inside.

I stare up into his concerned eyes once more before reaching out to close the door, cutting off any more conversation between us. But just before the door closes I swear I hear him say, "he still loves you, Peyton."

All the air comes rushing out of my lungs as I stare at the steering wheel, too afraid to look back at the expression on Leon's face. Although I'm not sure why. I'm not sure if I'm scared of what I thought I heard being confirmed or shattering hope that I might not have imagined it.

With what feels like lead in my chest, I put my car into drive and head for home.

I barely say three words to Aunt Fee who's still up waiting for me. Her brows pull together in concern as I grab a bottle of water and head straight upstairs to shower and collapse into bed.

I go to class Wednesday morning and then get straight back in my car to head home. The library would probably be a better option seeing as there is never peace and quiet in Aunt Fee's house during the day since Kayden and I moved in, and now with Elijah being there. But there was no way I was risking sitting anywhere on campus and risking having to talk to anyone.

I know that Leon, Letty, and I'm sure Ella, once she finds me, only want what's best for me. Our friendships might not have much—or any—history, but I know they're good people who only want to help.

It's why I really shouldn't be surprised when the doorbell rings at Aunt Fee's house when I'm helping her make dinner.

"I'll go," Elijah calls from the living room. Probably relieved to have a break from whatever Kayden is forcing him to endure on the TV right now. Kayden's infectious laugh keeps filling the house and melting my heart so I know at least one of them is enjoying it.

Elijah's deep booming voice fills Aunt Fee's small house as he greets whoever it is.

I don't give the visitor a second thought because there's very little chance it'll be for me. The only person who knows where I live is Luca and seeing as he sent Leon to be my bodyguard last night it seems he's not interested in seeing me himself. And that is more than fine by me because I'm not sure I've got any more fight left in me. I knew this semester would be hard, starting over in a new place, new classes, and all while trying to work to earn as much money as possible. Add Luca into all that and... I let out a long sigh.

"You okay?" Aunt Fee asks, looking over from where she's chopping vegetables.

"Yeah. It's just harder than I thought it was going to be."

She lowers the knife and turns to look at me at the same time Elijah calls my name.

He appears in the doorway a few seconds later. "It's for you. But if you don't wanna go, I'll happily keep the blonde entertained."

"Elijah," Aunt Fee snaps, sounding horrified, but there's a wide smile on her face. She knows all about what Marines get up to. Her late husband was one after all, and I heard a few stories about when she first met him from Mom.

"What?" He shrugs, pulling the refrigerator open and pulling out a beer. "So are you going or..." he says to me, pointing to the door.

"Uh... yeah." I wipe my hands on a tea towel and head toward the front door.

"Hey," both Ella and Letty say when I emerge.

"Uh... hey," I reply, looking between the two of them curiously.

"We hope you don't mind. We did a bit of detective work and found out your address."

"I-it's okay," I stutter, looking past them, half expecting Luca to jump out any minute.

"He's not here," Letty assures, clearly reading my thoughts.

"We knew it was your night off and we thought you deserved to have a bit of fun."

"Oh?" I ask, suddenly much more intrigued.

"It's not much but we thought you might like a trip around the mall and then grab some dinner."

Excitement fills me for the first time in a while as I look at the two women who've made an effort to come and make me feel better. I haven't had that... ever. They've no idea how much it means to me.

"I'd love to." I look down at myself in my ratty old jersey dress and leggings that are so old they're barely black anymore. "But I need to change."

"We can wait," Letty says.

"Okay." The words to invite them inside teeter on the tip of my tongue but then Kayden's smiling face pops into my head and I realize that I can't. "Let me just throw some decent clothes on and I'll meet you at your car. I'll be like two minutes."

They both look a little disappointed but I don't allow myself to dwell on it before swinging the door closed and running for the kitchen.

"Change of plan," I tell Aunt Fee. "I'm going out for dinner. Is that okay?" I ask in a rush, realizing that I'm totally bailing last minute.

"Of course it's okay. Go and have fun."

"Okay." I run up the stairs, rip my clothes off and replace my rags with a pair of skinny jeans, a plain white tee and my mom's old leather jacket I love that always makes me feel a little more like myself.

I swipe some mascara on my lashes and coat my lips in some gloss and figure that it'll have to do.

I say a quick goodbye to Aunt Fee and Elijah—who's escaped the cartoons—before poking my head in to see Kayden.

"Hey, bud. I'm going out for a little bit."

His face drops at my words and I immediately regret my decision. "But we're having dinner."

"I know. I... uh..." I look back when I sense someone join us.

"You've got the whole weekend with Peyton, Kay. Remember what Saturday is?" Kayden's face lights up as he remembers and I can't help but feel the same knowing I've got the entire weekend off work. It can't come soon enough.

"Okay," he says. "Have fun with your friends."

"I will, baby boy. Thank you." I hold him tight for a few seconds and place a kiss on his head.

This balancing act between work, college, having a life and being a part of this family is something I need to get a better grip on. I'm just glad we've got Aunt Fee because if she didn't reach out to help us after Mom died, I have no idea how we'd have coped.

"Go," Aunt Fee says when I linger a little longer. "And have fun."

'Thank you,' I mouth to her as I slip past.

She smiles at me, her eyes looking a little wet. She can never understand how much I appreciate everything she's done for us. I have no idea where to even start trying to tell her either.

"Hey. I'm ready," I say, dropping into the back seat of Letty's car that's idling on the road outside Aunt Fee's.

"That your aunt?" Ella asks, and when I look up, I find Aunt Fee watching us through the window.

"Yeah," I say with a smile.

"Okay, well... you ready to hit the store?" Letty asks, clearly sensing the heaviness in my response.

"Yes," Ella hisses. "Let's do it."

Walking in and out of each store while the two of them pick up different items, try some on and purchase others makes me feel more like myself than I have in a long time. Although I've never really had any girlfriends to do this with, spending an afternoon in the mall was one of mine and Mom's favorite ways to relax. Even if we never bought anything.

Ella's in the dressing room and Letty is looking at the shoes when a dress catches my eye. It's not my usual style, and it's way dressier than anywhere I have to wear it but it just speaks to me for some reason.

It's simple, classic and something you could wear for years and years and would never look out of date. Christ, I sound like my mom.

Reaching out, I run the soft fabric through my fingers imagining how it might look on me. Twisting the tag, I gasp at the price.

"You should try it on," Letty says, over my shoulder.

"N-no, I can't afford it. And I don't need it. I can hardly wear that to class."

"No, but you never know, someone might take you out on a hot date."

I scoff. "Unlikely."

"You never know. Stranger things have happened."

"Hey, how's it— Whoa, that dress is hot. You should totally try it on," Ella joins in when she finds us standing looking at it.

Glancing up at the two of them, I find them standing with their hands on their hips and a determined look in their eyes.

"Just try it. It might look awful and you can forget all about it," Ella quips.

"El." Letty laughs. "It will not look awful. Peyton's got a banging figure."

"I know." She shrugs, reaching out and pulling the correct size from the rack without even asking me. "Go on then." She smiles at me so sweetly and with so much determination that the only way to get out of this is to do it.

I blow out a breath once I'm alone in the dressing room. I know exactly what's about to happen, I'm going to fall in love with it even more the second it's on my body and I'm going to feel guilty for weeks for buying something so frivolous when I've got more important things to do with my money.

"So?" Ella calls through the curtain.

I stare at myself in the mirror, tears filling my eyes and a lump so huge clogging my throat that I can't respond.

"Peyton?"

When I still don't respond, the curtain moves a little and Ella pokes her head inside. She takes one look at me and throws it aside and invites herself in.

"Shit. Are you okay?"

I sniffle and nod, trying to get a grip on myself.

"Letty," Ella calls, startling me. In only a second, she also appears at the curtain.

"Okay, you're buying that," she states before coming over and taking my hand in hers.

"I'm sorry. Things just... things just hit me all of a sudden, you know. Mom and I, we used to..." I blow out a breath, unable to keep going.

They encourage me back so that I can sit down. Sharing a knowing look.

"Things have just been so insane since she had the accident that I haven't really had any time, and then standing there..." I blow out another shaky breath.

"It's okay, sweetie," Ella breathes, her hand squeezing mine in support.

We sit in silence for long minutes as I try to gather my emotions.

"I think you're right," I finally say. "I need to buy the dress."

"You do."

"She'd have loved it." I smile despite the pain slicing through my chest as I think about her and the fun we had together. "She'd have demanded that we went out dancing to show it off."

"Then that's what we should do."

"It's my birthday on the weekend," I blurt, regretting it the instant both of their faces light up.

"Then we are definitely taking that dress out dancing this weekend. Why didn't you tell us?"

"I don't want to celebrate. It feels all kinds of wrong right now."

"Bullshit. Your mom would want you to go out and paint the town red."

"It's not just that, though. There's all this crap with Luca and—"

"Fuck him," Letty snaps, the viciousness in her voice surprising me. "You don't get to be miserable because of him. That's bullshit. Saturday night, we're partying."

"I promised Aunt Fee I'd spend the weekend at home."

"That's fine. But as soon as the sun goes down on Saturday night. You're ours. She can even come if she likes."

"To a college party?"

Ella shrugs. "You know what crazy shit goes down. No one would probably even notice."

"As amusing as the idea is, I think she'd rather stick needles in her eyes."

"Fair enough."

"Right," Letty says, hopping up from where she was kneeling on the floor. "Get changed. Buy the dress. Then we're going for tacos and margs. My treat." She winks at me, and I can't help but smile.

I have no idea how I was lucky enough to find these two in all the bullshit that surrounds my life right now but I couldn't be more grateful.

With the bag containing the dress swinging from my fingers, Ella and Letty lead me toward a restaurant for dinner and we're seated in the middle of the vast space and handed menus. Letty orders a pitcher of margaritas before the server has a chance to escape along with a bottle of water for her seeing as she is driving.

They keep the conversation light and as far away from dead mothers and wicked ex-best friends as they can get.

Everything is great.

Fantastic.

Until he walks in.

23

LUCA

I spent what was left of Tuesday locked in my room. But as exhausted as I was, I couldn't shut it off. That only got worse once I knew that Peyton had started her shift.

Leon was there. I knew she was safe. But the thought of those men trying something and not being there to help her didn't sit right with me.

But I knew she didn't want to see me. She made that perfectly clear on Monday night when she used me for what she needed and then dropped me like a stone.

I deserved it. I know that. But fuck, it doesn't stop it from hurting.

I'm meant to be the one seeking vengeance after what she did. She shouldn't hold the power to hurt me. But she does. And she always has.

Despite Leon knocking to get my ass out of bed this morning for class, I didn't emerge from my room until long after everyone had left. I didn't want to deal with people and I really didn't want to go and sit in a class when I already know that I'm not going to hear a word of it.

What's the point? What's the point in any of it?

If I walk away from football like I've threatened to do, then I probably won't even have a place here at MKU.

It won't just be my football career that goes down the drain but my entire future.

Do I really want to start over?

A huge part of me says yes. To grab the chance of starting over without being controlled at every step by my father. To be me. Whoever Luca Dunn is without being QB1. I'm not sure he even exists.

Everything about my life for as long as I can remember has been about that, about the NFL, about success, about the win, the trophy, the high.

I glance at my shelf that holds all those trophies.

They mean nothing. Not really.

Sure, winning is great. Beating the other team is a rush. But that's not real happiness.

It's empty.

You walk away from that high of the win and what's left? The memory.

Okay, so I've got my team to celebrate with, and a desperate jersey chaser or two. But even that's getting old.

"Argh," I groan, shoving my head into my pillow so Leon doesn't hear me from the next room.

I hate all this unknown. All these questions.

I just want to be happy and to get on with my life, not have the past and the pressure dragging me down at every turn.

I startle when a knock sounds out on my door a few minutes later.

"You ready?" Leon asks, dressed, ready to head out.

"Err..."

"Colt's birthday."

"Fuuuck," I grumble, wrapping my hand around the back of my neck and pulling.

"I'm not making up a bullshit excuse about you being ill. You either pull your head out of your ass and come or you tell him yourself."

Since freshman year, we've always gone out for each other's birthdays. It's a tradition I started. One I wish right now that I really fucking hadn't.

Back then, I was gunning for the starting quarterback position and would do anything to show my leadership and to prove that I deserved it.

Now I'm considering handing it all over.

"Fuck, yeah. I'm coming. Give me ten."

I might be fucking up everything about my life right now, but I refuse to force my bullshit on the rest of the team. They might all be gutted about how our season ended but they're already getting ready to start all over again in a few months. To prove our place and make our senior year our best season yet.

I wish I shared their optimism.

I sit in the back of Leon's BMW while he, Colt, and Evan argue about some shit I have no clue about. Ignoring them, I just stare out of the window. I might have agreed to come but no one said anything about having to enjoy myself. My growling stomach, however, is totally on board with the tacos someone mentioned earlier.

I think back to last year when we rocked up to the same restaurant —the only one Colt ever chooses should he get the option—and wish things could be just like that.

A smile twitches at my lips as I remember us all flirting with our server to try to get some tequila out of her. She must have been in her thirties. She had a wedding ring on, but I don't think I've ever seen anyone blush as fiercely as she did all the while giving us just as much shit back as we gave her.

It was a great night.

We never got the alcohol we wanted. We made up for it when we got back to the house after, mind you.

This year though, more than half of us are legal which takes the fun out of it somewhat.

I follow the guys as we make our way through the mall, earning us more than a few interested glances, points and whispers.

It's not until we're being directed to our table inside the restaurant that I bother to look up. When I do, I lock eyes with her silver ones and I swear to God the world falls out from beneath me.

I stop, causing a couple of the guys to collide with my back and ensuring everyone else turns to look at me to see what's going on.

"Oh fuck," Leon breathes.

"I'll leave," I say, taking a step back, assuming the guys have moved.

"Where the fuck are you going?" Colt asks, totally oblivious to my life imploding.

I back up once more but he's not having any of it. His hand lands on my shoulder and he shoves me toward an empty seat directly opposite her.

I keep my eyes on her but her stare is fixed to her half-empty plate in front of her while Ella and Letty lean into her.

Letty glances up, finds me staring, and shakes her head.

Great, she's even got my friends wrapped around her little finger.

Letty nods toward the hallway where the bathrooms are and I push my chair out once more to stand.

"Where are you going?" Leon hisses.

Glancing over his shoulder, he follows my stare.

"Don't cause any fucking trouble."

"Me?" I ask innocently.

He rolls his eyes at me and I step around him.

"What the hell are you guys doing here?" Letty snaps the second I'm in front of her.

Lifting my hand, I push my hair back before wrapping it around the nape of my neck.

"It's Colt's birthday. This place is his favorite. I had no fucking clue you'd be here with her."

"She's got a name," Letty hisses.

"Fucking hell." I glance up at the ceiling, hoping I can find some strength.

"Firstly, you need to stay the hell away from her." I wipe any kind of expression off my face as I stare at her.

"I'm not a fucking moron, Letty." Her brow lifts in question. "You have no idea what went down between us. But it's nice to see you're already choosing sides."

"I'm not choosing anything, Luc. And that's rich seeing as you were the one who turned your back on me not so long ago. I have every right to be pissed at you for that alone without even mentioning what you've done to her."

"She's got a name," I quip, earning me a growl. "What was the second thing?" I ask, remembering she made her first point.

"Does Kane know you're all on a team night out without him?"

I shrug. "I don't want to be here. You think I was party to the fucking guest list?"

"Whatever. You hurt her again, and I'm coming for you."

I can't help but laugh at her serious face.

"Luca, this isn't funny. What you're doing right now isn't all that different from how Kane's treated me in the past, and you remember how you reacted to that? Well, you hurting her does the same to me. Prove to me that she's done something wrong. Prove to me that I shouldn't believe she's anything but innocent in whatever this thing is between the two of you and I'll walk away. But until you can do that, me, Ella, hell anyone who wants to be, are going to be her friend and support her. You might think you've got it hard right now, try being in her fucking shoes."

Her lips part like she wants to add to her ass ripping but she changes her mind, instead just shakes her head once before walking away from me and returning to her seat.

Whatever she says to Peyton causes a reaction because she looks up directly at me. My entire body jolts at the sadness in her eyes as if I've just taken a fucking bullet.

After long, agonizing seconds, she drops her gaze once more and continues poking around at the food on her plate with her fork.

Not wanting to cause drama by walking out, I return to my seat.

Until I've made a solid decision about my future, I need the guys to think everything is relatively okay.

"All good?"

"Letty's on team Peyton," I whisper to Leon.

"Fucking hell, Bro. There are no teams here. We're all here for both of you and just want you to sort this shit out."

I nod at him, not believing a word of it.

I know how they really feel, I can see it in their eyes. Despite not knowing anything about what happened, they all believe her. They just think I'm an asshole with a grudge that I can't get past.

Maybe I have. I don't fucking know anything right now. Maybe I have been wrong all this time. That the vengeance I've so desperately craved for five years was built on nothing but my own distrust and misplaced loyalty.

"Fuck," I bark, turning all eyes on me.

Not wanting to go into it, I grab a menu and stare down at it, although all the words swirl around the page in front of me.

Sitting with her in my eye line is torture.

Half of me wants to go over and try to talk to her, but the other half still wants to hurt her for all the pain she caused me. I can't deny that that side isn't shrinking faster than I can cope with as I watch all the people I care about quickly becoming her friend.

The thought of being wrong all this time terrifies me but Letty is right. It's time to find out for sure as to whether what she told me that day was all lies or not.

If only there was an easy way to figure it out.

Thankfully, once the girls have had their dessert, Letty pays the check and they get up to leave.

I've missed every single conversation that's happened around me. My entire focus on Peyton and what she might or might not be saying to Letty and Ella.

The three of them have no choice but to walk past me to exit the restaurant. I suck in a breath as Letty and Ella surround Peyton as if they can actually protect her from me.

I don't intend to do anything but the second her scent fills my nose I can't help myself and my hand flies out, my fingers wrapping around her wrist.

"Let go," she fumes.

"Luc," Lee sighs, frustration evident in his tone.

Looking up, I find her huge silver eyes. The exact ones that have featured in my fucking dreams for the past five years.

My chin drops to say something, but I don't have any words that aren't me pleading for her to talk to me.

Now that she's in front of me, I realize that all I want is her.

My heart pounds as we stare at each other. Her eyes hard and closed off, mine begging, but I already know who's going to win because it's going to take a hell of a lot more than this after all the shit I've pulled.

"Luca," Letty snaps. "Let her go."

My fingers loosen, but before I totally let her go two words fall from my lips. "I'm sorry."

She sucks in a harsh breath but she doesn't say anything as she pulls her arm away and marches off.

"Stay away from her, Luc. I mean it," Letty warns before giving Lee a hug and following the girls out.

I'm pretty sure I've never felt smaller in my entire life.

"I'm sorry," I say, pushing my chair out. "You guys enjoy your night."

"Luca, what the hell are you doing?" Lee barks, following me out.

"Don't worry, I'm not going after her. I just... I need to be alone right now."

I don't wait for his response; I just take off running through the mall.

24

PEYTON

The Mexican restaurant was the last time I saw Luca this week. He never showed up at work Thursday night, Leon did again, and I didn't see him around campus the last two days either.

I should be glad that he's kept to his word and stayed away from me. What I really shouldn't be is concerned.

But after learning from Leon that he spent Monday night exactly where I suspected and drank himself unconscious, and then the look in his eyes as he stared up at me on Wednesday night, I can't help it.

Deep down, no matter what Luca does, what he thinks of me, I'll still always remember him as my best friend. As the sweet boy who would do anything to protect me. It's ingrained in me.

I stare at my new little black dress hanging on the door of my closet but even the sight of that can't bring a smile to my face right now.

Today is too hard. Everything hurts too much.

Aunt Fee, Elijah, and Kayden have done everything they can so far to make it special, but Mom's absence in my life has never been stronger.

I thought I missed Libby when she went her own way, choosing a life of addiction over her family.

I drop my head into my hands. I thought I was lonely when we left Rosewood. But I had no clue.

Standing in that hospital alone, with the two people I loved most in the world in critical condition and unable to find my sister, let alone get a hold of her to tell her what was happening.

That was sheer loneliness.

It was also the only time I very nearly called Luca. The one time I almost caved to my need for the boy from my past who always picked me up when I fell, who always held me when I was hurting.

I sat for hours with his name right there, the call button taunting me.

I had no idea if it was even his number anymore. For all I knew, if it connected it could have been to some random person on the other side of the country. But in those hours where I knew nothing but sheer fear and desperation. He was the only one I wanted.

As I sit here now, thankfully being able to leave that hospital weeks later with one of those people and our guardian angel that is Aunt Fee, I wonder just what would have happened that day if I'd have gone through with it and told him the situation I was in.

Would he have come to help, or would he have called me a liar and turned his back on me once more?

The possibility of it being the latter only adds to the agony and loss that I'm feeling right now.

"PeyPey?" a little voice calls up the stairs. "Are you coming?"

"Yeah, one minute."

Sucking in a deep breath, I stand in front of the mirror and pull Mom's necklace from my jewelry box. Libby and I bought it for her one year for her birthday and she never took it off.

It's the one thing I have now that helps me to feel closer to her.

I place the white gold heart locket against my chest and run my fingers through my hair.

Schooling my features, I head out of my room hoping that my brave face will at least be enough to convince Kayden that I'm okay. That I'm enjoying the day he planned for me with Aunt Fee this week.

"You look pretty, PeyPey," he says when I emerge in the kitchen where he's helping himself to the plates of food Aunt Fee is in the process of taking outside.

I left the plans up to Kayden and he decided that I needed a picnic for my birthday this year.

It's January, but I guess we are in Florida so it's not so bad. Although we could be in Alaska and I'd go with it if it meant seeing him smile.

"Kayden," Aunt Fee chastises when she comes back to find him with his cheeks puffed out with food like a hamster.

"Wot?" he asks around all the food.

Rolling her eyes at him in faux exasperation, she walks over. "Shall I help you out?"

I watch them both go, scooping up the final few plates to take out.

It's totally over the top for the four of us but I appreciate the gesture.

Aunt Fee tried to convince me to invite Ella and Letty, or anyone really, but I couldn't. They're already in deeper with this thing with Luca and me than I want them to be. Them discovering the truth before he does would not go down well.

I might have told Luca the truth five years ago, but that doesn't mean I haven't kept something pretty fucking huge from him ever since. And I know that at some point I'm going to have to come clean and deal with the consequences. I just have to understand that it was about more than him or me. It's about that little boy out there. The one whose smile lights up every room he enters, and whose heart is pure gold despite the crap that's been thrown at him in his short few years.

"Oh wow, this looks amazing," I say, putting as much awe into my voice as possible when I see the banners and balloons that litter the backyard.

"Do you like it, PeyPey?" Kayden asks with hope shining bright in his eyes.

"I love it, lil' man. Thank you so much." I drop to my haunches and pull him in for a tight hug. Hoping that by the time I pull away I'll have got control over the tears that are desperate to fall from my eyes.

"Right, who's hungry?" Aunt Fee asks as if she knew that I needed an out before I fell apart.

"Oh whoa," I say, genuinely shocked when I see the cake. "Did you two make this?" I ask, taking in the two-tier cake with pink icing flowers all over it.

"We did," Kayden announces proudly coming up behind me. "The icing is just like Play-Doh but tastes better."

"It's a miracle there were any flowers left to put on it," Aunt Fee jokes lightly as we all take a seat at the table.

"Happy Birthday, Peyton," Elijah says, pouring me a glass of champagne, seeing as I'm now legal.

"Thank you."

"I know it's probably not quite what you imagined for your big two-one but I hope—"

"It's perfect, Aunt Fee. Thank you so much for... for everything."

"Anytime, girl. You know that, right? Dig in. I suspect you're going to need to fill that stomach before your big night out tonight."

I laugh at her, happy to pretend it'll be the first night I go out drinking. We can all fake it every now and then.

We chat away about nonsense. Elijah talks about shipping out again in a few days and Kayden regales us with every one of his crazy stories about the things he and Aunt Fee get up to when I leave the house.

Everything is as perfect as it can be given the circumstances until the back gate slams, turning all our attention to the other end of the yard.

"Oh my gosh," Aunt Fee gasps as my eyes land on the one person I did not want to see in this house—or yard—uninvited.

"L-Luc," I stutter, standing from my chair and coming to stand in front of Kayden in a pathetic attempt to hide him.

Luca is holding a huge bunch of flowers, way bigger than I've ever received before, and a birthday card. But exactly as I suspected, I'm not the object of his attention as he closes the space between us because his eyes are locked on the little boy I'm failing to protect right now like I promised myself I would.

"Peyton?" Luca whispers as he gets closer, his brows pulling together. Without any other option, I stand aside, allowing Luca to see Kayden properly for the first time.

Both gasp in shock, able to notice the similarities in each other's faces. Similarities I've been forced to look at every single day since Kayden was born.

"P-Peyton. Is he... is he mine?"

His question slams into me out of nowhere, shock rendering me speechless for a few seconds but before I get to respond, everything around me blurs, my head spins, and darkness consumes me as my body gives out.

Peyton and Luca's story concludes in The Destruction You Desire.

THE DESTRUCTION YOU DESIRE

MADDISON KINGS UNIVERSITY #5

1

———

LUCA

My hand trembles around the flowers I'm carrying as I walk around the house to the backyard.

Coming here is a risk. I knew that before I even left the house. But after avoiding Peyton—everyone really—since I walked out of the mall on Wednesday. I promised both Leon and Letty that I would give her some space. That I would try to figure my shit out. But my patience has run out.

I need her.

I need her more than I'm willing to admit, and that terrifies me.

When I first knocked on the front door, I assumed they'd gone out. But with all their cars parked out in front of the house, I figured they couldn't have gone that far. And as I walk toward the back gate, I hear joyful chatter and laughing, and I realize that I was right.

I have no idea what I'm expecting to find when I walk through the gate to the backyard. If I had to guess then I'm probably about to walk into the middle of all my friends celebrating Peyton's birthday as if they've all forgotten about me.

My chest tightens at the thought of them all taking her side in this fight.

It once again makes me question everything.

Has my loyalty been totally misplaced all this time?

Should I have believed her that day? Should I have told her that everything was going to be okay and pull her into my arms like I did every other time shit got hard for either of us.

I've spent all these years believing that she was the one to ruin us and everything we had. But really, was it me? Was I the dumbass who wanted to believe that those closest to me wouldn't hurt me like that?

My heart is in my throat as I stand before the gate, staring down at the latch.

Just walk through it and wish her a happy birthday, Luca. Don't be a pussy.

Squeezing my eyes closed for a beat, the image of her turning me away on Monday night slams into me. If I weren't so gutted by the move and the fact that she used me to get what she needed, then I'd probably be proud of her. But I can't move past the fact that I needed her, I needed my best friend at that moment and she turned her back on me.

I know I should have expected it. But fuck, my head was—is—a fucking mess.

All I knew was that I needed her to quiet everything down just for a little while.

She did. Kissing her, touching her, sliding deep inside of her, it gave me everything I was craving. It broke through the anger that had descended with Dad's surprise visit. But it wasn't enough. It was nowhere near enough.

Blowing out a quick slow breath, I reach for the latch and without thinking about it, I swing it open and step into the backyard.

The first thing I notice is that it's not full of people I recognize like I thought it might be. Instead, there are only four people sitting around a table at the other end of the yard.

The second is that one of those people is not only little, but in a wheelchair.

Time seems to slow down as the gate crashes closed behind me, alerting everyone to the fact that they've got company before all eyes turn toward me.

I hear people say things but I don't register any of the words because my eyes are locked onto the little boy who's staring back at me with wide shocked eyes.

He looks... fuck.

He looks just like me as a kid.

My heart thunders as my head spins at a mile a minute.

I know fuck all about kids, but he's gotta be what... four? Five, maybe?

My arms fall to my sides as I stride forward to get a closer look, but Peyton jumps up, immediately trying to block my view of the little boy with her body.

"Peyton?" I breathe, needing her to do something. To say something because right now I'm so fucking confused and beginning to jump to conclusions that I really don't need in my fucking head.

She hesitates for a beat, but clearly realizes that it's too late to try to hide him because I've already seen him.

She stands aside allowing me to once again stare at the little boy whose eyes are as green as mine and who looks exactly like the photos of me as a kid that hang on Mom's walls.

"P-Peyton. Is he... is he mine?" The words fall from my lips without me realizing but it's what makes the most sense to me right now.

My eyes are still locked on him when movement to his side catches my attention. But I'm not quick enough because as Peyton drops to the floor, the guy who was sitting beside her jumps up and manages to catch her before she hits the deck.

"It's okay, Peyton," the guy says, gently lowering her to the ground.

The lady at the table rushes around to her side as the little boy wheels closer.

Everything happens around me but it's like I'm not really seeing it, really experiencing it.

It's like I'm dreaming and I'm not really here.

I will myself to wake up but I know it's pointless because this is way too fucked up to be a dream. This kind of shit can only be real.

"I-I'm okay," she whispers after a couple of seconds.

"Peyton, thank goodness," the lady says, her voice full of relief.

"Seriously, I'm okay." She pushes away from the guy—her

boyfriend, I assume, and sits up, resting her elbows on her knees and drops her head into her hands.

It's like it takes her a second to remember what she's in the middle of. I know the exact moment it slams into her because her body tenses and her eyes fly up to mine.

Her lips part as if she's about to say something but she decides against it.

The tension in the air is so thick I can barely breathe, but I'm not leaving from the spot until I've been given an explanation and heard everything. I don't care how painful it is, I don't care how much devastation it's going to cause on top of everything that's already threatening to break me. I need it all.

"C-can you all go inside, please?" Peyton asks, her eyes still on mine.

"Are you sure, Peyton?" the lady asks as the guy stands from where he was on his haunches beside her.

"I'm fine. I just haven't eaten anything and—"

"I'll get you a glass of water. Come on." She gestures for the guy to go inside and after wrapping his hands around the boy's wheelchair the three of them disappear.

The air crackles between us once we're alone. My chest heaves as I fight to get a grip on myself and what all of this means.

"Here you go, sweetie," the lady says, passing a bottle over to where Peyton is still sitting on the edge of the deck with her feet on the grass.

"Thank you," she whispers, still not taking her eyes off mine. It's as if she can't believe this is happening as much as I can't either. The lady whispers something to her that I can't quite hear before Peyton assures her that she's okay. Accepting Peyton's answer, she squeezes her shoulder in support while shooting me one hell of a death glare, as she disappears once more.

The sound of the back door closing is like a gunshot echoing around us.

I wait two seconds before my need for an answer to my previous question gets the better of me.

"Is. He. Mine?"

She shakes her head, a sad smile curling at her lips.

"No, Luc. He's not."

I stare at her, my blood boiling as another possibility hits me.

"No," I bark, my hands coming up to my hair. The flowers and card that I was holding long forgotten as they tumble to the ground. "He can't be Leon's. Please, please don't tell me that you and—"

"What?" she screeches, jumping from the deck. "No, he's not Leon's. Jesus, Luc. Why would you..." She trails off as she begins pacing back and forth in front of me.

"Then whose is he, Peyton? Because you can't honestly stand there and tell me that he's got nothing to do with me. You've seen his face, right? He looks just like me."

"Yes, Luc," she hisses. "I've seen his face. I've had to look at his face for the last five years and swallow down the pain in my chest every fucking time."

"Who is he, Peyton?" I ask, ignoring her comment.

"He... He's..." She blows out a breath, turning away from me momentarily and pulling at her hair. Spinning back around, her eyes capture mine and she takes a step closer.

Her face is set in anger, her usually bright silver eyes are a dark gray.

"I never once lied to you, Luca. NEVER," she seethes. "What I told you that day, I told you because I loved you, because you deserved to know what I'd overheard. I had no idea if it was true at the time. But that didn't matter because I didn't keep anything from you."

"Peyton," I growl, my patience long shattered.

She throws her arms up in defeat.

"He's your brother, Luc. He's your little b-brother."

She covers her face with her hands as a sob rips from her throat.

He's my...

"FUCK," I roar. It's so loud that a couple of birds rush from the trees above us. "FUCK."

I pull at my hair until it hurts, until I swear it's going to come free as my world tilts on its axis once more.

Stumbling back, I collide with the fence behind me and drop to my ass. I'm trying to process what all of this means. But right now the only thing I can picture is fifteen-year-old Peyton with tears streaming down her cheeks, her bottom lip trembling as I shouted at her, called her a liar, told her that I'd never trust her again.

Emotion clogs my throat, tears burn the backs of my eyes, and I fight to keep them in. She curls into herself, lowering down to sit on the deck and sobs.

Tipping my head back, I stare up at the sky just watching the clouds move as I focus on just breathing.

My fists clench and unclench at my sides as I fight with myself not to just get up and walk away because fuck if that wouldn't be the easiest thing to do right now.

2

PEYTON

My body trembles with my uncontrollable sobs. I want to get a hold of myself but this has been a long time coming. Over the past five years I've let the truth totally consume me. Now that I've finally let it out, I'm overwhelmed by my emotions.

My hands are soaked with my tears, my nose is running unattractively but still, I don't lift my head.

The pain is too much. The knowledge that I've just exposed Kayden to all of this is just more than I can handle.

All I've ever wanted is to protect him from the truth. From his reality. But it's all about to unravel in front of me and I have no idea how to hold onto any of the threads to stop it from happening.

"W-what's his name?" Luca finally asks. His voice is rough with his own emotion and when I peek through my fingers at him, I find he looks as wrecked as I feel.

Good. He fucking should after everything.

I blow out a shaky breath, wiping at my face with my sleeves in an attempt to look less of a broken mess.

"Kayden. H-he's five." I hold Luca's eyes but it hurts to do so because I can see the pain in his dark green depths. Pain that I once would have wanted to take as my own to make it easier on him, but right now, a twisted, evil side of me wants him to feel all of it. All the hatred, betrayal, and desperation of the past five years.

"Five," he breathes.

"Is that the proof you needed to believe me?"

"Pey—"

"No." I hop up, anger once again taking precedence over the hurt. "You don't get to sit there and pull that face at me like you're innocent in all of this. That is not how this works, Luca."

"That's not—"

I march up to where he's sitting and loom over him. It's probably one of the only times in my life I've ever properly stood up to him, but that confused little boy inside gives me the strength to do what's needed.

"Six years ago, your sick cunt of a father got his hands on my sister. I have no idea what fucking game he was playing, or if he has a thing for high school seniors but he got her fucking pregnant, Luca. She was barely an adult and he fucked everything up. She was weak, you know that as well as I do, and he used it against her to get what he wanted. He's sick, Luca. And you stood there and told me that I was the one in the wrong when I told you about the conversation I'd overheard between Libby and Mom. I tried to warn you. To allow you to come to terms with it before whatever happened next. But you called me a liar. I'm not a fucking liar, Luc. I've never lied to you."

"Fuck that, P." He climbs to his feet, taking away my height advantage. "He's five years old for fuck's sake. At what point were you going to tell me that he even existed?"

"I don't know, Luc. Maybe when you weren't locking me inside people's pool houses and taking out all your anger on me."

"You should have told me."

I stare at him, my jaw working overtime as I try to keep my cool.

"That little boy in there is the only thing I care about right now. Libby is gone, Luc. She fucked off when he was a baby. My mom is dead and he—" A sob rips from my throat once more as I think about how small and vulnerable he looked in those early days after the accident. I already knew by then that Mom hadn't made it and I spent every second I could sitting by his bedside, holding his hand and praying that he wasn't going to leave me too.

"What happened?"

"Car accident," I grit out.

Silence falls between us and when I look away from his tormented eyes, I find Aunt Fee standing at the kitchen window watching us.

Straightening my spine, I swallow down my apprehension and force the words I need to say past my lips.

"I need you to leave."

A bitter laugh rips from his throat.

"You've got to be fucking kidding me. You can't drop a bomb like that and expect me just to leave."

"You weren't invited here, Luca, and you're not welcome. I need to go inside and make sure Kayden is okay. And you, you need to go and get your head straight because I can assure you that if I let you meet him properly, that you're not going to be in the state you are now."

"If you let me?" he spits, repeating my words back at me.

"Yeah, asshole. *If.* You lost any right to me or my family the day you called me a liar and walked away from me."

"Your family. He's mine too. Fuck."

I laugh but there's no humor in it. Just pain and anger.

"Yeah, so maybe you should think about how you want to deal with that because he deserves better than you. He's lost everything, Luc. Everything apart from me and there's no fucking way I'm letting you or anyone else hurt him any more than he already is."

Turning away from him, I storm toward the house needing to see my boy and make sure he's okay.

"Peyton, wait."

I don't want to do as he says, but the emotion cracking in his voice forces my body to stop at his demand.

"What, Luc?" I snap, looking over my shoulder, but not at him. I can't bear the agony and confusion in his eyes any longer.

"I-I'm sorry."

I scoff. "Too little too late, Luca."

Before he can reply, I yank the back door open and leave it to slam behind me.

The second our connection is severed, my knees give out and I start to fall, only what I fall into is a warm body as Aunt Fee's floral scent engulfs me as her arms wrap tightly around me.

"It's okay. I've got you," she soothes as I cry on her shoulder.

"K-Kayden, is he okay?" I finally manage to stutter once my sobs have subsided.

"He's playing with Elijah. He's fine."

Aunt Fee maneuvers me to a dining chair before pouring me a generous glass of vodka. I look up at her with my brow quirked.

"It'll take the edge off," she says, pushing it closer.

Wrapping my fingers around the glass, I decide I need more than the edge taking off and knock the whole lot back in one.

I groan as it burns down my throat but it's a welcome relief from the pain in my chest.

"I can't believe that just happened," I admit quietly.

"You knew it was going to eventually," Aunt Fee says, being the voice of reason.

"Yeah, I know but not like that."

Pushing the glass aside, I drop my head to my arm and suck in some calming breaths.

"Where's he gone?"

"No idea. I just told him to leave."

"You did?" The shock in her voice drags my head back up.

"Yeah, why?"

"N-nothing. It's nothing."

"Aunt Fee, now isn't the time to skirt around this shit. Just tell me whatever it is you want to say."

"I didn't think you'd have it in you. I know a lot has happened, but I also know that you still love him."

My chin drops as I stare at her in shock.

I already know that I'll always love Luca. The problem is that the Luca I love doesn't seem to exist anymore.

"He's not the same person anymore, Aunt Fee."

"Nor are you, sweetie. Just take it one day at a time. All of this, it's a lot to take in. What you're doing right now, it's not easy. You need to give yourself a break."

"I know but Kay—"

"Kayden is going to be okay, Peyton. He's got both of us, maybe some more family in the wings depending on how this goes. He's loved so much. You'll be surprised how far that will get him."

"I miss them," I confess.

"I know, sweetie. Me too."

"Why don't you go and clean up a little bit and then go see that sweet boy. He's been so excited for today. He wanted to make it so special for you."

The lump that's still lingering in my throat grows once more.

"I don't deserve him."

"You deserve the world, Peyton. And if Luca can't see that, then fuck him."

My eyes widen in shock at her words.

"What?" she asks innocently as she sets about making tea.

"Nothing. I'm just going to..." I point toward the door and push the chair out.

Today was meant to be about family, and damn it, that's what it's going to be.

I discover that my makeup is totally unsalvageable when I get to the bathroom and after washing my face, I completely redo it. I'm glad I do because when I walk out again, I feel stronger, more able to deal with whatever life is going to throw at me next.

I stop by my room, pulling my cell out of my purse to see if I have any messages. To my surprise, there's a group chat with Ella and Letty that's blown up in my absence about tonight's party.

My heart drops. I can't go out tonight with all this shit.

What I really need to do is man up and go and see Luca. Talk properly, but just the thought of doing that makes my stomach turn over.

There's no way we'll be able to survive through a conversation like adults.

I need to get Leon involved. Now that Luca knows the truth, Lee deserves it as well.

My hand trembles around my cell with the thought of sitting in front of both of them. I think about their mom. Maddie was always the sweetest person. God only knows how she ended up with an ass like Brett. But I know she was one of the many reasons why Mom packed up our stuff and dragged us out of Rosewood after she discovered the truth.

I wasn't meant to hear what I did that morning. They both thought I'd already gone out. I had, only I'd forgotten my cell and snuck back in.

There hasn't been a second of any day that's passed where I wished I'd never stepped foot back in that house. Ignorance is bliss, and I can't help but wonder how things would have played out if I didn't know the truth back then.

My sister was a nightmare at the best of times. She's two years older than me but listening to the things she got up to, you could easily think she was older than her almost eighteen years when we left. She didn't look her age either which is probably one of the only good things I can think of about the situation with Luca's dad. At least she didn't look underage. Granted she was only a few weeks off her eighteenth. But still. From what I've discovered, it wasn't just a one-time thing. They'd been spending time together for a while. Libby had been seduced by his status, money and power. I'm not surprised in the slightest. I love my sister dearly, but she had stars in her eyes, always wanting bigger and better. I can only imagine the kinds of things that Brett Dunn promised her.

The thought of what he could have said to her makes me feel sick. He knew how old she was. He knew who she was. Both of us had spent enough time at the Dunn's house for him to be well aware. It makes me wonder just how long he'd been planning something.

Disgust rolls through me once more.

I always knew Brett was a jerk. From as early as I can remember I hated him for the way he treated Luca, for the amount of pressure he put on a young boy's shoulders. But seducing a minor.

I shudder, opening the messages and tapping out something they're not going to want to read.

Peyton: I'm really sorry but I'm going to have to bail on tonight. Some family stuff has come up and I need to be here.

3

———

PEYTON

How do you tell a five-year-old who's already lost his mother and grandmother that the man standing in the yard earlier was his brother? A brother who may or may not want anything to do with him.

How do you even contemplate trying to explain the clusterfuck that is, that man's father is his father?

I lean back against the kitchen counter and just breathe.

I somehow managed to stumble my way through some kind of explanation that Kayden said he understood, but really, I barely understand it myself. How can I expect him to?

But I couldn't lie either. He'd seen Luca with his own eyes. The resemblance is too strong to deny any kind of connection there.

In true innocent kid style, all Kayden really wanted to know was if Luca was coming back.

His eyes light up just talking about him. As if he already knew Luca, and telling him that I didn't know if he was going to come back obliterated my heart.

"What are you doing?" Aunt Fee asks when she walks into the room with my half-eaten birthday cake.

"Sorry, I'll come and help tidy up," I say, feeling bad that I'm hiding away from it all.

"That's not what I mean. You're meant to be going out."

"I've canceled," I confess.

"Nonsense. It's your birthday. You deserve to go out and have fun."

"Yeah well, I'm not really feeling up to it after..." I trail off, not really wanting to talk about it again.

"Peyton, you only turn twenty-one once."

"I don't care, Aunt Fee," I say sadly. I just want to curl up in bed and forget today ever happened.

"I understand that, I do. But I think you'll regret not going. Plus, your friends are waiting."

"I told them I'm not going."

"Ah well... about that..." She rips her eyes away from mine, but not before I see them flash with guilt.

"Aunt Fee, what did you do?"

"Well, I was walking past your room and your cell dinged and... well... one thing led to another and..."

"You told them I was going, didn't you?"

"Yep. I told them you'd meet them in..." She looks at her watch. "Less than an hour so you really need to shift that ass into gear, girl."

"Aunt Fee, I can't—"

"You can and you will. Your mother would never forgive me for letting you mope around on your big day."

"She's not here, Aunt Fee."

"No, she's not. But I am," she says firmly. "And I say that you're going. You're going to let your hair down, get drunk and dance with a good looking boy because you can. Because you deserve it."

"But—"

"Nope, no buts. Elijah has offered to take you, he—"

"Of course he has," I say, rolling my eyes as I remember his comments about Ella.

"Please, Peyton. All this drama will still be here tomorrow. Stewing about it in bed all night won't make it go away, but—"

"Getting drunk will," I add.

"Well, that wasn't exactly what I was going for but yeah, I guess."

"Tomorrow you can talk to Luca. Invite him over here if you like so I can speak to him too."

"Thank you, but I think that's something I need to do alone."

"Okay, well the offer stands. If you want to go to Maddie too, all you need to do is ask, sweetie."

"Thank you, Aunt Fee. I don't know w-what we'd h-have—"

"Shush, Peyton. I wouldn't have it any other way."

I swallow down the lump and will my tears to subside once again.

"Now, get upstairs and shimmy into that sexy little dress. It deserves an outing." She winks at me before grabbing what's left of the champagne from earlier from the fridge and pouring us both a glass.

"When times are hard, go out with your girls and dance the night away," she says, holding her glass up to clink mine.

"You and Mom do that often?"

"More than I'm willing to admit to, sweetie."

Feeling a little lighter, I make my way upstairs to shower and dress in record time. Dread still sits heavy in my stomach but deep down, I know that Aunt Fee is right. I need this.

My determination wanes a little as I sit in front of the mirror in my small room applying my makeup. I'd hoped that sliding into the dress would give me the confidence I need to walk into a party tonight and figure out a way to enjoy myself, but it didn't have the magic effect I was hoping for.

I stare at myself with my mascara wand halfway to my face and let out a loud sigh.

Maybe this was a bad idea.

As if someone can hear my thoughts, a soft knock sounds out on my door.

"Yeah."

It creaks open before Elijah pokes his head inside.

"Whoa," he says, taking in the low-cut of the dress and my breasts that are damn near spilling out of it. "That dress is..." He trails off clearing his throat instead.

"Yeah, it's something," I mutter, looking back at the mirror and continuing with the job I started.

"How are you feeling?"

"Honestly?" I ask, shooting him a look over my shoulder as he lowers himself to the edge of my bed. My eyes linger on him dressed entirely in black and looking sinful. "I'm a mess. I have no idea if this is the right thing to do."

Leaning forward, he rests his elbows on his knees and watches me in the mirror.

"There are no rules here, Peyton. You just have to follow your gut."

"I need to talk to him."

He nods. "You do. But do you think going to find him tonight would be the best time?"

I think about Luca's hot temper both when we were kids and what I've witnessed recently. I know that finding him when he's probably still angry would be the worst thing to do.

I need to let him cool off. Get his head together. Then we need to sit down like sensible adults and talk properly. I almost laugh out loud at the prospect. I'm not sure either of us have it in us to manage it. We drive each other crazy whether we mean to or not.

"No," I confess, remembering that he asked me a question.

"Exactly. So, go out and blow off some steam. He's not going anywhere. This issue will still exist tomorrow."

"Great. Thanks for that."

"You know what I mean. This isn't the sort of shit that gets fixed easily or quickly. So just give yourself some time and trust that everything will work out in the end."

"I wish I could be so positive about things."

He shrugs. "I deal with life or death on a weekly basis, Peyton. No problem is ever as serious as that."

My stomach knots at the reminder of what he does for a living and I immediately feel awful for acting like the world is ending with my family issues.

"No, don't look at me like that. I didn't say it to make you feel guilty."

"I know, I know. It's just... ugh."

"Come on," he says, jumping up and straightening his shirt. "Finish up and we're going out and putting all your troubles behind you for a few hours."

"Okay." I nod at him, a small smile pulling at my lips.

"I want to get to your blonde friend. She's single right?"

"Jesus. I'm going to regret this, aren't I?"

"You'll never know if you don't hurry."

He leaves me to finish getting ready. When I finally stand in front of the full-length mirror out in the hallway before heading downstairs, I can't deny that I feel better.

The dress is killer and that along with my stilettos and makeup help me; it all feels like a layer of armor that I'm able to hide the truth behind.

"Wow, Peyton," Aunt Fee says, her eyes going wide when I appear in the kitchen doorway a few seconds later.

"Elijah's a lucky guy tonight." She winks at her son.

"Ready?"

"Yes, let's go before I change my mind."

"Have fun, kids. Don't do anything I wouldn't have done."

"We don't want to know what you got up to, Mom," Elijah groans, following me out of the house.

"An Uber?" I ask when I see the car idling at the end of the driveway.

"Yeah, you're already in no state to get behind a wheel and I do not plan on spending tonight sober so..." He gestures to the car, pulling the back door open for me. "My lady," he quips, making me laugh.

By the time we pull up outside the house where tonight's party is, I'm a nervous wreck. My hands are trembling, and my palms sweating. Despite the fact that I know I have a full stomach thanks to Aunt Fee insisting that I eat as much as I could this afternoon, I still feel like I might be about to pass out again.

"He's probably not even here after the bomb that exploded in his face this afternoon," Elijah says, unable to miss my hesitation to join him out of the car.

I suck in a breath, quietly thank our driver before sliding out.

"What the hell are you doing?" I gasp when his fingers tangle with mine. I immediately try to pull them free.

"You told me that he thinks I'm your boyfriend earlier. So, if he is inside let's allow him to believe it."

"E, I don't think that's wise," I warn, still trying to free myself.

"You want him to stay away, trust me. There's no better way."

Yeah, or Luca will delight in telling Elijah what a cheating whore I am and spill all our wicked secrets from last weekend.

"It's not a good idea."

"I can handle a college football player, Peyton." He lifts my hand and places a kiss to my knuckles. "You've got this, PeyPey." He winks and I barely contain my eye roll.

Unable to free myself from his grip, I walk alongside him and toward the open front door of the house.

The music booms, the scent of cigarette smoke and weed mixes together as we make our way into the crowded hallway.

"Peyton," I hear someone squeal before Letty races down the stairs so fast I'm sure she's about to face-plant on the floor any second. "Happy Birthday," she cries, slamming into me and throwing her arms around my body. Finally, I lose Elijah's grip allowing me to hug her back.

"Th-thank you."

"Ignore her, she's already wasted," a deep rumbling voice says. When I look up, I find Kane watching his girl with an amused yet satisfied smirk on his lips.

"You're aware you're wearing her lipstick, right?" I ask him, unable to keep the smile from my lips.

"Yeah, do you think it's my color?" He winks.

"Let's go get drinks."

"Are you sure you need another?" I ask Letty as she takes my now free hand and pulls me toward the kitchen.

"Elijah, Kane. Kane, Elijah. He's... kinda my cousin, I guess."

They nod at each other and follow us through the groups of people.

"Look who I found," Letty announces the second we're in the kitchen causing everyone to turn and look at me.

"What the hell happened this afternoon?" Ella asks, clearly more sober than Letty.

"Family stuff."

"Fair enough. Here you go, a very special cocktail for the birthday girl." She passes me over a Solo cup with God knows what inside it and encourages me to knock it back, which I do with a little hesitation. The second I swallow, I regret it because the alcohol burns.

"Jesus. What the hell is this?"

Ella shrugs, too busy staring at the person over my shoulder.

"You brought a friend," she says, clearly as interested in him as Elijah is in her.

"His name is Elijah. He's a Marine. Ships out again soon so do not get attached in any way. He's my aunt Fee's son."

"And he is hella hot. You mind?"

"By all means." While he's distracted with her, the less chance he'll be able to play big brother slash fake boyfriend with me.

"Giiirl, you are looking F-I-N-E," Brax says, coming to stand before me.

"Ah, the good-looking, smart one," I quip.

"I think I'm going to need a dance with the birthday girl tonight."

"I'm sure that can be arranged. Although, I'm pretty sure I remember you being firmly warned off me," I say, remembering Ella's demands when I went to their dorm the other week.

"Oh, she's fully distracted, don't worry." He winks.

My lips part to warn him about Luca. I know both Brax and West are on the team, which means they're his boys. But I don't want to think about him right now let alone say his name out loud.

I startle when a hand lands on my waist, but the second Letty's floral scent hits my nose I relax.

"Brax, stop looking at her tits," she slurs. "We all know you're desperate but Peyton is not for you."

"They're right in my face, I can't not look," he says with his hands up in defeat.

"The girls are looking good, Peyton. I bet Lu—"

"Don't," I growl, cutting her off before she lets his name slip past her lips.

"Has something happened?" she asks, clearly sensing that something is wrong even while she's intoxicated.

"It doesn't matter. I'm here to have fun and let go."

"Hell yeah. Let's go dance." She takes my hand before reaching for

Kane with the other. "El, bring your Marine. We're dancing," she shouts.

We blend into the crowd that are grinding it up in what I can only assume should be the living room and the second we come to a stop Letty pulls me into her and we dance together with Kane at her back.

Whatever Ella gave me added to the champagne and vodka I've consumed today ensures that my reality stays away as I lose myself to the music.

A guy who I'm introduced to as Letty's little brother and a couple of the other guys I recognize from the toga party supply us with drinks and with each one, I let go a little more. So much so that when some guy I don't know steps up behind me and begins dancing with me, I just go with the flow.

I don't care who he is. I don't want to think about anything. I just want to let go.

Resting my head back against his shoulder and moving my ass against him. His hand grips my waist, their burning heat turning my blood to lava.

I have no idea how much time or how many songs pass like that. It could be one or ten. I lose all sense of time and anything around me as I get lost to the music.

But the second he spins me around and I recognize a pair of green eyes, everything comes crashing down around me until my alcohol-fueled brain catches up with my reality. My body stills, my blood instantly cooling and my high from only seconds ago vanishing faster than I thought possible.

"Lee? What are you—?"

"Disappointed?" he asks, clearly reading my reaction.

"N-no, I just didn't... shit."

I drop my head to his shoulder, suddenly feeling like I've got the weight of the world on my shoulders once more.

4

LUCA

I stand in the driveway to the house where tonight's party is. It's only a short walk from our house on the next street over.

I told myself I wasn't going to show my face. Today has been the biggest shit show I've ever experienced.

My head spins with the vodka racing through my system and the house before me appears to move despite the fact I know it's not.

I can't even think about what happened this afternoon. If I picture his face, if I think about her confession, then I know I'm going to drown and never surface again.

I spent five years convincing myself that she was wrong. That my dad hadn't slept with my best friend's sister.

But it's not even just that. He got her fucking pregnant.

Lifting the bottle to my lips, I try to force myself to walk back home, to stay away from her, to stay away from everyone. But a photo I saw on Instagram only thirty minutes ago calls to me.

I have no idea if Letty did it on purpose. If she knew I'd be sitting at home stalking them all on social media to try to get a glimpse of her. Part of me thought she'd bail on tonight. But it seems what happened today hasn't affected her in the same way it has me because I know she's inside there right now, having the time of her life.

I guess she has every right. It's her twenty-first birthday, after all.

Pulling my cell out once more, I stare at the image as my confusion continues to war inside me.

I want her.

I need her.

I hate her.

My grip tightens until I worry I'm about to shatter the screen as I look at her smile at whoever is taking the photo. Letty? A guy?

My heart pounds as I think about her hooking up with someone else tonight, about someone else touching what's mine.

With another swig of vodka, I shove my cell back into my pocket and make my way inside.

A few people try to stop me as I walk through the house but most can sense the tension radiating from me and give me a wide berth. I don't blame them. I don't even want to talk to myself right now.

I scan the house for her pink hair, for Letty's bronze skin. Hell, even for Kane's smug fucking face. Anything that will help me find her.

I move through the crowds until I spot the flash of pink I've been craving. Just like at the toga party last weekend, she's in the middle of the dance floor, with the others close by. Ella has her tongue down some guy's throat while Letty rubs herself up against Kane as if they're in a room alone.

Ripping my eyes from everyone else, I focus on Peyton, desperate for the crowd to part so I can see who she's dancing with.

But the second that does happen, I wish it hadn't because a red haze like I've never experienced before descends upon me. I'm moving before I even realize my feet have left the floor.

Those who see me coming jump aside, those who don't soon find themself barged out of my way as I fly toward my brother.

"You motherfucker," I roar, pulling my arm back and slamming it into his cheek.

Peyton screams in shock as Leon releases her and goes stumbling backward.

Others cry and shout as I approach Leon once more but instead of coming at me, all he does is hold his hands up in defense as his cheek burns red.

"It's not what you think, Bro."

As he says the words, a flash of pink races past me as Peyton runs full speed through the break in the crowd.

"You fucking idiot."

"Peyton wait," Letty shouts but I'm faster than all of them despite the fact my body is entirely fueled by alcohol right now.

I take the stairs two at a time, hot on her heels. She flies past the line to the bathroom and dives inside right as someone exits, much to the complaints of the people waiting to go inside.

She slams the door but unfortunately for her, she's not quite quick enough. My palm connects with the wood and I push it open before she gets a chance to lock it.

"Leave me alone, Luc, please," she begs, wrapping her arms around her waist as if she's physically trying to hold herself together.

Slamming the door behind me, I cut off the complaints of the others who are waiting and I flip the lock.

I take a step toward her and she takes a hesitant one back.

"W-what do you want, Luc?"

I consider her question for a few seconds.

"Honestly. I have no fucking clue."

She gasps when she runs out of space behind her and bumps up against the wall.

"I-I'm sorry you found out like that. That wasn't—" Her words are cut off when my hand flies out and pins her against the wall by her throat.

She swallows nervously, her body trembling as tears pool in her eyes.

"Stop," I boom. "Just stop."

My chest heaves as I stare at her almost cowering away from me.

I hold her wide eyes for a beat before I drop mine to her pink lips. They're so full and I already know just how sweet they taste. Then I drop lower to her dress. It's the first time I really get to look at her and fuck.

"You look..." *Beautiful.* I swallow down the word as the confusion I've battled with all day only gets stronger.

Hurt her.

Take her.

Punish her.

Make her yours.

"Tell me he didn't touch you. Tell me he didn't take what's mine."

She shakes her head, her brows pulling together. "N-no, he—"

"Luca. Peyton. Open the door," a familiar, angry voice demands through the door.

"Fuck off, Legend," I bark. "This has nothing to do with you." I hold Peyton's eyes and I can't miss the relief that floods them that she's being rescued by that prick.

"No fucking chance," he shouts before there's a loud bang and the door rattles on its hinges.

"Fuck," I bark, acting on impulse and slamming my lips down on hers.

The second time he rams the door behind us, the lock gives way and he crashes into the room.

"Luca you need to—" Letty's concerned voice is cut off when she finds Peyton's hands wrapped around my shoulders, her nails digging into my skin as she kisses me back almost as fiercely as I do her.

Reaching down, I lift her so she has no choice but to wrap her legs around my waist, her tight dress riding up her thighs and exposing her ass for me.

"Stay out of my fucking business," I bark as I spin her away from the wall and holding Kane's eyes before drilling them into Letty as well. "This has fuck all to do with either of you."

Without waiting for a response, I march out of the bathroom and down to the quietest end of the hall.

"Peyton?" I ask when I stop, noticing that she's deadweight in my arms. "P, baby?"

Shifting her around so she's cradled in my arms, I look down at her sleeping face.

"Jesus fucking Christ, baby."

We get more than a few curious glances as I walk down the stairs with her in my arms. I could probably make use of one of the bedrooms in this place, but like hell is that going to happen. The only place she's sleeping tonight is in my bed. It's where she should have been last weekend. It's time to make up for that.

We're almost out of the house by the time someone alerts Leon to what's going on and he comes running up behind us.

"Luca, what the hell are you playing at?" I spin around.

"Nothing. I'm playing at fucking nothing. You need to stay away from her."

"Fucking hell, Bro," he mutters, scrubbing his hand down his face. "You have no fucking clue, do you?"

"She's passed out. I'm taking her home."

"By home, I really hope you mean her home and not locking her up somewhere to torture her again."

"I'm pretty sure she enjoyed every second of last weekend."

"You're a jerk."

"You're the one who's fucking clueless, Bro. You have no idea what the hell is going on here."

"Maybe you should tell me then."

I chuckle at him as memories from earlier today flicker through my mind.

"You'll regret suggesting that when I do tell you."

His brow creases in confusion.

"How about you put less time into worrying about me and go and try to get laid, huh?" I ask, turning my back on him and walking across the front yard with Peyton still in my arms.

The walk home is quick and the fresh air is enough to clear my head somewhat.

I make quick work of getting us up to my room. Thankfully, it's a Saturday night and the house is deserted. So in only minutes, I'm pulling my sheets back and laying her down on my bed.

Her pink hair fans out over my dark gray sheets and her dress rests high up on her thighs. I stumble back until my legs collide with my chair. Sitting down, I don't take my eyes away from her. Her chest heaves with her deep breaths and a little whimper rumbles up her throat.

She looks beautiful. Perfect. Everything I've fucking dreamed of for the last five years.

I lean forward, placing my elbows to rest on my knees and just watch her.

I can't count the number of times I imagined what it would be like to have her in my bed once again. Although I know for a fact that I never imagined it to be quite like this.

Every part of me wanted to believe that she wouldn't lie to me. After all our years together, I wanted to believe that I knew her inside and out, and that she'd never do that to me. But equally, I refused to believe that my dad could have done that.

I always knew he was a lot of things. But a... a pedophile? No. Never.

Okay so she was only a few weeks from turning eighteen, but he was what... forty?

My stomach turns over at the thought of him chasing after Libby. She was a kid. What was he even thinking? He had to know how much that would have hurt all of us. He also couldn't have been stupid enough to think we'd never find out. She was my best friend's sister, for fuck's sake.

My hands ball into fists as I try to figure out what his game plan was. My stomach knots with the knowledge of what he did, my anger once again threatening to get the better of me.

But as if she knows I need a distraction, Peyton pushes up onto her elbow. She looks directly at me, but I know she's not really seeing me because her eyes are glazed over.

"Luc, I—" She doesn't get to say anymore because she pukes all over herself and my bed.

"Fucking hell, P," I groan, jumping up and racing over to help her.

Scooping her into my arms once more, I carry her through to the bathroom and lower her feet into the shower.

"I knew I shouldn't have gone to that goddamn party," I mutter as I somehow manage to hold her up with one arm and undo the zipper at the back of her dress with the other, without us both ending up in a pile on the floor.

Turning the shower on, I let us both get blasted with hot water, it soaks my clothes as it washes away the puke covering Peyton.

She just about holds herself up with her arms wrapped around my waist and her head resting on my shoulder. And just for tonight, I tell myself that everything is okay. That we're just the old Luca and Peyton. I forget that anything else exists and let the alcohol still in my system wash away our reality so that I can just look after her for tonight. So that I can pretend for tonight.

I dry her off, my eyes lingering on her curves, my cock throbbing for her to wake up enough for me to take her, but I know she won't. She's out of it. And after pulling one of my jerseys over her head, I place her on the small couch in my room and strip the bed, something I had zero intention of doing tonight.

By the time I crawl in beside her in a clean and dry pair of boxers, she's curled up in a ball and snoring quietly.

I lay facing her, studying her just like I did last weekend as she slept. And just like last weekend, I see the worry lines on her brow that never used to be there, the dark shadows under her eyes. And for the first time since she confessed what she'd heard to me, I try to put myself in her shoes.

A huge part of me feels for her. Walking away from her ripped me apart, but I was the one who made the decision. I was the one who chose not to believe her. I chose my loyalty to my father instead of her. I was the one who made a huge mistake.

But despite being in the wrong.

I'm not the one who's kept a massive secret for the past five years.

A secret I'm not so sure I'm ever going to be able to forgive her for.

5

PEYTON

Anger burns through me like a wildfire, but the second his hand closes around my throat it turns into an inferno.

His hard, cold green eyes stare down into mine. The only thing I can think about is the explosion that's about to happen when he takes what he so clearly craves.

His chest heaves, his hot breath fanning my face, the scent of alcohol on it filling my nose, which makes my mouth water for a taste.

We might not be able to talk like sensible adults like we should, but it seems that since we reconnected, we're able to vent our anger in much more carnal ways.

My body melts into his touch. My impatience grows as my head and judgment becomes completely clouded by his touch and his scent.

Fuck, I need this. I need this badly.

Something startles me, but I have a feeling that the house could collapse around us right now and I'd barely even notice.

It's just him. Everything is him.

When his lips finally slam down on mine, I immediately give myself over to him. Drowning in the man—the boy I loved so hard has turned into. I forget at that moment that I don't like him. That I want to hate him for everything that he's done to me these past few weeks and I give in to what my body craves.

He kisses me deep, his tongue sweeping into my mouth. Claiming me, taking me, owning me.

My head screams yes, and my body demands for more as I wrap my arms around his shoulders and pull him closer. Although I fear that nothing will be close enough right now.

He sweeps me off my feet, both figuratively and literally. We move through the house, the music fading into the background behind us as I continue to drown in his scent, in his touch.

"Luca," I moan when my back presses against his bed, my body on fire to feel his lips on me once more. But he doesn't comply, instead, flipping me over in favor of getting me naked.

My dress is gone in seconds along with my underwear. His hands move around my body as if he doesn't know where he wants to touch me first.

He parts my thighs, staring down at me with hunger in his eyes. A hunger that I want to swallow me up and never let me go.

Ripping open his fly, he pulls out his hard cock, rubbing it through my wetness.

"Oh God, please."

He drops lower, pushing inside me in one thrust. I cry out in delight until something startles me and my eyes fly open.

My head feels like it's full of cotton, my mouth is vile and my body aches. Although the desire coursing through my veins is impossible to ignore.

What the—

Where am I?

My heart thunders against my ribs, my skin flushes with my... my dream?

"Shit," I pant.

I lower my head but movement on my thigh makes me jump once more and when I look down, I find a hand.

"Oh my God," I whisper, risking a look at the person who's beside me. "Luc? Shit."

I fall back onto the bed, immediately realizing that it was a mistake because everything around me spins. Throwing my arm over my face, I focus on trying to catch my breath.

However, that all goes to shit when his hand moves, parting my thighs once more and finding my slick core.

"Luc, what the hell—that wasn't a dream, was it?"

"Partly. Listening to you moan my name spurred me on."

He pushes two fingers inside me, and my body locks up.

"No." I try scrambling away from him, aware that none of this should be happening.

I can't even remember how I got here.

"Just give me this, baby."

"We can't... this isn't—"

Pushing up from the bed, he crawls between my thighs. He's only wearing a pair of boxers which doesn't hide the package I already know it covers.

His fingers curl inside me, hitting that part of me that makes me see stars.

"Oh God."

"You're going to let me watch you come, baby," he tells me, his voice rough and deep making butterflies erupt in my belly. "And then I'm going to fuck you so hard that you'll never forget having me inside you. You'll never forget what you've done to me." The edge to his voice hints to the new version I've met over the past few weeks that I'm not at all fond of. But then he folds himself over me. He runs his lips over my jaw as his free hand slips under the shirt I'm wearing until he finds my bare breast.

A thought flickers through my mind as to how I ended up here, in what I can only assume is his bed wearing nothing but his jersey.

Aware that it's probably something I'm going to regret, I push it all from my head. He pinches my nipple at the same time he presses against my G-spot and I forget about everything.

Our reality. How I ended up here. My raging hangover.

The only thing that exists in this moment is us.

Those two lost kids who crave to find the connection that we once had.

"Luca," I cry as his teeth sink into the soft skin of my neck as my orgasm crests.

He pulls back, staring down at me, captivating me with his hungry green eyes. But as much as I want to hold my steady gaze on his, I can't, and mine slam closed as I ride out the pleasure.

"Oh God," I pant as I come down from the high.

"So fucking beautiful," he breathes. He pushes the jersey up so he can feast on my breasts as he grinds his length against my pussy.

It's like we're horny teenagers once again desperate to go all the way but terrified to make that move that we both know will change things.

"I hope your stomach is feeling a little more settled," he murmurs against my burning skin.

My brows pull together in confusion but before I get a chance to ask what he means, his hands clamp down on my hips and a squeal rips from my lips. He flips me over, my face pressing into the pillow as his weight lands on me.

"I don't want to be cleaning up any more of your puke," he breathes in my ear.

"M-my wha—"

My words are cut off when his fingers thread into my hair.

"How much did you drink last night, Peyton?"

"Uh... I don't know. It was my birt—"

"Don't care," he snaps, pulling my head to the side so I can see him. "You passed out in my arms, P. You could have ended up in anyone's bed this morning."

A shiver of fear runs through me knowing that he's right.

I wouldn't usually drink as much as I did last night but it was my birthday and I had a lot of shit to drown out. I also trusted that Elijah and the others would take care of me. Clearly that wasn't what happened.

"Elij—"

"Don't even say his fucking name, Peyton. I know who he is. I figured it out after I walked away yesterday. He was the boy who used to spend time at your house as a kid. He was friends with your sister. What he is not, is your boyfriend," he growls in my ear.

"I-I never said—"

"No, but I have a very good reason not to believe a single word that falls from your lips."

Tears burn my eyes as he talks and my head continues to spin with confusion.

By all accounts he looked after me last night, cleaned me up after I threw up. How can he go from that to... to this?

My bottom lip trembles as I try to keep everything inside. I don't want to appear weak in front of him but everything is just too much to deal with right now.

"Don't even think about it, Peyton. I don't want your fucking crocodile tears."

"This isn't my fault, Luca. If you believed—"

"No. Don't you dare put this on me. I wasn't the one hiding a child, a brother, from me all these years. What did you think would happen, P? That I'd never find out?"

"N-no, of course not. I wanted to tell you but you—"

"Enough. I don't want to hear any more of your bullshit. You're going to do what I say, and then you're going to leave. You're going to walk out of my room and out of my house looking like the filthy slut that you are."

"No, Luc. Please."

His fingers slip between my legs once more dipping inside. As much as I want to feel nothing at his touch, it's not the reality because his fingers burn me from the inside out as he slides them inside me.

"So fucking wet, P. You're desperate for my cock again, aren't you?"

I bite down on the inside of my cheeks to stop me from responding because I'm not sure what words will come out if I do.

Part of me wants him to go fuck himself. But the other part, the dark and twisted side of me that Luca seems to have found in the last few weeks, wants everything he's threatening me with.

I want... The punishment. The pain. The torture.

His fingers dive deeper making my hips lift from the bed.

"Fuck yeah. Tell me what you want, P," he demands.

A growl rumbles up his throat when I shake my head in refusal.

His fingers slip around my throat holding me in warning.

"Tell me what you want, P," he grits out as if he's right on the edge of his control. "I want to hear you beg for it."

"I-I want you," I whisper, my hips lifting once more. My body is fully on board with what he's offering me while my head is having a harder time at joining the party.

"You want my what, baby?"

I suck in a breath, my defiance almost getting the better of me. But I know what will happen if I stand my ground. He won't give me what I need and not only will I leave here full of regrets, but I'll be frustrated as well.

"I want your cock, Luc," I say with a confidence that I know he'll get off on.

"Fuck yeah, you filthy slut."

"Luc," I scream as he lifts me with one hand and surges inside me without warning.

His intrusion burns as he stretches me wide open and bottoming out in one move.

He doesn't give me any time to get used to him, he pulls out of me almost immediately before he begins fucking me like a man possessed. The bed bangs against the wall as our bodies become slick from the exertion.

My head spins with my lingering hangover mixed with the heady desire only Luca manages to drag up inside me.

"Oh God," I cry as his fingers tighten in my hair. He shifts behind me and pulls me to my knees with only my hair. His length never once slipping from inside me.

"You shouldn't feel this good, baby. It almost makes me not want to do all the things to you that I've imagined for five long years."

His fingers tighten around my throat as he pins my ass back against him. His tight grip forcing my back to bend painfully as he continues to thrust inside me.

"Do them," I growl. "Punish me. Hurt me. Do whatever you want."

"Fuck, you drive me insane, baby."

"Good, that makes two of us."

He pulls me to one side so he has access to my neck and shoulder and he sinks his teeth into my skin.

"Oh shit, Luc," I shout as pain shoots from where I'm sure he just broke the skin.

"You're mine, Peyton. And you're not going to forget it."

He pistons into me, his movements becoming erratic as his cock begins to swell even larger inside me.

"Come for me, baby, or you're going to lose your chance. Who knows when I'll be feeling generous enough to give you two again."

"Luc," I cry as his fingers tighten on my throat until stars begin to appear in my vision.

He releases my hip and his fingers find my clit. The movement against my skin vicious but perfect and precise as he plays me to the perfect crescendo.

"Luca," I scream as the most powerful orgasm I think I've ever experienced slams into me. It turns my muscles to mush and makes me go limp in his hold as wave after wave races through my body.

He holds me up, thrusting into me three more times before his own roar of pleasure fills the room, sending aftershocks of ecstasy shooting around my exhausted body.

The second he's done, he releases me, giving me no choice but to flop on his bed in a heap. My muscles still quivering with my release.

"No better way to forget a hangover than to fuck it out. Thanks. You can leave now."

It takes everything I have to lift my head to look at him but the second I do, I regret it.

His face is an emotionless mask as he stares at me as if I'm nothing more than a piece of shit on his shoe.

I prefer it when he's angry and shouting at me, at least I know he's feeling something. But right now, he's downright terrifying and so much like I remember of his father that fear races down my spine.

Turning into his father was one of his biggest fears as a kid. He knew from an early age that Brett wasn't the kind of father most kids wanted. He never said well done, or told him he was proud. All the things kids need to hear. I can only imagine how he feels about him now that he really does know the truth.

But staring at him right now, I fear that he's getting closer and closer to becoming the man he feared he'd become.

"What are you waiting for? Get the fuck out before I throw you out."

My chin drops at the coldness in his tone before I scramble from his bed. I tug the hem of his jersey down in an attempt to cover up.

I look around for my clothes, my shoes, my purse.

"Get the hell out," he booms when I don't move fast enough.

Thankfully, I spot my purse on the nightstand beside where I slept. I grab it before he takes a menacing step toward me as if he's going to do exactly what he just threatened.

Part of me wants to stand my ground and see if he goes through with it. But the other part, the bigger part, is just too exhausted to deal with whatever he might deliver should I force that to happen.

Before he gets to me, I race toward the door.

I twist the handle but I don't open it. Instead, I look over my shoulder at his familiar yet totally unrecognizable face.

"You can keep pushing me away as much as you want, but we both know you want to hear what I have to say."

"Get the hell out, Peyton. I don't want you here."

I swallow down the emotion that threatens to clog my throat at how easily he can dismiss me after our time together.

I need to remember that this is who Luca is now. He's cold. Vicious and unattainable.

Just as I close the door behind me, something smashes against it right on the other side of my head. A scream of shock rips from my throat as my legs give out and I start sliding down the door.

"Whoa. I've got you." Strong arms wrap around me before I hit the floor and I'm lifted and carried inside another room.

"I need to leave, Leon," I say, dropping my head into my hands. I sit on the edge of his bed with the evidence of what his brother did to me only minutes ago leaking from my body.

Jumping up, I take a step toward the door.

"What's really going on here, Peyton?" he asks softly. The genuine concern in his voice forces me to look at him.

I wince at the darkening bruise on his cheek that only adds to the healing wounds from the last time they got into it over me.

"I shouldn't have come back here," I confess, my heart shattering with each word. "I knew it was going to be bad, but I never thought it would be like this."

Pushing from the wall where he was watching me, he drops down beside me.

"Why does he treat you like he hates you, Peyton?"

"Because he does," I state simply.

"Yeah, apart from he doesn't actually. He's loved you since before he even knew what it meant. That kind of love doesn't just die, Peyton. And don't even think about arguing with me because I know you feel it for him too."

My lips part to respond but I soon find that I don't have any words to say back to that.

"D-do you have a bathroom that I can use?"

He studies me for a beat, his eyes begging me just to spill everything, to put an end to all the secrets and the lies.

"Yeah, sure." He points to the only other door in the room aside from the one he brought me in through and I push from the bed. "Use anything you want. I'll find you some sweats or something."

I look down at my bare legs in a daze.

Is this weekend really even happening?

"Thank you," I whisper, padding across the room with my shoulders lowered and my heart in my stomach.

Slipping inside, I make use of the toilet before standing in front of the sink with my head down, too scared to find out what's going to be staring back at me when I do look up.

I suck in a calming breath before counting to three.

The second I'm on three I force myself to lift my head to look at my reflection.

"Oh my God," I gasp. No wonder Luca sent me away, I look like a train wreck.

My makeup is literally everywhere, my hair is a matted mess around my head and my neck is red with his hickeys and light bruising from his fingers.

"Jesus, Peyton. You need to get your shit together," I tell myself, reaching for the toothpaste that's sitting on the side and squirting a generous amount onto my finger.

Once my mouth is a little fresher, I feel a tad more alive. After washing my face, I run my fingers through my hair and call it a day. That's as good as it's going to get while I'm standing in a boy's bathroom.

A loud bang startles me, the floor shaking beneath me as the sound of footsteps thundering down the stairs sounds out. My stomach knots and disappointment floods me knowing that he's running away from all of this.

"Here," Leon says, holding out a pair of black sweats when I step back into his room. "I shrunk them, although they'll probably still be massive on you."

"Thank you," I whisper, my cheeks heating that he's once again seeing me in this state and attempting to pick up the pieces. "I shouldn't have gone last night," I say, unable to look at him as I make excuses for what happened.

"Bullshit, Peyton. You had every right to be there. He's the one who acted like a possessive jerk."

"I shouldn't have been dancing with you. I shouldn't have drank so much. I shouldn't—"

"Stop. Please. None of this is your fault."

A sad laugh falls from my lips. "You're damn right there."

"Talk to me, P." A shudder runs down my spine at his use of one of the nicknames Luca uses for me.

Dragging my eyes from his carpet, I stare into his concerned green eyes as he rubs the back of his neck almost nervously.

"Would you be able to drive me home?"

Disappointment floods his face, but after a second, he nods and reaches for his keys that are sitting on his desk.

6

―――――

PEYTON

The air in the car as Leon pulls away from the house he shares with Luca and some of the team is thick.

I know he has a million and one questions for me, and I know that I need to start answering them. But the thought of letting Kayden's existence be known by someone else connected with their father terrifies me.

I know it shouldn't. It's Leon. I trust him as much as I used to Luca.

Leon's loyalties have never been with his father. With every day that passed when we were kids, it became more and more obvious that Luca was Brett's favorite because of his chosen football position and I watched as Leon became more and more detached from his father. And even sadder, I was forced to watch his father not even care.

That's just one of the many reasons why I understand why Mom did what she did when she dragged Libby and me away from Rosewood.

She didn't want Libby, or her grandchild connected to that pathetic pig of a man.

I get it, I do. It just terrifies me that he could have repeated what he did with Libby over and over again and no one is any the wiser, other than those it directly affected.

I've prayed that Libby was the exception. That she was his one vice that he couldn't stay away from and broke all the rules for. But the fact that he didn't have any contact with her from the moment we left Rosewood forces me to believe that she could have been one of many.

He didn't care about her. He just wanted to get his rocks off with a younger model than he was used to.

My chest aches once more as I think about Maddie. The sweetest, most caring woman ever. How could he do what he did while she was at home being the parent Luca, Leon and Shane deserved?

I exhale a long breath, finally lifting my eyes from my lap to find that Leon's stopped the car in the line for takeout.

"W-what are you doing?"

"Getting coffee and breakfast. I'm starving and you look like you could use it."

Right on cue, my stomach growls.

"I think I might have puked all over Luca last night."

Leon throws his head back and laughs. "I really fucking hope you did. It's the least the asshole deserves after the stunt he pulled last night."

"What happened?" I ask. "My memories are hazy." And I have no idea what was a dream and what was reality.

"Well, you already know that we were dancing and he took offense to it," he mutters, rubbing at his bruised cheek.

"Yeah," I mutter.

"You ran, he chased you, and the next thing I knew he was carrying you out of the building in his arms."

"I drank too much. I was reckless."

"I don't know whether to be glad he looked after you or not."

"That makes two of us. I... I think he did look after me last night. But then this morning..." I trail off, my cheeks burning.

"No point trying to cover it up. I'm in the room right next door. I have a very good idea of what happened."

"Jesus, Lee. Not necessary."

He shrugs. "Sounded like my kind of punishment," he admits dryly.

A weird noise rumbles up my throat at his admission as he chuckles beside me.

"Don't worry, I've got no reason to punish you," he says with a smile, clearly sensing my unease.

"Christ," I mutter, dragging my hair away from my face as a thought hits me. "Have you two both been with Letty?"

"Uh... She tell you that?"

"N-no, Luc did."

"Huh." He scrubs his jaw as he thinks.

"What? Isn't it true?"

A smile curls at his lips. "Yeah, it's true. We've done a lot of stupid shit over the years. Most of it probably would never have happened if you never left."

"Is that a good or bad thing?" I ask despite the guilt already tugging at my insides.

"Who knows? Some of it's been fun. Other stuff not so much." Our conversation is cut off as he places our order. "He was never the same once you left, you know. You took a part of him with you. No one else saw it, or if they did, they didn't appreciate just how bad it was. Pretty sure there's not a day that's gone by where he hasn't wished you were still beside him."

"I don't know about that. It's not like he wants me here now."

"He does," Leon says confidently. "He's just working through whatever shit happened. Last night should be proof enough that he still cares."

I mutter some kind of agreement as he moves toward the window to pick up our order.

"It was too late for breakfast," he says handing the bag over as if he's only just realized that he ordered for me only minutes ago.

"It's fine."

Without wasting a second, I dig into the bag and stuff a handful of fries into my mouth.

He laughs at me as he pulls into a space in the parking lot and takes the bag from my lap, pulling out his own food.

"Time to start talking, Peyton."

I bite down the fry in my hand as I fight my internal battle about whether to confess or not. In the end, my mouth decides for me when the words just start pouring out.

"A few weeks before we left town, I told Luca something that I'd overheard my mom and sister talking about."

"Right," he says lightly, taking a huge bite of his burger as if I'm not about to turn his world upside down.

"She told Mom that she was pregnant."

"Holy shit," he splutters, damn near choking on his food.

I wait for him to swallow before I land the final blow.

"Libby told her that the father was..." Leon looks me dead in the eyes, I can almost see the wheels turning in his head trying to work it out.

"Luc?" he breathes.

A smile pulls at my lips because even now, I trust Luca to never have gone after Libby, not in a million years.

"No. Your dad."

All the air escapes from Leon's lungs as his face morphs into one of utter disbelief and shock.

He's silent for long seconds. He's still looking at me but his eyes have glazed over. It's as if he's not really seeing anything as he tries to process those three words I've just said to him.

"M-my d-dad?" he finally stutters.

"I'm so sorry, Lee."

"My dad slept with your sister and... and got her pregnant?"

No longer hungry, I push the bag of food onto the dash and curl myself into a ball on Leon's passenger seat.

"I'm so sorry."

"Fuck." He scrubs his hand down his face, leaning his head back against the headrest as he stares out of the windshield.

I want to reach out and comfort him in some way. But his body is locked up tight with tension and I'm not sure if he'd accept it right now.

Leon is a totally different person to Luca, and what I know might work with Luc could be an entirely different story with Lee.

His chest heaves as his fingers curl into fists. I just sit there awkwardly not knowing what to do for the best.

If I were wearing my own clothes, I might have offered to leave by now sensing that what he really needs is to be alone but selfishly, I continue to sit there in the hope he comes back to me.

"H-how old was she, Peyton?"

"Seventeen. She was a few weeks off—"

"Motherfucker," he booms out of nowhere making a startled little scream rip from my lips. Slamming his palms down on the wheel so hard it makes the entire car shake. "Fucking, motherfucking. Fuck. Fuck. Fuck."

His face turns red with anger as he takes it out on his car, spittle flying from his lips with every word that rips from his throat.

"Leon," I whisper, needing to break him out of the trance he seems to have lost himself in.

Resting his forearms on the wheel he drops his head to them and sucks in a deep, calming breath.

"I'm sorry." When he finally looks at me, the pain in his eyes makes me gasp. Unable to stop myself, I reach out and plant my hand on his exposed forearm in the hope the contact helps even a little bit.

"Hey, it's okay. I get it, trust me."

"Fuck, Peyton. That's what you told him?"

I nod, the lump in my throat from the look on his face too huge to talk around.

"And he called you a liar. All this time he's been walking around thinking you lied about... about that."

Again, all I do is nod.

"Fucking asshole. What happ— He could—" He sucks in a breath and looks away once more. "Fuck, Peyton. I don't even know where to start."

"I-it's okay. How about I just talk and hopefully it'll answer some of your questions."

He nods, sitting back in his seat and fixing his eyes on something in the distance.

I tell him about Mom making us leave, about getting us away from both Brett and the drama it would ultimately cause. Especially when she started showing and people began asking questions.

"Libby's pregnancy was awful," I confess. "You know what she was like. She was wild, always doing the opposite of what anyone said. Add some hormones into that mix and it was just horrendous. She wanted to be back in Rosewood. She was naïve enough to think that Brett would want to see her, would want to know about the baby. I have no idea if she ever managed to slip out of Mom's grip and get back to see him. As far as I'm aware, they had no contact since the moment we left, but this is Libby we're talking about."

Some kind of snort comes from the back of his throat telling me that he remembers all too well.

"Anyway, she had a little boy."

He gasps as if hearing that really makes it true.

"Kayden." He scrubs his hand down his face, his eyes closed for the longest time. "He's the most perfect thing, Lee. He was the best baby. Which was a good thing really seeing as Libby bailed a few months after he was born."

"She what?" he barks.

I shrug. "She was a mess. Her mental health was bad, really bad. She was already drinking and smoking weed then one day I found her with a line of coke. Two weeks after that, she was gone. No note, no goodbye, no anything. She just disappeared leaving me and Mom with Kayden."

"Jesus, Peyton."

"Where is she now?"

"Your guess is as good as mine. I don't even know if she's aware Mom died," I admit with a heavy heart. "I tried to find her. I did everything I could but... nothing. I don't even know if she's still alive. I can only assume she is."

"I'm so fucking sorry, Peyton."

"It is what it is. Too late to change any of it now.

"Mom brought Kayden up as if he was hers and between us, we just managed. When I was at school she'd look after him and when I was home, she would work. We figured it out."

"Why did she run? My dad's worth... a lot. I don't even know. She could have taken him for a fortune."

"She could. But if she did that, if she put it through the courts then it would drag it all back up for Libby, it would put all of us in the spotlight. Her priority was us and making sure Kayden was okay."

"I get that. But what if—"

"He did it to other girls? I know, Lee. I've battled with this for years. Mom and I argued over it regularly. I understand her need to protect me, Libby, Kayden, you three even, your Mom. But I never totally understood how she could walk away knowing that it could happen again."

"I didn't think it was possible for me to hate him any more," Leon mutters quietly.

"I'm sorry."

"I can't believe Luc didn't trust you."

"He didn't want to. I understand that. He didn't want to believe that your dad could do that. It was easier for him to call me a liar and to think it was all fake."

"Does he know it's true yet?"

Leon's immediate acceptance of my words, his trust in me, doesn't go unnoticed. It's exactly what I wished Luca did all those years ago.

"He invited himself to my birthday party yesterday and came face to face with Kayden."

"Fuuuck."

"Yeah. It was a disaster."

Silence settles between us, but while it's full of tension and anger, it's not uncomfortable.

"You want to meet him?" I ask eventually.

He turns to me, sheer panic written all over his face.

"You can say no. I just thought you might want to..." I trail off.

"Does he know... about us? About who his dad is?"

"Yeah, well... to a point. We never lied to him. He knows he has three brothers but he doesn't know who your dad is. He loves that he's got older brothers and is desperate to meet you. Apparently, I'm only so much fun because I'm a girl."

Leon laughs. Seeing a smile on his face melts my heart a little. "Well, yeah. I can understand that."

"Hey," I complain.

"I... I think I need to meet him," he confesses nervously.

"Okay."

"I need..." He blows out a long pained breath. So many things go unspoken in those few seconds as he tries to find his words. The pain that's oozing from him is palpable and I have to fight not to just pull him into my arms and hold him, to tell him that everything is going to be okay. But also, I think doing just that might freak him out even more.

He's clearly fighting some internal battle and I can't help but worry that my confession has triggered him somehow.

The Leon I'm looking at right now is different from the one who caught me before I hit the floor outside of Luca's room only an hour ago.

"I think I need to see that something good came out of all of this."

I nod, totally understanding that.

After giving him the directions to Aunt Fee's house, we both buckle back up and head that way, our breakfast—or lunch—long forgotten. Not that I'd be able to even eat it now with the way my stomach is churning.

"Before we go in there, I need to tell you something else," I confess.

"Fucking hell, Peyton," he groans, sounding like he's at his wit's end when it comes to secrets and shocking announcements.

"Kayden was in the car crash that killed my mom."

He turns to me so fast that I'm surprised he doesn't pull something. The speed of his reaction warms me from the inside out. He's not even met Kayden yet and he's already protective.

He's already proving what I've always known. The Dunn boys are going to be incredible big brothers to that little boy in there.

"Is he... Is he okay?"

"He will be. He's on the way to making a full recovery. But he's in a wheelchair right now."

"Fuck," Leon breathes.

"He broke both his legs, his pelvis. He's had a couple of surgeries to pin everything into place. Everything is looking as it should but it takes time, you know. He might never make the NFL like his big brothers, but it shouldn't limit him too much."

"Jesus fucking Christ."

"He's strong, Lee. So fucking strong. Brett doesn't deserve him."

"That cunt doesn't deserve anything fucking good in his life."

Knowing the only thing I can say to that is to agree, I push the car door open and climb out.

Nervous energy radiates from Leon as I pull my key from my purse and slide it into the lock. The second I push the door open, footsteps race toward us.

"There you are. Do you know where my son— Oh, Leon? Hi," Aunt Fee squeaks, changing her tone mid-rant.

"Uh... h-hi," Leon stutters, his brows pulling together as he tries to figure out how this woman knows him when he has no idea who she is, no doubt.

"Leon, this is my aunt Fee, she was my mom's best friend and she agreed to take us in after the accident. She's seen enough photos over the years to know who you are," I add lightly.

"Okay. Nice to meet you," he says politely, turning his megawatt smile on her.

Embarrassingly, Aunt Fee blushes.

"I have no idea where Elijah is," I say as she opens the door wider for us both to enter. "Last time I saw him he was.... You probably don't want the details," I say, thinking about him with his tongue down Ella's throat.

"Like father like son that one. Maybe one day he'll find a woman to nail his ass down. What happened to you? No offense, sweetie, but you look like hell."

"Luca happened."

"Ah, so my son wasn't the only one up to no good last night."

"Something like that. Anyway, Leon agreed to bring me home. I've told him everything Luca's failed to and he'd like to meet Kayden."

"Of course. He's watching TV, why don't you go on through and I'll put the coffee maker on."

She smiles at both of us, her gaze lingering on Leon a little longer than necessary as if she's trying to work out what his intentions are here but she obviously likes what she finds because she lets us move through to the living room.

"Hey, baby boy," I say when I find Kayden watching cartoons with his beloved stuffed lamb tightly in his grip.

"Hey." His eyes widen when he looks at me. Christ, I must really look a mess if I'm being judged by a five-year-old. "I've brought someone to meet you."

I stand aside and allow Kayden to see Leon standing behind me.

Kayden's eyes light up, although I can see a little hesitation there. After all, he thought he was getting his chance with Luca yesterday and I made him leave.

"H-hi," he says nervously. His eyes flicking from Leon to me, probably worried that I'm going to freak out again.

"Kayden, this is Leon. Your—"

"Brother," Kayden finishes for me.

"Hey, lil' man. What are you watching?" Leon asks, walking farther into the room as if they've met a million times before.

I stand leaning against the doorway as Kayden begins an in-depth rundown about the PJ Masks episode he's watching and who everyone is.

"That's a fine sight right there," Aunt Fee says as she stands beside me.

"Kayden deserves this."

"Girl, they all deserve this."

I nod, a lump clogging my throat and tears burning the back of my eyes as I watch the two of them together.

I did the right thing today. Getting this time with Leon will mean everything to Kayden.

I stand there for the longest time cradling the mug Aunt Fee passes me in my hands just watching them.

I have no idea how much time passes but after a while, my skin begins to tingle with awareness. It's a reaction I only get when one person is close.

Glancing away from Kayden and Leon, I look out the window. My breath catches as my eyes lock onto a very angry green pair standing out in front of the house.

7

LUCA

The farther I ran, the more clarity I found and the more I realized that I fucked up this morning.

Fuck, not just this morning. I've been fucking up for the last five years.

Ever since my first reaction to her telling me what my dad had done was to call her a liar.

Seeing her dancing with Leon last night lit a fuse that I had no control over.

Flashbacks of him with Letty played out in my mind and I knew I couldn't deal with that again.

Letty was one thing, but Peyton. My Peyton.

Hell. No. Leon wasn't going anywhere near her.

Knowing this morning that by kicking her out of my room I forced her straight into his arms once more was more than I could handle.

With her scent still clinging to my skin, I threw some joggers and a shirt on and I just started running.

I didn't have a destination in mind, but I soon realized that my subconscious had a plan as I got closer and closer to her house.

I thought that maybe by the time I got there, I'd have managed to clear my head and actually knock on the door and have something resembling a sensible conversation. Only, when I came to a stop out in front of the house, the first thing I saw was him.

My twin brother was exactly where I should have been.

I didn't want them to see me but I was powerless to do anything but to stand frozen right in the middle of the front yard, and watch as Leon introduced himself to our... our little brother and sitting beside him, chatting away as if they've known each other forever.

And Peyton, she just stood there staring at the two of them like they were the best people in the entire world.

My heart shattered in my chest as I vividly remember her looking at me exactly like that. Like I had literally just hung the moon in the sky just for her.

My chest heaves as I try to keep control of my breathing as I continue watching them.

My head screams to move, to stop torturing myself more than I already have. But my body... that refuses to cooperate. And that's why, when Peyton does finally look up, she finds me standing there like some kind of stalker watching her every move.

All the air rushes from my lungs the second her eyes find mine.

"Shit," I hiss through clenched teeth.

She says something and looks away for a second. It's my chance to escape, to run and pretend it didn't happen but still, my body remains frozen to the spot as Leon stands and looks at me through the window.

I can sense his anger, his frustration and confusion over all of this even with the distance between us. But he's in there. He's accepted her words for what they are—the truth—and he's being the friend, the brother, the person she expects. Hell, no, it's more than that. He's being the person she needs and it fucking rips me apart that he's taking my place.

I'm still having a silent argument with Leon when she opens the front door.

"Luc?"

Her soft voice sends chills down my spine and when I turn to look at her, the only thing I feel is the ache in my chest.

She's still wearing my jersey, my number. It should mean

something. But while she's in there with him, it means nothing. It's just a shirt because she's made her choice. It's why she's with him.

It's my fault. I'm fully aware of that, but it doesn't make it hurt any less.

"You look like the perfect little family," I spit, unable to keep the venom inside.

She rears back like I just slapped her, her arms crossing over her chest.

"What do you want, Luc?"

A shadow falls over her and when I look behind her, Leon steps up, his face set in a stone mask as if he's ready to fight this out again if need be.

I shake my head, a bitter laugh falling from my lips.

"It doesn't matter. It seems he's already slotted in and taken my place," I spit.

"There's no place to take, Luca. You're not a part of my life anymore. You made that decision for the both of us. So, unless you actually want something, you need to leave. None of us want you here."

Her words cut, but I know they're exactly what I deserve.

Ripping her eyes from mine, she turns to Leon, looking up at him like he's someone special.

My fists curl and I take a step forward but the second Leon looks at me, I stop.

The darkness in his eyes, the coldness in his green orbs rocks me to my core.

What the hell?

Before I get to do anything, say anything, I'm forced to watch as Peyton wraps her hand around his upper arm and all but pulls him inside.

Neither of them look back at me, they just dismiss me as if I'm nothing. No one. Insignificant.

It fucking hurts.

Spinning around, my fist finds the trunk of the tree at the end of the yard as an incensed roar rips from my throat and echoes down the deserted street.

Hanging my head, I take a second to revel in the pain that shoots up my arm from the hit, focusing on that instead of the agonizing ache in my chest.

I don't want to do it, but it seems my need to torture myself knows no bounds because before I walk away from the house, leaving Leon inside with my girl, I look back.

Neither of them are there but the older lady from the day before is. She stands in the doorway with her brows drawn together in concern.

Her lips part to say something but she quickly closes them again when I shake my head.

My body aches with exhaustion as I turn away from her worried stare and make my way down the street.

I barely slept last night. After she threw up in her sleep, I was too worried that she might do it again. Well, that's what I told myself. The reality was that I couldn't bear not to make the most of her sleeping beside me.

Just like last weekend in the pool house, I sat beside her and watched her every move. I studied every inch of her, once again noting the differences from the girl I used to know to the woman she's become. Not that any of those differences matter because I didn't fall in love with what's on the outside—although she is beautiful—what I really fell in love with was the girl on the inside. Her soul. And despite all the bullshit, deep down, I know she's still the same person.

Why couldn't I have just believed her that day? Why did my stupid loyalties have to lie with my cunt of a sperm donor instead of the girl who'd proved time and time again that she would do anything for me?

What the hell is wrong with me that I would spend the last five years convincing myself that I was right, that I did the best thing. That protecting my family—my father—was the right thing to do.

Deep down, I think I knew. But I refused to accept it.

I wanted to believe that there was something redeemable about my father. That the controlling, forceful man that I see, the one who will literally steamroll his way through anyone to get what he wants isn't all he appears to be. I wanted to believe that he wouldn't do something so... something so treacherous, that he would cheat on his entire family. And not just with some random ex-jersey chaser that we all knew followed him around like lost puppies, but a kid. Not just any kid, but Peyton's sister.

My stomach turns over at the thought of him going after her and I heave into the flowerbed beside me, bringing up what little is left over from last night.

My stomach convulses trying to expel the disgust that's rolling through me.

I have no idea what's going to happen next with Peyton. My chest aches knowing that she has every right never to forgive me for not only turning my back on her five years ago, for calling her a liar, but for the past two weeks.

I've been... I've been just like my father.

I heave once more. My throat burns as nothing but bile comes up.

A sob rips up my throat as the reality of the situation slams into me like a truck.

The way I've treated her, the things I've said, the things I've implied.

I'm him.

I get no clarity with that realization. If anything the dark cloud that has already engulfed me only gets darker.

I move, although I don't realize it, and I don't come to a stop until I'm somewhere I know I can make it all go away.

There are a couple of cars here already, so I take that as my invite inside and push through the main door.

The bar is deserted and thankfully, the lighting is low as if it's evening. The only main difference, aside from the lack of scumbags is that it smells like cleaning products, not alcohol and sex.

With no one behind the bar, I invite myself behind it and reach for one of the expensive bottles of whisky that Dad keeps on the top shelf to show off.

Cunt.

Twisting the cap, I throw it across the deserted bar and listen as it clatters against whatever it hits and finally bounces to a stop on the polished concrete floor.

I take myself to the booth in the shadows where I watched Peyton on her shift Sunday when those men stripped her bare with their eyes all night.

They're not here, yet my fist curls as I picture slamming it into each of their noses.

I'm almost halfway down the bottle before a door slams and footsteps echo across the room.

"Hello?" a familiar voice calls, clearly sensing that there's someone here. "We're not open yet."

"Don't need you to be open. Actually, I prefer it not to be."

"Luca? Fucking hell, man," he says, coming closer and finally finding me cloaked in darkness.

I tilt the bottle in his direction before lifting it to my lips once again.

"Where'd you—" He looks over his shoulder at the bar and stops mid-question, I assumed at finding the empty spot on the shelf. "Right."

He exhales in frustration before sliding into the booth in front of me.

"What the hell is going on, Luc?" He rests forward on his elbows and levels me with a look that tells me I'm not getting out of this easily.

Bry and I aren't exactly friends. Or maybe we are, I have no idea. But since I convinced security to let me in here before I was officially allowed, we've hung out and chatted. I don't know all that much about him, but it's nice to have someone away from the team and the pressure of all of that.

"Sit there silently all you like, but I know this involves Peyton and you can bet your ass that I'm going to do whatever I can to protect her. Me and you might have known each other longer, but that girl needs as much support as she can get."

"Fucking hell, Bry. You don't need to guilt-trip me. I fucked up, I know I fucked up. Okay?"

"You're here getting drunk on a Sunday afternoon with whisky you've stolen from my bar dand not with her, apologizing for whatever it is you've fucked up, so no, it's not okay."

"Fair enough." I think for a minute. "Peyton and I, we go way back."

"Yeah, I got that. I'm also assuming that you were the one to screw it all up."

"Good to know where your allegiances lay, Bry."

"She's hurting, Luc. She's desperate. Why the hell do you think she's working in a place like this? She doesn't belong here and you know it."

"Fucking right, I do. And I need to get her the fuck away before she realizes who her boss really is." A shudder rips through me at the thought of her being anywhere near my dad. It was bad enough last week after he suddenly showed up in town. But now, now that I know the truth. I don't want her anywhere near him.

"Why, what—" I pin him with a look that shuts him the fuck up instantly. "Oookay. Look, she needs the money. You can't just get her the sack and think it'll make everything okay."

"I know. Why do you think she's still here?"

"She's back in tomorrow night, and your father has already been in this weekend. If you want her out and away from him, then you need to act fast, man."

I nod, appreciating that his loyalty seems to be first with Peyton, and then me over my cunt of a father.

"I know."

"And getting wasted here isn't going to help. Especially once Helena turns up and decides to make you her little toy tonight."

"I'm not fucking interested in her and you know it."

"I do, it won't stop her from trying though, will it? She wants her taste of Maddison King's royalty. And the more you turn her down, the more desperate she gets."

Don't I fucking know it. She's like a dog with a bone.

"You've got three hours before she starts her shift. Sit here and drown your miseries if you want but I want you out of here before she shows her face. You've caused enough shit for Peyton already." I hear his warning loud and clear. It doesn't stop me from reaching for the half-full bottle on the table before me though.

8

—

PEYTON

The sound of Leon's cell cuts through Kayden's sweet voice as he continues to talk his new brother's ear off.

I didn't expect Leon to hang around long but his eyes lit up when Aunt Fee offered to feed him and well... he's still here. From the wide smile on Kayden's face, I'd say Leon's extended visit has made his year.

"Sorry, lil' man. I need to get this."

Standing, Leon pulls his cell from his pocket and looks at the screen before shooting a concerned glance at me.

My heart rate picks up at the concern on his face

"Yeah?" he asks as I sit forward on the couch. "Yeah, okay. I'll come get him now. Later, Bry."

Bry?

Leon hangs up and closes his eyes for a beat.

"I'm sorry but I need to head out," he says, dropping down to his haunches in front of Kayden. "But I'll come and hang out with you again soon, yeah?"

Disappointment darkens Kayden's eyes but he keeps a smile on his face.

"Y-yeah."

"Good boy." Leon winks at him and ruffles up his hair before walking over to me.

"What's going on?" I whisper.

"Luca is wasted at The Locker Room and they're about to open. I need to go and get him."

"Jesus Christ."

"What are you doing?" he asks when I shove my cell into my back pocket and grab my jacket off the back of the couch.

"Coming with you."

"No, Peyton. You don't need to, not after—"

"I'm coming."

He holds his hands up in defeat and waits for me to tell Aunt Fee where we're going.

"You two really need to talk," Leon says once we're on our way across town.

"Yeah, I know. It's just easier said than done."

"Well, you need to try harder because at this rate, Luca's not going to have much left to salvage. He came in the other night stinking of weed. If Coach finds out then—"

"I know, Lee. I know."

He glances over at me but whatever words were on the tip of his tongue die the second his eyes lock with mine.

"I'm on your side here, Peyton. But I'm worried about him."

"Same. I'm worried about both of you. You might have been wearing a smile all afternoon, Lee, but don't think I can't see beneath that," I confess, referencing the dark clouds that have been in his eyes ever since my confession earlier.

"I'm fine. It was just a shock."

"Sure," I agree, knowing that he's not going to want to talk to me about whatever it is. It's not like we've ever been close. "But if you ever need to talk or whatever, I'm here. Okay. I'm not—I wasn't—just Luc's friend."

"I don't think that's a good idea. As far as he's concerned, we've already spent too much time together."

"Well, he can go fuck himself. We're allowed to be friends. What happened with Letty, it's not going to happen here."

"Not into the twin thing, huh?" he deadpans.

"Lee," I breathe.

"Sorry. It's just easier to joke sometimes, you know?"

"I do," I whisper as he pulls into the parking lot for The Locker Room.

"Ready to go and see what state your boy is in?"

His words make my chest ache. He's not mine anymore.

With a loud sigh, the two of us climb out of Leon's car and head toward the main door which security opens for us.

"Where is he?" Leon asks the second Bry looks up from his place behind the bar.

Bry nods to the back corner and when I turn around, all I can see is a pair of feet sticking out into the walkway between the booths.

"Fucking hell. We'll get him out of your way."

I march over with Leon hot on my tail.

We find Luca passed out on the bench seat and still holding an empty bottle of whisky.

"You two really need to hash this out. He can't keep this shit up," Leon mutters, plucking the bottle from his brother's hand before pulling him so he's sitting up.

"Luca, asshole," he shouts, slapping his face with a little more force than probably necessary. "Luca, wake the fuck up. I ain't carrying your drunk ass all the way to the car."

Luca groans, his head rolling and his eyes remaining tightly shut.

"Grab an arm, I'll get the other. It's not that far."

Leon looks at me with wide eyes. "What? I'm stronger than I look."

"If you say so," he mutters, pulling hard on Luca's arm until his ass leaves the bench and lifts him into his body.

Wrapping his arm around my shoulder, we set about maneuvering him toward the exit and into Leon's car.

"If you puke in here, you're paying for a full detail," Leon barks before closing the door on Luca.

He groans in response and that's the last we hear of him all the way home.

The second we have him inside the house, one of their friends that I recognize emerges and thankfully takes my place. I might be strong and able to move Kayden around with little effort, but Luca is another story.

I lead the way, opening his bedroom door so the guys can unceremoniously dump Luca onto his bed.

"Come on, P. I'll take you home."

I stare at Luca passed out and then back at Leon who's standing in the doorway.

He must be able to read my mind because his brows pull together and he shakes his head.

"No, Peyton. He doesn't deserve it."

"I-I know but—"

"You should leave him to suffer after the way he's treated you."

"I know what I should do, Leon," I snap, irritated by his judgmental tone. "But things aren't always that simple."

His brow lifts. "You really want to do this? Fine, be my guest but don't come crying to me when he kicks your ass to the curb again."

"It won't come to that, Lee. I'm just gonna make sure he doesn't choke on his own puke." *Just like he did for me last night.*

As vicious and evil as he's been to me, I still desperately want to believe that there's a good person under all that hate and frustration at the world.

Leon leaves, slamming the door behind him to ensure I know how he feels about my decision to stay.

I understand why he's pissed at me.

Hell, I know I'm crazy. But I can't help it.

I just can't walk away right now and leave him in that state. I'd rather stay and make sure he's okay than lie in bed at home worrying about him.

I know I shouldn't worry, but it's Luca. No matter how wicked he is, no matter what he says to me, what he accuses me of, he'll always be under my skin.

With a sigh, I walk toward his bed and lower down beside his feet that are sticking off the end of the mattress.

I pull his sneakers off, then his socks and with all my strength, I manage to roll him over.

"You don't make this easy, do you, Dunn?" I pant out as I try to straighten him up.

Popping the button on his jeans, I wrap my fingers around the waist and attempt to pull them down over his hips. Only, I don't get very far because the second I clear his ass, his hand shoots out and wraps around my wrist.

My heart jumps into my throat in shock.

"Shit, Luc. I—"

When I look up, he's staring right at me.

The mask I've been used to staring at during the past few weeks is gone. He looks just like he did the other night when he came to The Locker Room after seeing his dad.

Exhausted. Lost. Utterly broken.

He blinks as silent seconds pass. His fingers retain their tight grip on me, and I start to think that he's still asleep and has no idea what he's doing. But then he lifts his arm and tugs so hard that I have no choice but to fall into the bed and on top of him.

Before I have a chance to scramble off him, he rolls onto his side, taking me with him and locking his arm around my waist.

His nose nuzzles into my neck causing fire to shoot through my veins and goose bumps to prick my skin.

Damn it, body.

"Don't leave me, Peyton. Please. I-I need you."

The vulnerability in his voice makes my breath catch.

"Please," he whispers, making a shudder race down my spine.

Squeezing my eyes closed, I fight back any kind of reassurance that wants to fall from my lips. He doesn't deserve to hear those words from me, he doesn't deserve to hear that I'm here for him, that I'll support him in any way through whatever it is he's going through right now.

Having said that though, as I lie there in his arms and surrounded by his, albeit whisky-infused scent, I find my body getting heavy with my own exhaustion.

I tell myself I'll just give it ten minutes, let him fall back into a heavy sleep once more and then I'll slip out confident that he's okay. I can call an Uber and get home to do work on my assignment.

I awake with a start sometime later and attempt to sit up but the deadweight of Luca still pins me to the bed. Forcing my eyes open, I find the room in total darkness, my brows pull together, knowing that there was a light on when I fell onto the bed.

Not allowing myself to dwell on it, I twist around to look at Luca.

He's fast asleep. His dark lashes resting down on his cheekbones, his full lips parted and the lower half of his face covered in weeks worth of scruff, hiding what I know is a square jaw beneath.

His brow is furrowed even in his sleep, showing just how tormented he is with everything in his life right now.

Knowing I need to leave before he wakes up, I slip out from under his heavy arm and tiptoe across the room.

It's not until I'm at the door that he moves. I freeze, holding my breath as he rolls onto his front but thankfully, he doesn't wake up.

I manage to get out of the house unnoticed, ordering an Uber as I do so. I only loiter on the sidewalk for a couple of minutes before a car pulls up to take me home.

It's long past midnight when I let myself back into Aunt Fee's house. It's dark, so the last thing I expect when I step into the kitchen is for someone to speak.

"Bit early for the walk of shame, isn't it?"

My heart thunders in my chest as I turn to the dark figure leaning against the counter.

Slamming my hand on the switch, I turn the light on.

"Jesus, Elijah. What the hell?"

"Sorry," he mutters, lifting a glass to his lips.

"Well, it's good to see you're still alive," I scoff, pulling the refrigerator open.

"Could say the same thing about you."

"Yeah, how'd that 'I'll keep you safe' thing work out for you?"

"A blonde happened," he confesses with a shrug. Although to be fair, he does look a little regretful.

"Yeah, I saw. Everything you hoped she'd be?"

"You have no idea. Listen though," he says somewhat nervously, lifting his hand to the back of his neck. "I'm sorry I bailed on you. Mom ripped me a new one when I got back."

"It's fine, E. I don't need a babysitter."

"What happened with Luca?"

I sigh, mimicking his stance at the opposite counter. "I dunno. He's a mess. I got trashed. He took me home, took care of me... kind of."

"Mom said Leon came to meet Kayden."

I can't help the smile that curls at my lips as the memory of the two of them playing this afternoon fills my mind along with Kayden's smiling face.

"Yeah. I'm pretty sure it was the best day of Kayden's life."

"How'd Leon take the news? I'm assuming good, seeing as he spent most of the afternoon here."

"Yeah," I murmur. "I'm not entirely sure. I mean, he believed me, so that's a start. I guess only time will tell." I think of the darkness that surrounded him as I explained what his dad had been doing and concern races through me.

I've experienced Luca's darkness before, hell, I'm living it right now. But there was something about Leon in those few moments that was absolutely terrifying.

9

———

LUCA

My first thought when I wake is of her, having her pressed against me as I slept. But the second I try to pull her tighter against me, I realize that it was all a dream because what I'm holding to my body isn't her little, curvy hot one, but a pillow.

Goddammit.

Rolling onto my back, I throw my arm over my eyes and focus on my breathing in the hope it'll magically make my hangover abate.

Just thinking about the taste of whisky makes me want to puke.

Once I feel like my body is a little more under control, I push myself up so I'm leaning against the headboard and look around my room.

My dream of her felt so real, the scent of her that fills my nose is almost enough to convince me that I'm not totally crazy.

Glancing around the room, I search for any kind of sign that she was here, but I find nothing.

The last thing I remember was sitting in the booth at The Locker Room and feeling Bry's disapproving stare burning into my skin. I have no idea how I got back here. Leon, I assume. Did she go with him? But why would she? After the way I've treated her, she should leave me to drown in my own drunken stupidity.

Reaching down, I find my jeans undone and around my hips.

The image of her delicate fingers wrapped around the fabric as she tried to undress me hits me out of nowhere as I push my hand into my pocket searching for my cell.

It's not real. She wasn't here, I try to convince myself.

Not finding my cell, I finally drag my pathetic ass from the bed and start looking. I finally find it under my pillow, all the alarms I had set canceled.

"Fuck," I hiss, taking in the time. Not only have I missed my chance to hit up the gym, not that I'm sure I could cope with a workout right now, but I've missed my first class of the day.

I still feel like death when I get to campus a little over an hour later, now late for my second class. I really don't want to sit in class and attempt to focus on anything but I figure it might actually be better than sitting in my room and replaying my dream over and over and trying to convince myself that it was real, that she was there, that she does care.

The building is empty as I make my way to the elevator, the doors open the second I hit the button and I slip inside.

Resting back against the wall, I tip my head back and close my eyes, wishing that I hadn't bothered and just stayed in bed.

The doors are almost shut when they jolt and open again.

I just about manage to fight the groan of frustration that wants to rumble up my throat at someone encroaching on my peace, but when I look up and find a familiar face wearing a determined expression as she stares back at me, I know that turning up today was a massive mistake.

"Well, well, well, look who decided to show their face," Letty mutters, stepping inside and letting the doors close behind her.

"I could really do without the lecture, Let."

"Well, that's a real shame, Dunn, because you're about to get one."

I stare at her, unsure if I'm impressed or just downright terrified by her attitude.

"You've spent too much time with Legend," I mutter.

"He's got nothing to do with how I feel about you messing around with Peyton."

"You barely even know her, Let. And you certainly don't know the details of what happened between us."

"I might have only known her a couple of weeks, but that's enough to know which one of you is in the wrong here."

"Wow, your loyalty astounds me," I deadpan.

"When you deserve it, you can have it back," she quips.

My chin drops, but I don't have anything to say in response. So instead, I just shut the hell up and stare at the doors, praying they'll open any second.

The tension in the small space is oppressive, even worse than the last time we were in here together.

"Go on then, hit me with it," I say, figuring that I may as well get this over with.

But before Letty gets to say anything, there's a loud bang and then the elevator bounces to a stop.

"What the hell was that?" Letty asks, her eyes wide as she looks around.

Reaching forward, I press the button again for the floor we want but nothing happens.

"Shit," I hiss, pressing it over and over in the hope it does something.

"Looks like there's no escaping this now then, Luc."

"Did you plan this?" I bark, turning to look at her.

An incredulous laugh falls from her lips. "You think I planned for the elevator to break so you'd be forced to talk to me. Are you serious?"

Reaching up, I rub the back of my neck. When she puts it like that, the accusation does sound ridiculous.

"I had no idea you'd even be late to class," she says with a sigh. "Press the call button and tell someone we're stuck."

"Sure thing, boss," I deadpan, doing as I'm told and explaining what happened to the bored sounding guy at the other end.

"I guess we may as well get comfortable then." Letty takes her jacket off, folds it up and drops it to the floor before sitting on it. "You look like shit, by the way."

"Thanks," I mutter, sliding down the wall. "You look amazing," I confess, taking in her sparkling eyes and constant smile.

"Thanks."

"How come you're late? You sure don't look like you're fighting a hangover."

"Kane, he had this morning—"

"Enough said," I cut her off.

"Luca, at some point you need to accept that this is how it is now. Kane is part of my life, and he's also a part of yours."

"I've accepted it."

"Sure you have." She rolls her eyes at me. "I shouldn't have to tell you that relationships are way more complicated than they often look. Kane and I, we have a lot of history. Things have happened between us that no one knew for a long time."

I stare at her, wondering if she's talking about the same thing Leon alluded to the other day.

"Everything you know about our younger years is true. I thought moving to Rosewood would get me away from it all, give me a fresh start. And it did, for a while. But Harrow Creek is my home, it's where my dad is. I was—I am—always going to go back there." She holds my eyes and I sit forward a little, resting my elbows on my knees, ready to hear what she's got to say. "Almost two years ago, I went to a Creek party. It was my old best friend's birthday. I was told he wouldn't be there. But he was. One thing led to another and... well... he got me pregnant."

"Shit, Let."

"Yeah. Well, I went back to Columbia, found out, thought I could deal with it all myself. I didn't tell anyone, I even managed to hide it from my roommates. I stupidly thought it wouldn't change much." She shakes her head. "I was an idiot."

"What happened?" I ask, assuming that she's not hiding a baby somewhere.

"I lost it at twenty weeks."

"Holy shit." She stares at me, her eyes glassy with tears, her pain tangible.

"I couldn't cope. Bailed on classes, lost myself. I was a mess."

"That's why you came back," I breathe.

"Yep. It got to the point where I was either going to do something I wasn't going to come back from, or I pull up my big girl panties and confess the truth. I came home, Mom found me someone to talk to and I worked through it all and restarted my life."

I scrub my hand down my face. "Fucking hell, Letty."

"Kane didn't know. I had no idea he'd be here. He already hated me and blamed me for Riley's death. Then when I told him about our baby... well, he drove his car into a truck."

"Shit."

"Look, Luc. I'm not telling you this for sympathy. I've dealt with it all now... mostly. What I'm trying to say is that things aren't always as they seem, and just because you think one thing, it doesn't mean you can't overcome it, change. Love isn't always easy, or pretty. It can be hard, painful, messy... dirty. But let me tell you, when you figure it out, it's so fucking worth it."

"What are you really trying to say, Let?" I ask with a heavy heart.

"Peyton is... she's not a liar, Luc. I don't know the details but I truly believe that she loves you and that she never wanted to hurt you."

"I know," I confess, much to her shock.

"Y-you do?"

"Yeah, I was wrong. She never lied to me. I just didn't want to believe it. What she told me... I had no idea how to handle it, so I picked the easiest choice and turned on her."

"O-okay. So, now what?"

"It's not as simple as me being wrong. She might not have lied to me that day when we were kids, but she's kept some huge shit from me."

"Shit she'd have kept from you if you'd have believed her back then?"

"Well... no, but—"

"There you go then. You can't blame her for protecting herself."

"Shit," I breathe, falling back against that wall and letting my head slam against it.

"Nothing is unforgivable, Luc. You just need to pull your head out of your ass and decide what you really want."

I keep my eyes closed but I feel Letty's stare burning into my face.

"Despite all the bullshit and whatever might have happened in the past. What do you want?"

"Her." That single word falls from my lips before I've even had time to think about it.

"So start making it right. Quit with all this drunken, angry bullshit. Stop with all the fighting, the pity parties for one. She needs you, Luc. She needs you to be on her side, in her corner. I don't know the details, I know she's lost her mom and she's still grieving. I also know that's only the tip of the iceberg.

"You want her, you need to prove it. You need to be what she needs, what she doesn't even realize she needs."

Dragging my head from the wall, I rip my eyes open and stare at Letty.

"I'm sorry I never told you about her."

Getting up, she moves closer to me and threads her fingers through mine.

"I understand, Luc. I know things have been fucked up, for both of us. But I'm here. I'll always be here for you."

Wrapping my arm around her shoulder, I drop my lips to the top of her head as emotion clogs my throat.

"Me too, Let. I'm sorry for all the shit I pulled."

"Me too. I should have told you the truth sooner. I shouldn't have used you the way I did."

I hold her tighter as the tension drains from the space around us and the silence stretches out.

"My dad fucked her sister. I've got a little brother out of it."

Letty's body tenses at my words but she doesn't say anything, and I appreciate it.

"I hate my dad. You know that more than anyone. But I refused to believe that he could do that, that he could stoop so low as to cheat on my mother with a high school senior."

"Shit, Luc."

"She was a few weeks from being eighteen but I have no idea how long it was going on for. If she was the first, if she was the last."

Releasing her, I lean forward once more, bowing my head in shame.

"She tried to tell me. Can you even imagine how hard it must have been for her to say the words? And then I turned around and called her a liar and cut her out of my life. I fucked up so fucking bad."

Letty remains silent beside me, giving me all the answers I need.

"Are you really serious about walking away from the Panthers?" she asks after long, agonizing seconds. Her change of subject gives me whiplash.

My brows draw together in confusion but I quickly figure out that Leon must have told her.

Dropping my head into my hands, I give her the truth. It's the least I can do.

"I don't know. I don't know anything right now. My life feels like it's spiraling out of control."

"Have you spoken to your father?"

My fists curl at the mention of him. "Not since I learned all of this," I force out through clenched teeth. "I want to fucking kill him, Let."

She turns to me, resting her hand on my forearm. "Still enjoying football and wanting success doesn't make you your father. Pushing hard to get to the NFL, to have all the things he's wanted for you—that you want for yourself—doesn't make you him."

I shake my head, not finding any words to respond with.

"I hate your dad, Luc. I've hated him for years for the way he's treated both you and Leon. Shane too. He's an asshole. But football is who you are. I have no doubt that even if he hadn't pushed you, that you'd be exactly where you are now. It's in your blood, Luc. Following in that path—in his path—won't change anything, it won't make him stop being the prick he is, and it certainly won't rewrite the past.

"The only person you need to worry about when you're thinking about what comes next for you, is you." I glance up at her. "Okay, maybe Peyton too if you're going to make that right."

"I am."

"Okay then, so what do you want, Luc? Do you want everything you've worked so hard for? Do you want football, the NFL, or do you want to start over, find a new path for yourself?"

My lips part to respond but she cuts me off.

"You don't need to answer that now. You've got time to figure it all out. We all just want you to be happy, Luca. We don't care if you're the NFL's next star quarterback or if you work in Dunkin' Donuts. We just want you to be happy, to figure this stuff out because you're killing us with this right now." Her hand slides down to mine once more and she uncurls my fist. "I just want my old Luc back. And something tells me that Peyton probably feels the same."

"I don't know who he is anymore," I whisper.

Placing her hand over my heart, she stares into my eyes with her big dark ones. "He's right here, Luc. You'll find him again."

Emotion clogs my throat and tears burn the backs of my eyes. I want to be able to agree with her, but I fear the person both she and Peyton remember is gone.

Leaning back against the wall, I blow out a long breath.

"Only time will tell, I guess."

Crackling from the small speaker on the control panel distracts both of us.

"An engineer is on his way. Hold tight, it shouldn't be too long."

"Hold tight," I mutter after Letty has thanked him. "Is he having a laugh, we're stuck in a metal box."

Letty shakes her head at me, a smile playing on her lips before her expression turns serious once more.

"So, Peyton. I guess we need a plan."

I stare at her for a beat, my chest tightening.

"I love you, Let. You know that, right?"

"Of course I do. We just need Peyton to know the same thing."

———

Our class is over by the time we're finally freed from the elevator. Letty heads off because she's got work this evening. I decide that it's time to get my life in order, I continue down toward my missed class in the hope of catching the professor to find out what I missed. No matter what happens next, I need all the credits I can get, and failing my classes this semester isn't going to help with that.

I turn the corner toward the auditorium when I collide with someone.

"Shit, I'm— Peyton?" Placing my hands on her shoulders, I push her back slightly until I can see her face.

Tears cascade down her cheeks as she keeps her eyes on the floor.

"What's wrong, P?"

A sob rips up her throat at my question and I pull her into my arms, holding her tight as she falls apart.

10

PEYTON

My cell buzzes in my back pocket as I sit and listen to Professor Lincoln. My fingers itch to get it. No one ever calls me unless it's important.

My heart pounds as I think about something being wrong with Kayden. I don't remember seeing a doctor's appointment on the calendar for him this morning. Then again it's not like I've really been on top of things the past few weeks, I wouldn't be surprised if I've missed something.

Glancing at the clock, I notice there are only ten minutes until the end of class. I convince myself to wait. That it's probably only a sales call.

I tap my pen against my notebook as I count down the seconds as the hands on the clock continue to tick around. I totally miss whatever Professor Lincoln says as my panic begins to build. There's something in my gut telling me that whoever is calling, bears bad news.

The second the class draws to a close, I run out of the auditorium like my ass is on fire, pulling my cell from my back pocket as I go.

I find two missed calls from an out-of-state number I don't recognize and a voicemail.

I'm about to hit play on the voicemail when it rings again.

"H-hello?" I ask, my heart in my throat.

"Hello, is this Miss Banks?"

"Y-yeah. W-who's this?"

"My name is Dr. Willis from St. Thomas Hospital in Atlanta. I believe I've been treating your sister."

Oh my God.

I stumble back against the wall as if the rug has just been ripped out from beneath me.

"L-Liberty?"

"Yes."

"Is she okay?" I ask in a rush, but the knot in my stomach from the tone in the lady's voice on the other end already tells me that she's not.

"Your sister was brought in following a drug overdose, Miss Banks. I highly suggest you find a way to get here if you'd like to see her."

Tears spill from my eyes at her unspoken words.

"Sh-she's n-not going to m-make it?"

"Her condition is critical, Miss Banks."

"O-okay. I'll get there as soon as I can," I promise before hanging up, not able to hear anything else. I stare at my blank screen for a few seconds as I try to process what I just heard. But the only words that repeat over and over in my head are that my sister might possibly die.

A sob rips from my throat as I push from the wall and all but run down the hallway, needing to get home and find a way to get my ass to Atlanta.

I don't realize there's anyone in front of me until I slam into what feels like a brick wall.

"Shit, I'm— Peyton?"

A large, warm pair of hands land on my shoulders and moves me back before his stare burns into the top of my head.

I suck in a shaky breath, wondering why it had to be right now that I run into him.

"What's wrong, P?"

The genuine concern I hear in his voice forces a sob up my throat. In seconds, I'm gathered in his arms, my face pressed firmly against his chest as his scent fills my nose.

Unable to keep myself under control, I let it all out and cried into him for everything I've already lost and everything I could be about to lose.

I don't realize we've moved until he lifts me onto his lap.

Lifting my head from his chest, I look around and find that we're still in the hallway but sitting on the chairs a little further down from the auditorium I was just in. Thankfully, the entire hallway is empty. It's bad enough that Luca just witnessed my meltdown, I don't need anyone else to see the mess I've been reduced to.

"Tell me what's wrong, baby." His voice is soft, and for a few seconds I forget all about the past few weeks, the past few years. I want nothing more than to confide in him and allow him to do what he can to support me.

But that's not who we are now.

His giant hands engulf my face when he cups my cheeks and wipes away my tears with his thumbs.

"Talk to me," he breathes, his eyes begging me to open up.

"I-it's Libby. She's—" A sob cuts my words off, but I find some strength from him and suck in a deep breath. "She's in the hospital. I think... I think I'm going to lose her, too."

"Shit." He pulls me into him once again but this time, I refuse to fall apart.

I can't because I need to get to Libby. I need to be there for her no matter what happens. I need her to know that she's not alone. That no matter what has happened in the past, I'll always be there.

I fight to get out of his hold and stand on weak legs.

"What are you doing?" he asks, taking in the determined look on my face.

"I need to figure out a way to get to Atlanta."

"Okay, let's go."

"W-what?"

Pushing from the chair, he stands before me, taking both of my hands in his despite the fact I try to fight him.

"We're going to Atlanta."

"No, Luc. You can't—"

"Watch me." Closing the space between us, he once again cups my cheek. "Let me be what you need, Peyton."

I open my mouth to tell him that what I need is for him to leave. But I can't force the words out because as much as I might not want him to be here with me right now, I also don't want to be alone.

Wrapping his arm around my waist, he guides me out of the building, successfully ignoring everyone who tried to engage him in conversation. It's the first time I've been around him on campus and it's my first insight into just how much of a celebrity he is.

I remember what it was like in high school always being in his shadow while he ruled the school, but here it's on an entirely different level. It is literally like he's God. I can understand why the pressure might be getting to him, especially after a less than successful season.

"In you go." I don't realize that we've made it to the parking lot until his words make me look up and I find his Audi in front of me.

"Uh... I have my own car. You don't need—"

"I said, get in."

He closes the space between us as if he's about to throw me inside if I don't do as he said.

"Luc, you don't need—"

"Let me do this, P. Please." His eyes plead with me, and as much as I want to say no, I know I'm not in any place right now to drive myself.

"But my car—"

"I'll get Leon and the guys to sort it out."

I nod, already too exhausted and too focused on just getting to Atlanta to care. I fold myself into the passenger seat and allow him to close the door behind me.

I watch him, feeling completely numb as he pulls his cell out and taps away on the screen for a few minutes.

I wait with my heart in my throat and my impatience growing with every second that passes.

By the time he pulls the door open, I've totally spaced out.

"There's a flight from Orlando in two hours. I managed to get us seats."

My eyes remain locked on a trash can across the parking lot, his words not really registering.

"Peyton," he says softly, reaching over and holding my hand that's resting on my lap. "Did you hear me? We're flying to Atlanta in two hours."

In a daze, I turn to him.

"T-two hours?"

"Yeah. I've booked us seats."

"You've booked... Wait, you're coming to Atlanta?"

He threads his fingers through mine and gently pulls me over the center console so he can press his lips to my forehead.

"Yeah, baby. I'm not letting you do this alone."

I nod, unable to find any words.

After another second, he releases me and starts the engine.

We're outside Aunt Fee's house in only minutes. Luca pulls up out front but hesitates to kill the engine.

Glancing over at him, I find his brow furrowed as he stares at the house.

"Kayden isn't home," I say, knowing that he's at kindergarten this afternoon. "Aunt Fee is though," I add, seeing as her car is in the driveway.

Hitting a button on the dash, the car shuts off and he throws his door open.

"This isn't about me," he mutters as he climbs out.

He opens my door before I've managed to gather my things and he reaches in for my purse.

"Come on. We don't have much time."

"Okay."

With his hand in the small of my back, he guides me toward the house.

"Peyton, you're home ear—" Aunt Fee's words are cut off when her eyes find Luca standing behind me but they quickly return to me. "What's wrong?"

"It's Libby. She's in a hospital in Atlanta."

"Oh my God, why? What's she done?"

"OD'd."

"Shit."

"I'm taking her to Atlanta. We've got a flight booked and leaving in two hours."

"Y-you are?" Aunt Fee asks, concern covering her face.

"Yeah," I say.

She looks between the two of us, obviously biting back what she really wants to say.

"Why don't you go and pack a bag?" Luca suggests, breaking the awkward tension that crackles around us.

Nodding, I bolt toward the stairs, more than ready to get to the airport so I can at least feel like I'm getting closer to her.

I hear Aunt Fee's soft voice behind me, but I don't hang around to hear whatever she might have to say to Luca. Right now, I don't care. I just want to get to my sister.

I'm shoving some leggings into my overnight bag when a shadow falls over me.

Glancing over my shoulder, I find Aunt Fee watching me with her arms folded across her chest.

"Do you think this is a good idea?"

"Right now, I really don't care. I just need to get there."

"But—"

"I know, Aunt Fee. Trust me, I know. But my priority right now is Libby and I'll take all the help I can get."

She stares at me, disapproval shining bright in her eyes.

"I'm not just going to forgive him because he's booked me a flight. It's going to take more than that."

From the way her brow lifts, I'm not entirely sure she believes me.

"She needs me, Aunt Fee. If she makes it through this, maybe it'll be the wake up call she needs."

Aunt Fee lets out a loud exhale. I know what she's thinking, and maybe she's right. Maybe Libby is a lost cause, but I refuse to give up hope on her. Kayden needs her. I need her. Addicts recover all the time, I can't lose hope that she could be one of them who does. I've already lost too much. I have to believe that there is a chance.

"You need to be careful," she warns. "I know you still love him, but you can't—"

"Is everything okay?" Luca's booming voice cuts through Aunt Fee's warning as he comes to stand behind her.

"Y-yeah. Aunt Fee's just reminding me that I hate you." Folding

Elijah's hoodie and placing it at the top of my bag, I throw it over my shoulder. "Let's go."

I push past both of them, already fed up with their meddling in my life.

Luca's fingers wrap around the strap of the bag over my shoulder and when he lifts it, I allow him to take it.

"I'll call you when I know something," I tell Aunt Fee as they both follow me down the stairs.

"Okay. Give her my love."

"Let's just hope I can, huh?"

"Shit, Peyton." She grabs my forearm and I spin around to her.

The tears shining in her eyes don't help me with my quest to keep it together.

"I'm okay. It's going to be okay."

She pulls me into her arms and holds me tight for two seconds before she releases me and pins Luca with a fierce look that I'm not used to seeing on her.

"You hurt her again and your life won't be worth living. I own a gun and my late husband ensured I knew how to use it."

If the situation weren't so dire, I might laugh at the look on Luca's face as all the blood drains out of it.

"She's joking. Let's go."

"Am I? I wouldn't want to test it if I were you, Dunn," she warns.

"Jesus. Come on."

"Call me as soon as you can."

I agree as I race down toward Luca's car. I don't bother to wait for him to open the door for me this time, I just impatiently drop into the passenger seat as he throws my bag in the trunk.

Aunt Fee watches us from the doorway with her brows pulled together in concern. I understand. I don't particularly want to fly to Atlanta with Luca but if it gets me there faster and safer, then I'm all for it right now.

"We'll swing by my place so I can grab some stuff and then we'll head to the airport."

"Okay," I say, strapping myself in and keeping my eyes looking out of the window.

"I just want to help, Peyton," he says after I ignore him for quite some time.

"I know," I say coolly. I might appreciate what he's doing for me right now. But that doesn't mean I'm going to give him a free pass after all the shit he's pulled.

One good deed isn't going to make me forget about all the pain he's caused me. How he's treated Leon lately.

"I'll wait here," I say when he pulls up outside of his house.

His chin drops as if he's about to argue. He must think better of it as he closes it again, nodding his head and climbing from the car.

I watch him as he makes his way toward the house. I take in his confident swagger, my eyes dropping down his body to focus on his ass.

I'm so lost in my thoughts that I don't notice him turning back to look at me until it's way too late.

His smirk when I look up at his face tells me that he caught me red-handed.

Rolling my eyes at him, I drag my gaze away and curl up into a ball on his passenger seat, wishing that I was already on my way to Atlanta, even if it meant driving. I can't cope with sitting still right now knowing that Libby is fighting for her life in a hospital bed.

My sister isn't the kind of person to just give up. She's stronger than that. Or at least... she was. I haven't known her since she was eighteen, hell probably a few years before that if I'm really being honest with myself.

She fell in with the wrong crowd at an early age. Although Mom refused to accept it, I fear she was using alcohol and drugs a lot earlier than we were even aware of.

I drum my fingers against my thigh, nervous energy racing through me.

I almost get out so I can start pacing to get rid of it, but I want to be ready to go the second Luca emerges.

The front door opens two seconds later, and my heart jumps into my throat but when someone emerges, it's not the twin I'm waiting for.

Leon runs down toward the car and I lower the window.

"Are you okay?" he asks in a rush the second he gets to me.

I shrug because I really have no idea what I am right now. Impatient. Terrified. Totally fucking lost.

"Are you sure this is a good idea, letting Luc take you?"

"I don't know, Lee. But I don't care right now. I just need to get there."

"I can take you."

I shake my head, knowing that even suggesting it to Luc would turn this shit show of a day into a complete fucking disaster.

"No, it's fine. Luc wants to do this and I'm happy to let him."

"But—"

"It's fine, Lee. I promise you that I'm not going to forgive him just because he got me a plane ticket."

"That's not what I'm worried about."

"I'm a big girl, Lee. I can look after myself. But right now, I need to be with her."

"Okay, I know." He reaches into the car and takes my hand. "Everything is going to be okay."

I try to swallow around the lump in my throat that tells me everything is very much not going to be okay and instead nod at him.

"If you need anything, you call me, yeah? I'll make sure that Kayden and Fee are okay without you. But I'm here okay. We're family now, Peyton. We take care of our own."

The tears that were burning my eyes threaten to spill over.

"Th-thank you, Lee. You're a good friend."

His lips part to say more but a door slamming behind him stops him. Luca's footsteps race toward us before the trunk pops open.

"Do I need to remind you again to keep your hands off my girl?" Luca growls at his brother.

"Fuck off, Luc." Lee's concerned eyes find mine once more. "Are you really sure? My car is right there and it's faster than his. We could totally outrun him."

I can't help but laugh at the serious expression on his face. It feels good to smile.

"I'll be fine. I really appreciate the offer though. We'll call you with news, okay?"

He nods at me as Luca drops into the driver's seat.

"You," Lee spits, his expression instantly morphing into something most people would be scared of. "If you so much as lay a finger on her, I'll drive to Atlanta and kick your fucking ass."

"Whatever," Luca mutters, totally unfazed by his brother's warning.

The car rumbles to life beneath us and Lee has no choice but to pull his head from the car when Luca puts the window up on him.

'Call me if you need me,' he mouths at me.

I nod once more before Luca floors the accelerator, sending me flying back into the seat.

"Jesus, a little warning would be nice."

"I don't like him touching you," Luca grits out.

"Fuck off, Luc. He's your brother. My friend."

"I don't care. You're mine."

I scoff. "I haven't been yours for years. It's time you got with the fucking program, Luc. There is no us. And you only have yourself to blame for that."

"I know who is at fault here, Peyton. You really don't need to rub it in my face."

"Really?" I ask, a bitter laugh falling from my lips. "I think you deserve everything I can throw at you. You called me a liar, Luc. After all our years together, everything we'd shared and experienced together. You threw all of that away because of him. Because of a sick fuck who can't keep his..." My words trail off knowing that saying them out loud won't help either of us.

"Don't." he spits.

Folding my arms across my chest, I once again focus my stare out of the window as he flies down Main Street toward the highway that will take us toward the airport.

"Why are you doing this?" I ask after a long silence.

"Because you shouldn't do it alone."

"Leon offered to take your place," I confess.

"Motherfucker." Luca's palm slams down on the wheel.

"I thought about taking him up on his offer. Getting out of your car, climbing into his and turning my back on you. I probably should have done that."

His teeth grind and his jaw pops at my words.

"When I told him everything yesterday, do you know what he said?"

Luca's grip on the wheel tightens, his knuckles turning white with his grip.

"He believed me, Luc. No question."

"Of course he fucking did," he mutters.

I let his words ring around us for a few more minutes as the airport becomes visible on the horizon.

"It ripped him apart, Luc. The look on his face. It took him to a bad place. I don't know what it was, but I'm worried about him."

He lets out a long sigh. "Leon's... complicated."

"That makes both of you. Is it a twin thing or is Shane hard work too?"

"It's a Dunn thing," he deadpans. "We're all related to that cunt. What do you expect?"

I don't answer that because there really is no response needed.

"Leon's... I don't know," he says, scrubbing his hand down his face. "He's hiding some shit. Has been for years. I don't fucking know what it is. I don't think anyone does."

"Shit. You think it has something to do with your dad?"

"I'd put fucking money on him being involved somehow. Long stay?" he asks, his sudden change of subject damn near giving me whiplash.

"Uh..." The sudden realization that I have no idea how long we could be about to leave town for hits me. "You really don't need to do this, Luc. You should be here, living your life not putting it on hold because my sis—" A sob rips up my throat, cutting off my words.

Reaching over, his hot palm squeezes my thigh.

"I wouldn't be anywhere else, P. We do this together, okay? Let me... Let me help you."

I nod, unable to do anything else. I might be conflicted as to whether this is the right thing to do or not. But right now I can't imagine demanding that he's wrong and that I need to do this alone.

"Okay, let's do this."

Luca pulls into the long-term parking lot and after finding a space, we both climb out.

I focus on my breathing as I stand beside his car while he grabs our bags.

I've spent years wishing I could see Libby again. I prayed that she'd found some peace, made herself a new life and was doing okay. I had to, the alternative was too painful to even think about. Luca might have been my ride or die until shit went south, but the relationship I had with Libby was a close second to that.

We fought, of course we did. We're sisters. But she wasn't just my sister, just like our mom wasn't just our mom. The three of us were a team. A unit. And in the blink of an eye, it became just me.

Reaching up, I wipe my tears away with the back of my hand.

With both our bags in one hand, Luca wraps his arm around me. His hand clamping down tightly on my waist as he pulls me into his body. His warmth, his scent, just his presence, calms me. Gives me strength, and I'll take every ounce I can get right now if I'm potentially heading toward a hospital to say goodbye to someone else I love.

"You've got this, baby. And I'm right here. I won't let you fall."

I manage to swallow down my sob this time as his lips press against the top of my head.

Sucking in a deep breath that's tainted with his scent, I pull up my big girl panties and take a step forward.

No matter how badly this is ripping me up inside, Libby needs me. No matter what happens next, she needs me by her side.

11

LUCA

I glance over at Peyton as she sits nervously chewing on her nails. Reaching over, I wrap my fingers around her wrist and pull her hand away from her mouth.

"Hey," she complains.

"You hate it when you bite your nails," I point out, much to her irritation.

As a kid, she tried all the tricks to make her stop doing it. It wasn't until our relationship started to change that she somehow managed to kick the habit. I like to think that even as a teenager, I was just that good at getting her out of her own head, but it was probably just a coincidence.

"Ugh, why do you have to remember shit," she complains with a huff.

"P," I breathe, reaching for her hand that she was just gnawing on. "I remember everything." Lifting her hand to my lips, I kiss her knuckles.

"Being all sweet and supportive is going to get you nowhere, Dunn."

"I-I'm not trying to get anywhere, P. I'm just trying to be here for you. Like I should be."

"The verdict is still out on that."

"Leon wouldn't have stopped you biting your nails," I point out, ignoring the wave of jealousy that surges through me as I think about him trying to convince Peyton to let him escort her to Atlanta.

I have no idea what the fuck he's thinking but when I get back, we need to have it out. All this shit needs to stop.

Her lips part to argue but we both know that he wouldn't have. He wouldn't have known.

"I never forgot anything about you, about us. I need you to know that, P. You might have left town. I might have been furious. But you've always been under my skin."

"You clearly forgot me while you were getting busy with all the jersey chasers."

I stare at her, unable to stop the smirk that twitches at my lips.

"You been stalking me, baby?"

"N-no, I—" She blows out a frustrated breath. "Okay, fine. I might have looked at your Insta every now and then."

I stare at her, lifting my brows for her to tell the truth.

"Fine. Daily. Okay?"

"And here I was thinking I was the stalker."

She stares at the back of the chair in front of her. "I just wanted to know if you achieved your dreams, Luc. No matter what happened between us, I still wanted that for you. I still do."

"Well, that makes one of us."

"You're not really going to quit? Not because of him?"

I shrug. "It's not just because of him. Things over the past few months have been..." I trail off. "I don't even know."

"You're not a quitter, Luc."

"I gave up on you, didn't I?"

Her lips part but she soon closes them again.

"Exactly. That person you remember, I don't think he exists anymore, P. The expectations, the pressure, the constant bullshit, it's tainted me. Hardened me. I mean, look at us. Look what I've done, the things I've said. I'm no better than him with the way I've treated you." My regret for how I've handled everything since she reappeared in my life threatens to swallow me whole.

"You think I'm the same person? Jesus, Luc. You aren't the only one who's had it hard."

"Shit, I know. I didn't mean... fuck."

"I know, I'm sorry. How long until we land?" she asks, looking out the window.

"About forty minutes."

"Okay."

Resting her head back, she closes her eyes and wraps her free arm around herself. I wait for her to pull her hand from mine but she never does. Knowing that she needs the connection, needs my strength gives me hope that we might be able to salvage something out of all of this.

I rest back, keeping her hand clamped tightly in mine.

I meant what I said to her about being whatever she needs. I've got a lot to make up for, and I figure that right now isn't a bad place to start.

She's still asleep when we start to descend, and as much as I hate to wake her knowing what she's going to have to face next, I know I need to.

"Peyton," I say softly, taking in her pale face and the dark circles around her eyes.

I've already put enough stress on her the past few weeks, this really is the last thing she needs right now. All I can do is pray that Libby pulls through this.

She has to.

Peyton can't lose anyone else. She just can't. It's not fair. Not while the man who caused all this walks around like he still owns the fucking world.

My free hand clenches in anger.

I haven't attempted to speak to him since I discovered that everything Peyton told me that day five years ago was true. I have no idea what I'd ever say to him. No words could ever be strong enough to really make him understand how little he means to me now and how disgusted I am with him.

He's fucking scum. The kind who doesn't deserve to breathe the same air as us.

I hate that all of this has gone on while his celebrity status and public image remain untarnished. It's wrong. Totally fucking wrong.

I vow there and then to do something about it the second all this shit has settled down with Peyton.

I'll speak to Mom, find out what she knows, and we'll somehow find a way to ruin him—to destroy him. It's the least of what he deserves.

"Peyton, we're about to land, baby."

Her eyes flutter open at my words and she looks over at me.

For the briefest of seconds, she looks happy to see me. It makes my heart hurt because I know that momentarily, she's going to remember everything I've done and the hate and disappointment I've become used to seeing in her silver eyes over the past few weeks is going to emerge.

"Shit, are we here?" she asks, distracting me.

"Yeah, we are."

Seeing as we only have our carry-ons, we're outside Hartsfield and heading toward a taxi in only minutes.

"St. Thomas Hospital," I tell the driver. I help Peyton inside who looks about two seconds away from running away from this whole situation.

I totally understand it. Leon's only ever managed to break an arm once when we were kids but that whole experience with him being in the hospital traumatized me for a long time. I can only imagine how Peyton feels right now knowing that Libby is in critical condition.

The second I'm in the car, I pull Peyton into my side and hold her tight. I'm hoping like hell that she will feel some kind of comfort in my touch.

She says nothing the whole journey to the hospital but I feel her tensing up the closer we get. She noticeably trembles when we see the first sign.

Dropping my lips to her ear, I whisper, "Everything is going to be fine."

"But what if it's not? What then?"

"You'll get through it. We'll get through it."

She twists in her seat and looks up at me. Her sad silver eyes staring up into mine before they very briefly drop to my lips.

Everything around us vanishes as I wait with bated breath stuck in my throat for what she's going to do next.

I want her to kiss me more than I want anything else in the world right now but I know it would be wrong to even allow her to do it.

I force myself to remember all the reasons she hates me, and why in reality, Leon, or even Letty, should have been the one to make this journey with her. Not that I'd have ever let them, but I shouldn't get this privilege after everything that's happened.

"Here you go, kids," the driver announces, bringing the car to a stop and breaking the moment between us.

Peyton jumps away from me as if she's been burned before climbing from the car.

"Thanks, man."

I pay the driver then join Peyton on the sidewalk and grab our bags.

She's once again chewing on her nails.

Taking her hand in mine, I hold it tightly as I take a step toward the imposing building before us, but she doesn't move.

"I-I can't do this."

Turning back to her, I drop our bags on the sidewalk and take her face in my hands.

"Of course you can, P."

"I can't," she whimpers. "E-even if she does make it, I've got to tell her that Mom is dead and I—" She sucks in a shaky breath, tears pooling in her eyes.

"Baby," I breathe, staring right into her eyes so she can hopefully see the truth in my next words. "You are so fucking strong. What you've been through, how you've handled it, it fucking floors me." Her tears drop and I catch them with my thumbs. "No matter what happens, I'll be right by your side. I swear to fucking God, I'm not going to let you fall, P. Not ever again."

She nods, her bottom lips trembling, but I'm not sure how much of it she believes. Hell, if our positions were switched, I wouldn't believe a word that comes out of my mouth if I were her.

"You need to know how bad it is. Standing out here and thinking the worst isn't helping anyone. It might not be as bad as you're imagining."

"Or, it could be worse."

I swallow nervously, knowing that she's right. Libby is a junkie according to Peyton so we could be about to walk into anything.

"Come on." I take her hand once more and grab our bags.

She walks silently beside me with her head down. All signs of the confident woman who stood up to me over the past few weeks have gone and I hate it. I want my little spitfire back. The one who called me out on my bullshit and refused to roll over when I treated her like shit.

"Hi, we're looking for Liberty Banks," I say to the lady behind the reception desk when Peyton makes no move to say anything.

"Okay, just give me a few seconds."

The lady taps around for a few seconds before looking up at the two of us with sympathy written all over her face.

"Oh my God," Peyton cries.

"She's in ICU. It's family only."

"I'm her sister," Peyton manages through her tears.

"And I'm—"

"My husband."

I nearly choke on my own breath at Peyton's words.

"Okay." The receptionist nods, looking between the two of us.

She gives us directions to get to the ward and sends us on our way.

It's not until we're in the elevator and heading for the fifth floor that I pull Peyton in front of me and grip her chin, forcing her to look into my eyes.

"Husband?" I ask, keeping my voice light.

"I'm not doing this alone. I would've said you were my brother if it didn't freak me out quite so badly."

"I appreciate that, baby. I think I can play a better husband than a brother, don't you?"

Leaning down, I brush my lips over hers, needing her to know that I'm totally here with her right now.

For better or worse.

"Luca," she sighs after a few seconds.

"I know. I'm sorry. I just want to make it better, P."

"You can't."

She turns her back on me. My arms move to reach for her, to pull her back into my body and hold her, but the set of her shoulders tells me not to. So instead, I stand there feeling like I'm drowning not knowing what to do to help, all the while her words from only a few moments ago echo around in my head.

I can't do this alone. Not, *I can't do this without you.*

The elevator pings with our arrival and to my surprise, the second the doors part, Peyton moves forward. She studies the signs hanging from the ceiling in the sterile hallway before marching forward. It seems she's found some strength from somewhere, and as glad as I am that she has, it also terrifies me because I know she didn't take it from me.

She's right. She really isn't the girl I used to know.

12

PEYTON

"Oh my God," I cry the second my eyes land on my big sister.

She looks tiny in the hospital bed, surrounded by harsh white sheets but it's not her size that's the most shocking thing because that is the state of her face.

I rush forward, taking in her dark sunken eyes, hollow cheeks and the sores and scabs that cover her once flawless skin.

As a teenager, I was always green with envy of her clear skin while I was always fighting acne.

"Libby, what have you done?" I whisper, finding her cold hand that's resting on the sheets. I hold it in both of mine as tears cascade down my cheeks.

The machines around us beep and whir. They're noises that I remember all too well from the last time I was in a hospital and sitting around both Mom and Kayden's beds.

"You can fight this, Lib. I know you can. I'm here, Sis. I'm right here," I cry.

Strong arms wrap around my waist from behind as I stand there staring at my sister in disbelief.

All my hopes and dreams about her finding a new life, some

happiness have been totally obliterated as I stare at my worst nightmare.

Luca holds me for the longest time with his lips pressed against the top of my head as my world crumbles around me.

She looks so weak, so frail, so hopeless, and I can't help but let it bleed into me.

She's not going to come back from this. How can she?

"Peyton Banks?" a soft voice says from behind us a few seconds later.

Luca turns with me as I look at the young doctor who's joined us.

"Y-yes."

"I'm Dr. Willis, we spoke on the phone."

I nod. "H-how is she?"

"Would you both like to come with me, we can get coffee and I can explain what's happening?"

I look from her to my sister. I don't really want to leave her now that I'm here, but I also need to hear what the doctor has to say, and the coffee. God, I need coffee.

"Yeah, okay."

I give my sister's hand a squeeze.

"We'll be back. Don't do anything stupid," I warn her before I leave her bedside. I follow the doctor out of the room and to a small family room a little down the hall.

She walks straight over to the coffee machine, but before she even asks what we want, Luca steps up beside her.

"I've got this."

"Thank you." I take a seat on the couch while Dr. Willis sits opposite me on a chair.

"How much do you know about your sister's life?"

"Not a lot. She left home five years ago, leaving her baby behind. She's always had an addictive personality, so I wasn't under any illusion as to why she vanished."

"Okay. Well, your sister was brought in yesterday following a crystal meth overdose."

"Jesus Christ." I drop my head into my hands. "Crystal meth. Seriously?"

"I'm sorry, Peyton. I know this must be a lot. Do you have any other family or anyone who could be here to help take the weight of this?"

I shake my head. "Our mom died a few months ago. It's just me and her son."

Luca places two cups of coffee on the table. He drops down beside me, pulling me into his arms.

"What happens now?"

"She's had a hemorrhage which has caused a mild stroke. She—"

"A stroke? Shit. She's only twenty-three."

"I know. But from her test results, it would seem she's been using for a while and it's more common than we'd like to believe."

"Shit. So what now? Is she going to make it? If she does, is she going to be able to function, what's the prognosis here?"

I stare at the doctor, not knowing what's worse, her not making it or her surviving and not being able to live a normal life.

"It's too early to tell really, and I'd hate to give you any kind of false hope. The next few days are going to be crucial. We'll see how it goes and if her vitals look okay then we can start to bring her around and see where we go from there. She's got scans booked in for the next few days and hopefully, they will help us see how things are going. But even if she's lucky, I'm sure you're aware that she's going to have a very long road ahead of her."

"I know," I mutter, mostly oblivious as to what that journey will entail, but I'm not an idiot. Recovering from this, if she gets the opportunity, and rehab if she accepts it, is going to be hell.

"I hate to bring this up, but I need to talk to you about insurance."

I shake my head, a sad laugh falling from my lips.

"She has none. I have none. It's—"

"I've got it covered. You don't need to worry," Luca says, his deep voice startling me.

"N-no, Luc. You can't—"

"It's the least I can do, P. It's the least *he* can do."

My argument is right on the tip of my tongue, but I can't deny that Luca's got a point.

"I'll make sure she has the best care. And when she gets to leave here, I'll ensure she has a place in an excellent rehab facility."

I stare at him, my eyes burning and emotion clogging my throat.

"N-no, you—"

"I can, Peyton. Please, let me do this for you, for both of you."

I nod although I still want to argue. No one has ever helped me and the prospect of someone doing so makes me feel totally uncomfortable. Even if it is Luca.

"Okay, well, she's not going to be going anywhere for a while so we've got time to get all that sorted."

"Okay, good."

"I'll let you get back to her. But right now, there's nothing you can do. Don't exhaust yourself trying to support her now, she's going to need that energy from you in the future."

I nod, knowing she's right, but hating that I'm going to have to leave her here alone.

"I'll let you drink those and get back to her."

"Th-thank you."

"You're welcome, Peyton. If there's anything I can do, please, just shout."

I nod again as she slips from the room.

"I'm so sorry, baby."

I blow out a slow, calming breath as I attempt to process everything I've just been told.

"Luca, I really don't expect you to—" His fingers lightly press against my lips, cutting off my words.

"I'll do anything for you, Peyton. For Libby. Please, just let me."

He holds both of my hands in his, sincerity pouring from his eyes as he stares down at me.

"I'm never going to be able to make up for what I did. *He* is never going to be able to make up for what he did. But please, let me make this easier on you."

"O-okay," I breathe, knowing that he's not going to let me refuse. I have a suspicion that even if I did, he'd find a way to make it happen anyway. May as well save the energy for something else.

"I need to go back to her."

"Come on then. I've got some calls to make."

Luca leads me back to Libby's room. But this time, he doesn't follow me inside, instead, he loiters at the window so I can see him as he talks to someone on his cell.

I can't explain just how relieved I am that he's willing to do this for me, for Libby. As much as my stubborn streak might hate it, I know it's the right thing to do if Libby has any chance of surviving all of this.

I hold her hand as I watch him pace back and forth, his brow furrowed. As if he can feel my stare, he turns to me, our eyes connecting and he blows me a kiss.

My breath catches and my stupid heart tumbles in my chest.

I shouldn't have that reaction to him. I shouldn't care. But I do.

I tell myself it's just my appreciation for what he's doing for us. But deep down, I know that it's more than that.

Him being here, him holding me up these last few hours.

It... it means everything to me. And at the same time, I hate that it's having such an impact after what we've been through.

Ripping my eyes away from Luca, I stare back down at my sister, barely able to believe that she's the same person as the girl I grew up with.

She was always so full of life and had an infectious laughter.

Is all of this *his* fault?

I knew that Libby was drinking and smoking weed before I discovered her pregnancy. But with what happened with Brett, is that what drove her to start on the harder stuff? The cocaine, the meth?

I shake my head, my brain trying to reject the knowledge that my sister's life has been reduced to this.

I run my gaze up her arms. They're bruised, covered in scratches and cuts but the needle marks are obvious.

Dropping my head to my arm, I try to imagine what her life must have been like since she walked away from her baby. I'm trying to understand how she must have felt to even be able to do that in the first place.

The thought of leaving Kayden damn near rips my heart out, and I'm only his aunt. How desperate for an escape from her own life, her reality, must she have been?

"We can fix this, Libby. We can. Me and you and your gorgeous boy. We can be a family again."

I don't hear Luca when he finally steps back into the room, I'm too exhausted both mentally and physically to know what's going on around me.

I startle when he places his hand on my shoulder.

"Everything is sorted."

Slowly, I turn to look up at him. My breath catching and my heart pounding in my chest as I stare at the man I hoped I'd find when I returned. The man before me is an older version of the boy I remember. He's sweet, thoughtful, caring. He just wants to take me in his arms and do all he can to make everything better.

And while I really appreciate that he still exists. That under all the hatred and anger he's still there. I'm not sure if I'm ever going to be able to forgive the other version of him that I've been acquainted with over the past few weeks.

His vicious words. They cut deep. Deeper than I think I even realized at the time. I'm not sure how I'm meant to be able to put them behind me.

Maybe I'm not meant to. Maybe it's a sign that all of this, us, it's all in the past.

"What's wrong, P? Has something happened?" he asks, concern laced through his voice.

I shake my head.

"N-no nothing's happened."

"Okay, good. I think."

Reaching out, he pulls a chair over and lowers himself down beside me. He grabs my hand that's not holding Libby's.

He lifts it to his lips, pressing a long kiss to my knuckles that sends heat racing through my arm.

"We'll do everything we can to help her, P. I promise."

I blow out a shaky breath. "If only that would be enough."

I might not have any experience with junkies or any of this. But I know enough to know that when—if—she wakes up, she's going to need to want the help Luca is promising she can have or it's all for nothing. She'll disappear again and the next time I see her will probably be the last.

Sensing that I'm losing control of my emotions, Luca lifts me out of my chair as if I weigh nothing more than a feather and places me onto his lap.

If I weren't so exhausted, I might fight him on it, but right now, having his warmth and scent surrounding me feels too good. So I shut down everything to do with us from my brain and just take what I need in this moment.

Right now is about Libby. She has to be my focus.

All this shit with Luca can wait. There's plenty of time to try to get my head around how I really feel about all of that later.

"Thank you for being here. I appreciate what you're giving up to support us," I whisper into his chest, needing him to know that I'm not taking this for granted.

"Baby, there's nothing I wouldn't give up to be here with you right now."

I nod, swallowing down the messy ball of emotion that only seems to grow larger in my throat.

13

LUCA

We sit in silence beside Libby's bed for hours. The doctors and nurses come in and out but each of them only repeats what the previous one said, that we have to wait and see.

Every time they say it, I see a little bit more of Peyton shatter. She needs some good news to give her hope, but I fear that right now, there really might not be any.

"Baby," I whisper when I notice she's closed her eyes. "We should head out."

It takes a couple of seconds but eventually her red-rimmed eyes open again and she stares up at me.

"I don't want to leave her, Luc."

"I know," I say, reaching out to tuck a lock of hair behind her ear. "But you need to remember what Dr. Willis said earlier, she's going to need you later. Running yourself into the ground right now isn't going to help."

She nods sadly, knowing that I'm right.

It would be so easy to allow her to sleep in this chair tonight. But what happens tomorrow night, the night after, the week after if Libby doesn't come out of this as soon as they're hoping she might.

I can't allow her to do that to herself.

I insisted I come here with her to take care of her and that's what I intend to do.

"I've already booked us a motel to crash in. It's the closest place to the hospital so if anything happens, we can be back here in minutes."

She nods once again but I'm not really sure she hears any of it.

Lifting her from my lap, I place her on her feet.

"I'll leave you to say good night. I'll be right outside the door."

With a kiss to her temple, I leave the room as she perches herself on Libby's bed.

The door clicks closed behind me before I hear whatever she's got to say to her sister.

"How's she doing?" Dr. Willis's voice from down the hall scares the crap out of me. "Sorry," she says when she sees my reaction to her. "I thought you saw me."

"I'm not really sure. Life has been a mess for a while. Their mom died a few months ago. Peyton doesn't think that Libby even knows. I'm not sure how she's going to handle it if this goes bad."

"People are usually much stronger than we give them credit for."

Rubbing at the back of my neck, I stare down at the doctor, knowing that she's right.

Glancing through the window to where Peyton is crying with her sister's hand still in hers, I can't help but agree.

After everything she's been through to this point, she's still standing.

"I guess." I watch them for a few more seconds before turning back to the doctor. "I've sorted out the insurance and I'm working on finding her a rehab facility, should she need it."

"Peyton's lucky to have you," she says with a smile.

"Yeah, I'm not so sure about that," I mutter.

"Just be there, that's all you can do right now. The rest we can figure out as we go." I nod, looking back at Peyton as she climbs down from the bed. "I'm off shift in a few minutes, but I'm back first thing. I'll check in and call if there have been any changes. Otherwise, I guess I'll see you both tomorrow."

"Thank you, Doctor."

"You're welcome. Try to get some rest."

With a smile that I don't feel, I watch her walk away.

"Did she say anything?" Peyton asks from the doorway.

"Nothing we don't already know. Come on. You need to get some rest."

Peyton glances back over her shoulder, clearly torn about whether leaving is the right thing to do or not.

"They'll call if anything happens, but she needs you to look after yourself right now."

"I know. I know," she whispers, her voice rough with emotion.

The motel I've booked is only a short walk away, but even still, the second I see a taxi loitering outside the hospital, I guide Peyton over to it. She's in no state to walk anywhere.

She looks at me curiously when we pull to a stop in front of a questionable-looking motel a few minutes later.

"Come on, baby," I encourage, taking her hand in mine after paying the driver.

"Here?" she asks, her brows pinching as she looks at the rundown buildings surrounding us.

"It's the closest."

"I know but... it's not really your style."

"What are you trying to say, P?" I ask in a mocking tone. She spent all our former years pointing out the little luxuries I had in my life in comparison to hers.

She's right. This isn't exactly the kind of place I'd choose given the choice.

"This isn't about me, baby. This is about making sure you're as close to Libby as possible. Come on, let's go get our key."

We step into the reception, fighting our way through the swollen door and the thick cloud of smoke that assaults us the second we're inside.

There's a man behind the desk with his feet propped up and a smoke hanging from his mouth. He's staring at something on a laptop that he doesn't so much as glance up at our arrival. But the moan that comes from the computer gives us a good clue as to what has him so distracted.

"I've booked a room." He startles and slams the laptop down in the rush, his smoke falling from his lip and burning his thigh.

"Shit. Fuck." He hops around, trying to get to the cigarette before it catches the ancient carpet beneath our feet alight.

"Okay, name."

"Dunn."

He flips over his clipboard and reaches behind him for a key.

"I just need a signature and deposit."

"Sure." Reluctantly, I take the pen from his outstretched hand, not wanting to think about where that's been already tonight and sign my name before pulling my wallet from my pocket and handing my credit card over.

Peyton stands silently at my side and when I glance over at her, she's looking around at the dated décor chewing on her nail.

The man passes a key over, and as quickly as possible, I get us out of there.

"I hope there's a deadbolt on the inside of the room," Peyton deadpans the second the door slams closed behind us.

"It can only get better, right?"

"Could today get any worse?"

"You hungry?" I ask, changing the subject when a neon pizza sign across the street catches my eye.

"Not really."

"You should eat."

"I know."

The room is about what I expected. Dated and smells faintly damp, but to my surprise, it is actually clean.

"Well, this is..."

"Close to the hospital," I finish for her, pulling her into my arms.

She nods against my chest, thankfully relaxing against me and allowing me to comfort her.

"I'm so sorry, baby."

She blows out a long breath and pulls away from me.

"Are you going to order that pizza?"

Pulling my cell from my pocket, I find the place and put in an order.

"It'll be here in fifteen."

"Okay." Without another word, she leaves me in favor of locking herself in the bathroom.

With a heavy heart, I kick off my sneakers and drop onto the bed. I unlock my cell once more and finding Leon's number.

"How's Libby?" he asks the second the call connects.

"Bad, man. It doesn't look good," I say, scrubbing my hand down my face. The doctors may try to be as realistic as possible but I can see in their eyes that they're not expecting a miracle here.

"Fuck. Peyton?"

"Falling apart. I don't know what to do," I confess quietly, not really wanting to have this conversation with him but knowing I need to.

"Just be there, Bro. Be the best friend she's needed for the past five years."

Pain slices through my chest.

"Fuck. How did I screw this up so badly?" I ask, not really expecting a response.

"I understand why you didn't want to believe it, trust me, I do. But you handled it really fucking badly, man. That cunt should never have had your loyalty over your girl."

"I know, I know. I just—"

"I get it. I don't want to believe it either. But it's true. And that little boy, Bro. He's fucking wicked."

A smile curls at my lips as I think about my very brief encounter with Kayden, our little brother.

"How are you really doing with all this?" I ask, knowing his MO of locking everything down and festering on it until he suddenly explodes. It's not happened for a few years, but if anything is going to set him off then it's going to be this.

"I'm... well, I'm sober right now."

I glance at the time. "That's... good, I guess."

"I just need some time. What are we going to do about it?"

"Right now, nothing. When I'm back, we need to talk to Mom, then we can make a decision. But I ain't letting this go. He's not doing that to Libby, to anyone, and getting away with it."

"I hear ya, man."

"Okay."

Silence rings out between us, a million and one things going unsaid.

"I know shit's been fucked up but I'm here, Bro. If you need—"

"I'm good." My brows lift as if he can see them because I don't believe a fucking word of it.

"Okay well, just in case. We can't let him win."

"Just look after Peyton. Prove to her that you're not just a prick these days."

"I'll do my best."

I hang up, lowering my cell to my lap right as the bathroom door opens.

My breath catches at the sight of her. She looks utterly wrecked.

"Peyton," I breathe, pushing forward, ready to go to her.

"I'm okay," she whispers, holding her hand up to halt my movements. "Who was that?"

"Leon."

She nods and lifts her fingers to her lips.

"You need to call Fee."

"Y-yeah."

Slowly she makes her way to where she placed her purse when we walked in and pulls her cell out. Dropping to the end of the bed, she unlocks it and finds her contact, lifting it to her ear.

"Hey," she says softly. The emptiness to her voice makes a lump crawl up my throat. Her body trembles as she listens to Fee.

I desperately want to reach for her, to help her somehow but I also know that I need to follow her lead.

I need to remember that she doesn't actually want me here. She never asked me to come. I gave her no choice. I think we both know that I'd never listen, but she could demand I leave at any moment. And that can't happen. I need to be here for her. I'd never forgive myself for leaving her to do this alone.

"She's in a bad way, Aunt Fee."

She sucks in a shaky breath as Fee says something.

"They don't know. She... she's had a st-stroke. She might not—" A sob rips from her and I move on instinct, caging her in with my legs. I take the cell from her hand and place it to my own ear.

"It's me," I say, so Fee knows I've taken it.

"Do you need me to come out there?"

"Not right now, there's nothing you can do. They're going to keep her sedated for a while yet, do some more tests."

"O-okay."

"I've handled the insurance. Once she's stable, they're going to move her back to Maddison so we can come home and you can be there too."

"Luca, you didn't need—"

"I did. It's the least I could do," I repeat the same words I've said to Peyton more than once today.

"Okay, well... we really appreciate it. I know Libby will too."

"Yeah," I breathe, hoping she'll come around and be able to do just that.

"Look after Peyton, Luc. She's already been through so much. I hate that I'm not there for her."

"I'll do everything I can."

"I know you still love her."

I don't respond to her statement. I can't.

"But you need to prove it to her because you've done a really good job at showing her just the opposite recently."

"I know," I whisper.

"You've got a good heart, Luca. Use it."

I nod despite the fact she can't see me.

"Call me if anything changes or if either of you need anything."

"We will. Thank you, Fee."

"Don't let me down, boy," she warns before hanging up on me. Leaving me with nothing but a blank screen and the ragged breaths of the woman in my arms.

"How much of that did you hear?" I whisper into her hair.

"All of it."

I hold her tighter, squeezing my eyes closed and breathing her in.

"She's right, you know," I confess.

She shrugs. "It doesn't matter."

Her nonchalance damn near rips my heart out.

"I don't know how to make it up to you, P," I admit, honestly. I fucked up so badly and I'm terrified that I'm never going to be able to come back from it in her eyes.

Unwrapping my arms from around her waist, she pushes from the bed and begins pacing.

"There's nothing you can do, Luc. What's done is done."

"No," I spit, standing in her way and forcing her to stop. My hands land on her upper arms, and although she doesn't look up at me, I know she's listening. "I'm going to find a way, baby. I'm going to figure out a way to make it up to you and to prove to you that you can trust me again."

She sucks in a breath as if she's about to respond when there's a knock at the door.

"Pizza is here," she mutters, slipping from my hold and walking farther into the room.

I watch her for a beat, her shoulders slumped in defeat. She drops into the old ratty chair in front of a small table on the other side of the room.

The pizza guy knocks again and drags me from my daze.

"Thanks, man," I say, taking the box from him. My stomach growls loudly the second the scent hits my nose.

Closing the door behind him, I flick the deadbolt that Peyton was worried about. I take the pizza over to her, sitting in the other chair. Although from the loud creak it makes when I put my weight on it, I'm surprised I don't end up on the floor.

I flip the lid and stare down at the cheesy goodness. My stomach growling once again but she makes no move to take a slice when I dive in for my first.

"Eat, P," I demand.

Her eyes fly up to mine. Her lips part to argue but she must remember why I'm being a bossy asshole because she sits forward and takes a slice.

With a small smile, I shove my slice into my mouth, demolishing it like a starved man.

I've eaten half of it by the time she finishes her first slice. She gives up on the crust and throws it back into the box.

"Pey—"

"No," she snaps, jumping up from the chair and pinning me with a look that stops me from saying anything else. "I appreciate what you're trying to do here, Luca, but I'm not a fucking kid."

She storms across the room and yanks open the door and disappears outside.

"Fucking hell."

My fingers curl around the arms of the chair in my attempt to stop me from chasing her.

I give her a few seconds before I walk over to the window and pull the curtain back.

She's sitting on the curb in front of a car with her head in her hands, her shoulders shaking with her tears.

"Shit."

Rubbing my hands across my face, I lift them to my hair and pull on it until it hurts.

I can't stop fucking up, even when I'm trying not to.

I stand at the window and watch her for the longest time. Eventually, she sits up straight, wipes her face with the backs of her hands, and stands.

She finds me behind the curtain the second she turns around and my breath catches in my throat at the unfiltered pain in her eyes.

Walking back to the room with her head held high, she says nothing as she steps up to me and takes my hand in hers.

Following her lead, I trail behind her as she walks into the bathroom.

I stand awkwardly in the doorway as she reaches into the shower and turns it on.

"P?"

She looks over her shoulder before her fingers wrap around the bottom of her tank and she peels it up her body.

Her jeans go next until she's standing before me in just her underwear.

My body heats, my heart rate increases even though I know it's wrong. She's having one of the worst days of her life and here I am getting lost in her already.

She turns to me and although she still looks utterly devastated and on the brink of falling apart, there's something else in her eyes.

Hunger. Determination.

Both of them stir something inside me.

I told her I'd be whatever she needs me to be. And I meant it.

Taking a step forward, I lose my fight and my eyes drop from hers in favor of her body.

Reaching behind her, she undoes her bra and lets it fall down her arms.

My cock swells at the sight of her breasts, her already peaked nipples.

She steps up to me, pushing her thumbs into her panties and letting them drop to her ankles.

She doesn't touch me as she stretches up on her tiptoes and breathes in my ear, "Make it all go away, Luc."

"Baby." My voice sounds pained even to my own ears.

"All I can see is her lying in that bed. Just for a few minutes, I need to focus on something else. Please." She pulls her head back and looks into my eyes. "I need you."

"Fuck." Those words fucking wreck me.

Reaching behind me, I pull my hoodie and shirt off in one go. I shove my jeans and boxers down my legs, kicking them off as I lift her into my body and walk us both into the shower.

Warm water rains down on both of us as I press her against cool tiles and slam my lips down on hers.

Her legs tighten around my waist. Her heels press into my ass, ensuring her burning pussy rubs against my cock.

"Peyton," I growl into our kiss.

"Fuck me, Luc." I pull back from our kiss and look at her, sensing she has more to say. And I'm right because her nose twitches.

"Say it, P," I growl.

"M-make it hurt." My eyes widen at her demand. "Pretend we're still in that pool house and that you hate me. Make it—" Her words are cut off with a gasp when my fingers wrap around her throat.

"Kinky little Peyton," I groan in her ear. "Fucking knew you loved that weekend."

"Oh God." I graze my teeth down her throat until I bite the soft skin of her shoulder.

I squeeze her ass in my palm until it has to burn before lifting her and thrusting inside her in one move.

"Fuck, Luc."

"What do you want, baby?"

"Yes, Luc. Yes. More."

I pound into her without restraint. Her back slides against the tiles behind her. I kiss her mouth with the same ferocity that I fuck her pussy with.

"Fuck, I missed you, you filthy little slut," I moan into her open mouth as she tries to catch her breath.

"More."

Pride for my girl surges through me. Fuck if her knowing exactly what she wants, what she needs, doesn't turn me the fuck on.

Pulling out of her, I place her on her feet and spin her around. I pin her to the wall with the length of my body.

Reaching up, I wrap the length of her hair around my fist and pull her head back until she's got no choice but to look at me.

"I hope you know what you're asking for, baby."

"I'm more than aware, Dunn." The challenge in her eyes turns my blood to lava.

My grip on her hip is tight enough to leave marks as I pull the bottom half of her body away from the wall and kick her legs wider.

"You're soaked for me, baby," I moan, running my fingers through her pussy and dipping them inside her.

Her hips grind against me in her search for more.

"You wanna come, baby?"

"Luc," she moans, her rough voice causing goose bumps to erupt across my skin.

"Be a good little slut and I might just let you."

Taking myself in hand, I find her entrance and thrust inside her once more.

She cries out, surging forward with the force. But my grip on her ensures she doesn't collide with the wall.

Pulling her hair, I twist her so she can see me as I pound into her.

"So beautiful, baby."

Her makeup is running down her face from the water cascading down on her. Her hair is plastered against her skin and her neck is already red from my fingers and teeth.

Her eyes hold mine, urging me on, demanding that I give her more, that I do whatever I'm capable of to get her out of her own head.

She screams when my palm collides with her ass cheek, her pussy clamping down around me and forcing a grunt of pleasure from my throat.

"Fucking heaven, P. Fucking." Thrust. "Heaven."

I spank her again, pull her hair tighter, making her back arch so my cock hits her deep and just in the right place.

Long before I'm ready, her body trembles in my hold and my balls start to draw up.

"I wanna hear my name when you fall, baby. Scream it fucking loud."

She nods, meeting my movements thrust for thrust.

The slap of another spank rings out around us and she crashes.

"Luca," she screams as her body convulses with her release.

I wrap my arm around her waist to hold her up as her knees threaten to give out. I continue fucking her through her orgasm but I pull out before I find my own.

14

PEYTON

My back slams against the wall, the hit smarts but I barely feel it or the cold tiles with the aftershocks of my orgasm still rendering my body useless.

Luca lifts me into his body once more and my legs wrap around him with instruction from my brain.

Before I can register what he's doing, his lips crash down on mine once more, his tongue plunging into my mouth as our teeth clatter with the ferocity of his kiss.

His hands move over my body, caressing, pinching, squeezing as if he doesn't know where to touch first.

I knew going into this that it could be a huge mistake. But it was the only way I could think without getting blind drunk that would help drag me out of my own head, and force my brain to think about something other than the image of Libby in that hospital bed.

"Peyton," he groans into our kiss, his deep voice sending a shudder down my spine.

Asking this of him was a huge risk, but I knew he'd never refuse me what I wanted. I might not know this new Luca all that well, but I know enough to know he wouldn't refuse me.

My hips grind down on him, my body already ready for another release, another few blissful seconds where nothing else but this moment, the two of us, exist. His hard cock brushes my clit and a thought hits me.

Pulling back from his kiss, I stare into his dark, hungry eyes.

"Luc, you didn't—"

His fingers press against my lips cutting my words off as a smirk curls at his lips.

"We're far from done yet, baby."

Parting my lips, I suck his fingers into my mouth, smiling as his lids lower with desire and his cock jerks against me.

"I know what you're doing," I confess once I release him.

"Oh yeah?" he asks, nuzzling my neck and nipping at my skin, enough to send a bolt of pain through me.

"I don't want you holding back, Luc."

He eases back from me and looks me dead in the eye.

"You think I'm holding back to punish myself?"

"Aren't you? It seems to be your favorite kind of punishment."

His eyes bounce between mine for a few seconds, I'm not sure if there's disbelief or pride within them that I've worked him out.

"Don't worry, P. I'll make sure I get mine."

He captures my lips once more before I have a chance to argue.

The water stops falling on us a second later and he pulls me from the wall, carrying me with ease through the bathroom and toward the bed.

Both of us drip all over the ancient, worn carpet but neither of us cares enough to do anything about it.

His kiss continues long after he lowers me to the mattress and climbs between my thighs. His still hard cock teases my entrance but despite grinding my hips in the hope of finding some friction, he doesn't move to take me again, much to my disappointment.

"You're a filthy little slut, Peyton Banks. You only want me for my cock, don't you?"

"Luca," I moan when he sucks on the sensitive bit of skin beneath my ear.

I want to tell him that I want way more of him than that, that I always have, but I slam my lips shut and swallow down the words.

That isn't what this is. This is me needing an escape. Nothing that is happening right now is in any way an indication of what the future might hold for either of us.

His lips descend my body, kissing, licking, and nipping, giving me just a taste of the pain I demanded of him in the bathroom.

"Oh God," I cry, my back arching for more when he wraps his lips around my nipple, sucking it deep into his mouth and sinking his teeth into the sensitive skin. My pussy floods with heat, the muscles tightening in search of the friction I need to lose myself once more.

Luca continues teasing me, switching from side to side just when I think a few seconds more might be enough to send me crashing over the edge he stops.

"Luca, please," I beg as he kisses down my stomach, dipping his tongue into my navel and staring up at me with his dark and determined eyes.

"You wanted me at my worst, baby."

"I-I know but—fuck, p-please," I whimper as he spreads my legs as wide and they'll go, blowing a stream of air across the heated skin.

"So wet for me."

I roll my hips, hoping it'll be the move he needs to drop his mouth to me.

"Tell me what you want, baby. Give me enough detail and I might just do it."

The cocky smirk he shoots me makes me wonder if I want to kill him or kiss him more at this moment.

"Eat me, Luc. Eat me until I'm screaming your name and our neighbors know exactly how good you are."

"Filthy slut," he mutters as he dives for me, licking up the entire length of me, lapping at my juices like I'm the best thing he's ever tasted.

"So sweet, baby. I'll eat you all fucking night if you need it."

My fingers twist in his hair, my hips leaving the bed in my need for more, for everything he can give me.

He eats me like a man possessed, bringing me to the brink over and over but never once letting me fall. It's the sweetest torture and everything I need right now.

Reality is long gone as he plays my body like it was made for him.

"Luca, Luca, Luca," I cry as my orgasm begins to crest once more. But just like I knew was going to happen, he rips his mouth away from me just at the last second, only this time, he doesn't wait for me to come down before starting all over again like it's some kind of game. This time, he crawls onto his knees and fists his cock before plunging it inside me.

I'm so sensitive after everything he's done to me that I can barely stand it. I wiggle around, not knowing whether to pull him closer or push him away.

"Oh shit." My eyes widen as his hand wraps around my throat. He's squeezing with just the right amount of pressure as his hips begin to piston in and out of me.

"Wanna know how good you taste?"

My eyes hold his, a smirk curling at my lips at his rhetorical question.

"Thought so."

His lips slam down on mine. His tongue parts my lips causing my own taste to explode in my mouth, making my almost lost release to race forward once more.

"Come for me, baby. Come for me right now."

He slams into me once more and I fracture into a million pieces.

"Luca," I scream as he continues to thrust a couple more times. Pleasure races through me, making my muscles quiver and heat to flood my entire body.

"Peyton, fuck. Fuck," he groans as his cock swells inside me. "Fuck, I love you."

My eyes widen in shock as his release rocks through him and he drops his entire body weight onto me for long seconds.

I love it, feeling him pressing me into the mattress but I'm too shocked by his confession to really appreciate it.

I mean, I know how I still feel about him. I came to terms with the fact I'd probably love him until my dying day some time ago, but to hear him say those words. Well, it has me shook.

After a few more seconds, he rolls onto his side, allowing me to suck in a deep breath.

"Come here," he murmurs, wrapping his arm around my waist and dragging me into his body.

Wrapping his hand around the back of my thigh, he pulls it over his hip, aligning us in the most intimate way as his lips brush mine. He slides his hand to my ass and palms it gently before brushing it up my back and threading his fingers into my still wet hair.

"I know you hate me, and I deserve it. I know that, trust me, I do. But fuck, I missed you, P."

I gasp and he uses the opportunity to deepen the kiss. His tongue strokes mine and I'm powerless but to allow him to consume me once more.

My head screams at my heart to stay locked up tight but it's really fucking hard not to let him slip back inside.

I focus on the movement of his lips against mine, the caress of his tongue and the heat of his body doing exactly what I asked—no, demanded—of him. Making me forget.

I allow myself to drown in actions, pushing any kind of feelings aside to deal with at a later date. Right now, everything is too much, but this, this intimacy with the one and only person I've ever truly felt myself with is everything I need.

———

I wake with a start not knowing where I am. I sit up, the sheets pooling around my waist but the second I realize that I'm naked, I quickly gather them up, holding them to my chest in a death grip.

Everything is a haze, reality right on the edge of my grasp like a dream that you can't quite remember. Then my eyes find Luca sitting on the chair where we had pizza last night with his cell in his hand and wearing only a pair of black boxer briefs and everything slams back into me.

"Oh God," I cry, falling back onto the bed and pulling the sheets with me.

"Well, no one has ever quite had that reaction to me the morning after, I've got to say," he deadpans as he climbs onto the bed beside me and drops a kiss to my cheek.

"It's not that, Luc. I just didn't... I forgot—"

I shove my face into the pillow, breathing in the unfamiliar scent and willing the tears away that are once again burning my eyes.

"Hey, it's okay."

I suck in a ragged breath, pulling my face out again and looking into his sympathetic eyes.

"You had your cell. Has anyone called?"

He nods and my heart jumps into my throat. "Dr. Willis called. They're taking Libby for some more tests and scans. She hopes that the results today might help to give an indication of where this is going to go. But she also said not to go in this morning because we'll just get in the way—"

"She said that?" I ask, my brows pulling together.

"Well, no. She was a little more diplomatic but that's what she meant. She said to go up after lunch and she'll give you the results as soon as she can."

I nod, accepting that I won't get to see her again until this afternoon.

"What time is it?"

"Almost nine. I thought that maybe we could go and get some breakfast. Find a store to get some supplies."

Reaching out, I rest my hand on his rough cheek. I really appreciate everything that he did for me yesterday, but I'm fully aware that he's walked out of his own life without a second thought.

"You should go back to Maddison."

He rears back a little as if I just slapped him. "No, P. I'm not leaving you here. No way."

"But your life. College, football, your—"

Leaning toward me, he rests his brow against mine. "I'm not going anywhere until you do. Once Libby is stable, we'll all go back to Maddison together."

"You've already done too much, Luc."

"Nothing will ever be too much for you, baby. Nothing." He threads his fingers through mine and dips his head to brush his lips against mine.

I don't react, realizing once more that doing what I did last night might have given him more ideas about our future than I wanted it to.

After a second, he realizes that I'm not going to return the kiss and he pulls back.

"Why don't you get cleaned up and we'll go and find some food."

I nod, unable to do anything but agree with him.

Luca takes me to a diner between our motel and the hospital. We're led to a booth right in the back of the restaurant away from anyone else. It's as if the server knows I need it. But one look at Luca, and I realize he did know and this is all part of Luca's way of looking after me.

I let out a resigned sigh as I drop down onto the bench, Luca sliding in opposite me after agreeing to the coffee the server offers.

Last night was a mistake. I knew that going into it. But I needed it. Hell, I still need it.

He made everything go away. All the thoughts and fears in my head vanished. It might have only been for a few minutes really, but it was the exact relief I needed from it.

The server returns to fill our mugs and still no words have passed between us. Although his concerned stare burns into the top of my head as I stare at the worn table before me.

Luca orders for us, and I'm grateful that I don't even need to look at the menu, let alone make a decision.

My stomach is in knots, dread and regrets from last night sitting heavy in it. I already know I'm not going to be able to force down much.

Luca continues staring at me across the table, and I feel myself closing down even more.

I don't want to be here. I want to be at the hospital, even if Libby isn't in her room and having tests. I just want to be there because she has no one else who's going to be.

I can't help her through this if she's alone.

I exhale once more, picking at the sore skin around my nails that I've bitten raw. I hate myself for doing it, but I've got to do something.

"Talk to me, Peyton."

"About what?" I reluctantly ask, my voice quiet and small.

"I don't know. Anything. South Carolina, your mom, Kayden. I just... I want to know everything, P."

My eyes lift, anger swirling in their depths. "A little late for all that, don't you think?" I spit, the venom in my voice surprising me.

"Probably yeah," he admits, rubbing the back of his neck nervously. "But... I want to make this right, baby."

I shake my head. "And you think that's possible?"

He shrugs, defeat clear in the way he slumps back against the bench. "Maybe not. But that doesn't mean I'm not willing to try. We didn't get a chance to talk about... about everything on Saturday. I want to know the truth, P."

A bitter laugh rips from my throat, making his brows pinch.

"I guess I should be grateful that you've realized what I say is only ever the truth."

"Deep down, I knew it all along. I just couldn't deal with it. I couldn't cope with my d— with Brett doing that."

"And you think I could? I lost everything, Luc. You, my home, my life, and I got dragged to another state, forced to keep this huge secret as I watched my sister lose control, only to lose her and then my mom a few years later. Libby is the only thing I have left, Luca." I sit forward, resting my arms on the table and hang my head.

"That's not true, baby."

I look up as his fingers manage to pry mine from the fist they were curled in and I allow him to lace them together. His warmth immediately settling something inside me.

"You've got me, Lee, Fee, Kayden. And once we've spoken to Mom and Shane, you're going to have them too. You've always been a part of my family, P. Always. Now it's just really time to take your place."

I scoff. "Jesus, Luc. It sounds like you're about to propose or some shit."

"If I thought it would help, I would."

My chin drops at his confession, that along with what he blurted as he came last night sends a shockwave through me once more.

"I'd do anything, Peyton. I need you to know that."

"I don't know anything, Luc. You can't go from locking me in a pool house torturing me to sitting here telling me that you'd marry me. It's fucking insane, Luca."

He shrugs. "I know." He thinks for a minute, his eyes glazing over as he goes someplace else. "Love isn't always easy, or pretty, Peyton."

I gasp at the truth behind his statement

"No, it's painful and full of regrets."

Hurt flashes through his eyes but I refuse to let it affect me. We both knew what last night was, and if he's thinking other things then he needs to seriously reconsider.

He told me he'd be what I needed, well... last night that was what I needed. No strings attached.

He's silent for a few moments. My hand is still in his as his thumb rubs along my knuckles. The move is irritatingly comforting.

"Before you ran into me yesterday, I got stuck in the elevator with Letty."

His words make me look up from our joined hands.

"Things have been strained between us since she came back and ended up with Kane. I thought... I thought she'd been sent back for me, fate or some shit, I don't know. I thought maybe she was a sign. Anyway, I fucked up with her. I was too focused on my own issues and fucked up life to really listen to what was going on with hers.

"Getting stuck yesterday was exactly what we needed. It gave us a chance to talk, to be honest with each other. She confessed what really happened with Kane and I told her about you, the truth."

My breath catches in my throat at his confession.

"It's okay, P. I'd trust Letty with my life. She's no threat to you or Kayden."

I nod, knowing that he's right. "I really like her."

"She's pretty awesome. She just..." He lets out a long sigh and falls back against the bench. "She just listened, understood. Told me what I needed to hear. I know I've fucked up. I know I should have believed every single word that ever fell from your lips, and I'm so fucking sorry that I didn't. But this, P." He lifts our hands. "What happened, it's doesn't need to be the end for us."

"If it was the end, I don't think we'd be sitting here right now." His eyes light up at my words and I realize that he read into them more than I expected.

"I don't know what you want from me, Luc."

"I don't want anything from you. I just want you."

"And if you can't have me?"

His lips part to respond but he thinks better of it. "Then I wait until I can."

Our server appears, breaking the silence that falls over our table, placing our breakfast in front of us.

With my eyes focused on my food, I let my mouth run away with me as I take a trip down memory lane. I tell Luca all the things I explained to Leon about Libby's pregnancy, her disappearance, Mom and Kayden's accident and all the things that have happened since that resulted in us living in Aunt Fee's house.

"I don't know how you're still standing, P. All of that would have broken most people."

"Meh. Maybe I'm not most people."

He laughs. "You got that right. You're one of a kind."

"I had him. I couldn't fall apart. I had to be there for Kayden. Until Aunt Fee agreed to take us in, I was all he had."

"You should have—" He swallows his words.

"Reached out? Oh yeah, because that would have gone down so well." I lift my free hand to my ear, mimicking being on the phone. "*Hey Luc, remember me. I told you that your dad got my sister pregnant and you called me a liar. Anyway, that kid is now in critical condition in the hospital and I need help.* I'm sure you'd have dropped the phone and come running right away," I deadpan.

"I—" He drops his head into his hand. "I'm sorry."

"You keep saying that, but those words don't fix anything, Luc."

"How much do you owe, for your mom and Kayden?"

"A lot. And there's more to come. Kayden still has a way to go."

"He's a tough kid."

"You have no idea."

"Can I meet him properly when we get back? Like Lee did."

"Can I trust you not to fuck it up?" I ask, knowing that if he loses his shit again and disappears, it'll rip Kayden apart. He's wanted his brothers in his life for a long time. I'm not about to let Luca into his life if he's not serious.

"Did you ask Lee that?" he asks, narrowing his eyes on me.

"Uh..." I hesitate, knowing that I didn't.

"Forgive me for being less concerned about your brother's intentions."

A scream rips from my lips, my entire body jumping from the seat when his palm slams down on the table.

"You have no idea what Lee is capable of. You don't even know him."

"Maybe not, but he proved his loyalty the second I told him what had happened between us, something you failed to do for five years."

"For a reason. Leon, he's..." I raise a brow, waiting for him to continue. "I don't know. He's hiding stuff. I don't know where his head is at with all this."

"Well, I can tell you for a fact that he's dealt with it better than you have."

"Touché. Just... don't take what you see on the outside with Leon as gospel. He's good at putting on a mask and hiding everything."

"Noted."

Luca finished his breakfast while I mostly pushed mine around my plate, my stomach still too knotted to even think about eating it.

15

LUCA

Things are still tense between us as we make our way to the hospital after paying for our breakfast.

Her words about not trusting me with Kayden are on repeat in my head as we stand in the elevator to get to the fifth floor.

Dr. Willis didn't say how long Libby was going to be with her doing tests and scans this morning. But I know I don't stand a chance of keeping Peyton away from her sister any longer, even if we spend the rest of the day sitting in an empty room.

She needs to be here, which I understand, but I also agree with Dr. Willis that this is only the beginning. She needs to look after herself, and if she's not going to, then she can bet her ass that I'm going to do it for her.

Her scent surrounds me as we ascend through the building, and my arms twitch to reach out and pull her into me but after the things she said to me this morning, I'm reluctant.

I knew what last night was. But still, I can't help hoping that somewhere along the way she's going to start forgiving me. It's probably naïve of me, but holding her last night, waking up to her in my arms this morning. That's what I need.

If I thought watching her at work, finding stolen moments with her, calmed the chaos in my head then it was nothing compared to just being us again.

We didn't have sex again last night, although both of us were more than ready for it, instead, we just made out like old times until she finally gave in to her exhaustion.

Everything was so much easier to deal with and process everything happening between and around us when she was pressed up against me.

Now, in the stark light of day, everything comes flooding back and I'm smacked in the face with our reality again.

Libby. My father. My little brother.

There's so much that I don't even know where to start processing it.

"Ah, Peyton. Perfect timing," Dr. Willis says, as we walk into the ICU a few minutes later. "Liberty is back in her room and I'm just about to go and find out the results. I'll come and find you as soon as I have some new information."

"Thank you," Peyton whispers before racing forward.

"Hey, Sis," she says, forcing as much lightness into her tone as possible. It seems like a wasted effort to me seeing as Liberty is still unconscious but whatever makes any of this easier.

Peyton pulls one of the chairs closer to her sister's bedside and once again clutching her hand in hers.

"Would you like another coffee?" I ask, knowing that this is going to be another long day.

"Sure, if you want," Peyton says without even looking at me.

"Okay. I'll be back in a bit."

I leave with a heavy heart, stopping beside the little window to watch her before I go in search of the nearest coffee machine.

"How's she doing?" one of the nurses who's been looking after Libby asks.

"She's..." Lifting my hand to my hair, I push the strands back, glancing through the window once more. "I don't know. She's strong but... I'm worried about her."

Her warm hand lands on my upper arm.

"This kind of situation can break even the hardest souls. Just keep doing everything you're doing and pray."

"I'm not really the praying kind."

"You never know what will help, sweetie." My eyes remain on Peyton, sadness for my girl coiling around my chest, making it hard to drag in the breath I need.

"I'll give it a go. Thank you."

"We're here for whatever you need. I know you have plans to transfer her as soon as possible, but if either of you needs to talk to someone in the meantime, just let us know."

Ripping my eyes from Peyton, I look into the nurse's kind eyes.

"Thank you."

Stepping around her, I walk away, feeling like I'm leaving a huge piece of myself behind.

My cell ringing stops me on my quest for coffee. The second I see Letty's name on the screen, I stop and fall into the nearest chair before connecting the call.

"Hey."

"Hey. I just spoke to Lee. How's Peyton? Her sister?"

Leaning forward, I rest my free arm on my knee and scrub my hand down my face.

"A mess. I'm so out of my depth right now, Let. I don't know what the fuck I'm doing."

"You're there. That's the biggest thing you can do right now."

"I didn't exactly give her a choice in that matter."

"So I heard," she mutters.

"We slept together," I blurt out, not really meaning to say it but needing to confide in someone.

"Of course you did. Luc, what are you doing?"

"It wasn't me. Well, it was but... she started it. Wanted to get out of her head."

"Okay."

"Fuck," I bark, startling an old woman who's walking down the hallway. I flash her a smile in the hope of making up for it, but she only looks more terrified by me and moves a little faster. "I want more, Let. I don't want to be just the person she can use to get out of her head when shit gets hard."

The line goes silent, but I know she's still there.

"Go on, you can say it."

"I don't need to. You already know that you don't deserve any better. Hearing me say it won't help in any way."

"I just want to fix it. I want her back."

"I know. But it's going to take work, Luc. A lot of work. And right now isn't the time for it. Her head is messed up. Evident by the fact she slept with you," she deadpans.

"Thanks."

"I'm kidding. I'm sure you rocked her world, QB."

I roll my eyes at her, wishing that she was sitting beside me having this conversation.

"I missed you," I whisper, needing to get everything out.

"I missed you too, Luc." She sighs as if she's fighting with whether to say something or not.

"Say it, Let. Shit can't get any worse right now."

"I'm worried about Lee."

"That makes two of us."

"Pretty sure he didn't spend last night at home. He looked... he was a mess."

"Fucking hell," I groan.

"I know. I'm sorry. I didn't want to say anything but–"

"It's fine, Let. I know shit's up with him. I can feel it. I just wish he'd fucking talk to someone."

"I'll try again but you know what he's like."

"Sure do. Stubborn, fucker."

"You should get back to Peyton, Luc. No matter what she says, she needs you right now. And if you're serious about proving yourself then you need to be there."

"I am. Could you do me a favor?"

"Of course. Anything."

After asking Letty to check in on Fee and Kayden, I hang up and rest my head back against the wall for a beat.

I barely slept last night. If I wasn't watching Peyton with my head spinning, filled with regrets and trying to come up with killer ways to prove to her that I really want this, I was waiting for one of our cells to ring with bad news.

I want to try to be positive for her, but I'm finding it hard when the situation seems so fucking dire.

I shoot Lee a message, inquiring as to who he hooked up with last night, something fucking normal before going for the coffee I was meant to be getting.

It feels like I've been gone ages by the time I push through the door to Libby's room balancing two coffees and cupcakes in one hand.

I was expecting to find Dr. Willis in here giving an update but it's still only Peyton in the exact position she was in when I left her.

"Hey sorry, Letty called and—" She turns to me, tears soaking her cheeks, her bottom lip trembling. "Fuck. What's happened?"

I all but throw the coffees to the table beside Libby's and drop to my knees in front of Peyton.

"D-Dr. Willis just left. Sh-she wanted to wait f-for you b-but—" She hiccups, cutting off her words.

"What did she say? What did the tests and scans show?"

"Th-they were good," she cries.

"G-good? Wait, what? They were good?"

She sniffs, pulling one of her hands from mine to wipe her cheeks. "Y-yeah."

"Holy shit, P. When I saw your face I thought—" I slam my lips shut. It doesn't matter what I thought, and Peyton certainly doesn't need to hear the words out loud.

"I'm sorry, I just—" She blows out a long breath.

"It's okay. You have nothing to apologize for."

Squeezing her hand in support, I release her and drag the other chair over so I can sit beside her.

"What did they say?"

She nods and holds her hands up for a few seconds as she tries to formulate the words.

"Brain activity was good. We have to wait for her to wake up, but they said they're more confident that there hasn't been too much damage and th-that..." She takes a moment. "She might have minimal damage from the stroke."

"That's fantastic news, P."

"They said she's got damage to both her liver and her... kidneys, I think. They said something about her heart, but I can't remember. It was a lot to absorb."

"I can imagine. Come here." I pull her into my arms and hold her tight.

"She might be okay, Luc."

With my fingers twisted in her hair, I pull her face from my neck and look into her tear-filled eyes.

"Luc?" she breathes.

Leaning forward, I brush my lips against hers. My need for her is too much to deny.

She tenses in my hold and I expect her to pull away. But when I move again, she doesn't back off, instead her lips mimic mine until they part and I'm able to slip my tongue inside.

"Okay, kids. Break it up," an amused voice says from the doorway.

Peyton jumps away from me as if she's been burned and looks over my shoulder.

"Hi, Doc. Sorry, we were—"

"It's okay. I've just got some paperwork for you to sign." She passes a clipboard over to Peyton, whose eyes briefly fly over the information before she signs her name at the bottom. "We've been in contact with Maddison County General and they have a room for Libby. Once we've woken her up and have been able to assess her we'll discuss the logistics of her transfer."

"Okay. That's great. Thank you so much."

"Did you need me to go over anything we said earlier?" Dr. Willis asks Peyton who shakes her head.

"N-no it's fine. I think I got it."

"It was good news, Peyton. The best we could expect given the situation. But there is still a very long road ahead for your sister."

"I know," Peyton agrees sadly. "But at least we're a step closer to the end."

"We are. Tomorrow, we'll begin reducing her medication and see how she goes. The detox is going to be tough, and we might find that she'll handle it better under sedation, but we'll have to wait to see."

"Okay. Whatever is better for her."

"I'll check in again later on. Keep it PG yeah?" she says with a laugh.

"Sure thing, Doc." I smile at her over my shoulder as she excuses herself from the room. "You okay?" I ask Peyton once we're alone again.

"Yeah," she says, resting back in the chair. "I know it's only the beginning but I can't help feeling that we might just go in the right direction."

I nod at her, looking over at Libby. I wish I could say she looked better, but the reality is that she looks as terrible as she did yesterday. To the point that if I passed her in the street like how she looks at this moment, I would never recognize her. It's heartbreaking.

"Letty called," I say after a few minutes, going back to what I was going to say when I first walked in. "She asked if she could do anything, so I suggested she stop in on Fee and Kayden. I hope that's okay."

"Of course. Aunt Fee will like that. I should call her and let her know the news."

"Why don't you go and get some air, take a minute after all that. I'll wait here with Lib."

She stares at her sister, reluctant to leave her.

"Nothing will happen, I promise."

"Y-yeah, okay."

"Take your coffee. I got you a cupcake too if you want it. Go and sit in that little garden we found yesterday."

She picks up the coffee but leaves the cupcake behind.

"I won't be long."

"Take as much time as you need, baby. All of this is a lot to process."

16

PEYTON

I rest back on the bench that's in the middle of the memorial garden we found out back of the hospital. The sun is shining, the scent of flowers fills my nose and the light breeze flows over my face.

For the first time since I received that phone call yesterday, I feel a little bit of hope trickle through my veins.

I take a sip at my now lukewarm coffee and focus on the taste instead of the man who got it for me.

Luca Dunn.

Fucking hell. He's been a part of my life, whether in actual person or just in spirit, all of my life. I have no memories of life before him, and I'm not sure I want to really admit it to myself, but equally, I don't want a future without making more with him.

I sit forward, dropping my head into my hands.

He's messing with my resolve to keep him at arm's length. Everything he's done since I ran into him yesterday has helped push what happened between us farther and farther back in my mind. But I don't want it to. I want to remember that vicious version of him. I need it to remind myself that I can't give in to the sweet boy hiding beneath. Because if I do, I'll be the one who's once again left heartbroken and alone. And it'll only be worse this time because it's not just my heart that will shatter.

Kayden.

A little boy who through no fault of his own has lost everything. If he were to lose Luca now, even though they've only seen each other across the yard... No. Just no. If protecting Kayden means keeping Luca at arm's length, then that's what I'll do.

I think about what I told Luca this morning about getting to know Kayden like Leon did, and I realize that I was a little harsh. I can't push my issues and my questionable relationship with Luca onto the one he could potentially have with his little brother. That's not fair.

I pull my cell out of my purse with the intention of calling Aunt Fee to update her, but when I land on another contact first, I know that I need to talk to her, to get a rational opinion on all of this.

"Peyton, how are you?" Letty says in a rush the second the call connects.

"I've been better," I answer honestly.

"I'm so sorry about your sister."

"Thanks."

"Any news?"

I give her the CliffsNotes version of what Dr. Willis and her colleagues said.

"That sounds positive."

"Yeah. She's got a long way to go. She's a freaking crank addict, Let," I confess, weirdly feeling lighter for having said the actual words.

"I know. She's got a long road ahead of her."

"I'm terrified that she's going to run straight back to it. If she does, the next time I see her, it's not going to be a bed she's lying in."

"All you can do is be there for her, Peyton. The rest is up to her."

I nod, although she can't see me. "I know. I just want to fix her, you know. I want my sister back."

"I can't even begin to imagine what you're going through right now," she says quietly.

"I just needed to talk to someone impartial. Thank you for answering."

"Of course. I hoped you might call."

I can almost hear the words she wants to say but holds back in the silence that follows.

"I know you've spoken to him."

"I know things are up in the air with your sister and everything, but where's your head at with him, Peyton."

"My head?" I laugh. "My head is telling me to run as far away from him as possible because it knows the kind of pain he's capable of causing."

"Smart," she deadpans.

"But it's not my head that's the issue," I admit.

"I figured as much."

"Last night, I—" I slam my lips shut, not really wanting to confess to what I did.

"I know."

"Shit," I hiss. "It was a mistake."

"Was it?"

"Y-yeah. It changed things. The way he keeps looking at me. He's got this hope in his eyes and it shreds me every time I see it because I can't give him what he wants, I'm not what he wants."

"You sure about that?"

"Jeez. I called you thinking you'd talk some sense into me."

"Peyton," she says with a laugh. "If you knew the whole story behind me and Kane and our history then trust me when I say that you'd never come to me for relationship advice. A lot of people would probably say that I did everything I shouldn't have, that I never should have forgiven him. But it's about more than just that. We both made mistakes. We both did things we're not proud of. But ultimately, life just makes more sense when we're together. Everything is easier when we're together.

"Things that might look bad to the outside world, sometimes are exactly what you need in your heart."

"But my head—"

"Your head and heart will come together at some point. You just have to trust it when it happens."

"And what if my head wins?"

"Then you walk away knowing that you're doing the right thing."

Just her saying the words literally feels like she's reaching inside my chest and pulling my heart out.

"And—"

"Trust yourself, Peyton. All this crazy shit with your sister, that needs to be your focus right now. Luca will still be there when it's all over. Something tells me it's gonna take quite a lot to get rid of him now anyway. It will all work out."

"I wish I had your positivity."

"One day you will. What he did, turning his back on you and all the crap since you came back. It was brutal. But maybe the time apart, the eruption when you collided again was exactly what you both needed."

"Everything happens for a reason," I whisper the words that Mom said to me more times than I can count over the years.

"Yep. I believe it does. MKU was our fate, Peyton. Written in the stars long before we knew anything about it. What you do with it now is up to you."

"Yeah, maybe."

"No one can make this decision but you, and you're the only one whose opinion matters. You're the only one who can control your happiness."

"Thank you, Letty."

"Anytime. It's nice to have someone listen to me. Kane, Luca, and Lee usually just grunt at me and pretend they're listening."

"I think you're listened to more than you think," I say with a chuckle.

"I should go. I need to update Aunt Fee."

"Okay. I'm here if you need me, okay. Judgment-free zone when it comes to bad decisions with me."

I laugh. "That's good to know. Thank you."

I pull my cell from my ear to hang up but Letty saying my name makes me pull it back.

"Yeah."

"Don't feel bad about using him for what you need. He owes you. Make the most of it."

"Letty, I think I love you." I laugh, feeling much more like myself.

"Feelings mutual, P. Speak soon, yeah?"

"Yeah."

—————

After calling Aunt Fee and then reluctantly my boss at The Locker Room to confirm what I'd already told him when I discovered what was going on, that I wasn't going to be there for at least the rest of this week, I make my way back up to Libby and Luca.

I feel lighter, less conflicted about everything that's going on between us after speaking to Letty. She makes everything sound so easy. It might be annoying if I didn't know she's just been through it with Kane. But I know she's talking from experience when it comes to complicated relationships, so I really appreciate it.

"Hey," Luca says softly. "How are you feeling?"

"Good. Better. Thank you for making me go. What's that?" I ask, taking in the battered purse that's sitting on the end of Libby's bed.

"Her purse. One of the nurses brought it in. They cleared it of... yeah. They kept it safe for you."

"Oh, is there much in it?"

"I haven't looked."

Walking over, I glance at my sister and then down at her purse. My need to know where she's been, what her life has been like, aside from the obvious, is too much to ignore and I pull the zipper open, peering inside.

I see that it's almost empty; other than a notebook, a tatty old wallet, and a lot of trash.

I pull out all the receipts and old wrappers and dump them into the trash. I find all the old coins at the bottom and drop them into her empty wallet.

"Oh my God," I gasp when I open the back section where her credit cards should be, although that part is empty. What captures my attention is the photograph on display.

"What is it?"

I stare down at a time that I remember like it was only yesterday.

"Is that the day he was born?" Luca asks, staring over my shoulder at the image of my sister holding a newborn Kayden in her arms and looking absolutely exhausted. No surprise there, she had the longest labor ever. Mom and I were there the whole way with her. It was incredible but long and painful for Libby.

"Yeah. Before everything fell apart. It's nice to know she's not forgotten that she's a mother."

"I'm sure that's not the case. She's just... lost, I guess," he says, sadness for my sister making his voice deeper than usual.

"Yeah, I know."

"What else is in there?"

"Trash mostly."

I pull the notebook out and stare at the words on the front, running my fingertip over the gold print.

Don't let anyone dull your sparkle.

A lump grows in my throat as I stare up at my sister.

She's certainly managed to dull her own sparkle.

"Anything exciting?" Luca asks, dropping back into the chair by Libby's bed as I flick through the pages.

A few loose pieces of paper fall free and scatter across the floor as I look at the pages of what looks to be some sort of diary.

"I think it's—"

"Motherfucker."

Luca's vicious tone forces me to abandon my sister's neat writing to see what's angered him.

Looking over, I find him standing with a photograph between his fingers.

"Wha— oh fuck," I breathe when I step up to him. I immediately understand his reaction because mine is almost as violent.

"I'm going to fucking kill him, P. I swear to fucking God."

I place my hand on Luca's forearm in the hope it'll calm him because he's trembling beside me with his restrained anger.

"He... he went after...." He lifts his hands to his hair and pulls so hard that there's no way it doesn't hurt. "He went after your fucking sister." His chest heaves and his eyes darken until they're bordering on terrifying. "What about any others? There could be other women right now across the country in this state because of him." The photograph in his hold screws up as his fist tightens.

"We don't know that."

His eyes shoot to mine.

"Don't we? Come on, P. Don't be naïve. Libby surely couldn't have been the only one. I know she's your sister and you love her, but she's nothing special. To him, she was just a young hot blonde who was willing to give him some attention. Add on the daddy issues and he was onto a winner."

My stomach turns over at his words but I can't deny that he's right.

"I know," I whisper.

"We have to figure out a way to expose this, to find other women. To make sure he pays for all this pain he's caused, continues to cause."

I nod, relief flooding me that he's saying out loud all the things I've wanted to do for years. Deep down, I know that Mom knew it was the right thing to do as well, but her priority was Libby, and I can't argue that she wasn't wrong there either. Having all this blow up, be all over the media would have made her worse. She might not have even been here now if that were the case back then, Kayden might not be here now.

I press my hand to my stomach, willing it to stop rolling before I have to run to the bathroom.

Plucking the photo from Luca's fingers, I stare down at the younger version of my sister. She's seventeen, I'd guess, wearing one of her favorite outfits from back then. Her hair is long and in bouncy curls, her eyes twinkling with happiness as she stares at him. I don't recognize where they are. The house isn't ours or the Dunn's. It's probably some hidden address that he used to use for meeting people.

"I think this is her diary," I confess, placing the photo back inside the pages and lowering myself to the chair.

I rest the book on my lap and look up at Luca as he begins to pace back and forth across the small room. A dark angry cloud surrounds him, one that I know will only end in destruction if I try to do anything about it.

A soft knock sounds out on the door before two of the nurses who have been caring for Libby slip inside.

"Hi, sweetie," the older one says, smiling at me. "Anything to report?"

I shake my head as they walk toward the end of Libby's bed and pull her chart from the bottom, studying it.

"We're just going to do her vitals. You're welcome to stay or—"

"I'll be back in a bit," Luca blurts, torment evident on his face.

Both the nurses look over at him and their brows furrow in concern.

"Y-yeah, okay." I force a smile on my lips but I know it doesn't help at all. He's too lost right now. But knowing how much getting away for a few minutes alone helped me earlier, I keep my mouth shut as he slips from the room.

"Is everything okay, sweetie? Things seem tense."

A bitter laugh falls from my lips. "Everything is fine," I force out.

"That sure is a fine young man you've got there, love," the younger one adds, her cheeks heating slightly at her confession.

"Yeah. He's something," I mutter.

"Oh, are you not together?"

I shake my head. "No. I'm not sure what we are."

"Well, Dr. Willis said—"

"Yeah? Well, things aren't always as simple as they seem. Excuse me." I storm from the room, my chest heaving and my hands trembling.

"Shit," I hiss to myself as I realize just how rude I was. "Fuck."

Needing a breather to calm down, I slip inside the empty family room and drop to the couch, my sister's diary still in my hands.

With trepidation, I flip over the first page.

Liberty Banks

KEEP OUT!

I smile as I think about teenage Libby writing that in the hope it would keep my nosy ass out. It might have worked back then if I was feeling nice, but it's certainly not going to work now. I need to know, and if what is on the pages within this book will help me discover what happened, help lead us to more, to the real truth then I'm all in. I'll just have to deal with the consequences later.

The first few pages are her gushing about the quarterback who preceded Luca on our high school football team. I remember him. Much like Luc, all the girls ran rings around him hoping to catch his eye, and my sister was no better. I don't need to read her words about how hot he is and how badly she wants to kiss him to know she was obsessed with him.

I scan the pages until I come to an aftergame party at the Dunn house. Brett was always trying to put himself right in the middle of the game long before Luca got captain, so it wasn't unusual for the parties to be there despite his own kids being too young. We were only sophomores but it didn't stop Brett from allowing his sons to party like seniors. I guess this is exactly how Luca and I ended up losing our virginity together earlier than I'm sure we should have. We were surrounded by it all. It was only natural that we started experimenting.

Shaking thoughts of our past out of my head, I keep reading until I find Brett's name.

My teeth grind at just seeing it. Knowing that he spoke to my sister, that he approached her, probably while she was wasted.

I keep reading despite the bile burning its way up my throat as she recalls just how sweet he was, how he told her how pretty she was and how the senior boys were lucky.

It's disgusting, and reading the bullshit that he fed her makes my skin crawl.

How did she fall for it?

Reading it now, it seems so obvious that he was playing her.

But I need to remember this isn't now. This was about six years ago. Libby was young, impressionable, and as Luca put it earlier, had daddy issues. I guess I shouldn't be all that surprised really.

She remembers our dad. She was just old enough when he decided to bail on us and Mom to remember him walking away. I, however, have no clue about the sperm donor who helped make me, and quite frankly, I'm happy for it to stay that way. It hurt Libby though. Believing that she wasn't good enough to make him stick around.

Ultimately, it was what all her issues as a teenager lead back to. And it's no different here.

I read through pages and pages of her former life. She was popular and had a lot of friends and I can't help smiling as I read through a happier time in her life, that is until every time I see his name mentioned.

He happened to be at Aces. At the beach. At football practice. At the store. At our goddamn house.

It's all too much, too forced but she didn't see any of it.

"Argh," I cry out in frustration. I wish that I could go back in time and warn her, show her exactly what he was doing to her, prove that he was grooming her and that really, he only wanted one thing.

I stop, slamming the book shut before anything actually happens, knowing that I'm not going to be able to handle it today. Just knowing that he was following her around town was bad enough, let alone him... I gag at the thought.

Holding the book against my stomach, I walk back to her room.

The nurses are long gone, the sun is setting outside but most noticeable is the fact that Luca isn't back and there is no sign of him.

"Shit." Digging my cell out of my purse, I hit call.

I knew he was in a bad place when he walked out. Maybe I should have stopped him.

17

LUCA

B y the time I walk back into Libby's room, the sun has long set and the hallways of the hospital are deserted.

I didn't intend on disappearing for most of the afternoon and evening. But seeing that image of my father with his arm around Libby, him staring down at her like she's the most precious thing in the world made my need to run unignorable. She was something precious, a fucking child. So what if she was only a few weeks short of eighteen. He was a grown-ass married man with kids. He should have been nowhere near her, let alone in a fucking hotel room or wherever that photo was taken.

Despite the hours that have passed, and the fact that I thought I'd managed to somewhat calm down, my fists curl once again as I think of that photograph.

The wounds on my knuckles from earlier this afternoon split open once more but I don't bother looking down to inspect them, I already know they're fucked. But the pain felt too good, too soothing. It gave me something to focus on other than my anger.

If Coach knew how much action my hands were getting right now that didn't involve catching or throwing a ball, he'd have my fucking ass. Fucking up my hands is a surefire way to have the decision I'm battling with about my future made for me.

Ignoring the sting, I push the door open, ready for Peyton to rip me a new one for my disappearing act, only when I do step into the dark room, no one so much as moves.

I find her curled up on the chair using the hoodie I left behind as a pillow.

She looks incredibly uncomfortable, and as much as I might want her to rest, I know she can't do it like that.

Dropping to my knees before her, I place my hand on her thigh.

"Peyton," I whisper.

She startles at my voice, her eyes flying open and finding mine.

"Where have you been?" she asks, that pissed off tone I was expecting in her voice.

"Cooling off. I'm sorry I bailed for so long."

She uncurls herself and sits up, stretching out the kink in her neck.

"It's okay. I get it." Her eyes drop to my hand on her thigh. "Shit, Luc," she gasps, picking it up and inspecting the damage.

"It's nothing."

"They're a mess. That's not nothing."

"How are things here?"

"Same."

"Okay. Did you wanna head out? I picked up takeout on my way back here."

Her stomach growls at the thought and I smile what feels like my first genuine smile all afternoon.

"You're cute."

"I'm not, I'm hungry. Let me say goodbye to Lib and we'll go."

I stand back and allow her to whisper something to her sister before she drops a kiss to her forehead.

We're almost out the door when she stops and doubles back toward a cupboard at the other side of the room.

"What are you doing?"

She rummages around a bit before holding up some white packets.

"Supplies for your hands," she states with a raised brow.

"Stealing from a hospital, P. That's low."

"It's a couple of bandages. After the amount you've paid for her care, I'm sure it'll be fine."

I want to argue and tell her that I'm fine, that my hands will heal, but the determined look in her eyes stops me from saying the words.

"Whatever makes you happy, baby."

Wrapping my arm around her shoulder, I pull her into my body and kiss the top of her head, breathing in her scent.

Everything inside me settles the second we connect. So much better than plowing my fists into a wall.

If only she could forgive me and let me really get my fix of her.

"What's that smell?" Peyton asks the second she walks into our room.

Stepping up behind her, I wrap my arms around her waist and brush my lips against her neck.

She tenses for a moment but after a second, she relaxes back into me.

"Your favorite."

"Luc," she warns when I part my lips and suck on her skin.

"I know, baby. I can't help it."

She sighs before pulling herself out of my hold. "I really need to eat."

I smile at her as she makes her way over to the bag that I left on the table before heading to the hospital.

"I hope it's still hot enough."

"It'll be perfect," she says, digging inside for the boxes and chopsticks.

She's almost shoveling rice into her mouth long before her ass even hits the chair.

"Oh my God, it's so good," she moans, her eyes closing in pleasure.

"Yeah?" I ask, unable to contain my smile that she's finally eating something.

"Come on before I eat it all."

"Wouldn't stop you, baby."

"You should. You don't want to ruin this, do you?" she asks with a smirk, looking down at her body.

Stepping up to her, I take her chin in my hand and tilt her face up so she has no choice but to look at me.

"Just you, P. I love your body, but that's not what I fell in love with when I was eight years old."

Her breath catches at my honesty, her eyes glazing over.

"You need to eat too. Then I'll fix your hands up."

Lowering down to her, I brush my lips over hers and thankfully she allows me to do it before I force myself to take a step back before I push too hard.

I need her so fucking badly right now, but I know I need to tread carefully. If I fuck this up then it really might be the final nail in our coffin, and that can't happen.

I know she says she regrets last night, but the darkness in her eyes when I stare at her across the table tells me otherwise. I just need her to stop worrying about the future, about the past and just focus on the right now when we're together because that's the only way I can see us getting through this.

She needs to remember just how good we can be together. Why we were always destined to be together. Why we were made for each other.

"Thank you for this."

"You're welcome."

I want to ask about the diary, if she read it or discovered anything but equally, I'm not sure I've got it in me to hear any more about it tonight. So instead of saying anything, we eat in comfortable silence, lost in our own thoughts.

The second she's done, she pushes the takeout boxes away from her, hops up and grabs what she took from the hospital.

"They'll be fine. You don't need—" She raises her brow and pins me with a look that silences me immediately. "Okay. Fine."

"Sit." She shoots a look at the end of the bed and I stand, pulling my hoodie and shirt off as I go and throwing it toward my bag in the corner of the room.

She rolls her eyes at me, clearly knowing what I'm doing. But I don't give a fuck. I'll use all the dirty tricks I can come up with right now.

"It's not going to work, you know?" she mutters, taking one of my hands in hers and inspecting the damage. The second her soft skin brushes against my callused fingers, sparks shoot up my arm heading straight to my dick.

"I'm not one to give up easily on something I want."

"Don't I know it."

I wince as she cleans the cuts on my knuckles, watching with amusement as she refuses to look anywhere but my hands.

I let her do her thing, knowing that she'll feel better once she's done it before capturing both of her hands in mine.

"Peyton," I breathe. "Look at me."

She keeps her head bowed, refusing to comply.

"What did you hit?"

"A wall. A few times."

"Shit, Luc. You can't do that. If you fuck up your hand then—"

"My dad will lose his shit? I don't really give a fuck about his opinion anymore, P."

"This has nothing to do with him and you know it. This is about you, about your future."

"I don't know if—" Finally, she looks up at me.

"It's your life, Luca. You can't walk away from everything you've worked toward your entire life."

"It's his life," I spit.

"You're nothing like your father, Luca. You're four times the man he is, if not more. You're kind, protective, loving. All the things he has no clue about."

I shake my head, not willing to accept that.

"Look at what I did to you, Peyton. I'm none of those things. Not anymore. I might have been before, but he destroyed all the good within me."

"Bullshit. You were angry, you wanted revenge. That's normal, Luca. Everyone feels those things."

"You're never going to forgive me though, are you?"

She shrugs. "Maybe I already have," she whispers, averting her gaze. "It doesn't mean I'll ever forget though."

My heart sinks because somehow, I think that could be worse. She's always going to look at me knowing what kind of a monster lives just beneath the surface.

"You're right though." My entire body jolts at her confession. "A dark part of me enjoyed it." Her cheeks burn bright red and her eyes leave mine as embarrassment surges through her.

Reaching out, I take her chin in my grasp.

"No point being embarrassed by it, baby. I already know. Your body told me exactly how much you enjoyed it."

Her eyes find mine once again and she swallows nervously, the silver I'm used to turning a dark gray.

"Luc?"

Sliding to the end of the mattress, I wrap my hands around her waist and lift her from the floor, placing her on the dresser opposite, and sweeping the contents to the floor.

"Luca, we shouldn—" My lips slam down on hers, cutting off her argument.

Her hands slide to my chest and she pushes gently, a pathetic attempt to do what she thinks is the right thing.

Pulling back, I rest my brow against hers.

"I need you, Peyton. Today has been—"

"I know, Luc." Her warm hand cups my rough jaw. "I know, but—"

"The buts don't matter right now. Just do what feels right."

My hands slip inside her shirt, connecting with the smooth skin of her waist and I push higher, brushing my thumbs over her nipples.

She gasps in shock and her lips once again find mine as she throws caution to the wind and dives in with both feet.

Her legs wrap around my waist, her heels digging into my ass and pulling me closer as I drag her shirt up her body and throw it to the floor.

"Luca," she moans when I kiss down her neck as I unhook her bra, freeing her swollen breasts.

"No pain tonight, baby," I whisper against her soft skin. "Only pleasure."

I suck one of her nipples into my mouth and her back arches as her head falls back, a moan ripping from her throat.

Lifting her from the dresser, I lay her out on the bed and rid her of the rest of her clothes before spending what's left of our night making the most of her. Proving to her why this is how it should be. The two of us against the world like it was all those years ago.

———

I come to, with her in my arms but the second I pull her closer, I know something is wrong.

Ripping my eyes open, I find her laying on her back and staring up at the ceiling, her body tight with tension.

"What's wrong, baby?"

She swallows, her lips parting ready to say the words I assume she's been planning for a while.

"I... I need you to leave."

All the breath rushes from my lungs.

"L-leave?"

"Yeah. I need you to go back to Maddison. Back to your life."

"My life is here. With you."

"No, it's not," she snaps. "You're only here out of guilt. You need to leave," she repeats, her voice rough with emotion as she throws the sheets back and attempts to get out of bed, only my grip on her is too tight.

"You don't mean that," I state, feeling like my world has just been pulled from beneath me once again.

"I do. Whatever this is," she says, gesturing between us. "It needs to stop. We're not those same people anymore and we don't have the future we once did."

"No," I say, refusing to accept what she's saying. "What about Libby? What about—"

"Libby is improving. She doesn't need both of us here putting our lives on hold."

"What if I don't want to go back?"

"I don't care, Luc. I need you to leave. I can't d-do this right now."

Reaching out, I cup her cheek, finally turning her toward me. It takes her a few seconds but eventually, her eyes find mine.

The pain and tears in her silver depths slay me.

"Please, Luc. I know you're trying to make things better but right now, you're only making my life harder."

I shake my head, unable to accept her words although knowing that she truly means them.

"I'm sorry, Luc. We're done. This is finished."

This time when she twists away from me to get out of bed, I release my arm and allow her to go.

I watch as she pads naked to the bathroom. She pauses in the doorway and looks down at her feet.

"I think it's probably best if you're gone by the time I get out."

Without waiting for a response, she slams the door closed and flips the lock.

18

PEYTON

I stand with my palms on the sink and my head lowered, fighting like hell to keep it all together until I hear the motel room door slam shut.

Then all hell breaks loose.

Swiping my arm across the counter, the few bottles that were littering the top go scattering across the small bathroom, ricocheting off the toilet and bouncing on the tiled floor.

"Argh," I scream, lifting my hands to my hair and pulling until it hurts. When that's not enough, I turn toward the door and rain my fists down on the chipped paintwork.

Part of me wishes that he's playing me. That he didn't just leave and is about to smash his way inside and show me that the decision I just made was wrong.

But that's not what happens because he left.

I knew he would the second I looked into his eyes.

Those words, me demanding he leave, gutted him.

He really thought that things were getting better here, maybe that we were embarking on the beginning of something. And that's exactly why I know what I just did was the right thing to do.

I can't let myself fall back into my old safety net that is Luca Dunn.

I'm better than that now, stronger. I refuse to lose myself in him, lean on him, rely on him.

Turning the shower on as hot as it will go—which admittedly isn't all that hot—I step under barely feeling the burn.

I don't even remember my journey to the hospital, and as I sit beside my sleeping sister once more, I'm completely numb. My brain refuses to focus on anything other than trying to convince me that I did the right thing. My heart, on the other hand, that feels like it's about to shatter into a million pieces once again.

The pain of him leaving is akin to the day he called me a liar and turned his back on me, only this time, it really is my fault.

Thankfully, my sister's vitals are still good so when Dr. Willis appears during her afternoon rounds, she confirms that they are going to start reducing her sedation so they can see how responsive she is.

The next four days are the most terrifying of my life, sitting alone and waiting for any kind of life from Libby. But still, I refuse to respond to any of the calls or messages I get from Luca. I speak to Aunt Fee, Letty, even Leon regularly and I know they're all feeding info back to him, but I just can't bring myself to reach out.

I'm still conflicted over the decision I made because having been here alone now longer than he was here with me, I know how much easier he was making it. Just to have him hold me when it was all getting to be too much. To feel the warmth of his thumbs as he wiped tears off my cheeks. The escape he offered me once we retreated to our motel room.

I expected to be kicked out of the motel room. I have no idea how many nights Luca paid for, but I know my time must be running out, and despite the fact it's probably cheap, I already know I can't afford to pay for it. All my spare money goes to Mom and Kayden's medical debts, and that's something that isn't going to be changing anytime soon.

I stare at Libby, unbelievably grateful to Luca for paying for all of this for her and not just piling more debt on my shoulders. I feel guilty for taking it, even if it is Brett's money at the end of the day. I never want to feel like a charity case, and although I know that that wasn't his intention, I still can't help feeling that way about it.

"Come on, Lib. Just give me a sign that everything is going to be okay."

Dr. Willis and the nurses have warned me about the state she could wake up in. Not only is she going to be totally disorientated, but we also have no idea how much memory she'll have of how she ended up here. Add in the detox from the meth on top of all that and it could be intense, to say the least.

I can't help hoping for the best though. For a miracle. It's the only thing I've got to latch on to right now while the rest of my world feels like it's falling apart.

My cell buzzes in my pocket and just like every time it rings, my heart jumps into my throat thinking that I'm about to stare down at his name and continue my internal battle as to whether I should just answer or not.

It's stupid, but disappointment floods me when I see Aunt Fee's name instead. I shouldn't care, it's what I wanted but the thought of him going back to Maddison and continuing on with his life like I told him to makes me feel physically sick. Has he gone running straight to another woman? A jersey chaser to make him feel better?

Bile burns up my throat as I accept the call and switch it onto speakerphone. I do it every time Aunt Fee calls just in case Libby can hear her.

"Hey love, any news?" Aunt Fee asks hopefully, but with every day that passes, it gets a little less.

The doctors have assured me that it's normal for people to take their time waking up. Libby's body has been through so much and it just needs this time to heal.

I want to say the words are reassuring, but every hour that passes without any progress only terrifies me more.

I can't lose my sister too. I just can't.

"Nope," I say sadly, my heart aching as I do. "Still nothing. They don't seem to be concerned though."

"She just needs time. When she's ready, she'll come back to us."

I'm trying to be as positive about all of this as Aunt Fee but with each hour that passes, it's getting harder.

"How's our boy?" I ask, hoping to steer the conversation to something lighter.

"He's good. He's right here."

"Hi, PeyPey."

"Hey, baby boy. How are you doing? Have you had a fun day?"

"We painted you a picture," he says. His soft voice washing through me and making me feel that little bit brighter.

"Oh yeah. What's it of?" I ask, curling into my chair but keeping Libby's hand in mine.

"We put your favorite flowers on it."

"Aw, I can't wait to see it."

"When are you coming home?" Sadness edges into his voice and it makes my heart crack a little.

"Soon, baby. I promise."

"Okay, good. I miss you."

As he says those final three words, something happens.

"Oh my God," I squeal, jumping from the chair. "Libby? Libby, are you awake?"

"Peyton?" Aunt Fee calls down the line.

"She squeezed my hand," I say, not knowing where my cell has gone. "She squeezed my hand," I repeat, already not believing that I really felt it.

"Libby," I breathe. "I'm here. I'm here and everything is going to be okay."

I stare at her, willing her to do something else. Anything to prove to me that she's finally coming back to me.

Come on. Come on, I will silently.

"What else have you done today, buddy?" I ask Kayden after long silent seconds, knowing that it was his voice she reacted to.

"Umm... we went to the store. Aunt Fee bought me my favorite candy because I've been a good boy."

"That's awesome, sweetie. Did you eat them all?"

"Nope. I'm saving some for after dinner." I smile at my sweet boy.

"Aw, that's good. Did you watch your cartoons today?"

That question sets him off and he embarks on a full rundown of what he's watched today.

Finding my cell still on the chair I was sitting on, I move it closer to Libby so she can hear him.

"That's your boy, Lib," I whisper to her, my eyes burning with tears. "If you're going to do this for anyone, do it for him. Please."

He chats away like nothing huge is happening while I wait patiently for another reaction from my sister.

Finally, he runs out of steam, and I have no choice but to bring the call to an end so he can have his dinner.

"You be a good boy for Aunt Fee tonight, young man."

"I'm always a good boy," he states.

"I know, baby. I'll see you real soon, okay?"

"Okay. I love you, PeyPey."

"I love you too, Kayden." I blow a kiss down the line and hang up.

"Did you hear that, Lib? That was your baby."

My breath rushes from my lungs as she squeezes my hand again.

"Oh my God, you did." The tears that were burning my eyes drop freely, soaking into the white sheets covering my sister's body. "He's so incredible, Lib. You'll be so proud of him. He's so caring, so kind. And clever too. He learns things so fast, he's so inquisitive. He's actually taught me a thing or two. I can't wait for you to see him again."

Her eyelids flutter and my hands tremble as I hold hers.

The seconds feel like hours as I wait, willing her to look at me. But nothing could prepare me for what I find when she finally does. Her eyes that are so much like mine and our mom's are cold, empty, and my heart shatters into a million pieces.

"Libby, it's so good to see you," I force out through my pain.

I know she's only at the beginning of this long and painful journey right now. I know that. But staring reality in the face is another story.

Her free hand lifts to the forearm of the hand I'm holding. The one marred with the most scars from years of abuse by both needles and blades it seems and she scratches at it.

"It's going to be okay, Libby," I say again, not knowing what else to say in such a dire situation. "You're going to get through this. I'll do everything I can to get you through this."

Her eyes hold mine for a few more seconds. Pain bleeding from them before her lids lower once more and she succumbs to her exhaustion and the meds being pumped through her body.

"Oh my God," I breathe once I'm confident she's asleep once more.

I hit the call button and wait for someone to appear around the door to tell them what happened.

I'm expecting a nurse but the person who appears is Dr. Willis.

"Everything okay, Peyton?"

"She woke up. Sh-she squeezed my hand and she looked at me."

"Okay, that's good. Do you think she recognized you?"

I shrug. "I don't think so. She just looked... broken."

I can't help but break down once more.

"I'm sorry," I mutter through my tears. "I'm just going to get some air."

"This is good news, Peyton. Things will get better. She probably wasn't even really awake."

I nod at her, knowing it's the truth but the look in my sister's eyes still haunts me, nonetheless.

My first reaction the second I get outside of the hospital and breathe in some fresh winter air is to call Luca and that reaction to what's just happened only makes me sob harder.

Every day since that first evening, Libby came around a little more and for a little longer each time.

Thankfully, by the next night, when she looked at me, there was a little more life in her eyes and I breathed a sigh of relief. Well, that was until she freaked out and tried ripping her IV out and the doctor on shift ended up putting her back to sleep before she hurt herself.

Yesterday, when she came to again, she actually said my name.

I sobbed like a baby as we sat there holding hands, crying together for everything we've lost. It might have been a harrowing experience, but it was the closest I've felt to my sister in years and I didn't want it to end.

Each time she wakes, she's stronger and this morning she spoke properly for the first time asking me where she was and what had happened. I skirted around the reality of the situation, unsure how she'd really deal with the truth right now and she seemed to accept it.

"Okay then, young lady," Dr. Willis says brightly after poking her head into the room to see if Libby's awake. "Are you ready to make your escape?"

Libby scoffs, already knowing that the only place she's escaping to is another hospital.

I have no clue what kind of strings Luca managed to pull when he sorted all this out. Now that Libby is awake and all her vitals are looking good, she's getting airlifted to Maddison County General where there's a private room waiting for her.

As glad as I am to finally be heading home, I'm terrified it's going to set her back in some way.

All the doctors and nurses have assured me that she'll be fine, but I still can't help worrying.

"I'm going to be right beside you the whole way, okay?"

She nods at me but I can see the torment in her eyes.

After packing everything up, we make our way up to the roof where we find a helicopter which is way bigger than I was anticipating.

"H-how?" Libby asks, her voice rough from sleep.

"You don't need to worry about that now, Lib. Just enjoy the luxury. A chopper all to yourself, not everyone gets to experience that."

A small smile curls at her lips but it's forced.

Dr. Willis and the two nurses who've spent the most time with Libby talk to the medical staff who are going to be flying with us and in no time we're all strapped in and ready to go.

"Thank you," I say sincerely to Dr. Willis, more grateful than she can ever know for everything she's done for both of us over the past two weeks.

She smiles at me. "Look after each other, you two." And with a nod, the sliding door is closed and we're on our way back.

Back to Maddison.

Back to real life.

Back to Luca.

I wring my hands on my lap as I think about having to see him again after ignoring all his attempts to contact me. Although, all of that vanished a couple of days ago like he totally forgot I existed. I don't know what's worse, the reminder that I possibly made the wrong decision or the fact he's moved on from it.

"Why do you look so nervous about this?" Libby asks me. She's not been awake all that long but already her eyes are getting heavy.

"A lot has changed in five years, Lib." I don't say it to be mean or make her feel guilty but from the look on her face as the words pass my lips, I know that's how she's taken it. "My life... it's... things are just really up in the air. Being here with you, it's been somewhat of a relief."

"You don't want to go back?"

Isn't that the million-dollar question.

"Of course. It's our home now, Lib." I smile at her, but she doesn't return it.

"I don't have a home, Peyton. Haven't for a long time."

"Then it's time to fix that, don't you think?"

Ripping her eyes away from mine, she blankly stares out of the helicopter as we move smoothly through the sky. My stomach twisting with all the unknowns we've yet to come across.

"What the fuck?" a familiar voice snaps from the doorway of my room two seconds after it swings open. "What the hell are you doing, Luc?"

"Go away."

She laughs as she pads across the room, throwing the curtains open and doing the same with the windows.

"If you think that's going to work then you don't know me as well as I think you do," she mutters. She turns back to look at me with her hands on her hips and a fiercely stubborn look on her face.

"Whoa, captain material right here," a deep voice rumbles, amusement laced through his irritating tone.

"Oh fuck right off, Let. You didn't fucking bring him." I push myself up against the headboard. The room is spinning around me as a bottle rolls off the bed and clatters against the floor.

"Talk to my girl like that again, Dunn, and this cloud of weed isn't what will end your NFL career before it's even started."

"Get the fuck out of here, Legend. No one fucking invited you to join the party."

"This isn't a fucking party, Luc," Letty spits as she begins tidying up around me. "Kane, go and wait downstairs. I got this."

He stands in my doorway with his arms crossed over his chest, his face hard and deadly.

"Kane," she urges.

"It was much tidier the last time I was in here. Smelled better too," he muses.

"When the fuck have you ever been in my room before?"

His eyes slide over to Letty. "You wanna tell him, Princess, or shall I?"

"Do as you're told for once, Kane."

"Fine. I'll leave it to you. Just don't forget to tell him how loud you screamed."

"Get out," she cries, throwing an empty beer bottle at him. He catches it with no effort before placing it on the dresser beside him.

"Going. Watch yourself, Dunn."

"I'm not gonna touch your girl, Legend." But despite his confidence, his eyes hold mine for a beat before he finally turns his back on both of us and leaves.

Letty walks over and closes the door behind him. Her presence in what's become my sanctuary over the past week or so is oppressive and no matter how much I might love her, right now, I just want her to leave me to my own misery.

"I'm done letting you wallow in self-pity. Your pity party for one is officially over," she states, dropping a few more bottles into the bag in her hand before placing it by the door, ready to go down to the trash. "It's time to sort your shit out."

She steps up to the bed and reaches for the sheets.

"You need to get up, get showered, shaved, and put your fucking game face on."

"Let, no," I cry, trying to catch the sheets as she pulls them from my body. But my alcohol-dazed brain means my arms don't coordinate with my head and they're gone before I get to stop them.

Instead, I'm forced to just cup my junk as I sit naked in the middle of my bed.

"Jesus, Luc."

"What? It's my fucking bed. I can sleep naked if I want."

"Whatever. Here," she says, grabbing a pair of boxers from my drawer and throwing them at me.

"You mind?" I ask when she just stands there.

"I've seen your cock before, Luc. It was nothing mind-blowing."

My chin drops in shock.

"W-when?"

Looking away, she walks toward my window, probably to get some fresh air.

"You were a whore in high school. I walked in on you and some cheerslut more than once."

"How don't I know this?" I mutter, wracking my brain for any kind of memory.

She rests her hands on the windowsill and leans forward.

"You were thoroughly distracted."

"Didn't stop you looking though, did it?" I deadpan.

"Trust me, I didn't hang around to watch."

"That why you fucked Lee?"

She turns back and pins me with a hard look.

"You need to let that go."

"I know. I have." Mostly. "I'm just curious."

"I was jealous, okay? Is that what you want to hear? I had a hella crush on you, but you never looked at me twice. You were too concerned with which cheerslut you were going to stick your cock into next. Lee knew, he saw everything. He always sees everything." I can't help but mutter my agreement. That asshole really does see it all. "He consoled me. We were drunk and one thing led to another."

"You're not his type. I think that's why I never even considered it would happen," I say, knowing my brother's addiction to redheads. Letty is actually the only one that I know of who breaks his mold when it comes to his chosen partners.

"I know. Neither of us were thinking about reality that night. We just needed comfort and we had each other."

"Okay. I get it. Enough about that." I shake my head, ridding the images of what the three of us got up to right there not so long ago from my head.

Any possibility of anything happening with me and Letty is long gone.

She's got Kane, and I've got... no one.

I drop my head into my hands as the mattress beside me dips as Letty sits down.

She places her hand on my shoulder.

"They're on their way, Luc. This... whatever this is, it needs to stop."

"She doesn't need me, Let. It doesn't matter that she's coming back."

"That's bullshit and you know it."

"Is it?"

I haven't told anyone the details of why I ended up leaving Peyton in that motel room. Letty doesn't need to hear it from me, I already know she's heard from Peyton.

Damn them for becoming friends. I've got no chance of drowning myself in vodka and weed with them teaming up.

"She's hurting, Luc. And you... you were making her feel things she wasn't ready for."

"She told you that?"

"Well, not in so many words, no. But I know it's the truth."

I scoff, not willing to accept that she actually cares at all. Especially after the way she sent me home and cut me out of her life as if I hadn't been there holding her hand since she found out about Libby.

"I don't care. We're done."

Letty shakes her head.

"What about Kayden and... and your d—"

"Don't," I spit. "Don't even think about calling him that."

"You can't just drown all of this under as much vodka as you can get your hands on."

"I don't know what else to do," I confess. "Everything is such a mess. I can't see him. If I do, I'll probably kill him. And she won't even respond to a message."

"Honestly, I don't have any advice about him other than you need to sort yourself out and go and visit your mom. As for Peyton, give her time, give her some space but show her that you haven't forgotten, that you haven't stopped caring just because you're not in the same room."

I stare at her. "Give her space but show her I haven't forgotten her. Contradictory much." I roll my eyes.

"Use your imagination, Luc. I know you've got one."

"Where's Lee at?"

"Right this second, no idea. But I'm worried about him. I'm not sure when he last slept in his own bed."

"So he's not spoken to Mom?"

"I don't think he's spoken to anyone. I can barely get anything out of him."

"All the redheads on campus better watch their backs, huh?" It's supposed to be a joke but it falls flat between us.

We both know it's how he deals with the hard shit. While I turn to the nearest bottle, Leon finds the nearest redhead and fucks her raw.

"Go clean up, I'll sort this place out."

Reaching out, I wrap my hand around the back of her neck and pull her to me, dropping a kiss to the top of her head.

"Thank you, Let. What would I do without you?"

"Die of alcohol poisoning? Now get in the shower, you stink."

By the time I emerge from the bathroom, my room looks less like a homeless guy is squatting inside it and once again resembles my own space.

"I made coffee," Letty says, nodding to the mug that's sitting on my nightstand.

I drop onto my bed and cradle it in my hands.

I feel better after the shower, but the effects of the vodka are still lingering.

"Talk to me, Luc. Whatever it is."

"I miss her," I confess, keeping my eyes locked on the coffee before me.

"So what are you going to do about it?"

"Follow your advice, I guess."

She laughs as if that's the most absurd thing she's ever heard and I have no choice but to look up at her. "What?"

"When have you ever listened to anything I've told you?"

"I have once or twice."

"Sure you have." She rolls her eyes at me as she sips on her own coffee. "Anyway. They're due about six-thirty. She's planning on going back to work tomorrow night, and—"

"Like fuck she is," I bark. "She's not stepping foot back in that place."

"You can't stop her working, Luc. That's not fair."

"Do you even know where she works?"

"Waitress in some bar?"

"Yeah, something like that."

"Well..." Her eyes widen as she waits for me to elaborate.

"The Locker Room isn't just a bar, it's an exclusive gentleman sports bar."

"Exclusive..."

"The waitresses, the girls. They... uh... make really good tips for their... waitressing skills." My stomach turns over at just the thought of those guys mentally fucking my girl.

"Nooo." Letty's eyes almost pop out of her head.

"Peyton doesn't do any of that, but still. The kind of men who drink there aren't ones I want around her."

"How do you know all this? Is it somewhere you drink?" she asks with her brow cocked.

Lifting my hand, I scrub it over my face before dragging my hair back.

"Brett owns it."

"Fuck off. Fuck right off, Luc. Does she know?"

I shake my head.

"Why the fuck haven't you told her? She'd never work there if she knew."

And here lies an issue I've been battling with for some time now.

"She's only working there to pay for her mom and Kayden's medical bills. If I tried to stop her—which she never would have allowed—then all I'm doing is making the debt worse."

"So? Pay it off."

"I have," I confess, and she holds my stare, waiting for me to explain. "When we got to Atlanta, I sorted Libby's insurance, dealt with her coming back here and cleared everything Peyton owes."

"But you didn't tell her?" she guesses correctly.

"She knows about Libby, obviously. But she didn't want to accept that, so I figured I'd wait to tell her about the rest."

"You need to tell her before she turns up to work for that scumbag."

"I know. I will."

"I'll speak to my boss. One of our girls is about to go off to have a baby. Maybe she can come work with me."

"Sounds like a much better option.

"Brett Dunn's life is already balancing on a knife-edge, the cunts from that bar are right behind him."

"Careful there, Luc. You're starting to sound like Kane."

"Never. Although I assume he has experience with that kind of activity."

She narrows her eyes on me. It's no secret that Kane was a member of the Harrow Creek Hawks and has probably put more bodies in the ground than I care to think about.

"The less you know the better."

"Well, that's not exactly reassuring," I deadpan.

"It wasn't meant to be. But he's done with all that. If you need help with anything, then you wanna go to the Harrises."

I stare at her in disbelief. "You're not actually suggesting that I—"

"Do what you need to do, Luc. I hated Brett before all of this. It would hardly be a waste to society."

"Who are you and what have you done with my sweet best friend?"

"I had a reality check, Luc. Life is messy and ugly. Sometimes you just gotta do what you gotta do."

She pushes to stand from the chair and walks over.

"If you need anything, call me, yeah? And no more hiding."

"Whatever you say, *Mom*."

She rolls her eyes at me.

"I'm going to look after Kayden for a couple of hours so Fee can be at the hospital for Libby and Peyton. I'll be done by eight." She winks, ensuring I miss the hidden meaning in her words. "And if you see Lee, slap him upside the head for me and tell him to get his shit together. You've both got big decisions to make and being continually fucked up ain't getting either of you anywhere."

She drops a kiss to my cheek before disappearing from my room and leaving me alone once more, only I'm much more sober and my room looks a hell of a lot better.

I get dressed and head out of the house, knowing that I've got shit that needs dealing with. Most importantly, I need to get rid of Peyton's fucking job, so she has no reason to step foot back in that place ever again.

The parking lot is quiet when I pull up, and as I make my way through the bar toward Bry, who I swear lives behind the thing, I find it just as empty.

"Evening. How's it going?"

Bry knows the basics after I called when we first got to Atlanta to let them know Peyton wouldn't be at work. And I've also been here drinking since I got sent back, so he's well aware that shit ain't great right now. He should just be grateful that those cunts, or my father, weren't here when I was because I was gunning for a fight.

"Yeah, you know. Julian here?"

"Yeah, he's out back."

With a nod, I take off in the direction of the staff-only door I walked through the night I came to find Peyton.

Fuck, that night feels like a lifetime ago.

I step into his office without knocking, although I really wish I fucking did when I find a pair of heels and fishnet-wrapped legs sticking out from under his desk.

He's sitting in his chair with his head tipped back in pleasure and his eyes tightly closed.

Clearing my throat, his head flies forward, his eyes widening in shock.

"We need to talk," I state, not willing to wait for him to finish.

"Get the fuck out," he barks at whoever it is under his desk.

The girl backs out, wiping at her mouth with the back of her hand before turning to me.

I recognize her, and she clearly does me too as a smile curls at her lips.

"You wanna join the party, sweetheart?"

"Do I... Fuck. Get the hell out."

"That's a real shame, doll. I just know we could have some fun."

"Helena?" Julian barks when she's about to disappear.

"Yeah, baby."

"Come back when he's done. I'm not finished with you."

"Sure thing. I'm more than ready for it."

She's barely past the threshold when I swing the door closed on her.

"Peyton is done here. Whatever shifts you have her scheduled for, wipe them off. Cancel her contract."

"E-excuse me?" he spits.

"You heard me. Find yourself another girl to sweet talk your customers."

"She's one of my best girls."

My stomach turns over knowing just how popular her little sweet and innocent look is.

"I don't give a shit, Julian. She's done."

"I know your surname might be Dunn, boy. But you are not my boss. Only your father gets to call the shots around here."

"Yeah well, things are fucking changing. Wipe her off the schedule. Better yet, forget she even fucking exists," I seethe, walking toward him, cracking my knuckles as I do.

"You threatening me, boy?"

"I'll do whatever is necessary to stop her from ever walking back in here."

I hold his stare, willing him to break first because I've got other shit to be doing.

In the end, he must get bored with the stand-off because he throws his hands up. "Fine. She's done. Are you finished?"

"Give me what you owe her?"

"W-what?"

"You haven't paid her for this month yet. Pay up." I hold my hand out, not willing to walk out of here without what she's owed. It's the least she deserves after putting herself through this hell for months.

He pushes his chair back and stands, obviously deciding that it'll just be easier to do what I say than to fight me on this.

"Jesus, you're just like your old—"

"NO," I roar, pinning him against the wall with my forearm against his throat, making his eyes widen in fear.

"I'm nothing like that cunt," I spit in his face.

"O-okay."

The second I release him, he rushes over to the safe and pulls out a wad of cash and passes it over.

"That should cover it."

I stare down at the cash.

"Good."

I turn to the door, glad to have got what I came here for.

"I'll tell him about this," he warns before I have the door open.

"I don't doubt it. It's time Daddy and I had a little chat anyway."

I blow out of there, stuffing Peyton's money into my back pocket as I go.

I whistle when I get to the bar getting everyone's attention.

Helena immediately looks over and I can't help but smile. "You can get back to blowing the boss now, darling." I smile at her before marching toward the door and leaving them all to it.

I get to the hospital just after seven-thirty and I sit in my car with my eyes locked on the entrance, hoping that Fee will emerge.

I only have to wait a little over five minutes before she does and I make my way inside.

The receptionist is a Panthers fan, so she's more than willing to hand me over all the information I need to find Libby, or more importantly Peyton.

The ward she's on is deadly quiet as I walk through, most of the pot lights are dimmed so the patients can get some rest.

The door to Libby's is cracked open, so I manage to open it without alerting the two people inside to my arrival.

I stand there for a few minutes, noticing the improvement in Libby in the days since I last saw her in Atlanta. But where she might look better, when I turn my attention to Peyton, I find she looks much worse. The circles under her eyes are darker than ever, her complexion pale, and when I look at her hands, I notice that the skin around her nails is red and raw.

Guilt threatens to bring me to my knees.

I shouldn't have left.

I'm still standing there at war with myself over my decisions when she must sense that she's got company and she turns to me. Her chin drops in shock when she realizes that it's me.

20

PEYTON

art of me hoped he'd come. The other part hoped he'd stay away because I knew that one look at him and everything I've felt since he found me in The Locker Room all those weeks ago would come crashing back like a fucking tsunami.

And I wasn't wrong.

All the air rushes out of my lungs as I stare at him in the doorway. His large frame takes up almost all the space.

"Luc," I breathe as if I'm checking that he's really there and not just a figment of my imagination.

"How is she?"

"She's... doing okay. There's still a long way to go but progress has been mostly good so far."

"That's good. I'm glad."

An awkwardness that I'm not used to feeling with Luca settles around us.

"Th-thank you for organizing all this. The chopper ride was kinda exciting, all things considered."

"It's nothing, P. No less than either of you deserve. Have you eaten?"

"Uh..." I hesitate, unable to lie to him.

"Let me buy you dinner. Just downstairs. Nothing crazy but we need to talk, don't you think?"

"Luca, I—"

"Please."

Unable to say no to him, I push to stand, grabbing my purse from the floor.

"I'll be back soon, Lib," I say to my sister, even though she's out cold, exhausted from our journey and the stress of the day.

I follow Luca out of the ward and we ride the elevator to the ground floor side by side, tension crackling between us but we remain in silence.

The kitchen has already closed for the night, so we end up in the coffee shop with sandwiches, chips, and cake, which is fine by me.

"Here, I got you an extra shot," he says, passing my coffee over as he joins me at the table in front of the window. I could have chosen to sit at the one in the shadows at the back but I didn't think that was a particularly good idea.

"How are you doing?"

I shrug. "Honestly, it's been tough."

"I'm glad you're both back."

"Me too. It'll be easier having Aunt Fee to share the visits with."

He studies me for a beat. I know what he's seeing, I'm shocked every time I look in a mirror.

"Eat, P. You look like you need it."

I do as I'm told, picking at my sandwich but with the tension surrounding us, it's hard to stomach anything.

"I'm glad you're back. I missed you," he says quietly.

"Really?" I ask curiously.

"P, don't do that," he warns, his voice low and dangerous in a way that makes tingles erupt from my lower belly. "Don't think that because I stopped messaging and calling that I don't care."

Guilt floods me at the broken look on his face.

"I-I'm sorry I made you leave like that."

"Why did you?" he asks, sitting forward as if he doesn't already know the answer.

"You know why, Luc," I whisper, stuffing a chip into my mouth because right now, eating seems like the lesser of two evils.

"See, that's the thing. I don't think I do. I know it's my fault, but it's like you keep pulling the rug from under me. I don't know which way is fucking up right now. One minute you need me, the next you're sending me away."

"Some might say that's karma."

"Yeah, and they'd probably be right," he admits. "So?"

I take a deep breath and stare down at the table. "You mess with my head, Luc. Being with you again, it's like no time has passed. When it's just the two of us, no bullshit, I feel like I'm fifteen again and with my best friend. But then reality kicks in and I remember that's not who we are anymore. I remember that I can't hand myself over to you anymore because I don't trust you not to rip me apart again."

"Pey—"

"No, Luca. You don't get to sweet talk your way out of this." I sigh, risking a glance at him, and immediately regretting it when I see the pain written all over his face. "Those first two days in Atlanta were awful, but having you there by my side, holding my hand, being just what I needed, it was everything, Luc. But I can't rely on that. What happens when shit gets hard again, are you just going to walk away because you can't deal?"

"No, I'd never—"

"Yeah, see, you probably would have said that the day before I told you what I'd heard back then too. But look what happened."

"I was a kid, Peyton."

"And only a few weeks ago?"

"I was angry. Confused. I'm a mess, P."

"Even more reason not to get carried away here, don't you think?"

"Nothing makes sense without you."

My heart pounds harder at his confession because I understand. I feel it too, but I'm not brave enough to do anything about it right now.

"I want this, Peyton. I want you. I want us. I want to be a part of Kayden's life. I want to move forward, put the past behind us. I want the future we always talked about. I've always wanted that."

"I can't, Luca. My life is a disaster. I can't make that kind of commitment to you, or anyone right now."

"I'm not asking for a commitment, P. I just want hope."

"Tell me about it," I mutter, lifting my coffee to my lips.

"I've got something for you," he says, lifting his ass from the chair and pulling something from his back pocket.

"What is this?"

"Open it."

Placing my mug back down, I take the envelope from his hand and pull out the letter inside. Unfolding it, I stare down at the words, the figures, staring back at me.

My head knows exactly what it is, but I still refuse to believe it.

He hasn't...

He wouldn't...

"W-what is this?"

"It's a receipt. Confirmation that you are now debt-free."

"No," I shout, pushing the chair out from behind me and causing an awful screech that turns everyone's attention on us. "No. This isn't fair, Luca. This wasn't your problem."

Before he can respond, I take off running. Thankfully the elevator is just about to close when I get there and I slip inside.

"Peyton, wait," he calls right before the doors close behind me.

The four other people in the car look at me with concerned expressions but I keep my eyes on the floor as my head spins.

He paid all my debts. All of it. Every single cent.

I'm pacing back and forth at the end of Libby's bed when he finally catches up with me. Dragging my eyes from the floor, I narrow them at him, silently begging for him to get out so I can process this.

"You're not running away from this, Peyton," he whispers, his chest heaving from presumably running up the stairs. Stepping inside and closing the door, he damn near takes all the air with him.

"You had no right to do that."

"I just want to help, P. Let me do this for you, please."

"My debt isn't your responsibility," I hiss.

"Peyton, please," he begs, taking a step toward me, reaching for my hands.

"No," I hiss, holding his stare and forcing him to stop moving. "This is too much. It's just—"

"L-Luca?" a quiet voice says from behind me, instantly cutting through the tense atmosphere between us.

"Libby," I say, racing over to her side.

"Hey, Libby," Luca says awkwardly behind me. I don't need to look to know that he's threaded his fingers through his hair. "How are you doing?"

She stares at him as if to silently say, *how do you think, asshole*, and I have to smother a laugh.

"Are you two..."

"No."

"Yes," Luca states. The confidence in his voice makes me turn back to him.

"Yes?"

"You know what I want, P, I'm not beating around the bush."

"You need to leave."

"And you need to stop being so damn stubborn and see what's right in front of you."

Anger burns red hot through my veins at his words.

"See what's right in front of me? Are you fucking kidding me? I am, Luca. I'm here, looking after what's important." I gesture to Libby. "I'm focusing on my family. Those who love me, believe me, trust me," I seethe.

"I fucking love you, Peyton," he booms, throwing his arms out to the side in exasperation. "I always fucking have."

I stare at him as he watches me closely, waiting for my response. His chest heaves, his eyes are wild, anger, irritation, determination swirling within them.

I startle when my sister's fingers twist with mine and squeeze gently as if she knows that I need it right at that moment.

"It doesn't matter, Luca. Even if I felt the same, right now, is not the time."

"If you felt the same," he repeats, rolling his eyes. "You do and you know it. I know it. I feel it every time I touch you."

Tears burn my eyes and emotion clogs my throat because he's right and he damn well knows it.

"Not now, Luca."

"Then when, huh, Peyton? Do we wait for the next time one of our lives gets thrown into chaos before we collide again? We're in this together, we always have been. You just need to let your head catch up with your heart and trust yourself. Fuck trusting me right now, I'll earn it back. I'll prove to you that what happened before was a massive mistake. That you, Peyton Banks, are the only one for me."

Silent tears cascade down my cheeks as he steps toward me.

He wraps his hand around the back of my neck and presses his lips to my head.

"Your job at The Locker Room no longer exists," he whispers.

My entire body jolts.

"Don't even think about going back there. You don't need it. Look after your family. I'll be waiting."

He kisses my head, nods in Libby's direction and then marches out of the room leaving me lightheaded and standing on legs that no longer know how to hold me up.

I crumple to the chair at Libby's bedside and drop my head into my hands. But I don't cry. I breathe through it and force myself to get a grip. Me falling apart is the last thing Libby needs right now.

"I know you're trying to protect me, Peyton. And trust me, I get it. I understand your reasons for wanting to treat me like glass right now. But you need to stop hiding things from me. Wrapping me in cotton and keeping out the ugly outside world isn't going to help me heal. It's just smothering me. I need the truth, Peyton. I need to know why we're really in Maddison. And don't give the bullshit excuse that it's because it's where you go to college. I know you went to Trinity Royal."

I gasp at her confession.

"I want to know why Aunt Fee is playing Mom and where our real one is. I want to hear you say my boy's name without wincing because you're worried it might set me off. And," she adds with a hard look. "I want to know exactly what is going on there."

"Not asking too much then," I mutter, trying to lighten the mood a little. But when she doesn't so much as smile, I nod. Accepting that it's time to stop beating around the bush and tell the truth.

Telling Libby about Mom's accident is hands down the hardest thing I've ever done in my life.

I thought experiencing it was bad, but at least I was there.

Watching Libby's eyes darken with disbelief and then grief a few minutes later when she realizes that I'm serious is utterly heartbreaking.

I know she thought she wanted the truth, that she could handle it. But right now as tears stream down her face, dripping to the sheets wrapped around her, I'm not so sure it was the best idea.

"K-Kayden?" she forces out.

"He's okay. He was hurt. He's still healing, but he's going to be fine, Lib."

"Fuck," she barks, her hands balling into fists. "Fuck," she screams, pain pouring from her as she pounds her fists down on the bed, the machine beside her beginning to beep incessantly.

"Lib, you need to calm down," I say, placing my hand on her shoulder in the hope it'll help soothe her. But instead, she shrugs me off and continues taking her frustration out on the mattress.

Five seconds later, two nurses come running in.

"It's okay, Libby. We need you to calm down, sweetie."

"She's gone," Libby wails, shattering my heart all over again. "She died thinking I was a total waste of space druggie."

"No, Lib. She didn't. Mom loved you more than anything."

"It's not fair. Why her? Why not one of the cunts who hurt people, who ruin lives?"

"I know, Lib. It's not fair."

Thankfully, with the help of the nurses, we manage to get her to calm down after a few minutes and the beeping returns to normal levels.

"If you need anything, just call, okay?" one of the nurses says before she slips from the room.

"Tell me the rest," Libby demands.

"Are you sure that—"

She stares at me. "It can't get any worse, right?"

"I guess not."

I tell her about Aunt Fee taking us in. The incredible job she's doing with Kayden and his recovery before I have no choice but to confess about The Locker Room and how I ended up reconnecting with Luca.

"Firstly," she states, sounding much more like my big sister than she has since she woke up. "Luca is right, you are done at that place. Mom would be mortified if she knew what you were doing with your body." She pins me with a look that makes me feel about an inch tall.

"I didn't have a choice, Lib. We had no insurance. I had to make money and fast."

"This is all my fault."

"No, Liberty." She instantly looks up at my use of her full name. "It's *his*," I hiss.

"I need you to know that... the only thing I really, really regret in all of this is how what I did tore the two of you apart."

"That's not on you, Lib. What happened between the two of us is his fault."

"But if I never—"

"No, I refuse to let you take on the blame for all of this. You were a child, Libby."

"I was almost eighteen."

"And he was an adult who should have known better."

She blows out a breath and falls back against her pillows.

"He made me feel so... special. I know it's stupid but I just really needed that back then."

"You don't have to explain yourself to me." I refrain from telling her that it's because I've totally invaded her privacy and read most of her diary from that time.

Those pages contain everything that could destroy Brett Dunn, we just need to be smart and figure out the best way to go about it.

"What now?" she asks, sounding totally exhausted.

"Now, we focus on getting you better and we rebuild our lives."

"And you and Luca?"

I shrug. "I'm not sure there is a me and Luca anymore."

"Bullshit, Peyton. I saw the way you two looked at each other, how you melted at what he confessed. He's right, you know? You're being stubborn."

"I'm protecting my heart."

"Yeah, same thing. It was always meant to be you two, Pey. Just give him a chance. He looked a mess and something tells me that has everything to do with you."

I open my mouth to respond but quickly find that I have no comeback for that, and when I look at her again, I discover that she's fast asleep.

"Well, thanks for that, Sis," I mutter to myself.

I sit there in her dimly lit room for almost an hour running everything around in my head. I eventually push away from the bed, kiss her brow and head for the door, more than ready to finally go home and get into my bed.

I call for an Uber as I ride the elevator down to the ground floor and instead of pocketing my cell, I pull up the chat that I've mostly ignored since Luca left Atlanta.

I stare at his words, his apologies for taking things too far, for pushing too hard. His concern for Libby. His demands that I reply just to let him know that I'm okay.

My chest aches knowing that he meant every single one. I know he did.

Without putting too much thought into it, my thumbs fly over the screen.

> Peyton: Thank you. You have no idea what a relief it is not to have to worry about that debt. I'll forever owe you. x

I hit send before I change my mind and fall back against the wall, closing my eyes for a beat.

My cell buzzes as the doors open and I ignore it until I'm safely in the back of the car I ordered and heading for home.

> Luca: Anytime. Anything. I can think of a few ways you can repay me. ;-)

With a smile, I lock my cell once more and rest my head back.

I don't realize that I fall asleep until the driver has no choice but to shout at me to get my attention to tell me that I'm home.

"Crap, I'm so sorry. It's been a long day."

"No, problem, darlin'."

I thank him and climb from the car, sighing in relief when I look at Aunt Fee's house. It might not be my real home, but it's as close as I've got right now and I can't wait to get inside and be surrounded by those I love.

The second I step into the kitchen and look into Aunt Fee's kind eyes, I burst into tears. The stress and exhaustion of the past two weeks suddenly is too much to deal with.

"Oh sweetie, come here," she says, wrapping me in a bear hug and holding me tight.

We stand there for the longest time, just holding each other, using each other's strength to stay upright.

"Can I do anything? Do you need anything?" she whispers.

"I need to see K, and then I need to sleep."

"Okay, I'll make you a hot chocolate to take with you."

"Thank you, Aunt Fee. For everything."

"You're more than welcome, sweetheart."

I suck in a ragged breath before slipping down to Kayden's room and quietly letting him know that I'm home. I want to see him desperately, but I also don't want to wake him.

I sit on the edge of his bed for the longest time watching him sleep and praying that Libby can get through this and become the mom she deserves to be.

21

PEYTON

The house is in silence when I finally wake the next morning, the only thing I can hear is the birdsong in the trees outside my window and just for a few minutes, I pull the sheets up a little higher and sink back into the pillow.

Knowing that I've got too much to do, and too many people relying on me to laze in bed all day. I eventually throw the sheets back and grab my cell from the nightstand that's beside the hot chocolate I was too tired to even sip last night.

> Aunt Fee: Kayden is at kindergarten today and I'm going to sit with Libby. Have a rest, do something for yourself for a few hours.

I lower my cell to the bed, feeling a little lost that someone else has organized everything. The past two weeks everything with Libby has fallen on my shoulders and I can't deny that sharing the load a little feels incredible.

Knowing she's right and that I do need to do something that doesn't involve hospitals, I lift my cell once more and hit call the second I find the contact I want.

"Welcome home. I wanted to call yesterday but I thoug —"

"Thank you. It's nice to be back. Do you have classes this morning?"

"I guess that all depends on what you're about to ask me."

I can't help but smile at her response and loyalty.

"I need to do something," I admit.

"Okay, something like..."

My reflection in the mirror on the wall opposite catches my eye and I wince at the state of me.

"I need to get my hair done," I blurt.

"Okay, we can do that. Let me call Ella, we'll set something up and come get you."

"Are you sure? I don't want you missing classes because of me."

"More than sure. Get dressed, we won't be long. I'll message when we're on our way."

"Okay, thank you." I hang up with excitement tingling in my belly at the prospect of doing something as normal as getting my hair done.

I jump from the bed with more energy than I've had in a long time and throw myself in the shower before dressing in clothes that aren't leggings and an oversized hoodie.

I pull my hair up into a messy bun and quickly do my makeup and put Mom's necklace on, holding it between my fingers for a few seconds.

"I'm more than ready to go when my cell buzzes a couple of minutes later letting me know that they're on their way and that they're bringing coffee. Could they be any more awesome?

I grab a cereal bar from the kitchen and head out right as they pull up outside the house.

Letty leaves the engine running but shoves the door open and practically flies at me, tackling me into a bear hug that I was not expecting.

"Whoa."

"I'm so sorry about your sister," she says, finally releasing me. "But I'm so glad you're back."

"Why? What have I missed?"

"Oh, just some stubborn-ass football player who needs you."

I roll my eyes at just how fast she's managed to bring him up.

"He's driving me insane with his pity party."

"Come on you two, I haven't called in this favor for us to be late."

"Let's go. We've got the perfect morning planned for you."

"You had like thirty minutes notice," I say, following her to the car and climbing in the back.

"Ella is nothing if not resourceful."

"Facts," Ella agrees. "Good to have you back, Peyton. Sorry about your sister."

"Thank you. Everything looks good right now. We'll just have to see if she can stay clean."

"Luc said she's got a rehab place ready for when she gets out."

"She does. Fingers crossed she'll accept the help."

"That little boy deserves it," Letty says with a smile.

"He sure does."

"Luca is dying to meet him but he wanted to wait for you."

"I appreciate that. He doesn't need any more upheaval. So where are we going?" I ask, changing the subject.

"Just wait and see."

They both turn the conversation to things I missed while being away. The parties they've been to and the classes I haven't attended.

I sit back and listen, beyond grateful that I'm not listening to nurses or doctors talking in medical jargon.

"Whoa, this place looks... expensive," I say when Letty pulls into a parking lot of an exclusive-looking hotel and spa.

"Yep. We're taking our job this morning seriously," Ella says with a wink.

"I'm not sure I can afford anything in this place."

"We've got it covered. All you have to do is relax."

I follow the two of them toward the entrance and listen as they talk to the receptionist in the elaborate building. Everything is purple and gold, and expensive. It's like nothing I've ever seen before.

"We have you booked in for facials first, mani-pedis, then hair and makeup."

"Sounds perfect. Thank you," Ella says.

"The lounge is through there, help yourself to food and drinks. We'll call you through when your estheticians are ready."

Together we walk into a conservatory that looks out over the rolling hills in the distance, the lake at the bottom sparkling in the winter sun.

"Wow."

"I know right. Ella has connections." Letty winks, making me wonder just how honest she's being about all this.

"Mimosa?" Ella asks, distracting me, and when I turn to look at her, I find her already holding two glasses out to us.

"I hope you are both aware that this is going to knock me on my ass."

"Yep. But here," Ella says, turning to the table of food behind her. "Have this too." She passes me a croissant over before stuffing another into her mouth.

"I don't know why she's so confused that she's still single," Letty mutters, laughing at her unladylike friend.

"Haven't found anyone who can handle me yet," Ella states around a mouthful of buttery pastry.

"Is that Colt's issue? Too much to handle."

"Fuck off," Ella scoffs, dropping down into one of the huge couches with her mimosa and another croissant.

"Ignore her. Lack of D makes her pissy."

"Missing Elijah?" I ask, remembering that the last time I saw her, she was grinding up against him with her tongue down his throat. Guilt sweeps through me that I've been too wrapped up in my own life to ask Aunt Fee if he's shipped back out again.

"Man, he was hot. Knew what he was doing, if you know what I mean." She winks.

"El, even the woman at reception knows what you mean," Letty deadpans.

"Surprising really seeing as he spends almost all his time with dudes."

Ella falls silent as images run around her head for a few seconds. "Imagine more than one of them..." She gets this far off look in her eyes and Letty and I leave her to it.

"You spoken to Lee?" Letty asks.

"Not for a few days no, you?"

She shakes her head. "I don't think he's been sleeping in his own bed either."

"He got a girl?"

"I don't think so. All this shit, it's messed with his head. I'm worried about him."

"Has Luc spoken to him?"

"He hasn't been in any state to stand let alone hold a conversation."

"What?"

"He locked himself in his room and drank and smoked himself into oblivion since he got back from Atlanta. It was only you coming home yesterday that got him out."

My chin falls open. No wonder he looked rough.

"Shit. I had no idea."

"I know. We didn't tell you. You had enough on your plate."

"He came to see me last night."

"Hi," a soft voice comes from the other side of the room. "Ella?"

"That's me." She hops up, and downs the rest of her drink. "Laters, bitches."

"Is she always so—"

"Insane? Yes."

"I kinda love her."

"Yeah, me too. Just don't tell her. It might go to her head."

I can't help but laugh as we both watch her skip down the long hallway to where I assume the treatment rooms are.

"So you were saying..." Letty prompts.

"He's paid off all my debts, Let. Everything. I can't let him—"

"You can, Peyton," she says, reaching for my hand and squeezing gently. "He just wants to help. Try to make things right."

"It's not his job to fix the past."

"Maybe not, but he wants to. Plus that money, it's not really his. It's Brett's."

"Does he know?"

"Not that I'm aware of. I don't think either of them have spoken to him since all this came out. That's a good thing if you ask me because I'm pretty sure there's going to be bloodshed when it happens."

I drop my head into my hands.

"I don't want that."

"It's out of your hands. He's their sperm donor. Let them do what they need to do."

I nod, knowing that she's right but terrified that they'll do something they'll regret.

"Scarlett, Peyton?" a lady says and the two of us stand and head toward them for our first appointments of the day.

———

Four hours later and I feel better than I have in a very, very long time. My hair is a fresh shade of pink, my roots nowhere to be seen, my face is cleaner than I think it has ever been in my life, my makeup is on point and my nails are a glittering deep purple.

I'm probably going to feel ridiculous later walking into the hospital like I should be going on a night out, but right now, I don't care. I'm flying too high after my girl time and pampering.

"I guess we should head back," Letty says after we've eaten the lunch they'd organized.

"Yeah, I need to take over for Aunt Fee."

"We can come with, if you like. Meet your sister."

"I'm pretty sure she'd love that, but maybe not yet."

"Okay, your call. Just remember that we're here if you need us."

"I know, and I really appreciate it."

We make our way out, thanking the lady who's still sitting behind the desk and toward Letty's car.

"Thank you for this."

"You know, you should totally make use of looking like that and maybe set up a date or something tonight," Letty suggests as a slightly tipsy Ella falls into the passenger seat claiming to need a nap.

"You think I should call him?"

"It's totally up to you, but a normal night out might be exactly what you need."

The thought of sitting opposite Luca in a restaurant and acting like civilized adults does have butterflies beginning to take flight in my belly.

Could we do it though? Could we push all the shit aside for a few hours and just try to be us. Find the two people who aren't drowning in all the drama that surrounds their lives.

"I'll think about it," I say, honestly.

"Come on then. I know one guy who's going to appreciate the shit out of this." She gestures to her face. "And his last class of the day is about to finish." She winks before joining Ella in the car.

I leave them with a heavy heart and the promise of hanging out again soon when Letty pulls up outside Aunt Fee's house.

I quickly run inside to grab a few things. I message Aunt Fee to let her know that I'm on my way via work to grab a few things out of my locker, seeing as I'm no longer an employee it seems.

I grab my keys and jump in my car for the first time in almost two weeks. I sit behind the wheel and remember that the last place I parked it was at college. I have a vague memory of Luca telling me that he'd get some of the guys to sort it out and I'm more than grateful that he pulled through.

He really did think of everything those first few days after that phone call from Dr. Willis.

Guilt floods me. Maybe I have been too harsh on him.

I battle with myself all the way to The Locker Room.

It's late afternoon when I pull up into the parking lot. Aunt Fee has already left Libby to get Kayden from kindergarten, so I need to get this over with as quickly as possible so I can get to her.

I know she's perfectly fine having a little alone time, it's probably good for her but it still makes me feel bad.

I'm going to need to get used to it though because I can't miss any more classes. I have got to go back next week and attempt to catch up on what I've missed.

The beat of the music is low, quieter than it usually is on a regular evening.

"Peyton," a familiar voice calls from behind me as I walk across the almost empty space. "It's so good to see you."

Turning around, I find Bry making his way over to me with a huge smile on his face. He pulls me in for a hug and holds me tight for a few seconds.

"How's your sister doing?"

"Yeah, I think she's going to be okay if she's willing to accept the help."

"That's good news." He leads me over to the bar. "So, I hear my favorite employee is no more."

"So I hear."

"Did Luc tell you?" he asks, leaning in and whispering.

"Tell me what? That I no longer have a job."

"Well that, yeah. But he walked in on Helena blowing Julian under his desk."

"No!" I gasp, although I have no idea why I'm surprised, that girl would blow anything with a pulse. "I guess someone is gunning for a pay raise."

Bry chuckles. "She clearly wants something. You couldn't pay me enough to go near his infested cock."

"Amen," I say with a laugh but both of us soon shut up when the man in question appears from out the back.

"Bry, don't you have a job to do?"

"Sure do, boss." Bry salutes before turning around but not before I spot his dramatic eye roll.

"Peyton, a word."

My stomach turns the way it always does when I'm in his company. There's just something so... gross about him. He's like Slick on steroids and I will happily live without ever having to see him again.

I follow him through the staff-only door and toward his office. The place smells the way it always does but knowing that I no longer belong here means the stench of stale sweat and dampness now turns my stomach even more than it always did.

"Today's your lucky day, Peyton. There's someone very special here to see you."

My brows draw together as I try to figure out what he's talking about as I step into his office.

My head spins the second I lock eyes with the man standing in the middle of Julian's office wearing a sharp designer black suit as if he's some kind of upstanding citizen of the community.

I turn, ready to run out of there and forget all about the few things that are in my locker, but I'm too late. Julian slams the door behind me, flicking the lock to ensure I have nowhere to go.

"W-what are you doing here?" I stutter, looking at the man I never want to look at ever again. The man who has single-handedly destroyed the lives of everyone I love.

"Aw, has he still not told you, darlin'?" My brows pinch as I wait for whatever bullshit lies are about to fall from his deceitful mouth. "I own this place. I'm the one who's been signing your paychecks all this time."

"No," I cry. "No."

He takes a menacing step toward me and a shudder of fear races down my spine.

Backing away from the monster, I bump into another.

"I thought we were rid of you and your white trash family."

"You asshole," I scream, my arm flying out to slap him. But he clearly hasn't lost his skills or speed because he has my arm in his grip before it moves toward him.

He steps forward again, pinning me between the two of them.

My fear freezes me in place, not that I think I stand any chance of fighting against them. They'll easily overpower me.

"W-what do you want?"

"Maybe I want to find out why my son has been so besotted with you all these years. I got rid of you so he could focus. It worked until you decided to step right into his path once more. You—" He lifts his hand and twirls a lock of my hair around his finger as bile swirls in my stomach and burns up my throat. "Are fucking everything up."

"You employed me," I spit. "You put me in his path."

"Julian employed you. Imagine my surprise when I saw your name pass through my files. My only regret is that I didn't get back here and get my hands on you sooner. I've waited years to find out if you're as compliant as your whore of a sister."

"Cunt." I spit in his face. But instead of being put off, his eyes only darken as a snarl curls at his lips.

"You stupid whore," he hisses. I don't see his backhand coming and my head snaps to the side. The pain burning through my cheek and down my neck, the taste of copper filling my mouth as hands touch me everywhere.

"No. No," I scream, trying as hard as I can to fight them off even though it's futile. "Help me. Bry."

"That little bitch won't come to your help, darlin'. You're ours for as long as we want to entertain you."

The sound of ripping fabric fills the room before cool air whips across my chest as my shirt is peeled away.

"It's time you pay for your inability to keep your trashy little mouth shut."

Brett grabs my chin, his fingers digging into my skin until it stings.

"I'm really going to enjoy this, darlin'. I'll enjoy it even more when he kicks your traitorous ass to the curb."

"He wouldn't. They wouldn't."

"Willing to bet on that, darlin'?"

22

LUCA

"Hey," I say, poking my head into Libby's hospital room and only finding the patient herself inside. I'm already on edge after finding a message on my cell from my father a few hours ago telling me that he was in town and wanted to see me. "Peyton not here?"

"Not yet, no. Aunt Fee said she was on her way after popping into work or something."

"She's going to work?" I ask, my heart rate picking up at just the thought of her walking in there after the conversation I had with Julian yesterday. Add Brett into the mix and fear races through me faster than I can control.

"Yeah, why?"

"Fuck," I bark.

"Luca?" she shouts as I bolt for the door. "What's wrong?"

"Hopefully nothing. I'll be back."

I take off running, my body trembling as I move. I fly down the stairs, using the handrail to help me take the corners at breakneck speed and nearly colliding with more than one other person. I'm too lost in my own head to care or apologize as I race from the hospital and toward my car that I only just parked.

"Damn it, Lee. Answer your goddamn cell," I shout. I slam my palms down on the wheel, running my second stoplight as I speed my way across town toward The Locker Room.

I slam my foot on the brake with my car blocking the entrance to the club. The sight of my father's Porsche in the lot makes me want to puke.

"Luca. Twice in two days. I'm gonna start getting used to—"

"Where is she?" I bark, cutting off his greeting.

"Uh... out back with Julian."

"Fuck," I bark, running toward the back door.

"W-what's wrong?"

I don't stand around long enough to answer his question. Instead I storm through the door making it slam so hard against the wall behind me that I'm surprised it doesn't fly off its hinges.

The sight of Julian's closed office door doesn't make me feel any better about what's going on inside.

Grabbing the handle, I twist and slam my shoulder against it, expecting it to swing open. So when it doesn't budge, anger and fear like I've never experienced before surges through me and takes control of my body.

I slam my weight against the door over and over until the wood splinters and I fly into the room. Immediately my anger has reached its boiling point after seeing the position they have Peyton in.

"Get your motherfucking hands off her," I scream, launching myself at my father, twisting my fingers in his shirt and dragging him back from where he has Peyton pinned against Julian's desk.

"Oh, hey, Son. Come to join the party?" he asks with a smirk that I want to rip from his face.

"I'm not your son, you sick fuck."

The crunch of his nose beneath my fist feels better than any other punch I've landed in my life.

"Luca, come on. We're just having some fun," he says, righting himself. Totally ignoring the fact his nose is gushing blood, staining his previously pristine white shirt.

"Fun. Your idea of fun is fucking sick. Did you really think I'd never find out about Libby, you sick bastard? How many other kids have you groomed, huh, old man? How many underage girls have you fucked with your pathetic excuse of a cock?"

He pales slightly but still doesn't back down an inch.

"You know nothing," he spits, covering Julian's already disgusting carpet with blood.

"L-Luca." Her terrified whimper cuts through me, turning my blood to ice.

"You're going to fucking pay for this," I warn, cocking my arm back once more and landing a solid punch to my father's temple that sends his toppling to the ground.

"Get off, please. Get off me." Her voice shatters my already broken and battered heart and I spin around with a roar but it seems I'm too late because Bry has joined us and has a chair careening toward Julian's head.

His grunt of pain sounds out before he hits the desk on the way down.

"Peyton," I breathe, rushing to where she's slumped on the floor, her eyes wide and terrified. "Baby, it's okay."

"Get her out of here," Bry instructs. "I'll sort this out."

"How?" I ask, looking at the two sick fucks passed out on the floor.

"I've got connections, don't worry."

I narrow my eyes at him but when Peyton shudders in my arms I forget all about it.

"Go out the back, no one will see you."

"Yeah, okay."

Standing, I pull my hoodie off before slipping it over her head to cover her up before lifting her into my arms and carrying her from the building.

As gently as I can, I place her on my passenger seat and strap her in. I run around to the driver's side, getting in and backing out of there as fast as I arrived.

"It's going to be okay, baby. He's not going to get away with this."

We're almost at the house when my brother finally decides to call me back.

"You at the house?"

"Yeah, just going out, why?"

"I'm just pulling up. I need your help with something."

He sighs, letting me know that I'm shitting all over his plans, but I don't give a fuck. This is more important than anything he was about to go and do.

I park as he emerges and walks over.

"What is it, Lu— What the fuck?" he barks the second he sees Peyton curled up beside me, staring ahead with glazed eyes.

"Help me get her in, yeah?"

"Y-yeah, of course."

He glances down at my fist, his brows pulling together.

We work in silence, me still trying to get control of myself as I lift Peyton from the car and Lee obviously trying to read between the lines to find out what the fuck has happened.

I jog up the stairs with her to my room, thankfully not bumping into any of the guys as I do so. I lay her out in the middle of my bed, pulling the sheets over her because I have no idea if she's shivering because she's terrified or cold or both.

"What the fuck is going on, Luc? What's happened?"

"J-Julian and—" I breathe out a long slow breath trying to calm the fuck down as the image of him with his hands all over my girl come back to me. "Brett."

"Dad. Dad did this?" he roars, disbelief all over his face.

"They were in the back room of The Locker Room."

"I'm going to fucking kill him, Luc. I swear to fucking God, I—"

"I left them out cold in the office. Bry is sorting it out."

"Bry? What the fuck does he know about dealing with that shit."

"I don't fucking know, Lee. But he offered and my biggest concern was getting her the hell out of there. They were gonna—" I bite back the words, trying to breathe through the fact I want to puke all over my bedroom floor at the thought. "They were gonna—"

"I got it, Luc. I'm going, okay. I'll sort it out. That cunt is going to pay for this."

I nod at him before he disappears from my room, leaving me with a trembling Peyton.

Pulling the sheets back, I lift her onto my lap and hold her against me.

"It's okay, baby. You're safe. I've got you."

I pull my cell from my pocket and find my last conversation with Letty about her plans for Peyton this morning.

Luca: Send Kane to The Locker Room. Lee will be there. He's going to need his help.

Letty: What the fuck have you done?

Luca: I'll call you when I can. I've got Peyton. She's okay.

Letty: Let me know if you need anything.

Dropping my cell to the bed, I look down at Peyton to find her wide silver eyes staring back up at me.

"Why didn't you tell me?" she whispers.

For a second, I wonder what she's talking about but then it hits me. She means Brett.

"Trust me, baby, it wasn't because I didn't want to." I cup her cheek and tilt her head so she has no choice but to look at me. I need her to see the honesty in my eyes, to understand how much I battled with this decision over the past few weeks. "I know how much you needed that job, the money that came with it. If I told you, you'd have ended up choosing between paying your debts and your integrity, and I didn't want that. As much as I hated you working there, spending time with those scumbags, I knew you felt it was what you needed to do."

"That's why you were there every night."

"Partly that, partly because I just couldn't stay away from you," I confess.

"I'd have paid your debt off the day I found out about it if I could have, but I knew you'd never accept it."

"I don't want to accept it now."

"I know, baby. But as much as you hate it, sometimes you just need to accept a little help. And at the end of the day, it's not actually my money either, and it's money that you and your family more than deserve."

She swallows nervously, her eyes once again filling with tears.

"W-what will happen to them?"

"I don't know, baby. Do you have any idea who Bry is connected to?"

She shakes her head.

"I've sent Lee and Kane over there to help."

Her brows pull together in concern. "Don't worry, if Bry doesn't know the right people, I can assure you that Kane does."

"To do what?"

I shrug. "Finish what I started."

As I say the words, she pulls her face from my hold and takes my fist in her hand.

"Has it even healed from the last time?"

"I don't care, Peyton. I'd do it all over again if it meant keeping you safe."

She drags in a shuddering breath. "I really thought they were going to—"

"It's okay."

"You saved me," she whispers.

"Always, baby." I lower my head to hers. "I'd go kill them both right now if that's what you asked of me."

She shakes her head. "Brett needs to pay, by doing what you really want to do would be the easy way out for him."

Our eyes hold, a million words we both want to say hanging between us.

"I really need to shower. All I can smell is them."

"Shit, baby. I'm so fucking sorry."

She swallows and drags up some strength from a deep place inside her.

"I'm okay. They didn't hurt me, not really."

I take her jaw in my hand, gently rubbing my thumb over the darkening bruise on her cheek and beneath the split in her lip.

"Did he—"

"Yeah."

My entire body tenses with my need to go back there, to ensure that he can't touch any female ever again. But as if she can sense it, Peyton wraps her hand around the back of my neck and stares at me with her big, silver eyes.

"Shower with me?" She leans forward, her lips brushing mine ever so gently.

"You sure?"

"I need to replace their hands with someone else's."

"Someone else's?"

"No, Luc. Just yours."

"You know I could never say no to you."

I stand with her still in my arms and walk toward my bathroom. Sitting her on the counter, I pull my hoodie from her body, careful of her face before ridding her of the rest of her clothes, relieved when I don't find any marks on the rest of her body.

"Okay?" I ask before stepping back so I can shed my own clothes.

She nods, sucking her bottom lip into her mouth as I drag my shirt over my head and drop my sweats and boxers.

She says nothing as I sweep her into my arms once more and back her into the shower.

"Oh my God," she squeals when we get blasted with cold water.

It soon warms up. She stands with her head resting on my chest and my arms locked around her body for the longest time as the water rains down on both of us.

"We need to talk to your mom, Luc. We have to get this all out in the open and figure a way out."

"I know, baby. We will."

With her still plastered against my body, I grab the bottle of shampoo from the shelf behind her. I squeeze some into my hand, and begin massaging her head.

"I was going to call you after I saw Libby."

"Oh yeah?"

"It was Letty's suggestion," she confesses. "She didn't think I should let the benefits of this morning go to waste."

"Did you have a good time?"

She pulls her head from my chest and looks up at me. "You paid, didn't you?"

"I wanted you to have a morning just to breathe. Mom goes to that place a lot so I just called and pulled some strings."

Her lips part and I brace myself for the onslaught of abuse, for making her out to be a charity case, but it never comes. Instead, her eyes soften and she says, "Thank you."

"You're welcome. I'm glad you had fun."

"I really did."

"Tip your head back." She does as I say and lets me rinse her hair out before I grab my shower gel and set about replacing any other scent on her body with my own. My hands caress every inch of her body, erasing their touch. My cock bobs between us, my need for her at an all-time high as I gently brush my thumbs over her peaked nipples.

"Luca," she breathes.

I stop, my heart thundering in my chest as I stare down at her.

Taking her face in both of my hands, I lower down until my nose is touching hers.

"I love you, Peyton. I never stopped. Please, tell me that there's something here. That we can at least try to find a way to figure out who we are again, together."

Her eyes shutter as she absorbs my words. When they open again, they're full of unshed tears.

It's not until she gives me the slightest of nods that I realize I was holding my breath.

It comes out in a rush as relief fills me and my lips curl into a smile.

"I... I love you too, Luc. Always will."

I pull her to me, capturing her lips in a knee-weakening kiss, but I don't take it any farther. After the events of the last few hours, it's the last thing she needs. Instead, I'm just going to look after her in the way she deserves.

PEYTON

Luca's warmth and strength seep into me as he wraps me in a thick fluffy towel and then scoops me back into his arms once more and out into his bedroom.

"I can walk, you know."

"I know," he mutters, lowering me to the edge of the bed and turning toward his dresser.

He pulls out a Panther's shirt with his name and number on the back and faces me.

"Trying to tell me something, Dunn?" I ask, quirking my brow at him as joy floods me. Because of him, I'm able to think about something other than the events of this afternoon, even if it is only for a few minutes.

"Yeah, I'm making things right. Arms up."

I do as I'm told before he pulls me to my feet, allowing the towel to fall from around me.

"Damn, my clothes look better on you."

"I'm not sure what Coach would think if I turned up ready to be his number one."

"Don't care what he thinks, you've always been my number one."

"So cheesy."

"Just the truth."

He captures my lips in a searing kiss that I feel all the way down to my toes. But he doesn't try for anymore, despite the fact he's got one hell of a tent in his towel.

My heart sings knowing that he's taking care of me. I mean, I didn't really expect him to do anything else. He always was the sweetest boy who always put my needs and well-being before his own. But the reminder of that person is exactly what I need right now.

"Get into bed," he instructs, resting his brow against mine and staring into my eyes. Anger and his need to hurt the men who hurt me still swims in the dark green depths, but I'm more than grateful that he's got a handle on it right now and is not out for blood like...

"Leon," I blurt.

"You're really thinking about him right now, baby."

"No, yeah... I mean. What's he going to do? You sent him to The Locker Room."

Luca tenses at just the mention of the name of that place.

"Lee will be fine. I've just sent him to help Bry, Kane's on his way, too."

"Kane?"

"Yeah, Letty's fiancé."

"I know. I'm just surprised."

"You girls talk too much," he says with a laugh that tells me he secretly loves it. "Kane has... a questionable past. If Bry's connections don't amount to much, you can be sure that Kane's do."

My eyes widen in shock.

"W-was he in a gang or something?"

"Yeah, baby. A gang or something."

"You can't just drop a bomb like that and then skirt around it." I sulk.

"I'll tell you everything I know, although not tonight." He pins me with a look that ensures I don't argue. "And then you'll have to ask Letty the rest. I only know the basics."

"But Letty is so sweet," I mutter, taking a couple of steps back and lowering down onto Luca's bed.

He laughs. "Yeah, don't let that pretty face fool you, she's capable of more than either of us are aware of. You don't get into bed with a guy like that unless you know what you're doing. You hungry?" he asks, doing a one-eighty on the conversation and sending me into a head spin.

"No."

"How did I know you were going to say that?" he deadpans.

"Let me rephrase. I'm going to get you food. Do not leave this room. Hell, do not leave my bed."

"Okay," I breathe as I watch him drop his towel and replace it with a pair of boxers.

He starts for the door, but I stop him before he pulls it open.

"You walk around like that in this house often?"

"Yeah, why?" He looks down at himself confused.

"Isn't it like... always full of jersey chasers?"

"Aw, baby. Are you a little jealous?"

"N-no, I just."

"Contrary to popular belief, this house isn't full of complete dogs." I stare at him, wondering just how he's going to convince me that that statement could possibly be true. "Okay fine, it is. But only girlfriends get sleepover rights unless it's a party night."

"Riiight so—"

"Fucking chasers have to happen elsewhere every other night of the week."

I look down at his bed, grateful that at least it hasn't had a different woman in it every night of the week.

"I haven't been with anyone for a long time, P. You don't need to worry, and you certainly don't have any competition."

I nod, not realizing just how badly I needed to hear those words from him right now.

"I'll be back. Hang tight."

I pull my knees up and look around Luca's room. It's not all that different from the one I remember from being a kid. There are discarded clothes covering the floor, and the laundry basket looks to be completely empty. There's football memorabilia everywhere, trophies, posters, random pages with plays sketched on them. But the thing I love the most about it is the smell. Okay, so there might be an edge of sweaty boy in the air, but everything else is pure Luca. The one person I was always able to rely on, the one who will always rescue me, and today is no exception to that rule.

His cell buzzes on the dresser and my eyes watch as the screen goes back to sleep once more, an idea hitting me.

Sliding from the bed, I walk on shaky legs to grab it, the realization that mine is probably still on Julian's office floor in my purse where it fell makes a wave of nausea wash through me.

If Luca didn't crash into the room when he did...

I heave as I think about what would have happened next. There is no doubt in my mind that both of them would have gone through with it. They're both as sick and twisted as each other.

Knowing that makes me feel better about whatever their fate is going to be. I have no idea what Bry is capable of, I don't really know who he is, but Luca sure seems to think that Kane is dangerous.

Which is why I pull up a new web browser the second I unlock Luca's cell and type in Florida gangs.

I scan through the hits until something catches my eye.

Harrow Creek Hawks.

I know of Harrow Creek. Everyone from this part of the state does. It's the pits of hell and a place most normal people will do anything to stay away from.

I click on the website and begin reading.

I'm so lost in all the allegations of the things the gang has done over the years that I don't hear Luca come back into the room.

"Hey, found anything good?"

I have to give him a double take.

"W-what?" I ask as he places a tray full of food down on the nightstand.

"You've got my cell. You snooping for evidence of jersey chasers?"

"Oh, shit. No. I haven't opened your messages or anything. I was just Googling."

"Googling what, baby?" he asks, jumping over me and sitting beside me.

"Digging up dirt that you wouldn't tell me."

He glances at the screen and laughs.

"What? I needed a distraction and you'd left so..."

"You thought you'd hack into my cell."

"Pretty much. I can't believe you never changed your passcode," I tell him, closing the browser down and locking it again before passing it over.

"Why would I? Only me and you know it, and I have nothing to hide from you."

"I really didn't go through anything," I say, needing him to believe me.

"I know. Like I said, I have nothing to hide. You can snoop away. And I trust you."

He leans over me, brushing his lips over mine as he reaches for the tray.

"I got a bit of everything I could find. There are pills too." He nods toward the small white bottle.

I stare down at the random mixture of food before me.

"We can get takeout if it's not what you want."

Reaching out, I squeeze his hand. "It's perfect, Luc."

I pop a chip into my mouth, mostly to make him happy because my stomach still churns as the memories of being inside that room with them refuse to leave me.

We sit in silence for a few minutes as we pick at the food before I remember something.

"Do you think your—" My eyes cut to his as I realize my mistake. He might have refused to call him Dad before today but I think he's really done now. "Do you think Brett meant what he said about getting rid of me before?"

He thinks for a moment, scrubbing his free hand over his face and dragging it through his hair.

"I want to say no, but I have a feeling that might have been the most honest thing I've ever heard him say."

My heart sinks into my stomach because as much as I didn't want to believe it when he said it, I do.

"He went after Libby on purpose," I mutter, needing to put the words out into the universe. "Do you think that means there aren't others?"

"I really fucking hope so."

Picking up a carrot stick, I munch on the end as a million and one things fly around my head.

"He couldn't have known that going after Libby would break us apart."

"No, but he clearly thought it was worth a shot. And as usual, I played straight into his hands."

Luca's fingers curl into fists. His knuckles once again split open.

"Stop that, please. I hate that you're hurt."

"I could say the same about you."

"I'm fine."

"He hit you, Peyton. He tried to... that will never be okay."

"I know, but it's over. You rescued me."

"I'm so fucking sorry, baby."

"Stop trying to take on blame that isn't yours. This is all on him, all of it."

He nods. "Whatever they do with him, I really hope it hurts."

"Me too," I confess. I've never wished anyone harm before in my life, but I'll make an exception for Brett. "What do we do now?"

"Wait for Lee to come back, find out what they've done, I guess. We need to go and talk to Mom. I want to meet Kayden. And I want to properly get to know you again."

His hand finds my neck and he kisses me gently.

"I need to go and see Libby. She's going to be waiting for me."

"Baby, I really don't think—"

I pin him with a look that I know he's not going to be able to ignore.

"Okay. But it's going to be a short visit," he insists.

"That's fine."

"We can swing by Fee's and grab some stuff."

"Can we now?"

"I know you live there. I know it's where Kayden is and probably where you want to be, but I'm not letting you go tonight, possibly not for a while. I just need you to know that."

"Okay, I think I can cope with that."

———

"Peyton, is that you?" Aunt Fee calls as I run for the stairs, still wearing Luca's shirt and a pair of his sweats that barely stay up on me.

"Yeah, give me a minute."

She doesn't and a second later, I hear her footsteps follow me up the stairs.

"Is everything— holy shit, Peyton," she says when she gets a look at my face.

"I'm okay. Everything is... f-fine."

Her brow lifts as she stares at me, clearly knowing that everything is not fine.

"I had a run-in with Brett Dunn."

"And he did that to you?" she seethes, the anger that emanates from her rivals that of Luca's.

"Luca saved me. Brett is... Brett is being dealt with."

"What the hell does that mean?"

"Honestly, I don't know but I trust those who are doing it to ensure he gets what he deserves."

"I'm not sure I like the sound of that," she mutters.

"You don't have to. You can just breathe easy knowing that he's not going to be showing his face anytime soon." Her eyes narrow on me. "Seriously, I have no clue what's going on. Other than that I need to get changed." I gesture at my current outfit. "And that I need to go and see Lib. I'm going to spend the night with Luca, if that's okay?"

"O-of course. Are you two..."

"I think we're going to be okay." I can't fight the smile that twitches at the corners of my mouth as I say those words.

I've been fighting it for so long that finally letting go and accepting that there really wasn't any other outcome for the two of us feels really damn good.

"Oh, sweetie," she breathes, taking a step forward and wrapping her arms around me. "He's a good boy, that one." I nod against her. "I'm so glad you found your way back to each other."

"We've still got a way to go," I say, releasing her and going back to my closet and rummaging around for something to wear.

"I know, but I've got a good feeling about it."

"Me too. Feels good after so long."

"I can imagine."

"Will you and K be here in the morning? Luca wants to meet him properly. Thought maybe we could take him for breakfast or something."

"That sounds like a great idea. Let me know what time and I'll make sure he's ready."

"Thank you."

In the end, after finding some clean underwear, I decide against replacing Luca's shirt. Being surrounded by his scent feels too good, so I just pull on a pair of leggings and tie the too-big shirt up around my waist. I shove my feet into my Chucks and throw Mom's leather jacket on the top. Despite the fact I've got a glowing bruise on my cheek and a split lip, I feel good. Really freaking good.

Kayden is watching his before bed cartoons when I poke my head into the living room. He's so absorbed in them that I'm able to kiss him good night without him actually looking at me, which is a relief.

After saying goodbye to Aunt Fee, I head back out to the car.

"Whoa, you look hot," Luca says the second I drop into the passenger seat.

"The badass look suits me, huh?" I ask.

"It does." He lifts off the seat a little and pulls at his jeans. "A little too much."

"I can't take you anywhere. Come on, let's go visit Libby, then if you're lucky, I'll fix that little situation for you."

"Little?" he asks, sounding affronted.

Reaching over, I wrap my hand around his thigh and squeeze gently.

"I've got no complaints, Dunn."

The smile that lights up Libby's face as we walk into her room hand in hand makes me realize just how badly everyone else wanted to see us put our issues behind us. That is until she catches sight of the bruise, then her face drops and her lips thin in anger.

"Who did that?"

Luca takes a seat beside her bed and pulls me onto his lap as my sister's eyes drill into him.

"You can stop looking at me like that, I wouldn't lay a hand on her, and you know it."

"Unless I ask him to," I add, unable to keep my mouth shut.

"Peyton Banks," my sister chastises. "What happened to my sweet little sister?"

"Lib, I've never been that."

"True. I haven't forgotten that day I burst into your room to find his white ass up in the air as he railed you."

"Are you two about done?" Luca asks.

"We'll finish this when we're alone," Libby says with a wink and a laugh that fills me with hope for what her future might hold. I know she's in pain, not from her overdose but from her withdrawals. I can see it in her eyes, but she's fighting it, and I can only hope that continues. "For now, just tell me what bitch I need to cut for laying a hand on you."

"It doesn't matter, Lib. It's done."

Luca tenses beneath me. I have no idea if that's because he was about to confess or if it's just the reminder of what we've both been through today.

Her eyes narrow on me as if she'll be able to read the answer in mine. "I will find out."

"Libby, can I ask you something?" Luca suddenly says.

"Uh... yeah, sure," she says, looking between the two of us with apprehension.

"I understand if you don't want to talk about it, but—"

"But?"

"Do you know if... if Brett—" A viable shudder rips through my sister at the sound of his name. "D-do you know if he spent time with other girls?"

Libby's jaw pops, her fingers curling around the sheets that are draped over her lap. "Was he fucking any other underaged idiots, you mean?"

"You're not an idiot, Libby," Luca says softly. "I know better than anyone just how far that cunt will go to get what he wants." His grip on me tightens and I snuggle into him.

"It was him, wasn't it? He hit you."

"Was there anyone else, Lib?" I ask, diverting away from her question once more. Although from the darkness in her eyes, she hears my unspoken answer loud and clear.

"Not that I was ever aware of. But I'm not naïve enough to think that I will have been the only one he played to get his rocks off. Why?"

"We assumed there were more. But he said something, something that made us wonder if he singled you out on purpose."

"So I was special then," she deadpans with a roll of her eyes.

"I'm so sorry, Libby."

"It's not on you, Luc."

"Maybe not, but he did it for my fucking benefit didn't he?" Libby's brow creases and we explain to her what he said tonight.

"He really thought that Peyton would stand in your way?"

"Women get in the way. They're a distraction. Only worth having around as a plaything."

Libby's head rears back, her eyes widening. I know exactly what Luca's doing, he's repeating all the bullshit he's been forced to listen to over the years.

"That's bullshit," Libby spits.

"I know. But nonetheless, it's what I grew up hearing. He didn't want us together. He thought it would stop me from following his dreams."

"And he knew I was impressionable. But he couldn't have known that you'd turn your back on Peyton."

"No, but the benefits clearly outweighed the risk."

All the blood drains from Libby's face. "That cunt needs to die."

Luca nods, his eyes glazing over probably as he wonders what's happening to his father right this second.

"Anyway..." I say in the hope of lifting everyone's spirits a little. "How have things been today, you seem brighter?"

"Yeah. I'm... I'm feeling better."

I smile at her, feeling just a little bit of the tension that was pulling at my muscles loosen a bit.

24

LUCA

Holding Peyton against me as we started to open up to Libby about what had happened helped to keep the beast inside me at bay.

I was desperate to find out where Lee, Bry, and Kane were and to discover what kind of punishment they thought was appropriate for our cunt of a father. But I knew that I was exactly where I needed to be. I had to let them deal with that while I was with Peyton.

She needs me more.

When she starts yawning with her head resting against my chest, I decide that it's time to head back and put this bullshit day behind us.

"Come on, baby. I'm taking you home to bed."

Libby groans, rolling her eyes at my announcement.

"Okay," Peyton whispers, looking up at me with heavy eyes. "Take me home, Luc."

Her words are like a baseball bat to the chest.

Home.

The only place I've ever truly felt at home has been whenever she's been by my side.

"I'll see you tomorrow, okay?"

"No," Libby states, making Peyton still.

"W-what?"

"Pey, you've given up your life for me the past two weeks. And while I appreciate every single second of you sitting by my side, even when I wasn't aware of it, I need you to have a break. Spend the weekend fucking Luca's brains out. Get out of town. Anything. Just... take a breather, yeah. I'll still be here on Monday, I promise."

Peyton's lips part to respond but no words come out. I know she's torn. I can feel her need to tell her sister that she's wrong, that she needs to be here but after a silent few seconds, she finally agrees.

"Okay, but if you need me, you call me. Yes?"

"Yes, *Mom*," Libby sasses before she realizes what she's said and her eyes fill with tears. "Shit."

Releasing me, Peyton rushes over and pulls her sister in for a hug.

I stand by the door, giving them some space, as they cry together for not only their mother but I'm sure all the time they've lost together over the past few years.

Peyton was right earlier, Libby does seem brighter today, and I only hope she's turning a corner and going to be able to come out stronger on the other side.

I've lined up the best place I could find close by for her recovery so that she could still see her family if she wishes to. I just hope it's enough because they've already suffered too much loss.

Eventually, they part and after another goodbye, Peyton tucks herself into my side and we leave Libby to get some rest.

"You okay?" I ask when she sniffles and wipes the tears from her cheeks.

"Yeah, I'm good. It's just hard watching her try to deal with everything, you know?"

"I can't even begin to imagine," I confess, dropping a kiss on the top of her head. "You up for heading to Rosewood for the weekend? Get away from all this for a bit."

"We're not really getting away if we've got to talk to your mom," she points out.

"True. But it'll be a change of scenery. And I'm pretty sure my mom is going to be stoked to see you."

"Yeah?"

"She ripped me a new one when I told her that we'd fallen out before you left. I think she'd had her heart set on you giving her her first grandbaby."

Neither of us needs to say it, but that is the exact reason why Brett did what he did. If I'd got Peyton pregnant young and I'd had to make a choice then I'd have chosen her and our baby any day, just like Shane did.

"You can meet my niece," I blurt.

She looks up at me with curious eyes as we step into the elevator together.

"You've got a niece?"

"Yep. Shane had a kid with Chelsea Fierce."

"Get out, he did not!"

"He did. Gave up football to be a dad. He's actually at MKU part-time right now."

"Well, shit. How did that happen?"

"Well, now you mention it," I say, backing her into the wall with a smirk playing on my lips. "I think he put his coc—" Her hot fingers press against my lips.

"That is not what I meant. All I remember of Chelsea is her following you around like a lost puppy."

"Yeah, well. She got bored of me and hooked up with Shane instead."

"Well, I can't wait to meet her."

"She's pretty fucking awesome," I confess, thinking of her sweet face and chubby cheeks as I lean forward for a kiss.

"I-if things were different, I never would have held you back, you know that right?"

I pause only a breath from her lips.

"I just needed you to know. If I never left and we stayed together, no matter what happened, all I wanted for you was to follow your dreams."

"I know, baby," I say, bumping my nose against hers. "But equally, I'd have given it all up for you, just like Shane did."

I'm never going to say that Brett was right in what he did. But I understand his fear because while football is literally his life, my future in football is his one main focus. It was only a small part of my life, and he saw that.

She shakes her head.

"I still would," I admit, finally capturing her lips.

I reluctantly pull back when the doors slide open and pull her from the small space.

"You never have to give up, or do anything for me, Luc. I want you to do things for you. If you still want football, the NFL, then you go for it. I'll be right by your side cheering you on from the sidelines. But equally, if you really think this is it for you, then I'll support what you want to do instead."

I don't say anything, I just let her words repeat over and over in my head as we make our way to my car.

Pushing her against the passenger door, I cage her body in, pressing my length against her.

Leaning in, I brush my lips against the shell of her ear. "The only thing I know that I want for sure right now is you," I breathe.

"Luc," she moans.

"I told myself I would let you rest tonight, but you're making it really damn hard to keep that promise."

"So don't. Break your own rule, Luca Dunn," she challenges.

"Get in the car, Peyton," I all but growl.

"You're going to need to move then," she points out.

"Jesus. You drive me insane, P."

The smile that curls at her lips melts my heart.

I stand back to allow her to open the door, but I snag her hand before she slips inside.

She looks up at me with her wide silver eyes that only sparkle brighter in the moonlight.

"I love you, Peyton."

"Yeah?" she asks with a wicked twinkle in her eye. "You'd better show me then."

She drops into the passenger seat and closes the door before I have a chance to respond.

Unable to wipe the smile off my face, I jog around to the driver's side and climb in.

"I hope you like it wild, baby."

"You know I do."

I floor the accelerator and throw her back into her seat, my impatience to get her alone once more becoming unbearable.

"Hey look," Colt announces as the two of us walk into the house only a few minutes later. "Luca's smiling."

"Fuck you," I bark, but I still can't wipe the smile off my face.

"He just needed to get laid, I told you this," Evan pipes up.

"Ignore them, they're just jealous."

"How's Ella these days, Colt?" I ask with a wink.

His face tightens before Peyton joins in, really rubbing salt in his wound.

"Last I heard, she was banging a Marine. First guy to really show her a good time, if you get what I mean."

Evan and a couple of the other guys damn near choke on their beers at my girl's response.

"Oh burn, bro. Luca, your girl is da bomb."

I pull her tighter into my body.

"I know. Turn the volume up, boys."

"Hell yeah, get it, bro," Evan calls, thrusting his hips for added effect as we leave the kitchen as quickly as we arrived.

"I can't believe you just said that."

"Why not? They all know what we're going to do."

"No need to spell it out for them then."

All the air rushes from her lungs, as I push her up against the wall.

"At least we know that no one will interrupt us."

I lift her up the wall and her legs automatically wrap around my waist. My cock lines up with her pussy and makes her moan in pleasure.

"You need me to stop, you just say the word, yeah?" I tell her, staring her dead in the eyes so she knows just how serious I am.

"I'm fine, Luc. I promise. Do your worst."

"Oh, baby. As much as I might want to, that's not how tonight is going."

I capture her lips before she has a chance to ask me any questions.

I figure it would be easier to show her exactly what my intentions are instead.

Dragging her from the wall, I walk her up the stairs and straight into my bedroom.

Seeing as Leon's car wasn't out front, I'm assuming that he's still out doing whatever the hell they're doing.

Fine by me seeing as he's the only one who'd be able to hear just how loud I intend on making Peyton scream in the next hour or so with his room being next to mine and the only other one on the top floor of our house.

Kicking the door shut, I flip the lock, just in case he decides on an impromptu visit and walk Peyton straight toward the bed.

I sit her on the edge before ripping my lips away from hers and dropping down to my haunches.

Pulling her Chucks off, I throw them over my shoulder before tugging her leggings down her legs and swiping her jacket away once she's shrugged it off.

Standing, I untie my shirt from around her waist.

"I like you wearing my number again. Almost a shame to take it off you."

"Plenty of time for me to work my way through your closet," she moans as I peel the fabric up her body, leaving her sitting in just her white lace lingerie.

"Fuck, I missed you so fucking bad, P."

"Same," she confesses as she rests back on her elbows. Her eyes dropping down my body and waiting for me to start shedding some clothes. "Now show me what I was missing, Dunn."

Reaching behind me, I pull my hoodie off at the same time I kick my sneakers off before ripping my fly open and shoving my jeans and boxers down my legs. My hard cock jutting out from my body, more than ready to see some action.

A small smile plays on Peyton's lips as her teeth skin into her bottom lip.

I walk toward her slowly, letting her get her fill before I wrap my hands around her waist and lift her up my bed. I crawl between her legs, skimming my hands up her body until I cradle her face in my hands and stare down into her eyes.

"Mine," I breathe.

"Yours."

Fuck.

I slam my lips down on hers and squeeze my eyes closed. They burn with tears at the reality that this really is happening, that we are getting this second chance to be together.

25

PEYTON

I'm just drifting off to sleep in Luca's arms when the sound of footsteps racing up the stairs has me sitting bolt upright in bed.

"W-what is it?" Luca asks sleepily next to me.

He seemed to pass out right after we cleaned up, but I couldn't stop the events of the day from spinning around my head.

I hate that they've made an impact on me. I want to push it aside and forget that it ever happened. That's exactly why I convinced Luca that I was fine because I needed normal, I craved normal. If I let him treat me like glass, if I allow them too much headspace then it'll give them the power to destroy me and I refuse to let that happen, especially now Luca and I seem to be somewhat on the same page.

That useless excuse for a man is not going to ruin this again, he's not.

"Lee."

That one word is enough to wake Luca up instantly and he sits up, throws the covers off, and drags a pair of discarded sweats up his legs.

"Stay here," he demands as I also climb from the bed.

"Fuck that, Luc. You don't need to protect me from this."

He holds my stare for a few seconds but he must realize I'm right because he hovers until I pull his shirt over my head once more then he jerks the door open and races toward Lee's.

He doesn't bother knocking, just swings the door open and marches inside.

"Shit, sorry," I blurt when we find him down to his boxers.

He looks over his shoulder at the both of us. His face is set in a stone mask and his eyes are dark. Terrifyingly dark.

"What happened?"

"Kane called some friends. They've taken care of it."

Luca crosses his arms over his chest.

"You've been gone for hours. You're stripping out of clothes that are..." He walks over and picks up his discarded shirt. "Yep, covered in blood."

"You left them with their noses gushing. What did you expect?"

"What did you do with them, Lee?"

He shrugs dismissively and Luca's shoulders tense, the muscles in his back rippling with frustration.

"Bull. Shit. Tell me the truth."

"That is the truth."

"Kane turned up as we were dragging them out, followed by some guy in a van. We loaded them in and they took off."

"And what, you and Bry sat in the bar drinking while covered in blood? Do you think I'm fucking stupid, Lee?" Luca steps up to his brother and shoves his shoulder, forcing Lee to face him.

The two stare each other down and the atmosphere in the room takes a dark turn.

"Please," I beg. "Please don't fight."

Lee flicks another look in my direction and this time he must have come back to himself enough to remember that I was involved in all of this.

"Are you okay, Peyton?"

"Yeah. Just tell us what happened."

"All you need to know is that they're not going to come near you again."

"Y-you killed them?"

"No. The cunts are still breathing."

"So, where are they?"

He looks between Luca and me, obviously battling with what he's willing to tell us, which makes me wonder just how bad it is.

"You know who Kane's friends are, right?" he asks Luca.

"Hawks, yeah. Why do you think I sent him to help?"

Leon nods, lifting his hand to rub at the back of his neck, but not before I get a look at his busted knuckles and the blood that's splattered down his arm.

"We taught Julian a lesson he's never going to forget. He may or may not manage to find his way back to Maddison."

"And Brett?" I urge.

"I ensured his punishment is much more painful and long-winded."

"What the hell is that supposed to mean?" Luca barks.

"It means that he's going to be the Hawks plaything for a while. There's nothing they like more than a bit of old-fashioned torture, apparently."

"Jesus. You should have just killed him."

"Where is he?"

"I don't know."

"But you went there?"

"Yeah, but I was in the back of the van. It was dark. Middle of nowhere."

Luca studies Leon for long seconds, assessing whether he's being completely honest or not. In the end, he must decide that he is, either that or he really doesn't care as long as Brett is gone.

"Okay," he finally says with a nod of his head.

"We're going to destroy him, Luc. We're going to make sure he loses everything he's ever loved."

"Money and fame then."

"Exactly. I've got some ideas, but they can wait. Right now, I need a shower." He looks over Luca's shoulder at his bathroom door longingly. I get it. He's covered in someone else's blood. He's probably more than desperate to get rid of that.

"Okay. We're going to Rosewood tomorrow to talk to Mom. You coming?"

"We're having breakfast with Kayden first," I add, remembering my brief conversation with Aunt Fee earlier.

"Are we?" Luca asks, his eyes lighting up in excitement at the prospect.

"Yeah. Lee, you're more than welcome to come. He'd love to spend time with both of you."

"Y-yeah, okay."

"Come on, P. Let's leave him to it." Luca reaches for my hand as he moves toward the door.

"Just give me a minute."

He watches me as I step up to Leon and throw my arms around his shoulder.

Lee is motionless for long seconds as I hold him before his arms finally wrap around me.

"Thank you for whatever you did tonight. But please, do not get in deeper than you can handle with this."

"Just doing what I need to do, P."

"I trust you. But if you need anything, I'm here, okay?"

"I'm fine. But you should probably let go before Luca blows his top."

"Seriously, thank you."

"We got your back, P. You're one of us, and we look after our own."

Hurrying back to Luca, I curl myself into his side as we both leave Lee alone to deal with whatever happened tonight.

"You believe him?" I ask Luc the second he locks us both inside his bedroom.

"Not a fucking word of it. You?"

"Bits of it. I'm worried."

Luca runs his fingers through his hair while my fingers automatically lift to my mouth, a habit I'm not sure I'll ever properly rid myself of.

"Yeah. Me too. Come on, let's sleep. Everything might be brighter in the morning."

———

I open my eyes the next morning and find Luca staring aimlessly at the ceiling, looking like he's not slept a wink. I realize that my words last night might have been wishful thinking.

"Hey, you okay?"

He glances over at me, his expression softening as he gazes into my eyes.

"You're in my bed, I'm more than okay."

He rolls over me, pressing me into the mattress as his lips find mine.

I fight it when he tries to part my lips with his tongue, aware of my morning breath but he doesn't seem to care.

"Open up, baby. I need you."

Unable to deny him, my lips part, his tongue slides against mine and his hand cups my face.

"How's your cheek?" he murmurs against my lips.

"Sore," I answer honestly, knowing that he won't let me get away with playing it off.

"I really hope that whatever they did do to them yesterday that it really fucking hu—"

I cut off his words and hopefully his thought process as I kiss him again and press my palm against his shoulder to roll him off me.

The second he's on his back, I throw my leg over his waist.

"Hmm, now this is the kind of morning I could get used to."

Lifting up on my knees, I take him in my hand and guide him to my entrance.

"Hmm... someone's horny this morning," he groans as I sink down on his length.

His giant hands skim up my ribs until he cups my heavy breasts, making my head fall back in pleasure when he circles his hips at the same time.

"So good," he moans.

There's a slight burn from the fact he was inside me until I almost passed out last night, but that added bit of pain only makes it that much sweeter. It reminds me that this is real, that we're really here, together, and have the chance at a future together.

"Luca," I moan, lifting almost all the way up before dropping back down, only harder this time.

He grunts, half in shock, half pleasure as his eyes shutter.

"Don't close them," I warn.

"Wouldn't dream of it, baby. I want to watch every second of you riding me."

He pinches my nipples, making me cry out and for my movements to pick up speed.

"Fucking hell, P," he groans, the muscles down his neck pulling tight with his restraint not to take over.

"Do it," I say with a laugh. Quicker than I thought possible, he flips us over, caging my head in with his forearms and captures my lips until we both moan our releases into our kiss.

"What are you smiling about?" I ask when I finally drag my eyes open and find him staring down at me.

"Well, aside from the obvious." He gestures to my naked body. "I'm kinda excited to meet Kayden."

"Yeah?"

"Yeah. I want to give him a family."

"Luca," I breathe, my eyes filling with tears faster than I want to admit.

"Has he seen Libby yet?" he asks, climbing from the bed and padding toward the bathroom completely naked, letting me feast on inches upon inches of toned football player.

He looks over his shoulder and laughs before lifting a brow and reminding me that he asked a question.

"No. We don't want him to get his hopes up yet in case she doesn't manage to get clean."

"Fair enough. Seeing him might help her though."

"I know. It's like a catch twenty-two. But ultimately, he's the child here, so he's our biggest priority. I'm just hoping that once she gets to the facility, they'll have advice on how to handle all this for the best. I'm way out of my comfort zone being a part of making all these huge life-changing decisions."

"You're doing a fantastic job, Peyton. Libby is lucky to have you."

"I just want her back, you know?"

"I do." He spins in the doorway and leans against the frame. His hand lifting to his hair, he pushes it from his brow, all the muscles of his torso rippling with the move.

"Jesus," I mutter, wondering how I managed to resist him for quite so long.

"You coming to shower with me or what?"

I'm out of the bed and flying toward him before he's even finished asking the question. He laughs as he gathers me in his arms and carries me into the stall where he blasts us both with ice-cold water just like he did the night before. Only this time I see it coming and brace myself for impact.

By the time we emerge from his bedroom, we're both smiling, happy, and sated. It's a really good feeling and I'm more than happy to push our reality from my mind for a few hours as we enjoy some family time with Kayden.

"Bro, you awake?" Luca calls through to Leon who just moans in response. "Get your ass up and out here in ten minutes or we're going without you."

He mutters something unintelligible, and we turn away to wait for him in the kitchen.

I'm not surprised to find the place deserted. It's Saturday morning during the off-season so I expect everyone under this roof to either still be drunk or sleeping off a killer hangover.

Luca pulls a stool out for me before he starts the coffee maker.

"We really gonna go without him?" I ask.

"I guess that all depends on how much vodka he drowned his lies in last night." Luca's voice is hard as he refers to what happened yesterday.

"Give him a little time, you might find that once he's processed everything that he'll open up."

"Unlikely, he's been hiding shit for years."

"Thank you," I whisper when he passes me a mug over. "He never said anything?"

He shakes his head. "Nope. I hoped that eventually, he'd talk to me, you know. But he just got more and more distant. I still have no clue what happened that summer."

I lift my hand to my mouth, ready to gnaw on the ruined skin around my nail but Luca quickly reaches across the counter and stops me.

"Sorry," I mutter.

I remember the summer he's talking about. I also remember the happy Leon before they went off to football camp and the distant, cold version of him that came back.

Luca and I came up with a few scenarios but as far as I know, he never brought any of them up with Lee in case we were wrong. Then everything with Libby happened and I guess I put it all behind me. It seems that Leon hasn't though, whatever it was.

"Has he talked to anyone?" I ask after a few seconds.

"Not that I know of. Letty has tried but never got anywhere."

"I guess the time just isn't right. You've gotta trust him."

"I know, and I do. But mostly I just want to help. Whatever it was, it left such an impact on him. He became—" Luca stops talking a second before an exhausted Leon walks around the corner.

"Don't stop on my account," he snaps, looking between the two of us.

"How are you doing?" I ask, although I don't know why I bother, it's written all over his face.

"Fantastic. Best day of my life," he deadpans.

"Did you get any sleep?" Luca asks, clearly seeing the dark circles around Lee's eyes just like I do.

He shrugs.

"Are we going to get the kid or what?"

"Y-yeah. Here, down this." Luca pulls an energy drink out of the refrigerator and throws it at Leon, who catches it easily.

He cracks the top and does exactly as Luca suggested.

The tension is heavy in the car as we head across town to Aunt Fee's house.

Leon sits in the back with an angry dark cloud hanging over him, it's so bad that I almost suggest that this maybe isn't a good idea. But I fear seeing Kayden might be the only bit of light in his life right now.

"Oh my goodness, look at you," I squeal when Kayden hops from the front door using a set of crutches.

"Surprise," he says with a beaming smile.

"When did you get these?" I ask. I knew he had an appointment, but Aunt Fee didn't say anything about him getting back on his feet.

"Two days ago. I wanted to surprise you."

"Baby boy," I breathe, pulling him in for a hug, emotion clogging my throat.

Aunt Fee stands by the front door with an equally wide smile on her face.

"Are you hungry?" I ask him as both Luca and Leon come up behind me. "We thought we could all go for breakfast."

"All of us?" he asks, his eyes sparkling with excitement as he looks between his two brothers.

"Yeah. That okay with you, lil' man?" Lee asks.

"Yesss," he squeals.

"Okay, why don't you show us how good you are on those things then. Luc and Lee will help you into the car."

He stares up at them both like they're the most incredible people he's ever seen in his life. It melts my heart.

I watch them for a few seconds before heading over to Aunt Fee. "You said the appointment went well but—"

"He didn't want me to tell you. Wanted to surprise you. He's gotta take it slow, just a couple hours a day, but he's so excited to be back on his feet."

"I can see."

"How is everything? Those two look... stressed."

"Yeah." I look back as they help Kayden. "This is a lot to process."

"They seem to have gotten revenge by the state of their fists."

"Yeah," I breathe. "Even if I wanted to tell you, Aunt Fee. I don't have any answers right now."

"I trust you, Peyton. And I trust both of them to protect you as well. But if you need anything, any of you, you talk to me, okay?"

"We will. We're heading to Rosewood for the weekend to talk to Maddie. Libby knows I'm not going to be around so—"

"I'll make sure she's fine. Go and enjoy your weekend, as much as you can, given the circumstances," she quickly adds.

"Thank you. I'd better go before they all starve to death," I joke when Leon joins Kayden in the back of the car while Luca heads for us.

"Luca," Aunt Fee says. "Thank you for looking after our girl here."

"Anytime. You ready?" he asks me.

"Sure. See you in a few hours."

"Enjoy yourselves."

Luca drives us to a diner that I've never been to before, but the second our food is delivered, I understand why he chose this place because the portions are huge.

All three of them clear their plates while I barely make a dent in mine.

"You three definitely are related," I deadpan, looking at their plates.

Kayden beams as he continues to look at both Luc and Lee like they can't possibly be real.

They chat away about football and all kinds of boy things, and I sit there with a smile on my face the whole time just seeing Kayden so happy.

He really needed this.

"You gonna come and see us play next season, Bro?" Lee asks.

"Yes," he squeals before looking at me. "Can we, PeyPey?"

"Of course, baby boy," I say with a smile before shooting a concerned glance at Luca. I can see that he's still torn about what he wants to do now. Reaching over, I squeeze his thigh in support. I meant what I said, no matter what decision he comes to, I'll be right beside him.

Disappointment covers Kayden's face when we make a move to leave.

"Can we do this again next weekend?" he asks hopefully.

The three of us look at each other before nodding. "Yeah, that sounds like a good plan, Bro," Luca says with a smile.

Although he might be sad that our time together is coming to an end, Kayden still doesn't come up for air from talking all the way home about all sorts of nonsense. Luca and Leon soak up every word.

They're going to be incredible big brothers to Kayden. I already knew that but seeing them together only solidifies it.

His bottom lip trembles as Aunt Fee comes out of the house to help him from the car. It breaks my heart but I know that we've got things we need to go and do, uncomfortable conversations to have.

26

LUCA

Leon drives his own car to Rosewood but he doesn't follow. Instead of taking a right at the intersection out of Maddison, he took a left and disappeared.

We both watched as he vanished into the distance but neither of us said anything. There really is nothing to say. Lee needs to deal with all of this his own way. And his way of coping with shit is shutting the hell up and banging a redhead. As much as I might want to shake him, demand he tells me how he's really feeling, I know it won't make any difference.

"You ready for this?" Peyton asks as we pull up on the driveway of my mom's place.

She sold the house we all grew up in after she kicked Brett out. I get it. There were too many memories inside those walls. I kinda miss it though. While she might not like to remember some of our years there, it was the place where Peyton and I spent most of our time. A part of me wants to reminisce in my own bedroom.

She downsized and bought a beach house just a couple of miles from our old home. The entire back wall is glass, making the most of the ocean beyond. It's pretty sweet, and definitely too small for our father's taste. It's probably one of the reasons why she bought it when she could have afforded something much more impressive after the deal her lawyer got for her following their separation. But Mom was never about that kind of life and needing to have the biggest and best everything. That was all him.

"Am I ready to shatter my mom's heart all over again? No, not really," I say, assuming that she's in the dark about the whole Libby situation.

"She knew he was unfaithful," Peyton says as if that will help soften the blow of the truth.

"Yeah, she's more than aware."

Hand in hand, we walk up to the front door and I let us inside.

"This place is really cute," Peyton muses before her breath catches when she gets sight of the view. "Wow."

"Yeah, Mom's got good taste."

"You don't say."

"Hello?" Mom calls from upstairs.

"It's Luc," I shout, leading Peyton over to the windows to get a better look.

Seconds later, Mom's footsteps race down the stairs.

"You should have said you were coming," she says a beat before she appears.

She's got a wide smile on her face as she sees me but that's nothing compared to what happens when she gets a look at who's standing beside me.

"Oh my God," she squeals. "Peyton?"

Mom damn near runs at Peyton, ripping her from my side and engulfing her in a hug.

"Why didn't you tell me?" she demands, gently slapping my upper arm while still holding my girl.

"Thought it could be a surprise."

"Well, I'm certainly surprised," she says, finally releasing Peyton. Although she doesn't let her go very far because she holds onto her arms and looks her over.

"Look at you, all grown up."

"Jesus, Mom," I mutter, running my hand through my hair.

"Oh shush. This girl right here is the daughter I never had, and I missed her almost as much as you did."

"I'm going to start the coffee maker," I say, ready to leave Mom to it.

"Don't you dare move. Oh my God, I'm so happy right now," she says. She cups her cheeks with her hands, and the widest smile I think I've ever seen on her face. I'm pretty sure even Nadine's arrival didn't make her smile quite like this.

She stares between the two of us, her eyes twinkling with excitement.

"Please tell me that you've put the past behind you."

"We have," I say, taking Peyton's hand and lifting her knuckles to my lips.

"I think my heart is going to explode."

"Overdramatic much, Mom." I roll my eyes at her.

"I need to know everything. Come on."

She takes Peyton's other hand and leads us toward the kitchen.

"Coffee. You want coffee?" she asks, suddenly nervous.

"I got it, Mom. You sit down before you have a coronary."

Walking over to the appliance, I watch as Mom sits at the table and just stares at Peyton like she can't possibly be real. The look on her face isn't all that different from Kayden's this morning as he looked at Lee and me.

"How long have you been back?" she finally asks Peyton who begins filling Mom in on some of the details of how we found each other again.

"I'm so sorry," Mom says when Peyton explains about her mom's accident. "I understand why you felt you needed to be close to home again."

"There's actually a lot more to it than that, Mom," I say, dropping down between the two of them.

"Oh?"

Dread sits heavy in my stomach.

"Peyton didn't move into Fee's house alone. She brought her nephew with her."

"O-okay. Where's Libby?"

"Right now," Peyton says. "Libby is in the hospital."

"She was in the accident too?" Mom guesses.

"No." Peyton lifts her hand to her mouth and this time I let her continue, understanding how she must be feeling.

"Mom, Libby was pregnant when they left town. Dad got her pregnant."

"What?" she screeches, standing so fast her chair topples over behind her.

"Peyton tried to tell me before they left but I didn't believe her. That's why we had a falling out."

"Your father s-slept with Liberty?"

"Yeah."

"M-my nephew, Kayden. He's Luc's half-brother."

"Holy fucking Christ," Mom says as she starts pacing.

Silence falls over the three of us as we allow her to process what we've just told her.

"L-Liberty was a senior when you left, right?"

"Yes," Peyton agrees.

"She was underage, wasn't she?"

"Yes."

"Motherfucker," Mom screams, picking up a vase full of flowers from the dresser and launching it at the wall.

"Whoa," I say, stepping up behind her and wrapping my arms around her. "It's okay."

She lets me hold her as she tries to get herself together.

"I hate him, Luca. I hate him so much," she sobs, sagging into my arms.

Guiding her back toward her chair, Peyton slides closer and takes her hand.

"We're really sorry to have to tell you this, Maddie. But it's time the truth came out."

Mom nods, tears cascading down her cheeks.

"Libby took off not long after Kayden was born. She's an addict. A couple of weeks ago, I got a call from a hospital in Atlanta to tell me that she'd OD'd. With Luca's help, she's now back in Maddison and will soon be heading to a facility where we really hope she can get clean and be a mother to Kayden."

"He drove her to drugs."

"Libby was an unstable teenager, you know that as much as we do." My mom and Peyton's were never close friends but with us being attached at the hip, they had little choice but to spend time together over the years.

The front door slams and footsteps head our way, but Mom doesn't seem to notice.

"Where's your father?"

"Uh…"

Leon appears at the entrance to the kitchen, looking just as much a mess as he was this morning.

"L-Lee?" Mom stutters.

"He's being dealt with," Leon says coldly.

"What the hell does that mean?"

"It means that his days of ruining everyone's lives are over."

"L-Lee you can't just—"

Leon walks over and drops down to his haunches in front of our mom.

"Trust me, Mom. I know what I'm doing."

I just about manage to swallow my reaction to that statement because I really don't think he's got a fucking clue what he's doing right now.

As if he can read my thoughts, he looks up at me, narrowing his eyes in warning.

"Does he know about the baby?" Mom asks.

Our silence is our answer.

"Motherfucker. He owes your sister a lot of money."

"We'll make sure Libby and Kayden get what they're owed Mom," I assure her.

"He needs destroying for this. Other women is one thing. But a child. No. We're going to fucking ruin him."

Her fire makes me smile.

"Glad we're all on the same page," Leon mutters.

———

We spend the afternoon in Mom's living room. Peyton and I sit next to her to support her while Leon sits closed off on the couch on the other side of the room.

No matter how gentle he's being with Mom, how supportive, it's like there's a brick wall built up around him that none of us are going to be able to scale.

I want to help, I want to listen. But all of that is pointless if he's not willing to accept it.

Shane, Chelsea, and Nadine came over and we had to recap the whole story to them once more and then watch as Shane bailed on the whole situation and ran for the beach.

Thankfully, Chelsea managed to talk him around and he came back after a while. But it was obvious that he wasn't dealing with it very well and after allowing me some cuddles with my beautiful niece, they left.

After drinking an entire bottle of wine to herself, Mom eventually falls asleep on the couch not long after the sun drops beneath the sea on the horizon.

"Help me get her to bed," I say to P who immediately puts her glass down and pushes up from my side.

I scoop Mom up in my arms and lift her from the couch.

"Don't worry, Bro. I got it," I snap quietly.

Pocketing his cell, Leon jumps up and marches for the door.

"I'm going out. Don't wait up."

Peyton and I stand there frozen as we watch him storm from the house.

"Well, okay then," I mutter, hating the way my stomach twists with concern for my brother.

Peyton looks at me, her own worry for Leon easy to read in her eyes.

She leads the way and opens Mom's bedroom door and pulls the sheets back so I can lay her down.

With a kiss to her creased brow, we leave her alone to get some rest.

"She's going to be okay," Peyton says, wrapping her arms around my waist and resting her head against my chest.

"I know. I just wish it could all stop, you know?"

"It will. We might be in the dark with what's going on right now, but one thing I'm sure of is that his days controlling your life are over."

"You know, I really want to be playing when you bring Kayden to a game," I say, pushing open the door to my room.

"Yeah? That's awesome."

"I want... I want to be someone he can be proud of," I confess. I drop down into the chair that's placed right in front of the floor-to-ceiling windows, showcasing the inky black ocean in the distance.

"You're his big brother, Luc. He literally thinks that both of you are the best people to ever walk the Earth."

"That's not true." She yelps as I pull her down onto my lap. "Because that would be you," I whisper before capturing her lips.

She melts into my kiss, sitting across my lap and allowing me the access to her that I so desperately need.

My hand skims up her thigh and under her skirt until I find the edge of her panties.

"Luc, we shouldn't," she forces out between heaving breaths.

"Why the hell wouldn't we?"

"Because it's your mom's house." Her eyes tell me that she's being serious, and I can't help but laugh.

"You're kidding. It didn't stop you when we were kids."

Her cheeks burn red.

"Yeah well, we were disrespectful kids."

"And now we can be disrespectful adults. Plus, she's in a wine coma, it's not like she'll even hear us."

"Oh God," she moans when I slip her panties aside and run my fingers through her already soaked pussy.

"Your argument might be a little more convincing if you weren't dripping for me, P."

I spear two fingers inside her, reaching up high and finding that spot that drives her crazy.

"Shit, Luc," she moans, throwing her head back.

I bite her nipple through the fabric of her shirt and bra, desperate to get her naked and laid out before me.

"You're mine, Peyton. And I intend on proving it at every opportunity I get."

Pressing my thumb against her clit, I pick up speed as she begins riding my hand, desperate for the release she's right on the cusp on.

"What the— Luca," she seethes when I rip my hand from her body and lift her from my lap.

"What, baby?" I ask innocently, lifting my fingers to her lips. "Open." She does as she's told. "Suck."

My cock jerks in my pants, desperate for release when she licks around my fingers, cleaning herself from them.

I stare into her dark eyes.

"We both know you love it when I deny you."

"If by love, you mean hate, then yeah."

"Whatever you say, but you know how much sweeter it'll be when I eventually let you fall."

Wrapping my hands around her shirt, I pull it up her body, quickly followed by her bra, skirt, and panties until she's standing before me bare.

"So fucking beautiful."

Her cheeks heat with my words, her arms twitching at her sides with her need to hide.

"Get on the bed. Legs spread."

Her chin drops at my demand but no argument passes her lips. Instead, she just backs up until her legs hit the end of the bed and then she crawls on, doing exactly as she's told.

"Fucking perfect," I mutter before reaching behind me and pulling my shirt off.

My pants and boxers join hers. But apparently, I'm not fast enough because before I drop them her fingers slide down her stomach to her pussy.

"Impatient, baby?"

"You're too slow."

Taking my length in my hand, I stroke slowly as I watch her play with herself.

"That how you do it when you're alone and thinking about me."

"Luc," she moans, pushing two digits inside herself.

"Fuck this." Marching forward, I press her legs as wide as they'll go and latch onto her clit. I'm sucking so hard her back arches off the bed and her fingers pull at my hair as if she's trying to rip it from my scalp.

Her concerns about my mom seem to vanish because when I spear two fingers inside her and find her G-spot once again. She falls over the edge with a scream loud enough to wake the dead.

PEYTON

I fell asleep last night with the image of Luca with his niece Nadine giggling in his arms in my head. The way his eyes lit up when Shane walked into the room is something I want to witness again and again. And then when he swiped her straight out of his brother's arms, I swear to God my ovaries exploded.

But when I woke late this morning, I was in bed alone. I soon found he'd left me something to wear though because when I looked at the end of the bed, I found his jersey waiting for me.

The memory of him telling me last night that he wanted Kayden to watch him play made me smile. It's the first sign that he might be starting to see things straight again.

"Good morning," Maddie says, looking much sharper than I was sure she should this morning after the amount she drank last night.

"M-morning," I stutter, feeling awkward standing in just Luca's jersey. I was expecting to find him down here. "Where's Luc?"

"Oh, he's gone to work out with Shane. You remember how they like to run on the beach."

I smile at the memory of watching them race back and forth when we were kids.

"Lee?"

She shakes her head. "I haven't seen him."

"He went out last night. I don't remember hearing him come back in."

"As much as I hate to admit it, Peyton. My boys are all grown up now. I've got to trust that they know what they're doing. Speaking of," she says, sliding a mug of coffee to me and nodding at the dining table. "I never got a chance to ask you about that bruise on your cheek yesterday."

I lift my hand to cover the purple mark on my face.

"It wasn't Luc," I say in a rush, needing to defend him.

"I know. If I had any suspicion that it was, I'd have kicked his ass by now."

I can't help but laugh. The thought of her even trying to get the better of any of her sons is amusing.

"It was Brett," I confess. Her fingers tighten around her mug, her knuckles going white with the force.

"Why don't you tell me all the bits you didn't get to last night? Like the truth about how you two got over the past. I know my son, Peyton. I know how much you leaving hurt him, how much he convinced himself he hated you. I can't imagine that he accepted you back into his life without a second thought."

"You got that right," I mutter, taking a sip of my coffee.

I give her a very PG-rated rundown of how we found each other again.

"Sounds like you've got the beginnings of a romance novel right there, young lady," she says softly when I've finished explaining, obviously not forgetting that I wanted to be a writer from as early as I can remember.

"I guess we just need to see if we'll get our happily ever after in the end."

"I have every confidence in both of you. There was never any question that you two weren't meant for each other. I just think that maybe you were both a little young to fully understand the strength of what you had. I think, in the long run, the bit of time you spent apart was probably for the best. You'll appreciate what you have again now so much more because of it."

I smile at her, understanding her point but still hating that we lost so much time together.

"I'm so sorry about all of this. There were so many times over the years when I just wanted to turn up on your doorstep and confess everything."

"Oh, Peyton." She reaches over the table to take my hand.

"I wanted Mom to do things differently. I thought she was taking the easy way out by running."

"Your mom was doing what all moms should do. She was protecting her babies. It's something I should have done for my boys a long time ago. But I stayed thinking that it was the lesser of the two evils.

"I knew Brett was an asshole. He was controlling, overbearing, just to name a few. But ultimately, I thought that having two parents would be better for them than one. I think maybe I was wrong."

"No. There's nothing wrong with wanting to keep your family together."

"Even if their father is a monster?"

"You didn't know."

She looks away, shame coming off her in waves. "I knew about the women. He was going behind my back for years. Every trip away he took, there was always another one. I just never expected—" She fights back a sob.

"I know."

Her eyes come back to mine and we both smile sadly at each other.

"Do you really not know where he is?"

I shake my head.

"Turns out, some of our friends have friends in high places."

"You mean dangerous places."

"Yeah, that too." I laugh but there's not much humor to it. "We just have to trust that everything will work itself out."

She nods. "If Brett is gone, wherever he may be, then it will happen. Hopefully, my boys will be able to find some peace without the constant pressure."

"Luca's been close to giving it all up."

"I know," she confesses.

"H-he told you?"

"No, Peyton. My boys don't tell me anything. But I'm their mom. I sense these things."

"Oh."

"You'll understand when you have kids of your own someday."

I nod, hoping that I'll have the insight that she seems to have.

"I'm worried about Lee," I admit.

"Lee is..." She lets out a long sigh. "He feels things deeper, harder, than the rest of us and he has no idea how to deal with it. Luca acts out with his anger and frustration. Lee just shuts himself off. Finds his release in silence."

"Why?"

"I don't know. But something tells me that's probably linked to Brett somewhere as well."

"You think Brett did that to him?"

"Maybe not personally, but he'll have had a hand in it, no doubt."

"Jesus."

"Trust me, Peyton. We're all better off without him in our lives. All I can hope for is that whatever they've done, it doesn't come back to bite them later."

I nod.

"Get dressed," she says, hopping up as if that conversation didn't just happen. "I need to go to the store and the boys will be gone for a while. Keep me company?"

"Of course."

I finish my coffee and take it over to the sink before heading for the stairs, but I stop when Maddie says my name.

I look back over my shoulder at her, still sitting at the table.

"I'm so glad you're back. My boy has been miserable without you."

"Me too. I didn't realize just how much until I was with him again."

She smiles at me and I slip away, my heart feeling so full it might burst.

———

"Isn't the store in the other direction?" I ask when Maddie takes a turn I wasn't expecting. I know I haven't lived here for six years but surely the store hasn't moved.

"I just need to make a pit stop."

"Okay," I say, sitting back and getting comfortable.

She talks to me about the town and the things that have changed since I've been gone as well as admitting that she's been spending time with Chelsea's biological birth father.

We chat away like the years haven't passed and that we're not surrounded by more drama than most people experience in their lifetimes before she pulls up into a parking lot for the beach.

"Here?"

"Yeah." She kills the engine and turns to look at me. "I'm sorry, Peyton. This is a total setup."

"O-okaaay," I say skeptically.

Surely, she's not about to kill me and hide my body at the beach... right?

"You remember your place?" she asks, dragging me from my crazy thoughts.

"Of course." I can't help but smile as I think about mine and Luca's spot at the end of the beach where we used to hang out when we needed to get away from people. I thought it was a secret, but it seems that might have been wishful thinking.

"He's waiting for you. Out you go."

My chin drops but I don't say anything. The excitement that explodes in my belly takes over all my thoughts.

I'm out of the car before I even know I've moved and running toward the gap in the hedgerow.

"Have fun," Maddie calls after me, but I'm already gone and running down the track that leads to our place.

Our solace.

My steps falter the second I spot what he's done.

In the space we used to spend so much time as kids, is a blanket, a huge picnic basket and a bottle of champagne. Next to it all is the man who's turned my world upside down in all the best ways.

He watches me approach as I take everything in with an easy smile playing on his lips.

"Working out, huh?"

He shrugs. "Surprise."

"What's the occasion?" I ask, making my way to him and dropping down onto the blanket with him.

"I just wanted to do something, just the two of us. Forget about all the bullshit for a few hours."

"Well, I'm surprised. Your mom gave nothing away."

"How is she?"

"I think she's going to be fine. Yesterday was just a shock."

"Okay, good. That's enough about all that. For the next few hours, none of it exists."

"Okay, I can get on board with that."

I crawl over to him when he rests back on the blanket.

"Hey," I say, cupping his jaw and brushing my lips over his.

"Hey." His eyes sparkle with excitement. The sight makes my heart beat that little bit faster.

"Thank you for this."

"I thought I owed you a proper date."

"It's perfect." I look around at a place that used to feel as familiar as my own home, noticing all the changes, mostly how overgrown it all is now.

My eyes land on the tree trunk behind Luca and I stare at the carving we did all those years ago.

"Seems like a lifetime ago, doesn't it?"

He leans back and looks up.

"I spent a lot of time here after you left. There were so many times I almost carved that out."

"I'm glad you didn't," I say, curling into his side and resting my head on his chest.

"I figured that if you were ever going to come back, then you might come here."

"I didn't think we were talking about that," I point out.

"I still want it all, you know?"

"All what?"

"Everything we planned back then. The house, the kids, the dogs, the life together."

"Me too, Luc. I never stopped wanting it, not really. But what about the other bit?"

He chews on the inside of his cheek for a moment, lost in thought.

"I think I still want the NFL too. But I want it on my terms."

"Then the NFL it is."

He smiles down at me and my heart flips when I realize that the person staring back at me is just an older version of the boy I once fell in love with.

"I've got something for you."

"Oh?"

Luca reaches into the picnic basket and pulls out a long black box.

"What's that?"

"Your sixteenth birthday present."

"My—" The lump that jumps into my throat stops any more words from coming out.

"You left before your birthday, and I never got a chance to give it to you."

"You kept it?" I ask, emotion burning at the back of my nose.

"I did. Deep down maybe I knew that we weren't over, not really."

He passes me the box, and I flip it open to find the most stunning bracelet inside.

It has a delicate white gold chain with a diamond-encrusted infinity symbol in the center.

"Luc, it's beautiful."

"Just like you. Can I?" he asks, taking the box from my hand and pulling the jewelry out.

Holding my wrist up for him, I watch enthralled as he works the clasp and secures it in place.

"I love it," I say, staring down at my wrist.

"I love you."

I part my lips to respond. He makes the most of the opportunity and crashes his to them, plunging his tongue inside my mouth.

"Whatever happens from here on out, there's one thing I know for sure," he murmurs into our kiss.

"Oh yeah?"

"Yeah. I'm never letting you go again, P. You're mine. Always have been and always will be."

"Always," I whisper but it gets swallowed up by his kiss.

And there, right in the spot we loved so much, we forget all about the picnic and everything going on in our lives. We focus on getting us back on track because he's right, we were always meant to be.

Written in the stars.

Or at least carved into the tree.

EPILOGUE

Leon

The slap of skin on skin echoes through the room seconds before she cries out in pain.

"Fuck, yeah," she moans, arching her back and offering herself to me, desperate for me to sink deep inside her.

I want to. Fuck, do I want to.

But even with the lights out and my eyes closed, I know she's not what I really want.

The one I wanted tonight got away. The redhead in the short skirt.

My cock finally swells as I imagine her on her hands and knees before me wearing my bright red handprint on her ass.

She was exactly what I needed, but she bailed before I had the chance to make my move.

"Fuck me," the girl beneath me moans, her voice desperate yet whiny. It's like nails on a chalkboard.

Not willing to bail, knowing that I've got a rep to keep. I lift my hand once more in the hope her scream of pain will get me hard enough to fuck her until I lose some of the tension that's keeping my muscles locked up tight. That it allows me to forget everything for just a handful of blissful seconds.

This hit is harder than any I've landed on her already and she screams like a banshee.

Shoving my pants down over my ass, I wrap my hand around my cock and pump vigorously, hoping it's the extra push I need.

I'm just about to slam inside of her when the door behind me swings open and the light above us illuminates the room.

"Charlie, what's— Oh shit," the girl says in a panic when she realizes why her roommate was screaming like she was being murdered. "Sorry, sorry," she says but she's not quick enough to escape because she gives me enough time to look over my shoulder.

What I find makes my cock rock hard instantly in a way that any girl couldn't, but it also makes everything around me grind to a silent halt.

It's her.

The girl who haunts my nightmares.

The girl who torments me relentlessly.

The girl who could have saved me.

Her eyes lock on mine and they widen as if she recognizes me.

I guess it's a possibility. Most people on campus know who I am, know my name.

But does she know? Does she really know?

And more importantly, does she remember?

She takes a step back but I'm faster.

I'm off the bed and in her space in a heartbeat.

"What's the rush, Red? Why don't you stay and have some fun?"

My hand finds the soft skin of her throat and I push her back against the wall. A gasp of shock ripping from her as I lean in. My nose almost touching hers as I breathe in her sweet scent that feeds the darkness that has festered inside me, growing each day since the last time I looked into her blue eyes.

"N-no," she stutters, attempting to release herself from my grip but I'm not having any of it.

I've spent years looking for Macie Fletcher. Years thinking she was nothing but a figment of my imagination. Someone to give me focus, to distract from reality.

Who knew she was living right under my nose?

Leaning in closer, my lips brush the shell of her ear as the length of my body presses hers into the wall. The unmistakable hardness of my cock pressing against her stomach.

"Maybe not tonight, Red. But soon."

"W-what?"

"Leon, what the hell are you doing?" a voice whines from behind me. But I've lost all interest in her now. She was only a means to an end, and a shit one at that.

I've got my sights firmly set on someone new.

"And that's a promise," I whisper before releasing her, grabbing my jersey from the floor and marching out of the room.

Until next time, Macie Fletcher.

And there will be a next time.

Want more Luca and Peyton? Keep reading for a bonus epilogue!

BONUS EPILOGUE

LUCA & PEYTON EXTENDED EPILOGUE

PEYTON

Two years later

I wake when the bed dips, and I sigh in contentment.

The scent of coffee and sea air rushes through my nose as the sound of the ocean, birds and my soon-to-be husband hit my ears.

"Good morning, bride," Luca says, his voice all rough and sexy from sleep.

"Morning," I whisper. I open my eyes to find him sitting beside me, resting back against the headboard with a mug of coffee in his hands. Oh, and he's shirtless, obviously.

Best freaking sight in the world.

"I love you," I blurt, unable to hold it in.

The most incredible smile curls up at the corners of his lips, making my heart flip, and butterflies taking flight in my belly. Just like it used to when we were kids.

From as early as I can remember, Luca has been the one. I never once looked at any other boy growing up. He was all I could see. I was fascinated by every single inch of him. I still am. And, even better, I'm able to get up close and personal with those inches too.

"I love you too, P. You still sure this is how you want to do it?" he asks as I push myself up so I'm sitting next to him. However, to his disappointment, I keep the sheets over my bare chest.

"Luc," I say, ripping my eyes from the open doors at the other end showcasing our private infinity pool and the ocean beyond that. "Everything about this is perfect."

"Still different to what we always planned," he says like we haven't had this discussion a million times since he proposed after his very final game as a Panther. A few months before both our lives changed all over again.

But this time, we were going on this journey together. A whole new life in a whole new state. Thankfully, though, one very important thing remained. Us.

Luca signed as a first draft pick to the Seattle Saints, and not long after we both racked up enough credits to graduate, we packed up our stuff and set about starting our new lives. Together.

Leaving Libby, Kayden, and Aunt Fee was hard. But I knew I was doing the right thing. They had their own lives and it was time for me and Luca to finally start ours.

Over the years, we'd spent a lot of time planning what our future would look like. We'd planned our wedding, what our house would look like, how many kids we'd have. He'd dreamed about the teams he wanted to be good enough to play for.

But we discovered that even years of meticulous planning didn't stop the wheels from coming off.

Brett Dunn had other plans for us. And I hate that he almost succeeded. I barely survived those few years without my best friend in my life. Sadness floods me whenever I think about the life Mom created for us in South Carolina.

She did her best, but the situation was even more fucked up than we ever could have predicted.

But all of that is in the past, and all we can do now is be grateful that we found our way back to each other. Even if part of the journey was full of more pain and loss than anyone should suffer.

"We were just kids, Luc. We had no idea what life was going to throw at us. Plus, that house is long gone," I say, reaching over to twist my fingers with his.

When we looked into the future, we had visions of our wedding being in Brett and Maddie's backyard. It was beautiful and a place that Luca loved. We wanted to invite everyone we'd ever met to watch us tie the knot, to celebrate with us.

But all these years on and things are very different.

The timing might be what Luc always wanted. A wedding after his rookie year in the NFL, but we're not in Rosewood, and we aren't about to say our vows in front of hundreds.

I think as teenagers, and despite Luca living a life with a famous father, we underestimated the level of interest we'd—he'd—receive from the media.

Not only has he had an incredibly successful year, but he's Brett Dunn's protégé. Everyone who has any interest in football seems to want a piece of him.

And that is the last thing either of us wants from our big day.

We've been waiting for this almost all our lives. The only people I want to witness it are those closest to us.

"I just want you to be happy," he says, studying my face for any sign that I might not be.

"Luc," I sigh. "I am so unbelievably happy."

I am. I love every single thing about our lives. Watching him live out his dream, working alongside Macie to help bring hers to life very soon. Living in Seattle, our incredible condo. Our friends. Our family.

We have the kind of life that as kids, we could only dream of. It is everything and then some. And I get to do all of it with my best friend right by my side.

"Good. Me too."

I smile up at him, my heart somersaults in my chest like it does multiple times a day.

"What time is it?" I ask after he's taken a sip of coffee.

It's unusual to wake up and find him in bed beside me. Even in the off-season, he's usually up first and in the gym, trying to make the most of his time. But being here, he's given himself some much-needed time off, and he's been right here for me to indulge in every single morning since we arrived.

We're in paradise. Quite literally.

Saint Lucia is... wow. When we booked it, the pictures looked incredible, but honestly, I didn't think that they'd pale in comparison to reality.

It's literally heaven on earth.

The ocean, the beaches, the food. Everything is just incredible. And the fact that our nearest and dearest and here making the most of a little bit of luxury too makes my heart swell with contentment and happiness.

"We've got an hour before you're going to be stolen away from me." He pouts, making me laugh.

"If Aunt Fee had her way, we wouldn't be together right now," I point out.

She was all for us being traditional and trying to demand that I crash in her room last night so we wouldn't see each other before the wedding.

It took a bit of convincing but eventually, she caved and gave in.

I don't know why she even tried. I already spend too much time having to watch my man on TV while he sleeps alone in a hotel room miles away. There is no way I'm putting any more distance between us than necessary.

I take a sip of my coffee, before placing it on the side and throwing the covers back.

"Where are you..." Luca's words trail off as I walk naked across the room toward the bathroom.

I stop in the doorway and look back over my shoulder.

He doesn't notice at first, his eyes are too busy feasting on my body. But the second he looks up, something crackles between us and my blood begins to heat.

"See something you like, Dunn?" I tease.

"P, baby, you have no idea."

I laugh. "I really do," I whisper before slipping into the bathroom to pee and freshen up.

By the time I emerge, he's ditched his coffee and thrown the covers back, leaving his incredible body exposed for me to enjoy.

"Well, well, well," I say, once again stopping in the doorway. "What do we have here?"

A cocky smirk plays on his lips as we watch each other.

"You've never looked sexier than when you're naked and wearing only my ring."

"What? This?" I ask, lifting the incredibly beautiful and inordinately expensive ring that adorns my finger, as memories of the night he gave it to me flicker through my mind.

I never forgot our childhood plans. But that didn't mean I was expecting him to follow them. So when he dropped to one knee outside the stadium in front of all his adoring fans who'd come to see his last Panthers game and wish him well in Seattle, I was floored.

We hadn't talked about anything other than finishing college and moving across the country. A proposal, marriage, was well off my radar at that moment.

But despite that, there was only ever one answer.

"Yes, that. If you could walk around wearing only that for the rest of our lives, I'd die a very happy man."

"I'm not sure about that," I tease, ripping my eyes from his godlike body and glancing down at my hand. "I think it needs another addition."

"Give me a few hours and I'll make it happen. You're mine, Peyton. Always have been, and always will be. Now get your sexy ass over here and let me prove it to you," he growls, sending a wave of heat through me.

"Oh yeah?" I ask, pushing from the doorway I was resting against. "And what exactly is it you want to do with me?"

His green eyes darken with every seductive step I take. I know every single thing there is to know about the infamous Luca Dunn. I can make him angry almost as easily as I can flip a switch. I know exactly how to make him laugh. And most importantly, I know how to drive him crazy with need until he loses control.

I love every side there is to him. The loving brother, the caring son, the supportive teammate. But there is nothing better than watching him ride the edge of unfiltered desire.

"Everything, P. I want everything."

The honesty in his tone makes my breath catch.

"Now," he growls. "Get up here and sit on my face. When you walk down that aisle later, I want to remember exactly how you taste. The noises you make as you fall."

"Luc," I breathe, unsure if I'm unbelievably turned on or mortified by his suggestion. "You can't say—"

"I can say what I fucking like, especially if it's true."

With seemingly little effort, Luca reaches out, wraps his giant hands around my waist, and lifts me off my feet, giving me little choice but to do exactly as he wishes.

"Don't hold back," he warns. "Scream my name as loud as you can so every motherfucker out there knows you're about to be mine," he demands before wrapping his hands around my thighs and dragging me down so he can suck my clit.

"Luca," I gasp when he instantly initiates a pace that is going to have me screaming in only minutes.

This man is on a mission, and I am here for the ride.

My grip on the headboard tightens as he works his magic. My hips roll as I shamelessly ride his face, chasing the incredible high that he's capable of delivering.

His fingertips grip my thighs with a bruising force, as he alternates between teasing my clit and plunging his tongue inside me.

"Oh God, Luc. Please," I beg as he holds me hostage right on the edge of my release. "Please, please. I nee— LUCA," I scream when he finally lets me fall.

My body quakes with the power of the release that surges through me, making my muscles spasm before turning them to goo.

"Oh my God," I gasp, trying to catch my breath.

"You've ridden my face, now you're going to ride my dick," he commands, once again moving me around like a rag doll.

His face glistens with my arousal but he doesn't make any kind of move to wipe it off as he settles me across his waist.

"Don't tell me," I rasp "You want to know that your cum is running out of me when I walk down the aisle."

His eyes flare with heat as he lifts his dick to line us up.

"Hadn't thought about it," he lies. "But now, that you mention it. Yeah, that is a really fucking good idea."

With a firm grip on my waist, he drags me down at the same time he thrusts up.

"Fuck," I cry as he stretches me open. I'm so sensitive from my release and admittedly a little sore from all the fun we've been having since we arrived here. But it's nowhere near enough to stop me. And in only a few seconds, I forget all about any discomfort and lose myself in the high of being with Luc.

It's always been electric between. Even when we were too young and exploring things we arguably shouldn't have been together. We had no idea what we were doing, but the high of each other's touch was too addictive to stop. It still is. And I hope it always will be.

Luca's hand locks on my waist. The other lifts to my breast, palming and pinching my nipples, adding to the sensations and making me squeeze down on him until he grunts in pleasure.

"Next time I fuck you, you're going to be my wife," he says, almost in awe.

"The next time I fuck you," I counter. "I'll own you."

He barks out a laugh ensuring he is even deeper inside me as his body jerks.

"Baby, you've always owned me."

He stares up at me with so much love in his eyes it makes my chest ache in the very best way.

"Same," I confess. "I'm yours."

"Fuck, yeah. You are."

Both of us pick up speed, our desperation to find our releases too much to ignore. Hands roam, teasing, and scratching as sweat begins to glisten on our bodies, quickly cooled by the light breeze blowing around the room.

I'm just starting to climb toward my release when a loud knock explodes from the door, making both of us still.

"Peyton, it's time to get your ass out," Libby warns.

My lips part to respond. To tell her to fuck off, but Luca sits up, changing the angle before he clamps his hand over my mouth stopping me.

"Just you and me, baby. Ready to finish this?"

He rolls his hips and I cry out into his hand.

"Your pussy is squeezing me so fucking tight, P. You feel so good," he tells me as the hand he still has on my hip helps me to move with his.

"You going to come for me like a good little slut?" he asks, making heat flood between us.

He groans as he feels it.

"Peyton?" Libby barks, unimpressed with being ignored.

Luc smirks and picks up the pace, fucking me with everything he's got.

Needing his hand, he drops it from my mouth and rests back on it to help give him leverage to take me as he wants to.

"Oh God. Oh God," I chant, uncaring about my big sister on the other side of the door.

She's experienced way worse than listening to her little sister get fucked by her soon-to-be husband anyway.

Luc circles his hips, his cock hitting magical places inside me.

"Yes. Oh my God, yes," I cry as my orgasm peaks.

"Come for me, Peyton. Show me what a filthy whore you are by coming all over my cock."

"Shit. Shit. Shit."

My body locks up as pleasure explodes within me. Lights flash behind my eyes and I scream out unintelligible words as Luca continues to thrust into me, following me over only a second later.

His thick arms wrap around me, holding me tight as his dick jerks inside me. A deep groan of pleasure rumbles in my ear and makes goose bumps rush over my skin. So fucking sexy.

We both startle when clapping starts up and when we look toward the doorway, we find my grinning, smug-looking sister inside the room watching us.

"Lib, what the fuck are you doing?"

"What does it look like? Watching a live porno."

"Private moment," I bark, grabbing the sheet as I climb from Luca's lap, immediately feeling empty without him inside me.

"Holy shit," Libby gasps, pointing out my mistake as I steal the sheet. I don't know why I bothered, she'd seen me naked plenty of times. My soon-to-be husband though... not so much. "So it's true what they say. Big hands big—"

"Get the fuck out," I bellow.

She's barely able to contain her amusement as she lifts her hands in surrender.

"Sorry. It's just, you're late and Aunt Fee is losing her shit so... If you could clean up and come with me, that would be awesome."

"Fucking pain in my ass," I mutter as I shuffle toward the bathroom on weak legs.

"That," Libby states, pointing at where Luc is still sitting in the middle of the bed with a pillow over his junk. "Is meant to be saved for later."

"Bite me," Luca hisses.

"Nah, I'll save that for my little sister. I've never really been into players," she teases.

"No, just dealers," Luca shoots straight back.

Shaking my head, I leave them to it and lock myself in the bathroom for a few minutes to gather myself.

2

———

LUCA

"So she just stood there and watched you both finish?" Leon asks with a snort of laughter.

"Can't say I'm surprised," Devin mutters. "Dirty bitch."

"You promised Mummy you wouldn't swear today," Kayden points out.

"Sorry, bud," Devin says, ruffling our little brother's head and messing up his hair.

"Hey, stop," he complains, twisting out of the way and running to the other side of the room. "It was all ready," he pouts, walking over to the mirror to fix his hair as if he's a fully grown ass man, not a know-it-all seven-year-old.

"How many times do I have to tell you? Devin sighs. "The chicks dig the messy bad boy look."

"So it was your hair that scored you Libby?" Shane asks with a smirk.

"Dude, you are so punching with that one," Leon jokes like he hasn't done a million times since their relationship was exposed.

"Don't I fucking know it. She's way too good for a scumbag like me."

"Language," Kayden chastises.

"It's like telling a kid not to eat anything while in a candy shop, lil' man. But full points for trying to follow the rules," Shane says with a smile. He and Chelsea tried stopping us all from swearing around Nadine when she was born but they soon came to realize it was a pointless activity.

"So are you ready?" Leon asks, watching as I stand next to Kayden fixing my hair.

All four of us are wearing navy cargo pants and light white cotton button-downs. Nothing fancy, just simple and understated. Exactly what Peyton wants.

"Yep. I am so ready. Been waiting all my life for this."

Devin makes gagging sounds before Leon smacks him around the head.

"Leave him alone. It's romantic."

"We don't all fall in love with our high school sweethearts," Devin mutters.

"Thank fuck for that. Have you seen the quality of the women who attended Harrow Creek High?"

"Once or twice," Leon mutters. "Slim pickings."

"Rosewood girls for the win," he announces happily. "Now shall we go lock this one in?" he asks me.

"Yeah, about that," I start as I step up to his side once we've left the hotel room.

"Oh don't start. We have all the time in the world. College first."

"You weren't saying that when you put a baby in her," Devin calls from behind like the obnoxious prick he is.

"Did we have to invite him?" Leon teases. "Ow."

"Fuck you, bro. You love me and you know it."

Kayden darts around them and steps up to my side.

"I'm really excited," he says with a beaming smile.

"Me too, bud."

"Peyton's going to look so pretty."

"She always looks pretty."

"When are you going to have babies. Aunt Fee said—"

I laugh cutting him off. "We haven't decided yet," I say before he can continue.

Kids are something else we had fully planned on as teenagers.

Propose on my last college game. Get married after my rookie year. Kids after my second year.

Yeah, we'll see. Right now, I'm enjoying life with my girl too much to think about bringing anyone else into it.

I'm living my dream playing for the Saints and while I do want a family, we're still young. There is plenty of time.

"You'll have to put up with Nadine in the meantime," Shane says, making Kayden groan.

"All she does is chase me around and force me to watch baby shows."

"She's only two, Kay.'

He hmphs. "I know."

"One day, she'll want to play the games you like too," I assure him as we make our way through the hotel lobby, where our relaxed-looking wedding planner spots us and walks over.

"Good morning, young man. Are you ready?"

"We are good to go, Carleen."

"Okay, fantastic. We've got an hour before the ceremony. So if you all want to go and help yourself to food, I'll come and grab you when it's time to head out. Peyton and the others had food delivered to their room."

With a nod, we take off toward one of the hotel's restaurants, and I spend my last hour as a single man with the most important men in my life. My brothers and... Devin, apparently.

———

"Can you make them Irish?" Devin asks with a flirty wink to the server who takes our coffee order.

"Dev," I complain.

This is the most important day of my life. There is no fucking way I'm doing it drunk.

"Just one. To celebrate."

"He's right, man," Leon says, clapping me on the shoulder. "You deserve it."

"Fine. But just one," I say, caving to their peer pressure.

"Good to know that you're not boring every day of the week," Devin snorts.

"Focused, professional athlete, thank you very much. There is fuck all boring about my life."

"Sure. If you say so."

Shaking my head, I ignore the idiot next to me and begin what I'm sure he thinks is a dull as fuck conversation about football with my brothers.

Before we know it, Carleen is heading our way with her headset in place telling us that it's time to move out.

I quickly drink the last of my coffee, enjoying how the hit of whisky warms my stomach, not that I'm going to let Devin know that, and push to my feet.

Carleen chats away about the plans for the rest of the day as we walk out of a side entrance to the hotel and down onto a private section of the white sandy beach that is reserved for private functions just like this.

There are a handful of chairs, just enough for our small number of guests. Each one is tied with a navy bow and there are bright yellow flowers tucked into each one. There's a matching runner that lines the aisle and more yellow flowers than I think I've ever seen in my life.

It's stunning, and so much more than I first imagined when Peyton suggested using Saints colors for our big day.

I thought it was going to be cheesy. But standing here right now, I realize it's far from that.

It's... perfect. Everything about it is just incredible. Just like my girl.

"Is it what you pictured?" Carleen asks as we come to a stop at the end of the aisle and look back.

"No," I answer honestly. "It's better."

"Phew," she says with a laugh. "I was worried there for a minute."

"She's going to love it. Thank you."

"My pleasure."

The sound of female voices filters down to us, and I look up in time to see Mom, Aunt Fee, and Chelsea emerge through the greenery that lines the path to the secluded piece of heaven.

"Oh wow," they gasp simultaneously.

"My boy," Mom says, finding me standing among it all. She practically runs down the aisle to get to me. "You look so handsome," she gushes before throwing her arms around me.

"You look good too," I say honestly. They all do.

We make small talk about the day and how incredible Peyton looks for a few minutes while Leon, Devin and I keep our eyes on the place our girls are going to emerge from.

The second I spot Carleen lifting her mouthpiece and speaking into it, my stomach erupts with butterflies.

"You ready for this, Bro?" Leon asks quietly, not missing the move either.

"So fucking ready. I've wanted this since I was fourteen."

"Fourteen? Nah, you fell in love with Peyton the first time you saw her. You were what, five?"

I smile at my twin brother. I miss the shit out of him with him playing in Chicago. It was inevitable that we'd end up separated. Doesn't mean I like it all that much, though.

Maybe one day we'll get to play together instead of against each other once or twice a year. Who knows what the future will hold?

As we get into position, I think back to my very first memory of Peyton. Kindergarten. We were five. She was a shy little blonde girl who spent the first few weeks hiding in the corner too scared to talk to anyone but the teacher.

Something about her called to me, reeled me in and I soon found myself asking if she wanted to play with me instead of tearing around outside with the boys.

Her smile practically knocked me on my ass. And it's been the same ever since.

Our friendship grew and grew and soon, other than Leon, she was the only person I wanted to spend time with. Of course the guys, my teammates, would always be important. But she was the first one I wanted to tell my news to. The one I wanted to celebrate my successes with. And soon, that need to share everything with her grew into something even more potent as we turned into teenagers and the hormones started raging.

I noticed the moment her body started changing, her moods began swinging from left to right with no warning. And I now know that she noticed the same in me. My muscles growing, my voice deepening.

Looking back, we probably started experimenting together too young. But to us, it was just a natural progression of our already incredible relationship. It made us stronger. We thought we were unbreakable.

I shake my head as regret seeps through my veins. I will never forgive myself for what happened. For the fact that I put my loyalty to my untrustworthy cunt of a father above my faith in her.

There's movement through the trees and my heart jumps in my chest. My need to see my girl, despite spending the morning with her, is almost too much to bear.

"Holy fuck," Leon and Devin gasp at he same time when Macie and Libby emerge side by side wearing matching navy dresses, holding small bouquets of yellow flowers.

They both stand to the side, Libby gazing at Devin like she's considering jumping him right here in front of our small gathering, while Leon whispers what I can only imagine are completely filthy promises in Macie's ear. I know what those two are like, we all lived together long enough.

"Daddy," Nadine cries, running down the aisle next, forgetting all about the flower petals in her basket. She abandons it on the ground and jumps into Shane's lap while everyone laughs.

"Turn around," Leon instructs, finally dragging his attention from his girl.

Despite my impatience, I do as I'm told and turn in the direction of the officiant, who's also waiting for Peyton.

A gasp rings out the second she emerges, and I lose my fight to wait it out.

"Fuck," I breathe the moment I spin back around and find her standing alone between the rows of chairs looking like an angel.

Her eyes lock with mine and everything else but the two of us falls away as she closes the distance between us. I don't even look down to know what she's wearing. All I know is that it's white. Or ivory. Or something like that.

"Hey," she says when she finally gets to me.

"H-hey," I stutter like a pussy. "You look—" I swallow, unable to get the words out past the lump that's crawled up my throat.

"You too," she says, gazing up at me with tears filling her eyes.

"I love you," I whisper.

"I love you too. So much."

"Okay, shall we begin?" the officiant asks.

Thankfully, Peyton seems to not have lost the ability to think straight and she agrees, getting the ceremony underway.

Our officiant says a piece about the joy of finding your soul mates and the happiness it brings to your life that makes both Mom and Fee sob.

"Peyton, would you like to say your vows?" she asks, focusing on my girl.

Peyton nods before sucking in a deep breath and taking a small step closer.

"Luca. The first time I met you, you terrified me." A smile curls up at my lips as I remember that little girl again. "And every single day since, I've felt the same. But for a very different reason. I fell in love with you long before I understood what it was. All my life, you've been by my side.

"It's been a few years since we started planning our lives together. And for a while there, I didn't think we were going to find our happily ever after. But just like we always knew, fate threw us back together to achieve everything we planned.

"There hasn't been a day that has passed where I haven't loved you. In fact, how I feel for you, our connection, it's only grown.

"Watching you live out your dream and build our lives together has been the most incredible experience, and I can't wait for it to continue.

"Luca, I love you with everything I am and everything I have. Just like most of the days that have come before, I want to spend every single one that comes our way by your side, loving you, supporting you, and giving you a kick in the ass when you need it."

A ripple of laughter rings through the air, but I'm too invested in her words to respond.

"I promise to always be your best friend, your partner in crime and your soul mate. I will forever be your number one supporter and push you to be the best version of yourself possible.

"I love you, Luca Dunn. Forever."

My vision of her blurs as I blink back tears.

'I love you,' I mouth.

"Luca," the officiant encourages.

I swallow thickly as all the words I've memorized over the past few weeks fly straight out of my head.

"Peyton." I shake my head and close my eyes for a beat, barely able to think straight.

Her tiny hand squeezes mine in encouragement. And when I open my eyes again, she's right there, staring right up at me and supporting me in the way she just promised she would.

"At five years old, I knew that you'd been made for me. From our very first meeting, you stole my heart and refused to give it back.

"Just being in your presence makes me a better person. And I can only pray that one day I'll be worthy of being the man to stand beside you for the rest of our lives.

"You're my best friend—sorry Lee—my everything. My girl. You always have been, and you always will be.

"I promise to always support your dreams, to hold your hand when times get hard, and to laugh until it hurts—even if it's at my expense.

"Everything I do, I do for you, to build our lives together and to live out everything we dreamed about when we were teenagers.

"I love you more than I can express, and I will forever be grateful that out of everyone, you chose to love me."

"It wasn't a choice, Luc," she whispers as tears cascade down her cheeks.

I shake my head, pulling one of my hands free from hers so I can wipe her tears.

"No, it wasn't. It was meant to be."

"Always."

"Forever."

"Peyton, do you take Luca to be your husband, to love him, to honor him, to comfort him, and to keep him in sickness and in health, forsaking all others, for as long as you both shall live?"

"I do," she says quietly as she takes the ring from the cushion between us and slides it up my finger.

"Luca," she says, turning to me, "do you take Peyton to be your wife, to love her, to honor her, to comfort her, and to keep her in sickness and in health, forsaking all others, for as long as you both shall live?"

"I do. A million times over."

I repeat her previous action and slide her diamond-encrusted wedding band up her finger, ready to sit beside her engagement ring.

"Congratulations, I am honored to announce that you are now Mr. and Mrs. Dunn."

A laugh of happiness tumbles from my lips as a few whoops and hollers come from our small crowd before I hear the magic words.

"Luca, you may kiss your bride."

"Fuck, yeah," I bark, wrapping one arm around her back and sliding my other hand into her long blonde hair. "I love you, wife."

"Love you too, husband," she just about manages to get out before I claim her lips in a filthy kiss.

3

——

PEYTON

The sound of the waves crashing behind us mixes with the music playing on the hidden speaker in the bushes. The greenery that ensures this part of the beach is totally private as I rest my cheek against my husband's chest, both of us moving in time to the melody.

Everyone we care about is out here with us, drinking, laughing, dancing and enjoying the gorgeous sunset as our day comes to a close.

It's been everything and more than I hoped for.

Lifting my head, I reach up on my toes and brush a soft kiss on Luca's lips.

"Thank you," I whisper.

"What have I done?" he asks, confused.

"Nothing. Everything. Today has been perfect."

"You're perfect," he counters, his hands sliding down my sides until they come to a stop on my ass.

The huge princess dress I once dreamed of as a teenager gave way to an A-line lace dress with spaghetti straps, a chapel train and a high split up one leg.

The second I saw it, I knew it was the one. It's simple, light, and perfect for our beach wedding.

"Do you think they'll notice if we slip away?" I ask, looking back at Leon and Macie who are dancing closest to us, then Libby and Devin, and Shane and Chelsea behind them.

"Nope. I think they're all lost in their own worlds."

Nadine is passed out under a blanket as far away as Shane and Chelsea could get her from the speakers, not that it really mattered, she was wiped. And by some miracle, Kayden is still playing in the waves with Aunt Fee and Maddie.

"I just need to…" I nod in their direction.

Taking my hand, Luca leads me toward the ocean.

"Hey, sweetie," Aunt Fee says with a wide, happy smile.

"We're going to head off."

"Okay," she says, lifting her arms to give me a hug. "Your mom would have been so proud of you today, kiddo."

Tears immediately burn the back of my eyes.

I banned her from talking about Mom this morning. Not having her here on my wedding day was always going to be unbearable. But I figured I might be able to get through it easier if we didn't say the words.

"Thank you," I whisper, a sob breaking through without permission.

In only seconds, Aunt Fee hands me back to my husband.

"Both of you," she adds. "She'd have been so happy to see you both reconnect and get back on track."

"Thank you, Fee. We really appreciate everything you've done for us."

Her eyes get suspiciously watery too.

"Now go before you turn this old lady into an emotional wreck."

Luca squeezes my waist as we quickly say goodnight to Maddie and Kay before leaving the other couples to each other. We disappear through the undergrowth in search of our room and some privacy to embark on married life the right way.

Luca practically drags me through the lobby of the hotel, much to everyone's amusement in his need to get me back to our room.

The second we're outside our door, he bends down and sweeps me off my feet.

My shriek of shock echoes down the hallway before he unlocks it and kicks it open.

It slams behind us, but he doesn't release me, instead, he marches over to the bed and lays me out in the center of it.

"My wife," he muses, crawling on beside me, his lips finding mine.

Despite our desperation to heat things up, we both just take a moment as we just make out like teenagers.

He looms over me, his hands everywhere, before he finally settles on making the most of the high split in my dress and finding my ass.

"Love this dress, P. You look so beautiful."

"Wanna see what's beneath it?" I ask, my impatience to get my husband naked too strong.

A deep groan rumbles in his throat. "Like you wouldn't believe."

I steal one more kiss before I shove him off me and get to my feet.

"Unwrap me then, husband."

"Best gift ever," he murmurs as he climbs off the bed and steps up behind me.

Collecting my hair, he drapes it over one shoulder before brushing his fingertips down my spine, making a shiver rip through my body.

Kissing across my shoulder, his fingers find the short row of buttons that start at my lower back.

They might be tiny, and his hands the complete opposite, but he surprisingly makes quick work of freeing them before he stands to his full height once more.

The heat of his chest burns my bare back as he pushes the thin straps from my shoulders.

The delicate lace falls from my body easily, leaving me standing in only a small lace g-string.

"Goddamn," Luca mutters before taking my hand and helping me to step from the pool of lace at my feet.

Spinning around, I let him see everything he's just agreed to enjoy for the rest of his life.

His eyes drop from mine in favor of my almost bare body.

My nipples pucker with his attention and my blood heats.

"See something you like, Mr. Dunn?" I ask as he begins to shed his own clothes.

"You have no idea, Mrs. Dunn. Fuck. That sounds good."

Hell, yeah it does. We've waited a long time and been through so much. But finally, we made it.

Mr. and Mrs.

"You want it?"

"Too fucking right I do. I own it, remember?" he growls as his boxers hit the floor, giving me an unobstructed view of what I now own as well.

"You're going to have to catch me first," I cry, taking off before I can think better of it.

The second I'm in front of our pool, I dive in, leaving his booming voice behind me as I'm swallowed by water.

There's a surge as he joins me and in only seconds, his hands circle my waist and I'm hauled into his large body.

We surface together and I find myself locked in his dark, hungry stare.

"Don't you dare run from me," he chastises.

"Only if I know you're going to catch me," I counter, threading my fingers through his wet hair, wrapping my legs around his waist, and kissing him until we're both breathless.

Moving us, he presses my back against the side of the pool and grinds himself against me.

"Why are you still wearing underwear," he groans, kissing down my neck.

"I don't have to be."

"Fuck. You're perfect."

As predicted, his fingers twist in the lace at my hips and no less than a second later, my last remaining item of clothing is gone and thrown somewhere, landing with a wet slap.

"That's better," Luca says happily. "Now to make you mine in every way."

Lifting me a little higher, he lines himself up at my entrance.

"Ready?" he asks.

"Been waiting my whole life, Luc. Yessss," I hiss when he thrusts forward, filling me in one swift move.

"Fuck," he bellows, letting anyone close know exactly what's happening here. "I fucking love you, Peyton."

My grip on his hair gets tighter as his thrusts pick up pace.

"Love you too, Luc."

His lips latch onto my neck, sucking on the sensitive skin there. The hand that's not gripping my ass finds my breast, pinching and twisting my nipple, sending bolts of electricity straight to my clit.

"Oh God," I cry as he hits me in just the right spot.

"Peyton," he groans against my throat, his cock already swelling.

We might not have had much foreplay, not physically at least, but I can't help feeling like every single second since I had to leave him in our room earlier has been building to this. And I am more than ready for him to consume me and show me every single move he has.

"Need you, Luc," I beg, digging my heels into his ass, forcing him to fuck me deeper.

"Yes. Fuck yes. Take my cock, baby."

"Luc," I cry as my release takes hold. "Fuck. Yes. LUCA." My scream echoes into the night as pleasure saturates every inch of me. And only a few seconds later does Luca bellow my name as he falls right over the edge with me.

"Best day ever," he pants into my neck.

"Just think, in years to come we can totally freak our kids out by telling them that we consummated our marriage in a pool," I laugh.

"Oh hell, yeah. But before we get to that. We've got plenty more practicing to get done."

"Bed?" I ask, more than ready to be on dry land.

"I'll follow you anywhere," he says, the honesty in his tone making my heart swell all over again.

At one time not too long ago, all of this was nothing but a fantasy. A dream I thought we'd let slip through our fingers.

But while those years apart might have been hard, they turned us into the people we are today, and I'm pretty sure we both love each other harder because of it.

And being here right now, with my best friend and soul mate right by my side, I wouldn't change any of it.

Get your copy of Leon and Macie's duet boxset, BITTER SWEET
RETALIATION now!

THORN

SNEAK PEEK

CHAPTER ONE
Amalie

"I think you'll really enjoy your time here," Principal Hartmann says. He tries to sound cheerful about it, but he's got sympathy oozing from his wrinkled, tired eyes.

This shouldn't have been part of my life. I should be in London starting university, yet here I am at the beginning of what is apparently my junior year at an American high school I have no idea about aside from its name and the fact my mum attended many years ago. A lump climbs up my throat as thoughts of my parents hit me without warning.

"I know things are going to be different and you might feel that you're going backward, but I can assure you it's the right thing to do. It will give you the time you need to... adjust and to put some serious thought into what you want to do once you graduate."

Time to adjust. I'm not sure any amount of time will be enough to learn to live without my parents and being shipped across the Pacific to start a new life in America.

"I'm sure it'll be great." Plastering a fake smile on my face, I take the timetable from the principal's hand and stare down at it. The butterflies that were already fluttering around in my stomach erupt to the point I might just throw up over his chipped Formica desk.

Math, English lit, biology, gym, my hands tremble until I see something that instantly relaxes me, *art and film studies.* At least I got my own way with something.

"I've arranged for someone to show you around. Chelsea is the captain of the cheer squad, what she doesn't know about the school isn't worth knowing. If you need anything, Amalie, my door is always open."

Nodding at him, I rise from my chair just as a soft knock sounds out and a cheery brunette bounces into the room. My knowledge of American high schools comes courtesy of the hours of films I used to spend my evenings watching, and she fits the stereotype of captain to a tee.

"You wanted something, Mr. Hartmann?" she sings so sweetly it makes even my teeth shiver.

"Chelsea, this is Amalie. It's her first day starting junior year. I trust you'll be able to show her around. Here's a copy of her schedule."

"Consider it done, sir."

"I assured Amalie that she's in safe hands."

I want to say it's my imagination but when she turns her big chocolate eyes on me, the light in them diminishes a little.

"Lead the way." My voice is lacking any kind of enthusiasm and from the narrowing of her eyes, I don't think she misses it.

I follow her out of the room with a little less bounce in my step. Once we're in the hallway, she turns her eyes on me. She's really quite pretty with thick brown hair, large eyes, and full lips. She's shorter than me, but then at five foot eight, you'll be hard pushed to find many other teenage girls who can look me in the eye.

Tilting her head so she can look at me, I fight my smile. "Let's make this quick. It's my first day of senior year and I've got shit to be doing."

Spinning on her heels, she takes off and I rush to catch up with her. "Cafeteria, library." She points then looks down at her copy of my timetable. "Looks like your locker is down there." She waves her hand down a hallway full of students who are all staring our way, before gesturing in the general direction of my different subjects.

"Okay, that should do it. Have a great day." Her smile is faker than mine's been all morning, which really is saying something. She goes to walk away, but at the last minute turns back to me. "Oh, I forgot. That over there." I follow her finger as she points to a large group of people outside the open double doors sitting around a bunch of tables. "That's *my* group. I should probably warn you now that you won't fit in there."

I hear her warning loud and clear, but it didn't really need saying. I've no intention of befriending the cheerleaders, that kind of thing's not really my scene. I'm much happier hiding behind my camera and slinking into the background.

Chelsea flounces off and I can't help my eyes from following her out toward *her* group. I can see from here that it consists of her squad and the football team. I can also see the longing in other student's eyes as they walk past them. They either want to be them or want to be part of their stupid little gang.

Jesus, this place is even more stereotypical than I was expecting.

Unfortunately, my first class of the day is in the direction Chelsea just went. I pull my bag up higher on my shoulder and hold the couple of books I have tighter to my chest as I walk out of the doors.

I've not taken two steps out of the building when my skin tingles with awareness. I tell myself to keep my head down. I've no interest in being their entertainment but my eyes defy me, and I find myself looking up as Chelsea points at me and laughs. I knew my sudden arrival in the town wasn't a secret. My mum's legacy is still strong, so when they heard the news, I'm sure it was hot gossip.

Heat spreads from my cheeks and down my neck. I go to look away when a pair of blue eyes catch my attention. While everyone else's look intrigued, like they've got a new pet to play with, his are haunted and angry. Our stare holds, his eyes narrow as if he's trying to warn me of something before he menacingly shakes his head.

Confused by his actions, I manage to rip my eyes from his and turn toward where I think I should be going.

I only manage three steps at the most before I crash into something—or somebody.

"Shit, I'm sorry. Are you okay?" a deep voice asks. When I look into the kind green eyes of the guy in front of me, I almost sigh with relief. I was starting to wonder if I'd find anyone who wasn't just going to glare at me. I know I'm the new girl but shit. They must experience new kids on a weekly basis, I can't be that unusual.

"I'm fine, thank you."

"You're the new British girl. Emily, right?"

"It's Amalie, and yeah... that's me."

"I'm so sorry about your parents. Mom said she was friends with yours." Tears burn my eyes. Today is hard enough without the constant reminder of everything I've lost. "Shit, I'm sorry. I shouldn't have—"

"It's fine," I lie.

"What's your first class?"

Handing over my timetable, he quickly runs his eyes over it. "English lit, I'm heading that way. Can I walk you?"

"Yes." His smile grows at my eagerness and for the first time today my returning one is almost sincere.

"I'm Shane, by the way." I look over and smile at him, thankfully the hallway is too noisy for us to continue any kind of conversation.

He seems like a sweet guy but my head's spinning and just the thought of trying to hold a serious conversation right now is exhausting.

Student's stares follow my every move. My skin prickles as more and more notice me as I walk beside Shane. Some give me smiles but most just nod in my direction, pointing me out to their friends. Some are just downright rude and physically point at me like I'm some fucking zoo animal awoken from its slumber.

In reality, I'm just an eighteen-year-old girl who's starting somewhere new, and desperate to blend into the crowd. I know that with who I am—or more who my parents were—that it's not going to be all that easy, but I'd at least like a chance to try to be normal. Although I fear I might have lost that the day I lost my parents.

"This is you." Shane's voice breaks through my thoughts and when

I drag my head up from avoiding everyone else around me, I see he's holding the door open.

Thankfully the classroom's only half full, but still, every single set of eyes turn to me.

Ignoring their attention, I keep my head down and find an empty desk toward the back of the room.

Once I'm settled, I risk looking up. My breath catches when I find Shane still standing in the doorway, forcing the students entering to squeeze past him. He nods his head. I know it's his way of asking if I'm okay. Forcing a smile onto my lips, I nod in return and after a few seconds, he turns to leave.

THORN and the rest of the ROSEWOOD series are now LIVE.

DOWNLOAD TO CONTINUE READING

ABOUT THE AUTHOR

Tracy Lorraine is a *USA Today* and *Wall Street Journal* bestselling new adult and contemporary romance author. Tracy has recently turned thirty and lives in a cute Cotswold village in England with her husband, baby girl and lovable but slightly crazy dog. Having always been a bookaholic with her head stuck in her Kindle, Tracy decided to try her hand at a story idea she dreamt up and hasn't looked back since.

Be the first to find out about new releases and offers. Sign up to my newsletter here.

If you want to know what I'm up to and see teasers and snippets of what I'm working on, then you need to be in my Facebook group. Join Tracy's Angels here.

Keep up to date with Tracy's books at
www.tracylorraine.com

ALSO BY TRACY LORRAINE

<u>Rosewood High Series</u>

<u>Thorn</u> #1

<u>Paine</u> #2

<u>Savage</u> #3

<u>Fierce</u> #4

<u>Hunter</u> #5

Faze (#6 Prequel)

<u>Fury</u> #6

<u>Legend</u> #7

<u>Maddison Kings University Series</u>

T.M.Y.M: Prequel

<u>TRYS</u> #1

<u>TDYW</u> #2

<u>TBYS</u> #3

<u>TVYC</u> #4

<u>TDYD</u> #5

<u>TDYR</u> #6

<u>TRYD</u> #7

<u>Knight's Ridge Empire Series</u>

<u>Wicked Summer Knight</u>: Prequel (Stella & Seb)

<u>Wicked</u> Knight #1 (Stella & Seb)

<u>Wicked Princess #2</u> (Stella & Seb)

<u>Wicked Empire</u> #3 (Stella & Seb)

<u>Deviant</u> Knight #4 (Emmie & Theo)

<u>Deviant Princess</u> #5 (Emmie & Theo)

<u>Deviant Reign</u> #6 (Emmie & Theo)

<u>One Reckless Knight</u> (Jodie & Toby)

<u>Reckless Knight</u> #7 (Jodie & Toby)

<u>Reckless Princess</u> #8 (Jodie & Toby)

<u>Reckless Dynasty</u> #9 (Jodie & Toby)

<u>Dark Halloween Knight</u> (Calli & Batman)

<u>Dark Knight</u> #10 (Calli & Batman)

<u>Dark Princess</u> #11 (Calli & Batman)

Dark Legacy #12 (Calli & Batman)

<u>Corrupt Valentine Knight</u> (Nico & Siren)

<u>Ruined Series</u>

<u>Ruined Plans</u> #1

<u>Ruined by Lies</u> #2

<u>Ruined Promises</u> #3

<u>Never Forget Series</u>

<u>Never Forget Him</u> #1

<u>Never Forget Us</u> #2

<u>Everywhere & Nowhere</u> #3

<u>Chasing Series</u>

<u>Chasing Logan</u>

<u>The Cocktail Girls</u>

<u>His Manhattan</u>

<u>Her Kensington</u>